PARANORMAL PAYBACK

Edited by Jim Butcher and Kerrie L. Hughes

SHADOWED SOULS
HEROIC HEARTS
PARANORMAL PAYBACK

PARANORMAL PAYBACK

Edited by

JIM BUTCHER

and KERRIE L. HUGHES

ACE
New York

ACE
Published by Berkley
An imprint of Penguin Random House LLC
1745 Broadway, New York, NY 10019
penguinrandomhouse.com

Library of Congress Cataloging-in-Publication Data

Names: Butcher, Jim, 1971- editor | Hughes, Kerrie, editor
Title: Paranormal payback / edited by Jim Butcher and Kerrie L. Hughes.
Description: First edition. | New York : Ace, 2025.
Identifiers: LCCN 2025008897 (print) | LCCN 2025008898 (ebook) |
ISBN 9780593816080 (trade paperback) | ISBN 9780593816097 (ebook)
Subjects: LCSH: Paranormal fiction, American |
American fiction--21st century | Short stories, American |
LCGFT: Paranormal fiction | Short stories
Classification: LCC PS648.P29 P37 2025 (print) |
LCC PS648.P29 (ebook) | DDC 813.0876208--dc23/eng/20250425
LC record available at https://lccn.loc.gov/2025008897
LC ebook record available at https://lccn.loc.gov/2025008898

First Edition: April 2026

Printed in the United States of America
1st Printing

The authorized representative in the EU for product safety and compliance is Penguin Random House Ireland, Morrison Chambers, 32 Nassau Street, Dublin D02 YH68, Ireland, https://eu-contact.penguin.ie.

Dedicated to the helpless amongst us,
who deserve better.

TABLE OF CONTENTS

INTRODUCTION

by Jim Butcher

People can be terrible.

We've all known someone like that. Someone who just doesn't seem to understand where the lines are, or who doesn't respect them even when they're pointed out. People who are thoughtless or careless to a harmful degree. People who are just . . . well. Stupid.

People who wrong us.

Figuring out how to respond to being wronged is the subject of a whole lot of human life. Religion, law, war, philosophy, violence—even art—are all facets of human beings figuring how to respond to being wronged. There is, in all of us, a need to see the scales balanced, if not for ourselves, then for others whom we see being wronged. It's innate.

From that common starting point, things diverge wildly. An eye for an eye, a tooth for a tooth, is one response. Taking back sevenfold what was stolen is another. Answering for ill action with one's money, freedom, or life is still another.

But we all have the same base idea: when the world is out of balance, we want it righted.

The first problem with that desire is our limited perspective. When we've been hurt, or seen others hurt, there's anger, and anger can make it hard to see when things are balanced again. Jurisprudence has been trying to figure that one out across the whole of human civilization for thousands of years.

The second problem is that every single one of us has wronged someone else, somewhere, sometime. We're flawed. Or sometimes broken. Or sometimes blind. Or sometimes stupid.

But in that moment, when we're the ones who are hurt and angry and afraid, we don't want balance.

We want to answer pain with pain.

We want revenge.

We want payback.

Here, dear reader, are stories of supernatural people and near people caught in those moments—when wrong has been done and must be answered. Here are tales of scales out of balance and the actions taken to right them—good, bad, and ugly. Perhaps it is a guilty indulgence, but what are stories of fantasy vengeance if not another attempt to consider the courses and ramifications of seeking to right the scales?

Justice, after all, is balance.

But payback . . . payback is *satisfying.*

FOREWORD

Move in the Shadows

Getting revenge is a difficult thing. You have to hold a space in your head to think about what someone has done, why they did it, and how they deserve to suffer. Then you have to do something to them that might get you in trouble. This is an imposition to your peace and well-being.

But who among us doesn't want justice for a wrong done to them? If you cannot allow a fool to go unpunished, you are better off moving in the shadows. This basically means keep it out of sight until the right time, place, and action can be decided. Revenge shouldn't be done unless you can walk away unscathed. To do otherwise just hurts you and possibly the people you care about.

Living a good life is really the best choice, especially if you make sure the person who wronged you knows you are living well, despite what they have done. I do know from experience, however, that people will continue to do what they do whether you get payback or not. Worse, they will make you the villain in their story. It's really all about the narrative.

And to that end, there's nothing wrong with enjoying a good payback story, especially when the paranormal is involved. It's good to live vicariously.

Move in the shadows and make good choices.

Best Witches,
Kerrie L. Hughes

PARANORMAL PAYBACK

MISTER PETTY

Jim Butcher

Monster LLC gets by on an extremely low overhead. My office isn't in the pricey part of Chicago, and I sleep there. I don't spend money on advertising. My receptionist works for nothing for reasons that aren't any of your business.

It isn't that I don't have money. You've been alive since most business was done in coins, you have money. It's the principle of the thing. If you're running a business, you should be writing numbers in black ink—which is why not every job I do costs one dollar. I mean, sure, paying The Rent is important to me, but I gotta make enough to use the black pen too, and when you're running a low-end private investigation business, that means doing a lot of divorce and adultery cases, finding small-time embezzlers, that kind of thing.

And sometimes, someone's heard about my real skill set.

My name is Goodman Grey, and I am a professional monster.

She came into my office around eleven on a Thursday morning, a thirtysomething woman who wore clothes that would have looked stylish and well fit maybe ten years or pounds before, giving her an overstuffed look. She'd started pregaming for the weekend by the smell, though she moved with that kind of self-aware precision that experienced drunks can sometimes achieve. She'd cried at least once since putting on her mascara, and her short blond hair was tousled in an attempt to be chic. She carried a lit cigarette in a bejeweled bright pink plastic holder. Old school.

The woman stopped at my receptionist's desk and said, in a quavering voice of melodrama, "My name is Sheryl Petty. I am looking for Goodman Grey, if you please."

My receptionist, Viti, looked up from her tablet. She was a blandly attractive young woman, one you'd hardly notice going by. Her dark eyes tracked ash falling from the pink cigarette holder to the spotless office floor with calm, severe disapproval. "May I ask what this is regarding?"

"Reven—!" The woman slammed her open hand down on the desk, but she wobbled on one of her heels when she did it and wound up almost falling. She recovered and drew herself up with deliberate dignity and sniffed. "Revenge."

Viti put her hand on the weapon she kept tucked into a holster under her desk and glanced at me hopefully.

I shook my head.

She frowned in disappointment. Viti is a little fuzzy on the details of how moral decisions get made. It's one of the reasons she's with me.

"Ma'am," I said. She had enough ice for a hockey game on her left ring finger. "Why don't you step into my office. Mrs. Petty?"

"I suppose that is who I am, legally speaking," she said. "I have a husband." She gave me a small, friendly leer. "Technically."

I gave her a bland smile and opened my office door with a small inclination of my head. She swayed in on the heels. I hoped she didn't roll her ankle. I had her pegged as the sort to make a production of it. I held out the seat across from my desk for her and she sat down, making a display of crossing her legs.

"My husband has ruined my life," she said. "I wish to even the scales. Word has reached me that you are exactly the sort of man I need."

"Justice is a noble pursuit," I said in a very neutral tone. "Why don't you tell me about what has happened?"

She took a long drag from the cigarette holder, exhaling smoke along with her words. "I married Maurice fifteen years ago. When I was younger and far more foolish."

I had my personal doubts on that score. I got a biography after that. Rich older man, beautiful young woman, happiness, then boredom, then distance, then contempt.

"Honestly, what did he expect?" she said. "That I would just sit in the house and wither away instead of enjoying the fruits of life? Of course I didn't."

"I take it Maurice didn't react well to news of your infidelity?"

"He *canceled* my *credit cards*," she snarled. "Look at this," she said, waving a hand in the general direction of her chest. "I must have worn this outfit four or five times now."

I'd grown up with people who'd owned a shirt. "That sounds like a difficult change for you."

"Oh, you've no idea. None at all." She tilted her head back and put her fingers to her forehead as if fighting off a headache. "I think he's cheating on me. I wish evidence, for everyone to know. And I wish you to make him sorry he has treated me like cattle."

I think the word she'd been looking for was "chattel." Not enough people read. "For all intensive purposes," I said, "I think we can work together. I'll need to talk to him."

Wariness went over her face. "Why? What for? I just told you what he did. What would be the point?"

"I always verify targets," I said. "Makes things simpler afterward. I can leave you out of it if you like."

She leaned forward, her eyes viperish. "Oh, let him know. I want him to know. I want him to be afraid of it coming. I've heard about the things you've done."

I smiled at her. It wasn't the polite smile. It was the one I used to make people uncomfortable. It worked.

"I . . . I've brought a cash retainer," she said, reaching into a tiny, expensive-looking designer purse to pull out a thick sheaf of Benjamins. "Ten thousand." She set it on my desk and drew her hand back quickly as if she'd been concerned about being bitten.

Like I said, the smile makes people uncomfortable.

"You're hiring me for vengeance," I said quietly. "You don't get to decide how the scales get balanced. I do that. I'm sure someone of your sophistication can see why."

"To protect us both in case the cops get involved," she said, nodding.

Honestly, it was more because if you're seeking to unleash someone like me on another human being, your judgment probably isn't in the best place to start with, and I sure as hell wouldn't trust her judgment over mine. But I nodded and took the money. "So be it. I need his name, picture, Social Security if you have it."

"Maurice Petty," she said firmly. She licked her lips and looked at me. "If you give me your number, I'll send you his picture."

I gave her a smile that promised things I had no intention of following up on, passed over one of my business cards, and said, "I'd like that."

"I don't know his Social Security," she said, taking up her phone. It too was pink and bejeweled. "Maurice does all the numbers things."

My phone chirped. I looked. I'd received a photo of naked

Sheryl standing in front of a mirror and turned just so as not to be entirely revealing, the arm of the hand holding her phone pressing her breasts against her chest.

I glanced up at her.

"Oh," she said. "Was that not the right picture?" She glanced at her phone and blushed artfully. "How embarrassing. I must have tapped the wrong one. Here."

My phone chirped again. This time I had a picture of a whip-lean older man with streaks of silver at his temples.

"I hope you won't think me terribly inappropriate, Mister Grey."

"It's the twenty-first century, Mrs. Petty," I said. "Such a thing doesn't change my opinion of you in the slightest."

⤜⤛

Sheryl Petty didn't close the door all the way, and Viti rose to shut it behind her and lock it. My secretary slash driver slash subcontractor locked it and turned to face me, her expression disapproving.

"She's so . . . obvious," Viti seethed.

"She's smarter than she's letting on, and meaner than she looks," I said. "What did you get while we were talking?"

"Sheryl Petty, née Montecrist. She was Miss Illinois until that scandal with the university football players," Viti said.

"Oh, I remember that, I think. While ago."

"Seventeen years," Viti confirmed. "She lost her tiara, went into exotic dancing, two convictions for solicitation, disorderly conduct, reckless endangerment, misdemeanor assault, possession of narcotics, six months in county. Her husband—"

"Yeah," I said. "Maurice Petty, who used to be Maurice Petralucci. He's one of Gentleman John Marcone's accountants, left over from the Vargassi days."

"The creative one," Viti said. "Going after him may put you at odds with Marcone."

"Except he's the creative one," I said, waving a hand. "Marcone will have cutouts built into their relationship in case the IRS feels froggy someday." I waved the stack of bills. "And I have a living to make."

"One wonders where she got the cash if she's been cut off as she claims," Viti noted, taking up her phone.

"One does indeed," I replied. "Get me an address for—"

My phone chirped, and Petty's address appeared on the screen, ready to be followed.

I tossed Viti the cash, grabbed a coat and a cap, and headed for the door.

Viti quickly squared and began counting the money. "Do you want me on this?"

"Keep digging on both of them," I said. "See what you can find out online. I'll call in after a bit."

Viti walked back to her desk. "Are you going to subtract him?"

"Too early to say. Let's see where the day takes us."

⤜⤛

Maurice Petty lived in a luxury place in the Gold Coast. I hung around outside until he came out in a white tennis outfit carrying a bag and got into a town car waiting for him. I'd taken my bike into town, and I set out calmly into traffic to follow him.

I look human, but I'm not. My muscles don't work the same way yours do. It wasn't hard to keep up, not that anyone ever really got to drive around town terribly quickly. Whoever Maurice's driver was, they weren't trained security, because I pretty much had to stand out to anyone who was actually looking, keeping up with them on my mountain bike.

I followed them to a ritzy tennis club Maurice could have walked to in fifteen minutes. I tucked my bike into the closest space between buildings, where it would have a chance of not being taken if I was quick enough, and jogged to go see Mr. Petty.

I changed my face as I went. I had a default face I used that might have been the original. I wasn't sure anymore. Being born with shape-shifting as a legacy gave me a certain number of advantages, but the largest was the ability to vanish into crowds whenever I needed to do it. That meant I had to do a little planning ahead.

"Excuse me, Mr. Petty?" I said to Petty in a friendly tone as he reached for the club's front doors.

He paused and looked back, a tall, lean man maybe in his early sixties, with sharp, severe features and teeth that looked like they'd cost him at least six figures. He arched an eyebrow at me. "I am."

"I wondered if you might have a moment to speak to me," I said. "It regards Mrs. Petty."

He rolled his eyes, took a slow breath, and exhaled through his nose. "Ah. So, we've gotten to this part."

"What part is that?"

"I've been expecting either hired muscle, a process server, or a private investigator, hmm?" He opened the door to the club and waved his hand for me to precede him. "And since you aren't large enough to be the kind of bruiser she'd choose, and you aren't carrying an envelope, I'm going to assume you're an investigator."

"Sharp guy," I said.

"Your name?"

"Not terribly important," I said, and handed him one of my phony cards.

"Jake Stonehard," he said, amused. "Sounds fictional."

We went into the club, and he turned left into a small coffee shop. He greeted the barista, who began an order without being told, and then he went over to a table in a back corner of the shop, sat down, and invited me by gesture to join him.

"Very well," he said when we sat. "What is she upset about now?"

"Money," I said.

His mouth quirked wryly. "I'll need you to be more specific."

"She's upset you've cut off her line of credit," I said.

"Perhaps she should have taken a few dozen fewer lovers," he noted. He waved a hand. "I'm not sure what she's told you, but I can tell you from extensive experience that she's unlikely to have been honest with you."

I frowned. "If that's the case, why not simply divorce?"

"Our prenuptial agreement," he said. "If I end the marriage, standard divorce law will decide the division of assets."

"And if she ends it?"

He smiled faintly. "She gets little. She has been trying to provoke me for years with her behavior." He studied my face with sharp eyes. "She didn't mention that part to you, did she?"

"She did not," I said.

"She's playing to form," he noted. "What are you here to do?"

"Getting an idea of what's going on," I said.

The barista came over with a small cup of thick espresso and put it down in front of Petty. He didn't look at her, picked up the cup, and eyed it. "In a clean cup, if you please," he said absently, putting the cup down and pushing it toward her with his fingertips.

"Yes, sir," she said in a very neutral voice. "My apologies. Just a moment."

"Mmm," Petty said, not really listening. He wasn't the kind

to pay much attention to the help. "I assume she paid you a retainer?"

I shrugged.

He regarded me for a moment and then said, "Ah. She's angling for divorce via adultery." He pursed his lips. "I'll pay you five times what she did."

"To do what?"

"Take some time off," he said.

Ah hah. So he was cheating, too.

People can get into such weird relationships.

"Wouldn't be professional," I said.

Something flickered in his eyes. I'd crossed him and he didn't like it.

"I assume," he said, "that you know who I am, 'Jake.'"

"Yes."

"And who I work for?"

"Yes."

"Reconsider."

I frowned. "Okay." I paused. "Still wouldn't be professional."

The barista came back. Petty spoke quietly to her. Then he examined his new espresso and sipped it, giving me a hard look. He knew how. "This can be profitable for you," he said, "or it can cost you."

"Mr. Petty," I said, "I've got nothing personal in this. I'm just a guy doing a job."

"It's rather personal to me," he said. "We'll both be happier if you take the money."

Maybe something in his tone annoyed me. Or maybe I don't react too well to being crossed, either. "I'm a pretty happy guy, naturally."

"Things change."

"You don't know the half of it," I replied amiably from behind my false face.

Light footsteps came from behind, and a young woman in a tennis outfit, blond, fit, and pretty, threw herself into the seat beside him and planted a kiss on the corner of his mouth. "Good morning," she burbled.

He glanced from me to her, his expression frustrated. "I'm doing business, Cammy."

She blinked at him, and then flushed, scowling. "Oh. Oh, then excuse me," she said in a stiff tone. She glared at me. "I can't believe you'd speak to me like that in front of strangers."

Petty started to snap something and then visibly controlled himself. "Stop talking. Now. I'll meet you on the court in a few minutes and explain."

"You'd better, stupid," snapped Cammy. "You don't want things to get out of control." She stood up and walked away. I watched her go. Great calves.

When I looked back at Petty, he was staring after her with a mix of venom and lust in his eyes. He noticed me watching him.

"Push this," he said, "and you won't need a five-year plan. Work with me, I could arrange more business for you."

"Generous," I said. "But."

A couple of sets of heavier footsteps approached, and a pair of beefy security guys showed up in white shirts with epaulets and walkie-talkies and belts with gadgets. Ah. He'd asked the barista to call them.

"This conversation is over," Petty said. "Think about my offer. While you can."

"You're kinda fun," I said. I smiled up at the security guys and stood. "No problems here, fellas."

Petty nodded at them. They took me by the arms, one on each side.

"Oh," I said. "It's like that."

My origins aren't pleasant. My father was one of the more savage species of beings on the planet. I had a sudden and violent urge to start snapping off hands at the wrists. Maybe with my teeth.

But I pay The Rent for a reason, so that I have a choice.

I chose to stay calm and let them walk me out.

⤚⤙

Outside, I got on the phone. I was shaking a little from adrenaline. I don't like it when hands get laid on me without my permission.

"What else did you get?" I asked Viti.

"It's only been two hours, Grey," Viti said with a sigh.

"But what else did you get?"

There was a moment of piqued silence. Then Viti said, "It would appear that Mr. Petty has recently become a gambler. He's placed a number of large bets on sporting events in the past six months."

"How's he doing?"

"If what I've found is representative, he's down five percent," she said.

"So, he's having money troubles recently," I said. "Hoping for a lucky windfall?"

"That seems plausible."

"Huh. I wonder if he cut Sheryl off for reasons other than marital issues."

"Finding out more on his financials will take more time," Viti said. She knew a lot about information system security. She wouldn't be getting it legally.

"Well. Keep on it. Oh, and let me know if you come across the name Cameron, Camille, Camden, anything that would shorten to Cammy."

"'Cammy' is not shorter than 'Camden.'"

"Fine," I sighed. "Anything that might familiarize to Cammy."

"Why?"

"He's seeing someone by that name, and it might tell me something."

I heard her writing it down. "Understood. What is your plan?"

"I believe I'll talk to the help."

⤚⤙

I lurked about outside until the barista got off her shift. She came out and started walking toward the nearest El station. I came hurrying up to her and said, "Hello, miss. Would it be all right if I spoke to you?"

She glanced at me and frowned. College-age girl, brown hair, a little taller than average. "Oh . . . you're from earlier, right? They kicked you out?"

"I'm sure their hearts weren't in it," I said, grinning. I offered her my hand. "My name is Jake. I'm a private investigator."

"Oh," she said, shaking. "I'm Tracy. Um. I had to sign an NDA when I got hired at the club."

Of course she had.

"I can't talk about members' business."

"I'm not really looking to hear about their business," I said. "Just wanted to know what you could tell me about Maurice and Cammy."

Her expression flickered. "Oh. Those assholes."

Being a terrible person comes with costs you never know you have to pay. "Wow. That bad?"

"Oh em gee," she said. "You can't imagine. Him having you dragged out is just standard for him. They're both the worst. Just the worst."

"Like Maurice sending his first espresso back?"

"He usually sends it back twice," she sighed. "Cammy forgets what she ordered and claims I got her order wrong maybe every other day. I just have to smile and nod."

"They're a thing, then?"

"They're some kind of thing," Tracy said. "I mean, they say horrible things to one another like they're having a normal conversation."

"So why are they together?"

"She's hot and kind of slutty. He's a dog. So, they have that in common. I mean, he's married, you know? And not to her."

"You ever see his wife?"

"No. I guess she's not the athletic club type."

I couldn't imagine a chain-smoking alcoholic would have much fun playing tennis, but I could have been wrong. "Anything else you might be able to tell me?"

"I don't know," she said. She looked over her shoulder warily. "Cammy likes her snow. I know that. I've walked in on her in the bathroom."

"Ah," I said. "She rich, too?"

"She's some kind of financial person, I think," Tracy said, "but she doesn't carry designer bags. You know?"

"Starting to get a picture," I said. We had reached the El station. "Thank you for your candor, Tracy."

"You're not going to tell anyone I talked to you, are you?" she asked.

I held up three fingers with my thumb folded over my pinky. "Scout's honor."

⋙⋘

I thought about calling Viti again, just to be annoying, but she had occasionally shot me out of pique, and I didn't feel like healing up another wound. Viti is very good about establishing boundaries. Monster LLC had plenty of shady contacts, but it would take her more time to dig around the more legitimate, private parts of the net.

Having nothing better to do, I hung around across from the tennis club, waiting to see what happened. Mostly what happened was older men and expensive-looking women coming and going, and Cammy came out looking freshly showered in business casual attire. She waited for a few minutes, looking at her phone, then got into a car that had a ride service sign in the window. What the hell. I got on my unstolen bike and followed her.

Traffic was slow, and if anyone had been looking for me, it would have been a problem to blend in believably rather than blowing past stalled traffic. No one was. I did a lot of loitering. Cammy and her pretty calves wound up getting out of the car at an office building on the north end of the Loop. I changed my face again, put on a ball cap to make me really unrecognizable, and hurried ahead of her to open the building's door for her.

She took no notice of me. She was talking loudly to someone on the phone as she walked, wearing wireless earbuds. ". . . and where do they get these drivers? He just sat in the traffic and did nothing at all to get me there faster. One star, bitch. And a review that says he was staring at me like a creep. That's what he gets . . . I know, I know, right?"

I followed Cammy, still without being noticed. Don't get me wrong, I'm good at not being noticed, supernaturally good at it in fact, but I could have been wearing a poster-board sign that said,

"I'm the guy from the club today" and Cammy wouldn't have seen it.

So I got in an elevator, pushed the button for the top floor, and stood quietly while Cammy kept chattering. "Uh-huh, I know. I know. Good, that was exactly what you should have done to the bastard. He deserves exactly that. Right. Okay. Okay." She hung up without saying goodbye, gave me a withering glance, and said, "Don't even think about it, buddy."

I didn't move, look at her, or otherwise show that I'd heard her at all.

"Fucker," she said, and got out on the fourth floor.

I rode the elevator to the top and back down, found the office index on the wall of the ground floor, and scanned over which businesses had the fourth floor: an orthodontist, a title company, an engineering consulting firm, and a tax attorney's office, Acumen, Inc.

Ah hah.

That would seem to be some kind of financial person's business.

I went back out to my bike, which admittedly looked pretty junky—I just buy old used ones so when they get lifted it's not a big deal—and got on it for a leisurely ride back to my office.

⤚⤙

Viti looked up from her laptop when I walked in. She was straight-up mortal, but she'd been working with me long enough to know me in any shape, unless I'd gone really deep—something I avoided, unless absolutely necessary, because going that deep into a form meant that I might lose track, myself.

"Grey," she said, "we need better internet."

"It's expensive," I said.

"Then I need a boss who isn't so cheap."

"Harsh," I said, "and creating a hostile work environment. Keep it up and I'll report you to human resources."

"I'm the only human here," she said.

"Hmm. You have a point. Draw it from petty cash."

"Do you mean from the ten thousand in cash in your desk drawer?"

"I do," I said.

She frowned for a moment and then said, "Oh. You're attempting humor again."

"Thank you," I said. "I accept your apology."

Viti gave me an exasperated look and followed me into my office. I sat down at my desk, took about half the stack of bills from the drawer, and slid it across to her. "I assume better internet is expensive."

She took perhaps a quarter of that and slid the rest back. "This will do."

I tucked it back into the drawer. "What did you find?"

"Little," she replied. "Stunningly, a skilled accountant working for organized crime is quite apt at concealing his financial affairs."

I leaned back in my chair and pursed my lips. "Did you find a Cammy anywhere?"

"I did not."

I nodded. "See what you can find out about a company called Acumen, Inc." I told her about Cammy.

"Interesting," Viti mused absently.

She vanished to her desk. I'd done my part of the legwork, so I let her do hers, fired up my game console, and spent some time battling digital aliens.

She appeared a bit later and said, "Acumen, Inc. is owned by a Ms. Cameron Montecrist."

I hit pause and lifted my eyebrows. "Oh ho."

Viti frowned. "Oh ho?"

"I can't say 'ah hah' every time," I said. "I'll sound like a jerk. I assume her last name isn't a coincidence."

"Correct. Ms. Montecrist is Mrs. Petty's younger sister."

"Heh," I said. "Heh, heh, heh."

"What's so funny?"

"Right now, I'm guessing," I said. "But what an ugly little triangle we have going."

"There's something else."

I tilted my head.

"Acumen, Inc. is a subsidiary of the LaChaise group."

"Ghouls," I murmured. "At a guess, that's how a schmuck like Sheryl heard about me."

Viti leaned her hip on the edge of my desk, frowning. "I don't like guesses."

"For good reason," I said. "But now we know where we need to look next."

Viti nodded. "Tonight?"

"Tonight."

"Burglary?"

"Exactly."

She smiled. "I'll bring the laptop. You bring the lockpicks."

⤚⤙

"Well?" I asked Viti. It was about eleven, and we were parked a block from the office building where Acumen, Inc. was located. We'd been sitting there for an hour.

She stared at the screen of her laptop, adjusted one of the bits of electronic skulduggery she had in the car, and chewed on her lip thoughtfully. It was one of her few uncalculated mannerisms.

"They didn't use store-bought," she said. "But they didn't spend a lot more, either." She picked up a tablet and tapped it a few times, entered something on the keyboard, and said, "Oh, that makes it simpler. Here."

She twisted in the driver's seat and leaned back to a black box in the back seat of her safety-minded Volvo. It spat out a plain plastic card with a magnetic stripe and a security chip on it, and she passed it to me.

"Front door?"

"Office door," she said. "You'll need it after hours."

"There's a security guy on the front door," I said.

"Yes." She picked up the tablet and showed me a security camera view of an overweight, bored-looking man sitting at a desk with his feet up, watching something on his phone. "He just got back from a sweep, so you'll have about forty-five minutes. I recommend you go in through the roof."

I grunted and picked up an earbud. I knew enough to turn it on at least, and slipped it in. "Check, check."

My voice came tinnily out through a handheld communicator on the dashboard. Viti nodded, picked it up, and clicked a button on the side twice. I heard it in the earpiece, and I swung out of the car. "You got the circuit on the top door?"

"I doubt the security guard has had to fend off many looters seeking to break into an orthodontist's office," she said primly. "However, I am somewhat offended to be asked such a thing."

"My mistake," I said. I kicked off my shoes and socks and tossed them into the passenger seat.

She nodded, mollified, and I shut the car door and moved silently through the night toward the back of the building. I shifted my fingers and toes into climbing claws as I went, nails thickening, lengthening, becoming pointed with a low rustling sound as

I approached the building. A bit more went into it than a simple face change. Muscles in hands and forearms, feet and calves swelled. Tendons thickened. Pangs of discomfort flickered through me in time with my heartbeat.

It was a ten-story building, and I went up it with little difficulty. Once on the roof, I took out my lockpicks, went to the access door, dealt with the dead bolt, and used a jimmy in one hand and my claws in the other to swing it open. I'd been doing this kind of thing for a long while. I didn't leave marks on the door or the lock.

Once inside, I dilated my pupils wider, turning the near darkness into a cloudy afternoon, and started silently down the stairs. At the fourth floor, I bypassed another lock, slipped inside the hall, found Acumen, Inc., opened that door with the key card, and slipped into Cammy's business.

It wasn't much. A small reception area and an office beyond it.

"Grey?" Viti said.

I try not to talk too much when I'm doing burglary. I clicked my teeth together once in acknowledgment.

"A town car just pulled up outside the building," she said calmly. "Two men are approaching the front door. I don't think they're human."

"Damn," I murmured. "Keep me posted."

The door to the inner office was locked. I had it open in three slow heartbeats and went in. Filing cabinets, a desk, a personal computer, monitor, keyboard, and mouse. The computer was shut down. I slipped the little portable drive into a port and booted it up. "Drive is in."

I heard the clicking of Viti's keys through the earpiece. "They're showing ID to the guard."

"Maybe they're orthodontists," I said.

A soft snort came over the earpiece. "You only have a few moments."

I went over to the filing cabinets. They were locked, too. There wouldn't be time to go through all of them.

If I was an attractive, self-absorbed crooked tax attorney, where would I keep my most incriminating things?

There was a door at the back of the office, to a small bathroom. It had a mirror.

I went to it, ran my claw tips around it, pried gently, and popped it off its mount. There was a hollow space behind it in the wall, roughly formed. A brown legal folder rested inside.

"I'm in," Viti said. "So are they. They're getting in the elevator now." Keys clicked. "Oh, she's rather obvious as well. Copying files to the thumb drive."

I took the folder, slid it into my shoulder bag, and carefully replaced the mirror. Then I went back to the computer and grasped the thumb drive. "Ready to go when you are."

"Fifteen seconds," Viti reported. "Ten. Five. Now, Grey."

I popped out the thumb drive, shut down the computer, and paced back the way I'd come.

I got to the stairwell and slid into it just as the elevator doors opened, wafting out the scent of ghoul, an acrid odor with a faint reek of decaying flesh, buried under too much cologne. I shut the door silently and froze as the ghouls passed me and went into the office of Acumen, Inc.

Then I went back out the way I came.

"So," Viti said. "The ghouls have Ms. Montecrist under surveillance."

We were back at the office. I produced the thumb drive, and she seized it like a raven with a peanut. Then I took out the legal folder from my shoulder bag. "Apparently," I said. "But what is she doing that's worth surveilling?"

Viti put the thumb drive into her laptop, sat down at her desk, and cracked her knuckles while her machine booted up. "Shall we find out?"

I started going through the contents of the folder. Viti took the thumb drive.

Ten minutes later I looked up to find my assistant looking back at me.

"What you got?" I asked.

"She's Petty's accountant," Viti said. "He's lost a great deal of money in bad investments in the last eight or nine months. Sixteen million."

I held up several pages. "I have here records of sixteen million dollars in assets in an offshore account."

Viti sat back slowly in her seat. "Embezzlement."

"She's taking Petty for everything he's worth," I confirmed. "Including a ten-thousand-dollar wire transfer taken out in cash the day before yesterday."

"Sheryl Petty's retainer," Viti noted. "She is Sheryl's accountant as well. Mrs. Petty has also lost a great deal of money in the markets."

I went to the next section of the folder. "Uh-huh. Here it is. Cammy is scamming them both."

"Hmm," Viti said, her face thoughtful. "This behavior seems somewhat less than ethically ideal."

"Correct," I said.

She smiled faintly. Viti was not insecure about much, but she often had trouble grasping fundamental ethics.

"So," I said. "Sheryl Petty, besides sleeping around on her husband to get him to divorce her so she can take his money, is also siphoning a lot of money from him and using it to hire me to deliver unto him a fate worse than bankruptcy. Maurice Petty is sleeping with his wife's little sister to get her to divorce *him* so he can keep his money. But he can't, because Cammy is embezzling his balls right out from his pants, while simultaneously cleaning out Sheryl, too."

"Which is . . . wrong?" Viti guessed.

"Wrong to the third power, at least."

She nodded firmly. "Where do the ghouls fit in?"

"Must be where she heard about me," I said. "Cammy tells her sister about me, to keep Sheryl focused on Maurice. Even provides her with the money to hire me, because what are sisters for?"

"What a tangled web we weave," Viti said solemnly.

"Very nice. And LaChaise and his people have Cammy's office wired, because she's coming into about twenty million bucks and they want to know when and where and how she gets it."

"So that they can subtract her and keep the money for themselves," Viti finished.

"And as a bonus," I said, "Petty has nothing left. And his wife has me after him. They offer him enough money to keep him going, and they own Marcone's money guy."

"Couldn't he go to Marcone for help?"

"Maybe," I said. "But guys like Petty look out for themselves first. And Marcone doesn't tolerate much nonsense in his organization. I think Petty would do anything to hide it."

I pursed my lips thoughtfully.

"What are we going to do about it all?" Viti asked.

I thought about it for a moment and then smiled slowly.

Viti tilted her head.

"I have, after all," I said, "been paid, and paid well, to balance the scales."

⤚⤙

I got my meeting with Baron Marcone at dawn the next day, in a building that was under refurbishment. He sat behind a battered old desk, a mature man in a tailored suit, with silver at his temples and no signs of weakness. His square, strong hands were folded into a steeple, his pale green eyes were calm, and a Valkyrie in a business suit lurked over his left shoulder, watching me closely.

"Mister Grey," Marcone said, his tone pleasant and meaningless. "What brings you to me today?"

"I'm walking in your yard," I said. "I wanted to let you know about it."

"Mmm," he said. "Please explain."

I did. I laid everything out, including a report that Viti had generated for me.

Marcone glanced over the report. He was a speed reader. I suspected he had much in common with Viti, because he gave a micro-nod of approval as he finished.

"You are being uncharacteristically candid," he noted.

"No reason to be coy," I replied. "The ghouls are about to own your accountant."

"So it would seem," he said. "Petty has allowed himself to become a liability." He closed the report and squared it carefully with the desk's surface. "Why bring this to me?"

"Petty's about to cause turbulence for your organization," I said. "I thought I'd ameliorate things for you."

He tilted his head. "Why?"

"I've been hired to balance the scales."

"Not by me."

I shrugged a shoulder. "That's why we're talking."

"Respectful," he noted.

"There's no point in unnecessary conflict. I assume you have measures in place for when you would need to move on from Petty's services. I thought it would be polite to let you know it was time to use them."

"Are you telling me how I should run my business?"

"I am merely the messenger of an unfortunate reality," I said.

Marcone steepled his fingers again for a moment, and then let them fall apart briefly, an acknowledgment.

"Why not simply walk away?" Marcone asked.

"First, I have been paid," I said. "Second, the ghouls are using me without paying me. I can't tolerate that."

"What did you have in mind?" Marcone asked.

I told him.

He had a shark's smile. "That hardly seems heroic."

"I'm not a professional hero."

⤜⤛

After the meeting with Marcone, I stopped in the open street and called Viti. "Well?"

"You were right. The ghouls have realized things went south and they're trying to clean up," she said calmly. "They're on you."

"How many?"

"Six."

"Only six?"

"Grey."

"I know. I have an ego. Where?"

"Two cars, three each. Beige sedan. Black SUV."

I glanced around until I'd spotted both cars. "Okay. Have they noticed you?"

Viti sounded mildly annoyed. "Grey."

"We always check, don't we?" I said.

"Hmph."

"You pick a spot?"

"The silos."

"Always charming," I said. "Security?"

"Paid them out of petty cash."

"See you there."

And I got on my bike and started riding.

It was still early, and a weekend, so not much was moving. I rolled along at the speed of traffic, got onto Damen, and headed south.

Chicago is what passes for an old city in America, and I'll give the place this much—in its lifetime it has lived a lot. Rapid changes in technology, demographics, economics, industry, and politics have built the city in layer after layer of repurposed construction, which, for the most part, has resulted in a busy metropolis. Here and there, though, there are loose ends. Purpose-built locations that simply could not be readily made over to suit current needs. One of those places is a complex of old grain silos on Damen.

An explosion in the late seventies left the site unusable, and it simply never caught up with the rest of the town. Several hundred yards square of gutted red-brown brick buildings, steel girder skeletons, tunnels, and round concrete towers create one of those spaces where graffiti artists, urban explorers, and shady investigators go to pursue their craft. In the middle of a thriving city, it is an island of silence and stillness where weeds and trees have begun to reclaim the ground.

It just wouldn't have been believable to the ghouls following me if I hadn't noticed them in the morning stillness, so I waited until I was a few blocks away, glanced over my shoulder, goggled theatrically—ghouls not being known as the brightest pixels on the screen—and began to pedal quickly in an obvious attempt to escape.

The property was fenced off, of course, and I drove right to the sign that read "State Property, No Trespassing" to ditch the bike and climb the fence. The cars roared up and the ghouls piled out, while I dashed into the abandoned cityscape.

I broke visual contact and opened up into a full sprint, maybe forty, forty-five miles an hour. I found an entrance to the tunnels, tossed my shirt and jacket one way, and went the other. I'd gained enough ground to take a moment, and I did.

Little changes, faces, hands, feet, they don't take a lot of effort. Compare it to a regular person jogging up a couple of flights of stairs. Even becoming a completely different person, height, weight, and so on, that's only moderately difficult. Run a mile at a moderate pace.

Turning yourself into a monster, though. That's harder. A lot harder. And it hurts. It hurts a lot.

The part of me inside that isn't so nice, the part that wants to tear limbs and rip flesh, capered about in glee as the pain started. My face burned and ached and twisted. My spine lit up viciously as every single vertebra dislocated simultaneously. Bones in my arms and legs cracked and stretched and swelled. My heart rate went up enormously. Heat bubbled through me, my flesh covering itself in sweat even as hair dropped away and scales began to slide out of the pores and unfurl.

Objectively, it took seconds. From my point of view, it was a bad, bad hour. My body pulled in energy from everywhere, drawing extra mass from the spaces between realities. And when I was done, I was nine feet tall, covered in black scales, a thousand pounds of muscle and claws and fangs.

Steam curled up from my scales. Air heaved in and out of my massive new lungs, pluming in the cool subterranean air. Slabs of gorilla-like muscle quivered to be used.

And I was feeling grouchy.

The ghouls showed up a minute later.

They'd done some shifting of their own. Arms had lengthened, backs gnarled, claws extended. Muzzles had thrust out from their faces, fangs growing. Hungry, slavering, carnivorous monsters.

But when I came out of the dark, half a ton of steaming black scales, ripping claws, tearing fangs, and red, glowing demonic eyes, the monsters found out the difference between amateurs and professionals.

It got ugly.

It also got all over the walls and ceiling.

One of the ghouls got away by tearing itself loose from its own arm, clenched in my jaws. It ran while I finished off a couple of wounded. Ghouls are like roaches. They take a lot of killing, generally by dismemberment. I made sure the job was done, and about the time the fleeing ghoul got to the surface, there was a loud boom, and then two more.

I ambled up to the mouth of the tunnel, where Viti stood, holding a semiautomatic shotgun over a badly wounded ghoul. It had taken one round to the chest and one to each leg and was trying to drag itself away on its remaining arm.

I came out of the tunnel, bloodied, because you don't tangle with half a dozen ghouls without paying a price. Viti's eyes widened, and she almost raised the shotgun. Hard to blame her.

I grabbed the wounded ghoul's leg and dragged the ghoul back down into the tunnel with the others. It yowled weakly, thrashing.

Then I finished the job.

⤚⤙

Later that night, I met with Sheryl Petty on the waterfront in the Port of Chicago. Barge shipping traffic from the city isn't what it was back in the town's heyday, but it still exists. It's slow. Which suited my purposes perfectly. You work with the shady side of Chicago, you know guys at the port, especially the ones there late at night. I made sure she got let through.

Mrs. Petty pulled up in her sporty little European car (pink, obviously), tires crunching on gravel as she stopped under a buzzing halogen light outside one of the many, many warehouses. She'd dressed for the part, in a long coat, sunglasses, and with a kerchief over her hair, as if she'd been sent over from central casting as "clandestine meeting Barbie."

"Mister Grey," she said. She tried to look cavalier as she fitted a cigarette into her holder and lit it, but her hands were shaking. "Are you going to make me a happy woman?"

"Depends on your point of view," I replied. My arm and belly burned silently from wounds that would take a few more meals and several more hours of sleep to heal, and it might have made me ill-tempered. Even so, she'd hired me. She deserved a chance to turn aside. "You want bad things to happen to your husband?"

Her eyes narrowed. "That's right," she snapped. "That's right, I do."

"And you're sure about that?"

"Completely."

I exhaled through my nose. "So be it. Come and see."

I led her into the warehouse, past a clerk's office, and into the dim, cavernous main storage area where cargo containers and large shipping crates were stacked twenty and thirty feet high.

"My God," Mrs. Petty breathed. "I mean. There's no one here."

"Not entirely true," I said. We went to the far end of the warehouse, where vast rolling doors were closed snugly against the night, and there, in a frozen goods shipping container the size of a tractor trailer, were Viti, Maurice Petty, and Cammy Montecrist.

Maurice and Cammy sat on the floor back-to-back. They'd been restrained with zip ties, their mouths covered with adhesive tape. Viti stood over them both, holding a silenced pistol down by her side.

Sheryl Petty took in the sight, her eyes widening. "What? My God, what? Cammy?" She rushed over to her sister.

"I thought you'd want Maurice's lover to suffer as well."

Maurice sighed through his nose. Cammy's eyes widened, and she started shaking her head.

Sheryl froze, shocked. Then her eyes went even wider, and glassy, and her face turned very, very red. With a birdlike pounce, she closed the distance on Cammy and began slapping her across the face, hard, repeatedly. One of the blows tore the tape off the corner of Cammy's mouth and she began cursing.

Viti and I traded a look and walked back to the entrance of the cargo container.

"You bitch!" screamed Sheryl Petty. Then she started slapping Maurice, too. "You bastard!"

Maurice noticed when I took hold of the cargo container door. He screamed through the tape, nodding desperately toward me.

Sheryl whirled around.

"Balanced scales," I said quietly. "Sheryl, you were siphoning off your husband's money and you hired a genuine monster"—I put my hand on my chest modestly—"to make him miserable and/or kill him horribly. Maurice, you make a lot of things possible for bad men doing bad things, and you were banging your wife's sister. And, Cammy, you were conspiring with ghouls to steal from both of them and planning to leave them high and dry. You're all . . . just terrible people."

All three of them stared at me. Sheryl began to take a step toward the exit of the storage container, but Viti raised her pistol and gave her a flat, emotionless look.

Sheryl froze.

"Your coat. Scarf. Sunglasses. Please," Viti said in a neutral tone.

Sheryl goggled. Then woodenly removed the mentioned items of clothing. Viti collected them, her eyes cold.

I nodded. "Now. Had Sheryl not hired me, Cammy would have run off with all the money. The ghouls would have killed her, taken the money, blackmailed Maurice, and used him to get at Marcone, and I think you know how that would have ended for you, Maurice."

"What about me?" Sheryl demanded. "What would they have done to me?"

"I dunno," I said. "Killed you and eaten you, maybe? If they noticed you at all."

"Oh," she said in a much smaller voice.

I gave them all the unsettling smile. "Of course, Sheryl did hire me. So. You're not going to be killed and eaten by ghouls. Instead, I'm sentencing you to Sartre's hell."

"What?" Sheryl demanded. "What do you mean?"

"You'll see," I said.

And I shut the shipping container door and locked it.

"How thick is that insulation?" I wondered aloud.

"Eighteen inches," Viti said promptly. "Can't you hear them screaming and banging?"

"No," I said.

"Precisely," she said.

"You put the supplies in there?"

"There is enough water and enough calories to keep them alive until they reach St. Louis and the container is opened. Assuming they share them rationally."

"They'll have a lot to talk about on the way," I noted.

Viti slipped her pistol away and put on Sheryl's coat, scarf, and sunglasses. She fished Sheryl's keys out of the coat pocket. While I walked, I put on Maurice's face. Security cameras would take pics of us on the way out, but they would only see the Pettys. "What we have just done is illegal, is it not?"

"Very."

"But right?"

I waggled my hands. "For some values of right, I suppose. They're awful people. They deserve one another. I'm just making sure they get what they deserve."

"When they are freed, they may seek vengeance," Viti noted.

"Have a hard time with that," I said. "I'm fairly sure Marcone's people have already cleared out their bank accounts, using the information from the report you wrote up."

"Ah. Sheryl might kill the other two while they are restrained," Viti noted.

"She might," I agreed. "That will be her choice. She did hire me to get even, after all. Of course, if she does, she'll deserve the ride while the bodies stink, and what happens to her when she's found in there with them in St. Louis."

Viti frowned. "So, we have delivered justice?"

"We have delivered appropriate vengeance and fulfilled the letter of my agreement," I said.

"Which is good?"

"Which is complete," I said. "Honestly, you're going to find that good and bad get really fuzzy, really quick, outside of very simple equations," I mused. "Besides, I'm not the kind of monster you hire for petty crap like this."

Viti frowned as we got into Sheryl's car, with her driving. "Is their fate not rather severe for such a thing?"

"I'm not above being a little petty myself, I suppose."

"Is that balance?" she asked.

I shrugged. "It's life. You hungry?"

"Starving."

"We made money," I said. "Let's eat."

THE UNDERGROUND GODDESS

Kevin Hearne

There is a certain joy when the temperature dips in the fall and everyone in Poland decides it's time for a nice scarf. You see riots of colors and fabrics, conservative wraps and devil-may-care danglers, and very casual attitudes about it like it's no big deal, but secretly everyone is happy about scarf season. We get ideas from one another, like, *Ooooh, I want to try wearing mine like* that *tomorrow.* We admire each other like we admire the trees turning colors in Pole Mokotowskie: Every day we notice something a little bit different but entirely beautiful.

At least that is how it is in Warsaw—perhaps it is different in other parts of Poland. I wouldn't know, since I have traveled so little. But in Warsaw, when the scarves come out, you notice.

And I think there is a pride to it as well, a societal preparation for winter, an acknowledgment that tough days lie ahead, and we say to one another with our scarves, *I am ready*, and also, *Because I am ready, I will be able to help you if you need it.*

I have many theories on the nonverbal cues of scarves—

some are bait for compliments, some are cries for help, some are warnings, and some are meant to project professionalism or any number of other things. I could write a thesis on the Scarves of Warsaw.

But mostly they make me think of tea and Babcia, who knitted me a scarf every year, clucked and pinched my cheek whenever she saw me, and made me hot tea with honey and lemon. When she set down a cup and saucer in front of me and then groaned as she lowered her arthritic bones into her accustomed chair, she always did so with a satisfied smile, tucking her joy into the depths of her crow's-feet to be carried with her forever. Her eyes sparkled as she watched me take my first sip. I knew that having tea with her kochana wnusia, Anna, was her primary joy in the sunset of her life.

Teatime with my babcia reminded me of a verse from a poem by Wisława Szymborska, for which my rough English translation would be:

There is no such life
That is not immortal
For at least a moment.

I could see that for Babcia, tea with me was her immortal moment. She had no idea I was a witch. I did plan to tell her someday, but tearfully, while standing over her grave. My membership in the Sisters of the Three Auroras was a secret to be shared only with the dead. She had survived one hell of a lifetime, enduring occupations by fascists and communists and another round of fascists, and now Russia was threatening our borders again with its war in Ukraine. I could tell that she woke up every morning tired of the world's endless shit, but at least she had me, her one perfect thing. I would never rob my babcia of that illusion.

There was someone out there, however, who had no scruples about robbing her.

I could tell something was wrong as soon as I entered the door—the crying was a pretty obvious tell, but her posture slouched in defeat, and the entire aura of her house had become a wet gray dishrag of despair.

"Babcia, what's wrong?"

"Oh, Anna, I have lost everything. This man on the phone convinced me something was wrong with my bank account and I told him the number to confirm and they cleaned me out. It's all gone."

"What's all gone?"

"My money. I have nothing to live on now."

"Okay, Babcia, listen. First, you don't have to worry. I will replace every penny. But I want to know everything he said and when this happened. Tell me everything."

"How will you replace everything?"

"I have hidden resources. Come. Let's fix this."

She talked me through it, and I carefully kept my face neutral and concerned while inside I was screaming with rage. I had heard of criminals using phone scams to take advantage of the elderly, but had always dismissed it with a perfunctory "Oh, that's terrible" sort of brush-off. Now that I personally saw what devastation it wrought, I could not dismiss it—not for anyone, but certainly not my babcia. This was a particularly modern plague for which the sisters could provide a cure.

We often skimmed the accounts of rich men who exploited others, and took especial pleasure in targeting misogynists, but we never ruined them—at worst we delivered a little humiliation and perhaps a lesson. Law enforcement would view our coven's activities as organized crime, but we thought of ourselves as a set of extrajudicial scales.

After reassuring Babcia in calm tones that she would be fine and replacing her savings would be no trouble, I left and worried about how much trouble this would be. I may have screamed a bit in the car and administered some abuse to my steering wheel that it didn't deserve, but I needed to release that pressure a bit before driving.

I lived in a large old house with the rest of the coven, two or three of us in a room, because there were thirteen of us. Located in the Radość neighborhood across the Wisła River from Warsaw, it was surrounded by a rock wall and offered an acre or so of land screened by trees that provided a nice private space to conduct our rites.

I am the youngest of the Sisters of the Three Auroras, though eight of us are still in our natural twenties. It's the original five that are at or near the century mark but still look to be in their thirties. They were around in World War II. They fought the actual Nazis and endured Russian occupation in Warsaw, and now they have lived long enough to see Russians threaten us again.

The old sisters even call the Auroras—the goddesses who grant us power—the Zoryas, owing to their time growing up saturated in Russian language. The younger witches and I keep reminding them to use the Polish name, the Zorze. And they have to be coached on how evil has mutated and twisted itself into a different shape in recent decades. It does not manifest on our frontiers as a blitzkrieg—though the Ukrainians may beg to differ, facing the tanks and artillery fire of the Russians now. No, it rather slithers online and burrows into brains with memes and other verbal poisons. It nests in technology and hatches its malevolence there, striking digitally. Look at what happened in America: They elected a puppet and now they are a client state of their old enemy, losing their status in the world because the battlefield was social media and their military could not help them fight misinformation.

Our coven leader, Malina Sokołowska, dismissed my plea at first. But I went to the other seven new members, who agreed with me that this was a legitimate concern. We conducted some research of news articles, and together we convinced the original five—Malina, Roksana, Klaudia, Kazimiera, and Berta—that phone scammers in Poland needed a serious pruning. They were leeching millions from Poland's populace. The old witches needed that kind of old-school evidence-based persuasion to act, but I just really wanted to avenge my babcia.

Together we performed a divination ritual to locate the source of the call to my babcia. But once we had it isolated, the location pulsed with ethereal warnings and disturbances that went beyond mere human evil. Something was seriously wrong there, and we all felt the collective push from the Zorze to address it. We would have investigated anyway, but this was the equivalent of a divine command for us, so we were all in.

"Anna," Malina said when we emerged from our trance, "I apologize for being so dismissive at first. Thank you for bringing this to our attention. That something this disturbing could be living in our own shadow upsets me. Gear up. We're going now."

Gearing up for us wasn't like those montages you see in military movies with guns clacking and combat boots being tied and muscles flexing. We were more into cutlery and charms. We simply stabbed what could not be subdued with magic. And we tended to look fabulous while doing it, dressing mostly in black with purple accents of some kind. I had a purple scarf of diaphanous material that I wrapped around my neck like a soft twilight cloud. It said, *I may look soft, but I am ready.*

The call center, when we arrived at the address provided through divination, was an abandoned brick tenement that the elder witches recognized. It was in the Wola district, ul. Wolicówa 14, its windows boarded up with sheets of plywood. Fencing around the property was covered in rather unimaginative if colorful graffiti.

"I remember this place," Kazimiera said. "It was part of the Warsaw Uprising."

The other old witches nodded and grunted in agreement, and you could watch their eyes go glassy as they accessed old memories of World War II, seeing the building as it used to be under Nazi occupation, instead of the decrepit hulk it was now.

"Yeah, I killed a Nazi here," Klaudia said, a sleepy smile on her face. "That was a good day. Of course, it was a near thing back then. I wasn't so powerful at the time." She looked at me and the other young witches. "I was a baby witch like you lot. We all were. Can you imagine if we'd been as powerful then as we are now, Malina?"

"It would have turned out much differently," Malina said.

"They can't be using the apartments for a call center, right?" I wondered aloud.

"Doubtful," Roksana said, blinking through her oversized eyeglasses. "I imagine they're using the basement space, which is largely open except for furnaces and water heaters and things. We'll probably find some vampire cables leading in there that are giving them electricity and phone access."

"Well, let's circle the perimeter and cut those first," Malina said. "Over the fence and wards up, knives out."

Once on the property, we split into six and seven; I went left with Malina, Roksana, Martyna, Ewelina, and Dominika, while the others went right. We spied no cables, but once we met up with the other group in the rear of the building, they confirmed that they had found some and sliced them. That would most likely rouse the scammers into investigating, which was not ideal for us, but it did have the benefit of immediately ending the progress of any scam they had going at the time.

The back entrance was not only boarded up but had chains twined around the doors with a padlock.

Roksana, Berta, and Ewelina joined forces on that to cast a spell called Passage, which unlocked the padlock and the dead bolt on the doors as well. Some clanking and rattling ensued as Martyna unwrapped the chains, and Malina told us all to cast kinetic wards on ourselves before entering.

"We don't know if they're armed or what might be down there. It might not be an entirely human threat."

That was the first time I'd heard that interpretation, but I'm glad she said something. I cast the protective ward and was bathed in a cone of violet light that filtered the world in shades of indigo.

Martyna hauled open the doors in a scrape of dust, and we filed in, daggers out, and immediately heard a chorus of cursing coming from downstairs. It was utterly black inside because the cutting of the cables not only disabled phones but robbed them of electricity. We had to pause to cast Night Vision, which showed us the dim contours of walls and staircases, but very little else. We were in a foyer or lobby with staircases heading up and down. We headed down, with Klaudia taking point, and I was in the middle of the pack; the violet light from our wards aided us somewhat as our eyes adjusted.

The muffled shouting increased abruptly in volume as Klaudia opened a door at the bottom of the staircase that gave egress to the basement area. We rushed in to shouts of "What is that?" and "Who is that?" because our wards were visible to the humans down there.

Had it only been humans, we would have had little trouble.

But there was something else hiding underground, and once we presented ourselves as targets, they attacked, horned and hooved.

I did not understand the fullness of that at first—I got rammed and it staggered me, but the ward did redirect much of the force at the attacker, and he pinged off me like a pinball on a purple bumper. They kept coming, however, but on their second attack, we were ready and bloodied some of them, got a better look at what lunged out of the darkness, and heard their bleats of pain when we stabbed them: They were fauns. Or satyrs, as I first thought, because that was the word I most commonly associated with chimeras made of man and goat.

I was not the only one to mutter a "What the fuck?" under my breath, because while this manifestation or infestation certainly explained the deep weirdness we'd sensed about the place in our divination, no one could fathom *why* such creatures would be lurking in a Warsaw basement.

Upon their third advance, the fauns demonstrated that they could learn: They came up close and reached out with their hands to grapple with us—specifically attempting to disarm us. One simply approached me with slow steps and watched my knife hand the whole time, no eye contact, just waiting for me to strike. I straight kicked him in the face with my left booted foot to make him understand the knife wasn't all he needed to worry about, and he blinked, snorted blood, and grinned as he kept coming.

I feinted with the knife overhead, and his hands shot out to intercept but annoyingly tracked as I spun and tried to stab from the other side. He caught my forearm in an iron grip, bent down, and sank his teeth into my flesh, all of these movements too slow to trigger the kinetic ward.

I screamed, dropped the knife, and wasn't the only witch screaming. My sisters were also suffering similar attentions.

But I heard Malina say, "Fuck this," before a searing flash of light assailed our eyes in the gloom. She had summoned her hellwhip—an arcane weapon that could dispatch most anything unprotected by god-level wards. It was the equivalent of igniting a lightsaber in a room full of foam rubber swords, and normally she wouldn't summon it where humans could be tagged with it, but so far we'd seen no humans, only fauns.

She swept it in a counterclockwise scything motion, and the white-hot blade of it juicily separated human torsos from goatish nethers, ropy intestines and bean-shaped kidneys spilling across the floor and bleats of agony and dismay filling the space as the fauns splashed into pools of their own blood.

The whip licked harmlessly off our wards, and Malina swept the whip back once more before flicking her wrist and allowing it to loll in electric menace.

"Someone cast Starlight, please," she said, and I think it was Patrycja who obliged, calling down the brilliance of the Zorze to shine from her hands and penetrate the dark, revealing a crowd of humans farther back in the basement, all cringing away from the sudden glare. They had on useless headsets and stood near little cubbies arranged on a couple of long tables. We also saw shelves and a furnace and several water heaters—it was fortunate that Malina's hellwhip hadn't burst any of those. "Charm them into submission," she said. "We'll take our time interrogating them."

Stepping over and through the viscera of goat-footed men, I hoped at least one of the humans could explain the fauns' presence, because it made no sense for them to be there. They were creatures out of Greco-Roman myth. They should be pursuing naiads and dryads on the slopes of Mount Olympus, not slumming in a Polish basement, guarding a criminal call center.

Each of the sisters had a feature that she used to charm others; it was primarily a defensive measure, because no one lashed out at someone they liked, but it could also get people to talk because they wanted to please us. Malina had long, straight golden hair that was nearly irresistible, Klaudia used her lips, and Ewelina actually used her right ear, which I thought a bizarre move, but there was no denying its mesmerizing effectiveness. Like many of the other young witches, I used my eyes.

But I didn't go straight to the cluster of frightened men and women, because I was curious about the shelves—why were they even there? What was being stored on them?

Cardboard boxes of indeterminate contents. A dusty sleeve for carpenters' tools—hammer, screwdrivers, pipe wrench. And a human head.

Wait—

Yes, a head. A woman's head situated on a small marble base. She herself looked to be of marble, so pale and bloodless was her skin, but she had eyes and real nostrils, not the dead white of statues, and there was a shy blush to her lips, at least. Her dark hair might be a wig, but it looked real. And she *blinked*.

I froze and locked my gaze on her, trying to determine whether I was really seeing this or if my brain was playing a cruel joke born of hormones and stress chemicals.

But no, her eyes were tracking the movements of my sisters,

and when she noticed me staring at her, she returned my gaze coolly.

I stepped closer, pouring some energy into my eyes, attempting to charm her.

"And who might you be?" I asked.

The disembodied head blinked a couple of times, gave me the tiniest smirk on one side of her face, but made no reply.

"Come on, tell me your name," I said with all the persuasion I could muster.

The smirking intensified.

And so did the din of voices from the scammers: They should have been quietly falling under our coven's sway as our charms hijacked their minds, but instead they were resisting—not physically, because they were unarmed and we still very much were, but rather with spirited suggestions that we perform anatomical impossibilities.

"I don't understand," Roksana said. "They should be charmed. How are they not?"

"I think it might have something to do with her," I said, pointing a finger at the woman's head on the shelf, "though I don't know who she is."

"Watch them," Malina said to the coven. "Roksana, with me."

The two of them left the cluster and came back to where I was. Roksana turned on her phone's flashlight and shone it at the head of the woman, who eyed them with the same contemptuous amusement she'd given me.

"Is that . . . ?" Roksana began, but almost immediately trailed off, her eyes shifting uncertainly to Malina. Our coven leader stepped forward and cupped the left jaw of the woman, her thumb brushing softly across her cheekbone.

"Yes," she said. "It's her."

"Why is she here?"

"We won't get an answer until she's gone," Malina said. "They won't respond to our charms until she's taken care of."

"Pardon me, but who is that?" I asked.

"She has several names, but is most often called Laverna," Malina said. "Roman goddess of thieves and grifters. The fauns were protecting her. And she is protecting those phone scammers from our charms."

The smirk of the goddess widened into a full smile of brilliant teeth. "Always a pleasure to know my work is appreciated," she said, dry menace hidden behind a tone of wry amusement.

"Knowing your work and appreciating it are two very different things," Malina said.

"How did you find me?"

"Divination."

"I am shielded from divination."

"That is no doubt true in most cases. But the goddesses who protect Poland are nearly impossible to deny when it comes to identifying threats in our lands, and we are blessed by them. Why are you here?"

"Why am I anywhere? For the money."

"Money you cannot spend and which will never make you whole."

"I simply don't have enough yet."

"There will never be enough. The world's billionaires are obviously broken people incapable of recognizing their own immorality. And you are no different." Malina turned to me. "Laverna is the reason this group was so effective. Remove her, and justice can proceed. Would you like to do the honors?"

"I'm sorry, what?"

"She's an Olympian. Unkillable except in the very short term. Destroy this current vessel, and she will respawn like monsters in a video game, because the Olympians are truly immortal. But she'll respawn in Olympus, effectively ending her influence in our lands. That will allow us to make some progress with the scammers. If you want vengeance for your babcia, it should—no, it needs to—begin with her."

"Good." I wanted that very much. Stealing from an innocent woman, putting that strain on her heart for personal gain? Unforgivable. I held up my knife so that Laverna would be sure to see it. "One of your minions here preyed upon my babcia, the sweetest lady in Poland. I am not half so sweet—not even a little bit when it comes to her—so I will do what she could never contemplate. Your immortal moment in Poland is at an end. Do not ever come back. It is under our protection."

The contemptuous smile disappeared. "Wait, who are—"

I did not wait. I shoved my knife into her eye and punched it through the socket to penetrate the brain, then I twisted the blade around to scramble everything well. Golden ichor spilled out of the wound, and the jaw went slack. If she was foolish enough to return, we would dispatch her again.

"Try the charms now," Malina called over her shoulder, and soon the protests of the scammers died down and they said nicer things in softer tones, entirely agreeable and willing to confess their crimes. Which we would absolutely have them do in front of police.

Under questioning, the scammers told us that one of them had taken a road trip to Italy and come back with Laverna's head resting in the passenger seat. The scam had been conceived and set up on the drive, and the fauns had been summoned over the course of some weeks to provide extra protection. More important, though, was the crypto wallet the leader handed over along with its password.

We would be draining all of that for sure; my babcia's funds would be restored, and we'd try to return as much as we could to all the other victims we could find. Or rather, I would.

I volunteered for the project, as I felt that healing the wounds caused by such malevolent greed would be my grateful service to the Zorze in return for their aid to us. The goddesses above gave us the strength to defeat the goddess below. They were the keys that unlocked our dreams—a phrasing that I borrowed from another Szymborska verse in translation:

Dreams have keys.
The real world opens on its own
and can't be shut.

We certainly could not shut out the real world. But we could, for a small while, put on a scarf and make tiny corners of it cozy and safe. Especially when you had a sisterhood at your back. Babcia and I would have many happy teatimes ahead of us.

DYING ISN'T JUST FOR THE YOUNG

Holly Black

Excerpted from the diary of Beryl Finch. Published with the permission of Nora Lee Amin, executor of Ms. Finch's literary estate.

March 3, 2004

I sat by Nigel's bedside at Mount Sinai Hospital all today, his papery hand in mine. His lungs were bad for years, then got much worse overnight. When he inhaled, I could hear them crackle, as though someone were wadding up a piece of wax paper. When he exhaled, there was a sound like a dog pouncing on a squeak toy. I told him we were going home in just a few more days.

Our marriage has always been full of polite lies, but this might be the final one.

March 4, 2004

"Beryl," Nigel wheezed tonight, awake and conscious enough to want to talk. "What would you do differently if you had a chance to live your life over again?"

A dangerous question. Before I could even begin to answer it, he cut me off, his gaze on the screen above us.

"That can't be real, can it?"

The news anchor was desperately trying to explain some outbreak of a new disease in Springfield, Massachusetts. There's a Springfield in every state, isn't there? Wasn't that some kind of joke on *The Simpsons*?

Going Cold, they called the illness, because chilly skin is an early symptom. Another is wanting to bite people. That's how they think it spreads, like rabies.

The night nurse believes it has something to do with drugs. There was that whole thing with people becoming like zombies from doing something—snorting? smoking?—bath salts, so maybe she has a point.

I went and looked online and it wasn't *really* bath salts, but some kind of drug nicknamed "bath salts," which is very confusing. I feel foolish, but in my defense, in my day when people said they were sniffing glue, they were actually, for real, sniffing glue.

March 7, 2004

No new insight into Nigel's condition, but the news is full of this Cold thing. They're saying infected people *die*, but somehow don't *stay dead*. The president of the United States addressed the nation using words like "undead" and "vampires" with complete seriousness.

Nigel and I watched together, then he dozed off again. Nigel was always a force of nature. It seems impossible to me that he can't find a way to wriggle out of death when he's managed to wriggle out of a bankruptcy, two heart attacks, and at least three scathing reviews of his plays in *The New York Times*.

The world is upside down and ridiculous, and I want to stomp my feet like a child until it stops.

March 23, 2004

I am left with the news as my companion most nights in the hospital.

The infection seems to be spreading. The National Guard is in Springfield, but instead of helping, they're erecting a barricade around the outside. It's awful. There are people inside taking video of what's happening in there, and there is so much terror and heartbreak. And blood. There's a lot of blood.

Although I shouldn't admit it, the screams on the screen are still preferable to the bagpipes of Nigel's lungs. That's one of the terrible paradoxes of humanity. The suffering of one person can be inexpressibly painful to us, while we can feel so much less than we should about the collective suffering of thousands.

Nurses and doctors come through the hospital room and try to reassure us that the outbreak of whatever-it-really-was can be contained and will certainly never make it to New York. They prescribe new medicine for Nigel and reassure us about that too.

Oh, and one of the doctors finally explained how this Cold thing works. If you're bitten by a vampire (yes, they're calling them that officially now), you become infected, your temperature drops, and you crave blood. Biting someone in that infected state doesn't spread the infection—but it's the trigger for the infected person to die and then be reborn as a vampire (again, yes, really, a *vampire*, like Dracula or *Sesame Street*'s Count). Then they can spread the Cold.

There is a growing belief that the body can shake off the infection, though, if blood is unavailable for long enough. Maybe there is a way to stem the tide of horror after all. Despite the efforts to wall off Springfield, new cases were discovered in Texas and Seattle just this week. Someone has to do something, and soon.

April 3, 2004

Alarm bells rang through the hospital tonight.

Nigel woke up disoriented, and while I was trying to quiet him down, a nurse rushed into the room and locked the door behind her.

"Get down," she said.

I am ashamed to say that I just stared at her. It was only when she hit the floor that I understood and slowly got to my knees. At my age that's not easy.

"What's going on?" Nigel complained.

"One of them got loose," the nurse said. "Shhhhh."

"What are you talking about? What got loose?" I demanded, trying out all the possibilities running through my head. A lion. A serial killer. One of the monsters from the television.

Nigel began coughing.

I could see the tension in the nurse's expression. She clearly wanted to tell him to stop but was enough of a professional to understand that would be useless. He couldn't.

"One of the infected ones," she told me, now that quiet was off the table.

"Why would one be *here*?" I hissed at her.

She made a gesture of exasperation. "Because some of them have money. A lot of money. They put her in a coma and—"

I heard the crash of a door opening so hard it hit the wall. Footsteps. Our doorknob turned before catching on the lock. I caught my breath. Nigel coughed harder, tears leaking out of his eyes. His hand covered his mouth, trying to muffle the sound. The nurse moved toward the attached bathroom, and I could tell that bitch was clearly planning on locking herself inside if our door opened.

The doorknob rattled. It rattled again. Then the steps went on, looking for doors that hadn't been barred.

From the room beside ours, there came a scream so horrible that it made the hairs on my arms stand up. I wish I could say that was the end, but it wasn't. The man pleaded for help, then screamed some more, cries that went on and on and on. The nurse wept, while Nigel and I looked at one another in shared horror and grotesque relief.

April 9, 2004

Despite death passing us by that night, Nigel's lungs still failed him. By the time he died, the *Times* reported that one whole floor of our hospital had been devoted to locking up infected people. It was a terrible scandal—front-page news week after week—but what did that matter to me? Nigel was gone.

Curfews had started by then too—no one was supposed to go out after dark—and burials of intact bodies had become fraught.

I was sent back to our Upper West Side apartment with a box of ashes.

April 11, 2004

Our daughter, Diane, came down from Massachusetts, with a story about passing a mall beside the Springfield "Coldtown" that rebranded itself as the Dead Last Rest Stop. Although many people were trying to get out of the Coldtown, it seemed that some were trying to get in. To them, vampirism meant living forever. Vampirism meant never having to be afraid.

Our son, David, flew in from Florida, where there hadn't been any reported outbreaks yet. He was terrified to be in New York, and told Diane and me so, many times. He said that anyone who'd nearly been attacked by one of the infected was insane to stick around and I was just lucky that he was such a dutiful son.

For her part, Diane informed me that she'd left her three-year-old daughter and eighteen-month-old twins with her husband, so whatever we were doing for her dad couldn't take long. Diane takes after Nigel; she has no time for sentimentality.

April 12, 2004

We held a celebration of life in Central Park at midday, swiftly assembled, but full of touching speeches. In addition to writing his own plays, Nigel taught at the New School, and so, along with actors, rival playwrights, directors, costume designers, and all of the people involved in a production, there were a whole host of devoted students ready to mourn Nigel and hold forth on his lost wisdom. It turned out that no one enjoyed making a tragic speech like an actor, except for a playwright yet to stage their first production and who hoped to catch the attention of someone important.

"Nigel once told me that we create not for the people who've come before or after, not for our friends or lovers, but to tell the truth," declaimed a curvy actor who'd been in several of Nigel's plays and with whom I suspected him of having an affair. "He believed that it was the small moments that conveyed the greatest emotional weight."

"Nigel explained that if I didn't stop writing scenes with close-ups that were supposed to be performed on a stage, he would smash his coffee cup and cut my throat with the jagged remains," said a former student. I had to admit, that did seem much more like something Nigel would have said.

"Dad said that living well is the best revenge," said David, heaping clichés on his poor father's grave. "And he sure did that."

Afterward, half of them took the subway to my apartment and we drank wine for an hour or two and cried. I cried *a lot*, I am not ashamed to say. I drank a good deal as well. The curvy actor who had probably, maybe, almost certainly had an affair with Nigel put her arms around me, and I sobbed on her blouse. People are complicated. Relationships are complicated. Nigel's death felt horribly, monstrously uncomplicated.

April 15, 2004

Two days later, David and Diane sat on either side of the couch and told me how they saw my future.

"You should come live with me, Mom," Diane said. "At least

until things settle down in the world. It's not safe to be in a city anymore. Besides, everything costs so much here. And I could use help with the kids. If you were covering part of the mortgage, we could get a bigger place."

"You live in *Massachusetts*," David reminded her. "Fang central. Mom should get a place in Florida. A condo in a retirement community."

"I will come visit you both when I can," I told them. "But your father and I put away enough in the bank for me to stay here in Manhattan. I'll be fine. You don't have to worry about me."

They exchanged looks. "You're not used to being on your own," my daughter said.

Nigel's loss already felt like a black hole, dragging everything toward it. I couldn't imagine my future without him. But at least I would have our familiar places. I could get a bagel at the same corner store. I could browse the books at our local bookshop and visit my favorite gallery. I could write poems in the corner of the room where Nigel and I had worked on his plays. Giving up New York wouldn't erase my grief; it would only give me a new thing to grieve. "No," I said. "I'm not."

"We have to talk about Dad's estate too," Diane said, changing her angle. "Do you have the number for his lawyer?"

I did, of course. Harry was also my lawyer. I felt vaguely insulted by the assumption that *they*—who had not even seen most of Nigel's plays—were going to take over as executors of his estate, but that would all be in the will. If Nigel had entrusted them with the rights—very unlikely, but possible—and they wanted to allow some sketchy Hollywood producer to option his plays for a pittance, well, why not? It couldn't hurt him anymore.

"This place has to be worth millions." David glanced around the apartment, which was overstuffed with books and papers and midcentury furniture. But it was true that if you hung on to a piece of New York real estate long enough, you would almost certainly turn a profit, and we'd had this place for fifty years. "Mom, you should really think about selling. You could invest the money. My business—"

"I like it here," I reminded him. "And it's not like the value is going down."

"We just lost Dad. We want to make sure you're safe," Diane said, although she mostly sounded annoyed I wasn't going along with their plans. "Please just consider it."

"No," I said sharply, surprising all of us. I could not remember the last time I had given anyone an unequivocal no, without so much as an explanation.

Diane and David left the next day with a lot of kisses and some sighs and reminders that I could change my mind. When I met friends for lunch the following week, they told me I was lucky that my children wanted me to be close to them.

May 9, 2004

It's been a month since Nigel's death, and I have been working on his final play. I have added what I hope will be a touching bit of fiction about him dictating the last parts of it to me in the hospital, to cover the timing. I only wish I'd had the presence of mind to say something about it during his celebration of life.

I realize that part of my doing this is to give my mind something to focus on other than his being gone. Perhaps in some way he feels less gone to me when I can do this familiar thing with him one more time.

When I'd drafted parts of his plays before or even when I'd

done extensive revisions on them, I was always bound to his belief about how plays ought to work. He thought that excessive emotion had no place in a truly great production and often remarked how my work veered into melodrama. He said it was still useful to him because in paring it back, he could discover interesting possibilities. With him gone, I find myself acting as both of us—the passionate one and the one trying to strip all the passion away.

January 1, 2006

Goodness, it's been a long time since I wrote in this journal. I suppose the play somewhat took over my life. It turned out to be quite successful—staged quickly, perhaps because of his death and the importance of it being his last work. In particular, it was praised for its warmth and greater humanity, which I've tried not to be smug about.

At night, I've watched the news much the way I did in the hospital. Of course, I saw footage of Coldtowns springing up all over the US: zones of infection, walled off by government edict, trapping the infected and uninfected together in grisly disharmony. I gaped in horror along with the rest of the world. I witnessed the protests and the cruelty. Saw the footage from those who couldn't get out but could still livestream video of what was happening inside via satellite. Newly created vampires understood how to set up cameras and cell phones. Soon *they* were speaking to us directly, staring into the cameras with their garnet eyes and talking with the faint lisp of recently formed fangs.

It's a frightening new world. I've adjusted to a curfew at nightfall. I've also adjusted to life without a husband. I started to write for myself again, something I hadn't done in many years—there had always been too many projects of Nigel's. I got rid of half of our old furniture and all of our drapes. I put Nigel's papers in bins and then sent them off to the university to which he had deeded them, for some grad student to sort through. I binged all the British murder mystery shows I wanted. I went to plays and ate bagels and listened to music. I lived.

I will attempt to keep this journal with greater frequency going forward.

February 3, 2006

Attended a play about vampires today. The sort of thing Nigel would have hated. Portrayed them as cursed to eternal misery, when it seems clear from the livestreams out of Coldtown that they're having a great deal of fun. Only a young person could complain about being young forever.

Went out with George and Eunice and had champagne after. While she was in the bathroom, he put his hand on my thigh and started talking to me about how I must be lonely. It's all the same rubbish. I removed his hand and told him that I appreciated his concern, but I was just fine. Men! You'd think they'd be different after seventy, but you'd better think again.

February 7, 2006

The writer of that melodramatic vampire play sent me a message that she was a fan of Nigel's and she'd love to get coffee and chat to me about her career.

Nora—that's her name—complained about all the usual things, and I gave her all the usual advice. Gossiped a bit, which I think we both appreciated. She offered to send me her new play, and I told her I would give her some notes. She seemed so young! Just a baby!

After, I couldn't help but wonder if I was a coward never to have written on my own. Even if I was a flop, even if it hurt my marriage, I would have had something that was all mine.

November 1, 2008

Lunch with Harry. We went over my will and the conditions of the estate. He worries about a lot of things that I would never have considered, but of course that's why he's a lawyer and I am just a retired homemaker. He's set up trusts for the grandchildren and a trust for me that separates the bulk of the financials into investments, leaving what I live on separate, so that the principal can continue to grow. Set up the future of Harry's literary estate. And mine, even though it's just a smattering of unpublished poems and notes for projects I will never complete.

One never likes to contemplate one's own demise, but a few martinis make everything easier to wash down.

November 19, 2009

Nora the playwright escorted me to a photography show featuring a journalist who'd been covering the outbreak in Coldtown when he wound up on the wrong side of the barricades. He was bitten by one of the infected but survived and became a vampire.

No one is sure how he smuggles his film out of the city, but according to the curator of the show, he has an old friend who develops it. The photos are stunning and horrifying, a close observation of what's happening inside, from the perspective of the monster.

After, I gave Nora notes on her new play. She was surprised by my insight, and I worry it gave away the level of my involvement in Nigel's work. It's been tempting over the years, of course, to admit that I wrote a particular line or two that critics praise, but I dismissed those feelings as vanity. This time when I bit my tongue, though, it was because I couldn't bear to see Nora's disappointment. With Nigel. With me. With the past. With every compromise I hope no one ever asks of her.

June 23, 2014

One disastrous afternoon a week ago, I moved the wrong way, fell, smashed up a few ribs, and hurt my back.

I managed to call the ambulance, but what followed was a haze of pain medication and surgery. Diane and David both came, with a lot of paperwork to sign. And I, fool that I was, signed it.

After I was discharged, I was given a cane, and then my children brought me back to my apartment to pack. I walked stooped over, as though I had become an ancient crone overnight. Oh, the ridiculousness of knowing that you're old, but somehow not thinking you *look* old until you find yourself hunched over a cane.

Not to mention the ridiculousness of your children tricking their way into authority over you and then behaving as though that wasn't what they did.

"You need to accept the facts," Diane said. "Don't make this harder on me or yourself. You heard the people at the hospital.

Someone has to take care of you. You're not supposed to be on your own yet. And I can't stay in the city."

"*Take care of me*? That sounds ominous," I told her, already thinking back to the paperwork in the hospital. "I am sure I can manage. I can order groceries. Have my pills delivered."

"You're being unreasonable," Diane told me, her voice stern, as though she were the parent now.

"I warned you about falling," David told me, although he had done no such thing.

"I don't see how living anywhere else would have made a difference to my sense of balance," I said tartly.

"I'm sorry, Mom." David put his hand on my shoulder. "You're right. We're just upset because of how worried we got when we heard you fell."

"You might be able to come back here in a few weeks," Diane said, but I could hear the lie in her voice.

I leaned heavily on my new cane.

I haven't been entirely truthful in this journal about what it was like to live with Nigel. Not that I didn't love him. Of course I did! And it wasn't as though he meant to be cruel, although sometimes he was. It was just hard for Nigel not to see what he needed as more important than the needs of anyone else. And it was hard for Nigel to see a thing he wanted as anything but rightfully belonging to him. Mostly, that was fine. But sometimes it wasn't. Sometimes it went too far, usually when the thing he wanted wasn't going to be given up easily by the person who had it. Going too far had cost him professional relationships in the past. It had cost him personal ones too.

That was the way of moving through the world he'd modeled for our children. And there they were, taking that lesson to heart.

July 14, 2014

My daughter's house is in a place called Belchertown, which, as names go, is just embarrassing. It's a perfectly lovely town, though, and Diane has an acre of green grass surrounding her home and a view of a tree-covered valley out the back, near a rusted firepit.

Inside, white shiplap covers most of the walls. Beneath the detritus left by my three grandchildren, a large beige sectional rests on top of a greige rug. Nothing with much color, really, as though Diane sought not to draw the eye to anything at all.

She and Keith, her husband, installed me in a ground-floor bedroom with my own television. I managed to pack a few of my favorite dresses, along with art supplies, some costume jewelry, and books. They brought my laptop and phone but "forgot" both chargers. They've promised to get me new ones, but so far those have not materialized. What they did give me a lot of was pain medicine, which helped. And wine, which, combined with the pain medicine, knocked me sideways.

When I wasn't sleeping, I got to spend more time with my grandchildren. I supervised them sewing fresh garlands of garlic, which we hung along the windows. My eldest granddaughter, Mary, was very serious, while her two little sisters, Susan and Willow, obviously believed they were playing a game. They complained about the stink of the garlic and begged to go outside, even though dusk was coming on.

"Nana, are the vampires going to come here?" Mary asked me later that night. At thirteen, she was full of the kind of restless energy that created poltergeists.

"No," I said, gesturing toward our creations. "We've got garlic on the windows."

Someone probably gave her that answer before. She looked unsatisfied. "Maybe I want to be a vampire."

I raised my eyebrows. "Oh?"

She shrugged, looking defensive. Waiting for me to scold her. "I'd get to do what I wanted. Forever."

That made me smile wistfully. I imagined myself as the ambitious young woman that I was in my twenties and thirties. Writing into the night, espresso shots and—admittedly, look, I don't recommend it—a few bumps of cocaine for company. Working in a restaurant as a server by day, so we had something to live on. Running from work to one of Nigel's performances with barely enough time to wipe the sweat from the hollow of my throat. Barely enough time to put on a fresh coat of lipstick and slick back my hair.

Back then, plastic cup of wine in my hand, laughing backstage, I wanted *everything*.

"Oh, sweetheart," I told her. "We all dream of that."

"And I could make you a vampire too," Mary volunteered.

I smiled and opened my arms for a hug. She smelled like cherry lip balm and the faintly oniony underarm scent of a teen who wasn't diligent about putting on antiperspirant. She felt so alive in my arms that it seemed even sadder that she was dreaming about death.

"Then you wouldn't have to go anywhere," Mary went on.

"When I go back to the city, you can come visit like before," I told her.

Mary looked confused, though. A chill went through me. "Sorry—where am I going, honey?"

Mary shrugged. "Because you're getting older . . . I don't know."

That night I didn't take my pain medicine. I didn't drink wine. And I didn't sleep.

July 15, 2014

Tonight, sober as a church mouse, I managed to overhear one of Diane's calls.

"You got it listed yet?" She stood in her upstairs hall, pacing back and forth near the top of the staircase. "Harry can't do that!"

Oh, I wasn't going to like this.

Diane went on. "I faxed him the power of attorney she signed. *Again*. The guardianship papers. What else can he possibly need?"

She listened for a few minutes, making noises of agreement. "No, we're doing the right thing. What does she need the place for—or all that money? Dad meant for us to have it."

So David was on the other end of the line, then.

"No, I haven't told her about the home yet."

Right up until that moment, I hadn't accepted how bad the situation could get for me. In my defense, she's my daughter. I knew she loved me. I just forgot that people can love you and still convince themselves to do some truly terrible things.

"Yeah," I heard Diane say with a sigh. "But once it's happened, she'll accept it. What choice will she have? We're her kids. She wants what's best for us, right?"

Fine, I admit it. I cried after I heard that. I cried a lot.

July 17, 2014

In addition to the windows being hung with garlic, they locked mechanically. The door locked that way as well. I found that out by attempting to go outside this afternoon, only to have an alarm go off.

I managed to seem confused by the whole thing, so I don't think Diane believed I had any intention of escape. I don't think she thinks of me as a prisoner, exactly. She didn't let me see her punch in the code to turn the alarm off, though.

July 18, 2014

All those British murder mystery shows must have been good for something. How annoyed Nigel would be if he knew.

I hid my pain pills in my cheek and flushed them down the toilet. I even managed to log in to my email on one of the grandkids' iPads. From there, it was simple to send a message to Harry. We were able to schedule a Zoom over the Wi-Fi, with my television turned up to cover the sound of my voice.

"Tell me my options," I said as soon as he came on the screen.

He tried, although it was difficult for him to be brief or inexact. I had signed a financial power of attorney and appointed Diane as my health care proxy while I was in that hospital. She'd used that to get a guardianship—which meant power over my health care—but so far, the trust Harry put in place kept Diane from being able to get at the bulk of the money. (It did, however, allow for the sale of the apartment.) Unfortunately, she also had power over *me*. And she was applying for a conservatorship, which would give her even more.

I noted that David was really trusting Diane to manage the whole thing and give him his cut. I doubted that was going to go well, but it was clear that neither of them were interested in my opinion.

"What do you want me to do?" Harry asked.

I told him, although I admit, I let him believe I had different plans than the one already forming in my mind. Maybe I wasn't ready to admit what I'd decided, even to myself.

July 20, 2014

There was no point in delaying any further. I waited until everyone else in the house was asleep, then put on the least pajama-y looking pajamas I owned as well as the slippers with the thickest heels.

Then I went into the little bathroom and used a razor blade and a safety pin (sterilized in peroxide, don't worry) to make two marks in my throat. The process was painful and not particularly convincing, but blood from my leg (hence the need for a razor blade) helped add verisimilitude. I trusted panic to cover the rest.

Then I got a meat tenderizer from the kitchen and used it to shatter the glass of the window in my bedroom.

The house alarm bleated loudly, and I stashed the tenderizer under my pillow, thinking of all the reasons why this wouldn't work. But then Keith rushed in. Diane was beside him, yelling.

"It bit me!" I screamed as loudly as any actor playing to the cheap seats.

"Is it gone?" Keith demanded, looking around the room as though there might be a vampire hiding behind my shower curtain.

"I don't know!" I shouted, because more confusion is better. I turned toward Diane. "The kids! You have to keep them away from me. They can't see me like this."

She must have realized that they would eventually come down the stairs. Already, the twins cried out for her, demanding to know what they'd heard. Their voices alone probably would have propelled her into the hall, but I like to think that what I said helped. Diane turned back to Keith in the doorway. “Cover the window with something. Nail up some wood.”

As soon as she was out of the room, I took my chance. “I can’t stay here,” I told Keith, grabbing my dead phone off the nightstand. “I need to be away from the family before the hunger hits.”

He hesitated. He was used to doing what Diane said, and he had to know that Diane wouldn’t like it if I was gone.

“I don’t want to hurt the children,” I said, with as much gravitas as I could muster. “I can already feel it coming on.”

My daughter would never have married a particularly strong-willed man. Looking horrified, Keith nodded, went with me to the front door, and punched in the code.

“You’re going to be all right?” he asked, a ridiculous question. If this really were all true, I would definitely not be all right, but he needed absolution.

“Of course. You’re doing the right thing for them—and for me,” I reassured him as I headed toward the road. As soon as the door shut, I hobbled as fast as I was able into some nearby bushes and cut through a yard into the stretch of woods that ran behind the homes. I couldn’t move fast, and it wouldn’t be long before Diane noticed that if a vampire really had broken the glass on the window, the shards would be primarily inside the room instead of outside.

I cut across to another street and stayed off the road as much as possible. Inside brightly lit houses, I occasionally caught a glimpse of neighbors drawing their drapes. Then I heard a siren and veered off into a copse of trees.

A police cruiser stopped. One of the cops—a young woman in uniform—got out, looking up and down the road.

“They don’t die right away,” her partner said from inside the car. "But they move fast once they do. Let's come back in the morning."

"She's not really infected, the lady said. She's pretending."

"Yeah," the guy inside the car said sarcastically. "A seventy-eight-year-old woman ran out into the night, long past curfew, without her cane, to play a prank on her daughter? Or what, she has dementia but is also a manipulative liar? Either the caller didn't want to admit to herself that her mother's infected or she thought we wouldn't look as hard if we knew. I am going with the second."

The young cop took one last look down the deserted street, got back in the car, and drove away.

The walk to a nearby gas station was grueling. By the time I got there, I'd managed to clean the blood off my neck using a backyard hose, so at least I didn't look dangerous. Still, I am sure I looked deranged. The clerk blinked at me from behind bullet-proof glass.

"You need me to call someone?" he asked.

"What I need, young man," I told him, as sternly as a school-teacher, "is a charger cable and fifteen minutes of grace. Do you think you can give that to me?"

"We're not really allowed—" he started, but I'd already ripped open the box with the cable inside. He blinked at me balefully as I plugged it into the wall.

As it charged, I got myself painkillers, a new cane, a large coffee, and a Danish. Then I used Venmo to pay for my haul and called myself a Lyft.

"The Dead Last Rest Stop?" the driver asked when I got in, eyebrows raised.

"That's right," I told him.

It was a little after three when we got there. Floodlights washed the parking lot in a bright glow beneath a neon sign proclaiming the name of the structure. Despite the late hour, the Dead Last Rest Stop was obviously full of people.

Limping toward the front doors on sore feet, I felt a shocking burst of anger at Nigel for, of all things, not writing plays in which a person like me would ever do anything like what I just did.

I don't know why that made me so furious. Perhaps because Nigel thought his plays were smarter because no one in them did anything epic or strange or loud. Everything was toned down, representing the small moments of real lives.

Except sometimes, it turned out, real lives could be really fucking melodramatic.

Inside, I walked across black polished floors, past screens broadcasting Lucien Moreau's Eternal Ball along with other popular Coldtown feeds, to the information kiosk. A map showed the offerings—rental showers, coffin-shaped pods to sleep in, lockers, restaurants, bars, a salon, and various boutiques selling long black column dresses with fluttery sleeves as well as a great deal of velvet. And the place I was looking for—a FedEx ShipCenter.

I went to the desk, gave them the tracking number, and got my package from Harry.

It was large and long and difficult to rip open. Inside was a vintage leather suitcase that had belonged to me for a long time and a more modern, cheap duffel. There was also a beautiful cane with mother-of-pearl roses and a note attached. A gift from Harry. "For your new life," he wrote, which was very sweet.

Inside the duffel were several envelopes of cash and the clothing I'd asked for. One of my black suits with a skirt, a favorite pin, a hat, and earrings. The shoes I'd requested weren't particularly practical, but they were very nice.

I changed in the showers. From a kitschy souvenir shop, I got a package of water-purifying pills and several overpriced tins of food—two things I'd heard were prized inside.

The floppy-haired blond boy behind the register stared at me with wide eyes. "*You're* not going inside, are you?" he asked, clearly taken aback.

"What?" I asked him. "You think dying is just for the young?"

He blinked in surprise, then took my hundred-dollar bill and counted out my change without further comment.

Outside, I spotted a girl with hair dyed flame red walking toward her car, a lacy black parasol over her shoulder. The mascara under her eyes had run a bit, as though from tears.

"Heading to the gates?" I called after her.

"Yes," she said defensively, frowning. "What's it to you?"

"I'll give you fifty dollars if you give me a ride," I told her.

"Oh," she said, taken aback. "Okay. Sure. Hop in."

On the drive, the girl—Margot, she called herself—told me about her reasons for wanting to enter a Coldtown. A girlfriend and a bad breakup and a dead-end job. As she talked, she kept wiping her eyes and apologizing for crying.

"There's nothing to be sorry for," I said. "You're young. You're supposed to love hard and be devastated when the person you love turns out to suck." I told her a little about being young in New York and Nigel and some of his affairs. I told her how she seemed smart and funny and kind.

By the time we got to the gates, she'd decided she wasn't going inside after all. I was relieved to hear it. I left her the cheap duffel bag with my pajamas, slippers, and five thousand dollars inside. I hope it helped.

The de-registration paperwork was perfunctory and dull. It ought to have felt profound, to sign my name to something like that, giving up my rights. But by then it didn't feel like anything at all.

"No one is going to turn you," a guard said, looking me over. "You look like a nice old granny, but those vampires—they don't even want the young, hot chicks. They just want blood."

"Well," I said. "I suppose you have everything figured out."

Once it was done, I passed through several heavy doors, then into a cagelike elevator. As they lowered me, I could see the whole city sprawled out before me in all its hungry glory.

I'd seen it on the news, but it was different to be there in person. The smashed windows. The burnt husks of cars. Elaborate graffiti covered the walls, paintings of dragons and other, darker things. From inside the buildings, I could tell that Coldtown's citizens were watching, to see if I was worth bothering with.

I took the cane top and pulled it up, exposing two inches of the steel sword encased inside. Truly, Harry gave the best presents.

After that, I managed to pay for directions with the water-purifying pills and tins of food, then headed directly to Lucien Moreau's Eternal Ball. There was a wait at the door, but an ancient crone stooped over a cane was exotic enough to get waved inside—especially after I produced a small bribe to sweeten the deal.

One thing about spending so much time among playwrights is that I have observed a lot of negotiations over the years. Vampires had good reasons not to make more vampires, but I had three things that most other candidates for vampirism didn't.

One, I had a lot of money in a suitcase. Cash, which was hard to come by inside and useful if you wanted to buy things from the guards, which everyone did.

Two, I had access to enough entertainment contacts that I could get some real promotion going for a deserving livefeed, not to mention the potential for better distribution.

Three, I had the presence of mind to hide the suitcase so that when I made the offer, the vampire couldn't just kill me and take it. Truly, some people really ought to watch more British crime dramas.

June 24, 2014

This will be my last entry, I think. Tonight, I can't stop thinking of Nigel's question: *What would you do differently if you had a chance to live your life over again?*

I can't stop thinking of David speaking at Nigel's celebration of life. *Living well is the best revenge.*

Let's turn that cliché on its head, my darling child. Dying well is the best revenge. It's mine, anyway.

I stare at the reflection of my own red eyes in the glass and smile.

What would I do differently? Let's find out.

A MIDSUMMER NIGHT'S SCHEMING

Delilah S. Dawson writing as Isla Jewell in the world of Arcadia Falls

It all began with a donkey. A stubborn, dirt-spackled, flop-eared donkey ruled by his many appetites. A donkey named Gary. A donkey who, for some unknown reason, chose to rear up on his little black hooves and attempt to make sweet, sweet donkey love to the booted foot of his beloved mistress, Keelie King, as she rode her palomino mare through the forest and contemplated revenge against the man who had hurt her sister.

The town of Arcadia Falls had been named for a single waterfall, and not even a particularly big one, but it was a lovely place to stop along the trail and think about how to ruin Mark Ranger's life while Marigold drank from the pool and pawed in the clear water. Gary the donkey always came along on Keelie's trail rides, and, usually, he behaved himself. He was the loudest thing in the county and didn't like men who got too close to Keelie, so she felt well protected. Being on a sixteen-hand horse with hooves the size of dinner plates also helped with the safety aspect of traveling alone through the summer woods, as did the squirrel-chasing dog who completed their little party. Peach Pit, a chestnut-brown pit bull, would defend Keelie with her life. Gary would, too, she was fairly certain.

But just because Keelie had no fears about being alone in the national forest didn't mean she was safe—at least not from stealthy donkey loveplay. Gary reared up onto his back legs and wrapped his front hooves around Keelie's paddock boot, braying his most romantic love song, and Marigold startled and bolted directly into the pool as Peach Pit barked her fool head off. Honking his dismay, Gary fell forward into the pool, too. The poor mare couldn't find her feet on the rocks, so Keelie bailed off her back, scraping her elbow in the process, and flailed into the water—directly into the path of the waterfall.

The water that emerged from a spring far overhead should've been quite cold, even on a summer day, but to Keelie, it felt like warm honey cuddled her shoulders and filled her with a strange golden glow. At least for a few seconds—and then reality came crashing down along with the icy water and she spluttered and stood, instantly reaching for her phone. Marigold dragged herself back up onto the bank to shake off the water, and Peach Pit stopped barking to cock her head quizzically and unhelpfully back and forth, but Gary just stood there silently, which wasn't something he generally did.

"What the devil?" someone said—a male voice with a cultured English accent.

Keelie staggered out of the water, clutching her phone and preparing to dial 911 if the creeper dude turned out to be a threat . . . but she didn't see anyone around the pool, especially not a confused British tourist.

"Hello?" she said, doing her best to sound aggressive even though she was a hundred and twenty pounds of silly goose, according to her older sister. Keelie wasn't the kind of person who could intimidate Jell-O, but that didn't mean she was going to just lie down and become a victim of opportunity. "I have a gun."

"No, you do not."

That voice again.

Definitely male. Definitely nearby.

Definitely sounding a lot like Mr. Darcy.

"Who said that?" Keelie barked.

"Me."

"Me, who?"

A pause. "It is I, my beloved. Gary."

Keelie looked at the donkey. He stood chest-deep in the water, dirty gray fur soaked, left ear pointing out to the side, while his right ear pointed straight up. He looked . . . disturbingly earnest.

"Say that again," Keelie whispered.

"After all these years, after all my sonnets and songs, my heart is on fire, for finally my lady love can hear my words of adoration."

She was staring directly at the donkey as she heard the words, and although his dark brown eyes were full of emotion, Gary's lips were not moving. He took a step toward her, tripped, and flopped face-first into the water.

"This isn't funny," Keelie said, rubbing her sopping wet phone on the driest part of her T-shirt. It was an old phone, and it appeared to be dead, but nobody else had to know that. "I'm calling the cops."

"The cops," the voice snapped as Gary found his feet and pinned his ears. "I *loathe* Officer Ed. I hate Officer Ed with the fire of a thousand suns. I despise Officer Ed like—"

"Shut up." Keelie sat on the ground and took off her helmet, feeling all around her head for a painful lump. "Shut up. I think I have a concussion."

As Marigold watched warily, Gary the donkey struggled up out of the pool and staggered over to Keelie, gently nibbling at her hair. "A concussion. Surely not. Perhaps you are overcome with passion, as I am."

Keelie swatted Gary away from her hair, as always, and he took a step back. "Gary?" she asked, feeling like a goddamn fool.

"Yes, my sweetness?"

"To be clear, you are Gary the donkey, and you are talking to me right now?"

He moved in to tenderly lip the shoulder of her shirt. "The very one, my love, and my soul is filled with poetry for you."

Keelie gently moved his nose aside; if he was suddenly sentient, she felt the need to be slightly more polite, even though he had never, ever been polite. She held up three fingers. "How many?"

Gary wrapped his donkey lips around her fingers. "Three. Three perfect, delectable fingers."

Keelie yanked her slobber-covered hand away.

"What the hell is happening? Am I hallucinating? Why are you talking? And if you're talking, why aren't Marigold and Peach Pit talking? And why do you have an accent?"

Gary looked from the mare to the dog, his lips curling back. "Marigold is a haughty virago, and Peach Pit keeps her secrets, but I, I shall always answer when you call. I will guard your gates and eat your dandelions and stomp any coyotes that dare trespass upon your domain, my love. I will—"

"Lord, and I thought you were loud when it was just a bunch of hee-haws."

"It was never just hee-haws to me, darling."

Keelie squeezed the water out of her hair and squelched over to Marigold, who looked at her distrustfully, as if all of this was Keelie's fault. It was true that the mare was haughty and headstrong, but they got along well enough. After cinching her saddle and checking her bridle, Keelie put her helmet back on and swung up into the saddle.

"Can we head home now?" she asked. "Anybody else got anything to say?"

Marigold switched her tail, and Peach Pit gave a joyous bark that suggested she was ready to bound down the trail, chasing twitchy rodents into the brush.

Gary looked up at Keelie adoringly. "Thither thou go, shall I go, too," he said.

Keelie shook her head and nudged Marigold toward the path. "For somebody who just started talking, you sure have a lot to say."

Gary trotted along at her side, looking up at her with glowing eyes. "When you love deeply, you can only speak from the heart."

"God, you're hot to trot. Didn't I have you castrated?"

For a long time, Gary was silent. And then, in a tiny, prissy voice, he said, "I forgive you."

The trail ride home took an hour, and although Gary didn't attempt to assault her boot again, he certainly wasn't quiet. Keelie was accustomed to hearing him honk and bray, watching him charge into the brush and gallop after Peach Pit, but now he stayed chivalrously by her side and attempted to make polite conversation like a Victorian beau. She was fairly certain she didn't have a concussion, which meant she was probably losing her goddamn mind. That didn't change the fact that she had to be at work at five for the dinner shift at MacGillicuddy's. Her boss, Farrah, was fair but firm, and "My donkey is in love with me and won't shut up" was not a valid excuse for tardiness.

Once they were back home on the farm and she'd brushed Marigold and put her back to pasture, Gary casually attempted to follow Keelie into the house.

"Absolutely not," she said, blocking the doorway. "I don't care if you can talk. Donkeys stay outside."

"But—"

"Can you control your plops?"

After a moment of embarrassed silence, Gary turned and ambled back toward the barn, head hanging.

Without a working phone, Keelie had no way to call her sister, Cash, and ask her if they had a family history of being bugnuts crazy. As she showered and got ready for work, her mind ran a mile a minute. Lately, most of her thinking time was dedicated to two things: wondering if Noelle Halloran would ever text her again after their breakup and hoping for some way to get Mark Ranger and his wife, Samantha, to leave town, or at least to embarrass them so much that they'd lie low and stop taunting Cash. Six years ago, Sam and Cash had been best friends and Cash and Mark had been high school sweethearts, and then Mark cheated with Sam. When she found out, Cash left town, and Keelie had missed her big sister every single second that she was gone. Now Keelie, sweet Keelie, innocent Keelie, wanted to punish the people who had decided to make Cash's life hell ever since she'd come back home.

Today, of course, all she could think about was the fact that her horny rescue donkey was reciting love poems in a British accent from just outside her bathroom window while she put a Band-Aid on her scraped elbow. He kept rhyming "friend" with "end," which made her wince.

When she got to work, she found her sister already at the bar and uncharacteristically happy. Cash was like that every time she spent the afternoon with her new boyfriend, Riley. Keelie knew that if she told Cash what was happening with Gary, her big sister would stop smiling and start worrying, so instead, she sought out the woman who'd stepped in as a mother figure over the past three years: her boss, Farrah.

Farrah MacGillicuddy was the toughest woman Keelie knew and also the most bedazzled. She loved rhinestones, sequins, electric blue glitter eyeshadow, clanky jewelry, and making sure nobody messed with her servers. She also loved her truck, which Keelie had unfortunately backed into a few months ago, but that was in the past now.

"Farrah, can I talk to you?" Keelie said.

Farrah looked up from the corner table she used as an office and guard tower. "Of course, hon. I'm guessing you want privacy?" When Keelie nodded, Farrah led her out to her truck, and they clambered up into the high cab. "You pregnant?" Farrah asked right off. Keelie shook her head. "Good. You quittin'?"

Keelie noted Farrah looked a lot more worried about the second option, which was gratifying.

"No. It's just . . ." She looked down. "If I tell you something personal, do you promise you won't tell Cash? Or anyone?" Farrah nodded, and Keelie gathered up her gumption. "Something funny happened today while I was at the falls, and—"

Farrah's whole damn face changed, from concerned to . . . delighted? Amused, even?

"Something happened at the falls?" she prodded.

"You're not going to fire me if I tell you something totally bananas, right?"

Farrah reached over and grabbed Keelie's hand in her plump, beringed ones. "Honey, something funny happened to me at the falls once, when I was younger. Did the water feel . . . different?"

The weight lifted off Keelie's chest.

"Yes! Like . . . like honey and sunshine. For a minute, it's like I wasn't even wet."

"And let me guess. Then you heard a voice, but there was no one there." A significant look. "No human there, that is."

Keelie was so relieved she felt her eyes tear up. "Yes. Yes, exactly. It's Gary."

Farrah's crinkled eyes were dancing. "Your donkey? You took your damn donkey to the falls?"

"He goes with me on all my trail rides, and he tried to hump my foot, and my horse ended up in the pool, and I bailed into the falls, and now my stupid donkey won't stop hollering sonnets at me."

Farrah did not call her crazy or shove her out of the truck or fire her. Farrah threw back her head and laughed. "And you weren't expecting any of this?"

"Why the hell would I?"

"Oh, honey." Farrah squeezed her hand. "Your mama was supposed to tell you all about this—" Her face fell. "But your folks passed before they could tell you, didn't they? Both your folks."

Keelie nodded. How could she forget the worst day of her life?

"And nobody else in the family ever mentioned it?"

"Nobody told me anything about talking donkeys."

Farrah released Keelie's hand and settled back in her seat. "Okay, I'm gonna give you a quick explanation for something real complicated because I can already see that we're gonna have a busy Friday night, but . . . you're a witch."

She paused for effect, and Keelie gasped and said, "Me? But I try to be so nice—"

"No, honey. An *actual* witch. Arcadia Falls is full of 'em. Throw a rock at dinner service, and you'll hit one. If you're from one of the old families, they dunk you in the falls when the time is right, which activates your powers, along with a dab of blood. Most folks take an animal they like, a cat or a dog, because if you're lucky, you get a familiar out of it. That's why your donkey is talking. You're an Arcadia Falls witch, and that donkey is your familiar. He'll live as long as you do, not that anyone else will ever notice."

Keelie's head fell back against the headrest. "A witch. You think I'm a witch."

"If your donkey is talking to you, yes. That's pretty much the only reason. I just can't believe nobody told you."

Keelie's mind was reeling. "Well, my parents died, and my grandma and Cash took care of me. Are they witches, too?"

Sadness shone in Farrah's eyes. "No way to tell. Sometimes it skips a generation. But if you leave, you lose your powers."

"What powers?"

Farrah glanced longingly back up to her restaurant, and Keelie wished they had hours to talk about it instead of maybe three minutes. "Everybody has a different knack—something you're good at—but it's not like in the movies. My mama told me it was like math. If you're good at math, you're probably not Einstein, but you'll get good grades and make a fine accountant. If you study and read up, you'll be even better, and if you get the right calculator and notebook, you'll be even better than that. So once you find your knack, there are ways to improve your power and reach, but let's just say Arcadia Falls has a lot of nice accountants and no Einsteins. D'you understand?"

"Not really—"

"Well, we can talk more later. For now, I need you in your apron. My power is with animals, which means it's no help running this restaurant. For that, I need great servers like you." She opened the truck door and looked back fondly. "But I'm happy for you, honey, and I'm sorry it caught you by surprise and gave you a scare. Be nice to that donkey, and he'll be your friend for life." She reached into her truck's cup holder for a nickel and closed her hand around it. When she opened her fist, a polished stone was there, a heart-shaped piece of rose quartz. Keelie plucked it off her palm, marveling at it.

"Keep that for luck," Farrah said before heading inside.

Absolutely stunned by, well, everything, Keelie put the stone in her pocket and followed her boss. Was it possible Cash knew about this and just hadn't told her?

There was no way.

Cash would never.

Did that mean that if she took Cash out to the falls, her tough older sister might end up with magical powers and a devoted talking chipmunk companion? Keelie could only shake her head. She was relieved to learn that she wasn't losing her mind, but that didn't make anything she'd heard easier to believe. And how would she find out what her knack was? She hoped it wasn't math. She'd never liked math. Although at least then she'd save on taxes.

Despite her addled brain, she easily shifted into her role. Even without magic, she was great at her job, and MacGillicuddy's had a full house. Each time she took an order to the bar, Cash smiled at her and made the usual sisterly small talk, and Keelie did her best to reply in kind even though, internally, she was shaken to her core.

"Can we chat later?" she asked Cash.

"Sleeping over at Riley's," Cash said, waggling her dark eyebrows. "Maybe tomorrow?"

"Maybe tomorrow," Keelie echoed, but . . .

She sounded exactly like Cash.

Exactly like her.

Her older sister gave her A Look. "Are you mocking me?"

"Not on purpose. Tomorrow would be great. I hope you guys have a good night."

It sounded weak because it was weak, but Keelie hated confrontation and arguing and hurried back to her table with the beers Cash had supplied. Most likely Cash would try texting her later, but since she didn't currently have a working phone, that wasn't going to accomplish much. She had to let Cash know so she wouldn't worry—and she had to get a new phone immediately.

The night flew by, the tips flew in, and then she was driving home in her old truck. "Before He Cheats" by Carrie Underwood started up on the radio, and without really thinking about it, Keelie sang along. She knew the words by heart because she'd long ago learned that it was the kind of song that got the crowd going at karaoke, so even though her voice wasn't particularly nice, the whole room ended up singing along with loud and supportive passion, drowning her out. But this time, her voice blended seamlessly with the song. She hit every note, trilled every growl, and grinned at how powerful she felt, how right. She wanted to slash all four of Mark Ranger's tires, take a Louisville Slugger to the headlights of his old Impala, and remind him that even if it had been six years ago, what he'd done to Cash was neither forgotten nor forgiven. She held the last note until the song cut out, feeling it resonate in her bones.

And that was when it hit her.

Accidentally mocking Cash. Singing this song flawlessly in a voice that was not her own.

It didn't feel like a coincidence.

She changed the radio station to some guy advertising pizza and mimicked his voice, word for word. On the next channel, she sang along with a Bon Jovi song *as Jon Bon Jovi*, then found a new station and matched her voice to Cyndi Lauper's.

Each time it happened, she felt that warm sunshine in her heart like she had at the waterfall and was unsurprised to hear another voice entirely coming out of her mouth.

This must be it, she thought. *My knack. Or whatever. I'm a mimic.*

At first, her spirits rose because, well, magic! But then they fell a little, because it would've been more helpful if she could've turned rocks into gold or made the wheels on a slot machine stop on her whim. And then her spirits splattered on the ground because this skill seemed totally useless to someone with high morals who was honest to a fault. What use would she ever have in her life for mimicking a sound? She wasn't even a hunter who could use such a talent to attract prey, although that would make her extremely popular around town.

How odd, to go from thinking she was losing her marbles—

To getting excited about possibly being a witch who could solve all her problems with actual magic—

To realizing that her special gift was utterly useless.

As soon as she turned down the long gravel drive to the farm, she could hear Gary braying happily. Except now, instead of the usual atonal hee-haw, she could hear the words underneath it. "My love!" the donkey shouted. "My love, you've returned!"

It honestly would've been a lovely voice if he hadn't been a donkey.

As she drove along the fence, he trotted along with her, ears bouncing. "Every time you leave, I think to myself, 'What if she never returns? What if the light of the sun were to wink out, leaving me in perpetual darkness?'" he called.

In their brief talk, she had neglected to ask Farrah what a witch was supposed to do when her familiar was desperately in love with her. She got out of the car and went to the gate.

"I'm going to pet you like usual, but don't make it weird," she warned him as he skidded to a halt and tenderly nibbled her hand.

"There is nothing weird about true love. Yes. Right there. Oh, yes. Scratch it, you minx."

Keelie stopped scratching behind his ear and stepped back. "Gary, we need to have a talk."

"So long as your voice fills mine ears—"

"Listen."

He went silent, ears quivering.

"You have been my pet donkey for, what, two years?"

"Two glorious years, the best of my life—"

"Seriously, listen. I rescued you from that horrible old man's mud pit of a yard and brought you here, and I take care of you—"

"Such good care!"

"Shut up, Gary. I think we get along great, and I appreciate how you get rid of coyotes and let me know whenever anyone is near the yard. I did not appreciate it that time you chewed all the wires on the side of the house. But I need you to understand that my love for you is strictly platonic."

The donkey gasped. "You . . . you merely wish . . . to be friends?"

She put a supportive hand on his back. "Yes. A human and a donkey can only ever be friends."

"But the way you brush me—"

"I brush Marigold and Rico, too. Grooming is just part of livestock care."

"You run your hands so sensually down my legs . . ."

"To pick out the rocks so you won't get sore hooves."

"And you sometimes let me—"

"Gary, I absolutely do not 'let' you hump my boot while I'm riding. I just can't stop you most of the time."

The poor little donkey seemed to deflate, his head hanging and his ears dangling limply.

"So that one life-changing time that you touched my—"

Keelie blushed and had to look away. "Also a part of equine husbandry. It gets dirty up inside your—your—you can get an infection if I don't clean the sheath." She coughed. "I didn't enjoy it."

"So that's why you wore gloves."

The moment grew very, very awkward.

"I'm going to need some time to sit with this," Gary said, turning his back to her.

"I understand."

It felt so much like a breakup that Keelie almost cried. Nothing like when Noelle had broken up with her, because that was devastating. She liked Noelle so much more than the guys she'd dated in high school, possibly loved her. Keelie had just recently come to terms with being bisexual, and now she had a talking donkey hitting on her?

Unbelievable.

Keelie went inside and prodded her phone, trying desperately to get it to function, but it was really, really old and very, very dead. She'd heard newer phones were water-resistant. She didn't have a ton of extra cash, but the next morning, she went out to buy a decent model that wouldn't poop right out the second she fell into a magical waterfall. Gary did not chase her truck along the fence out to the road as usual. When she scanned the pasture, she saw him moping in the far corner. He'd been missing at breakfast, but she left a chunk of pineapple in his feed bucket, hoping his very favorite treat would remind him that he was loved, even if not in the way that he'd hoped.

As she drove, she sang along with every song she heard, enjoying the bizarre pleasure of being able to wail like Christina Aguilera or rap about thrift stores in a gravelly voice along with Macklemore. It was a longer drive than she usually took, as the cell phone store wasn't in Arcadia Falls but down the highway a couple of exits. She soon had a model several generations newer than her old phone, plus a decent rebate thanks to turning in her waterlogged one. She immediately texted Cash to let her know what had happened, but she knew full well that after a long night of bartending and then Riley-tending, Cash was likely going to sleep until noon.

As she stepped out of the phone store contemplating a nice little treat for lunch, the hairs along the back of her neck rose, and she scanned the immediate area for some kind of Stranger Danger. There was no one nearby, no magical voices, no threats, no lascivious donkeys. But then her eye was drawn to a familiar figure in the burger place next door.

Mark Ranger.

Detestable cheating jerk Mark Ranger, he who deserved to have all four of his tires slashed.

But sitting at the table next to him was not Samantha, not his wife, not the woman who had helped break Cash's heart and sent her running across the country to heal.

It was a girl Keelie had never seen before—a suspiciously young girl.

Like, possibly even a high school girl.

A girl who seemed pretty happy to have Mark's hand on her thigh.

And sure, Mark was the hottest guy in town, if you ignored the fact that he was a cheating sleazebag. But someone who wasn't from Arcadia Falls might not know that, might actually fall for those baby blue eyes with no one to tell her the truth, and—

Wait.

Wait.

Keelie could use this.

With a few clicks of her new phone, she had several pictures of the burger joint tryst, including the girl feeding Mark a handful of fries like an absolute goober. Of course, she could show these pictures to Sam and know that her sister was avenged, but . . . well, for a seemingly sweet and silly goose, Keelie held quite a grudge against this man. Just blowing up his marriage wasn't good enough. Several of Cash's old friends had known about Mark and Sam and had kept the secret from Cash, and now all of Arcadia Falls had accepted their marriage; hell, most folks had attended the ceremony and had gifted them the same toaster. Keelie wanted the whole damn town to know, once and for all, that Mark was a cheater and Sam wasn't much better.

As she drove back home, she formulated her plan. It was the perfect moment to discover Mark with his hot young thing. Saturday night was always the busiest time of the week at MacGillicuddy's, especially since Farrah had hired a guy from Scorpion Hollow to run bar trivia at five. That meant that the restaurant would be packed. Keelie just had to run a few errands, send a few texts, and put on her acting face, as her tenth-grade drama teacher had called it.

The first thing she did was go to the Biscuit Barn, where Sam worked. Keelie hated Sam and Sam knew it, but everybody in town loved those biscuits. As she walked in the door, she homed in on Sam behind the counter and put on her friendliest smile.

"Six biscuits, please," she said when it was her turn.

Sam gave her a dead-eyed glare. She'd been one of the prettiest girls in high school and Keelie had thought of her like a second big sister, but Sam now looked older than her years, with grown-out highlights and bags under her eyes.

"That'll be ten," Sam said. It was the bare minimum, but it was enough.

Keelie had been playing with her newfound magical abilities, and she just needed to hear something once to mimic it. Three words from Sam, and now it was like she'd trapped Sam's voice in a jelly jar and could open it right back up anytime she liked.

Plus, now she had biscuits.

Next, she took the biscuits to work, where Farrah was overseeing the lunch shift. Farrah took a biscuit from the box with a warm smile.

"You trying to butter me up?" she asked, but not like she minded.

"I wanted to ask the trivia guy a question," Keelie said. "Can you give me his number?"

Farrah stared at her for a long moment, the sort of stare that said, *You're up to something, but I reckon I trust you.* She wrote out a number on a sticky note and handed it over. "Remember: be like Superman," she said. "Use your powers for good."

"Why, I don't know what you're talking about." Keelie slid the biscuit box fully across the table. "And there's honey butter in there, too."

Now this next part? Keelie wasn't looking forward to it, but it had to be done, and at least it would be quick. She did an online search for Mark's lawn-care business, On Your Mark Yards, and called his number.

"On Your Mark, this is Mark," he said.

In the background, Keelie could hear the girl's laughter.

She hung up and blocked his number. She didn't need to say anything.

He'd already given her everything she needed.

Back home, she found Cash drinking coffee at the kitchen table with Peach Pit curled up at her feet. Cash looked up with a light in her eyes that Keelie had missed for years. "You still need to talk?"

Keelie sat down and chose her words carefully. "Did Mom ever say anything about the falls?" she asked.

"Just to be careful at the swimming hole because drunk kids drown easy. Why?"

Keelie teetered on the edge of telling Cash everything. The falls, the betrayed donkey who was currently avoiding her, what Farrah had told her about witches, her strange new power.

"No reason. I was just out there riding and wondered if it had any old stories I might've missed because I was too young."

"Not that I know of. The old crew tried to get me to go swimming there once senior year, but it wasn't my thing. The rocks look slimy."

They are, Keelie wanted to tell her. *Slimy and slippery.* But she just said, "They do. I wonder why the town is named after one little waterfall."

Cash shrugged. "I guess whoever started the town needed water? This land belonged to the Cherokee originally. Maybe it was important to them. We need more historical signage. It's all over the place out west."

"You're working tonight, right?"

Cash chuckled and swigged her coffee. "Of course. Bar trivia means great tips."

Keelie hugged her sister's shoulders and headed off to her

room to get to work. Cash thought of her as an innocent little sweetheart who couldn't hurt a fly, and if Keelie played it right, things would stay that way.

It took several tries and multiple online searches to accomplish the job, but soon she had the file she needed stored on an old thumb drive. She texted Jerry the trivia guy, telling him who she was and what she needed. He texted back immediately, telling her a new guy would be running trivia tonight but that he would pass on the message and that her request would be no problem.

And then, all she had to do was find some way to make four hours fly by before she chickened out. The answer, of course, was a trail ride, her favorite way to relax and spend time.

Usually, she would have zero reservations, but now, everything had changed.

Gary had *thoughts*.

"I'm a human being," she told herself. "This is my farm. I can ride my horses whenever I want to, and the donkey can join us or stay behind, but I will not be held hostage by guilt for turning him down." It was the weirdest pep talk of her life.

She went through her internal checklist outside, bringing Marigold in and grooming her, waiting to see if Gary would continue sulking in the back corner of the pasture. As she saddled her sturdy mare and fetched her helmet, she listened for the clip-clop of sharp little hooves or the eager braying that usually met her preparations, but the barnyard was silent.

"Gary, I'm going for a ride," she called. "You're welcome to join me."

She was about to swing up into the saddle when he appeared at the gate, looking hangdog. She silently let him through. When she reached out to scratch his ears, he turned away.

"How long are you going to pout?" she asked.

"I'm not pouting," he said crisply. "I'm having an existential crisis."

Keelie mounted her horse and walked her down the long gravel drive. Gary trotted along, just a little behind her.

"An existential crisis, huh?"

"Suddenly I can converse, and one of the first things I learn is that the creature I love most does not return the sentiment and never has. I thought you felt the same way. I am grieving what I have lost."

Keelie took a big breath. She'd never been to therapy, and her life had been pretty easy, outside of losing her parents young and then being abandoned by her sister, but she genuinely cared for Gary and wanted him to be happy, or at least not depressed. He looked way too much like Eeyore at the moment.

"Well, maybe you should celebrate what you've gained. We can talk now. Have conversations while we ride. Every time you greet me, I'm happy. I always laugh. You know that. You make my heart feel light when I see you, and when I'm at home, you make me feel safe. That's a lot more than lots of folks have."

A snort. "Forgive me if I wanted more."

"What more, Gary? Were we gonna make out? Get married? Have babies with long ears and human fingers?"

He was silent for several moments. "I . . . admit I did not think that part through. I merely longed to hear your words of love."

"Okay, then. I love you, Gary. I love you *platonically.* You are my favorite donkey in the entire world, the best donkey I've ever known. I never want another donkey but you in my life, and I never want you to leave me."

He trotted to her side and looked up, brown eyes shining.

"And I love you, Keelie. I love you with all of my heart, with my soul, with my loins—"

"Stop it with the loins stuff."

"I love you completely. I always have, and I always will. And if friendship is all that you can offer, then I will gladly take it." They turned onto the asphalt and headed toward the cow pasture that would lead them to the forest trails. "But if you'd like to enumerate more things you love about me as we go, that would perhaps be soothing to my ego."

⤞⤝

That night, Keelie got to work a little early and made a beeline for the bar trivia setup. The usual guy, Jerry, was in his late sixties and looked like a member of the Grateful Dead, but the new guy, Eli, was in his early twenties and distractingly hot, with blond surfer hair and sweet brown eyes.

"Jerry said you could help me play a quick video at halftime?" she asked, feeling her cheeks flush. Arcadia Falls was not a big town, and she'd known pretty much everybody around since the day she was born. Any new guy, especially if he was straight and not tied down, was news.

"Of course. Celebrating an anniversary, Jerry said. Want to do a quick run-through to check?"

"Oh, no need," she said too quickly. "It's just a basic MP4. All you need to do is click on it and press play."

He grinned. "That's sweet of you, to put it together for them."

She bit her lip. It really wasn't, but if she lost a chance with this guy for telling the truth and avenging Cash, then it was worth it. "Well, believe me: they deserve it," she said before hurrying on to the next step of her plan.

Everything was going off without a hitch. Gary was back to his mostly normal if British-accented self, Cash was in a good mood behind the bar, and all the elements of Keelie's scheme were in place. Folks began filling the tables and booths a little before five, and relief swept through Keelie's heart when she saw Mark and Sam walk in, along with their friends Carter and Trip and Emmy. Keelie had asked the hostess to seat them at a booth right in front of the trivia projector screen. They were all in good moods, but Keelie could sense an undercurrent of confusion, which made total sense. Supposedly, Mark had invited everyone else . . . but now Mark swore he hadn't done it.

Trivia started up, and Keelie was busy but distracted as she waited for the halftime mark, when the trivia guy took a break and put short videos on the screen while folks ate and drank. Finally, finally it was time, and she went to the bar to stand with Cash.

"What's up?" Cash asked her. "Got an order for me?"

"Nope." Keelie was practically shaking with nerves. "Just watch the screen."

"And tonight we've got something special," Eli said into the microphone. He had a nice voice, Keelie thought. Not Gary nice, but nice. "Mark and Samantha Ranger, this one's for you. Happy anniversary!"

"What the—?" Cash started.

Keelie covered her sister's hand with her own. "Just watch."

The video started, and it was just a loop of the ten photos Keelie had taken at the restaurant earlier today. Mark and the young blond girl laughing, her feeding him fries, him kissing her hand, both of them leaned over to kiss in front of the entire restaurant, the cashiers, and God. There was no music, but one very recognizable voice spoke as the pics cycled past.

"Hey, man. It's Mark. Look, I need your help. I'm seeing this girl—real young, such a hot piece. Natural blonde. She has no idea I'm married. Obviously Sam has no clue. She'd kill me. And I know I cheated on Cassia King, too, back in high school, but that doesn't make me a serial cheater. A man has needs, you know? That's one of the great things about running a lawn-care service. I can flirt with the wives and check out the underage daughters. Anyway, here's what I need you to do."

The voicemail cut out.

That voice—it was clearly Mark Ranger. There was no doubt.

Whispers started up, but the slideshow wasn't done, and neither was the audio.

"Hey, it's Sam," Sam's voice said. "I'm worried Mark might be up to something. He's smiling at his phone way too much. He doesn't smile at me like that anymore, you know? He did at first, back in high school, when we were sleeping together behind Cassia's back. It was so fun, having our secret, getting one over on my perfect best friend. And everybody knew, but they covered for us because my brother told them to. Anyway, once we were married, things kinda fizzled, and we both let ourselves go, and now I'm totally insecure. So . . ."

The audio cut off and the final frame flashed, showing Mark kissing the blond woman. *How old is this girl? Looks underage, doesn't she?* the text along the bottom read.

The screen went dark.

The entire room roared with voices, and every single eye turned to Mark and Sam.

"That wasn't me! I didn't say that!" Mark hollered.

"Then who the hell else was it?" someone shouted.

"Are the pictures fake, too?" someone else added.

"Mark, is it true?" Sam asked, standing.

"Of course not, baby! I would never hurt you!"

But Sam had apparently heard and seen enough, as she stomped out of the restaurant with every single eye following her.

"Screw y'all! That wasn't me. I never said any of that!" Mark shouted, throwing down his napkin. He pointed at the screen. "And she told me she's turning twenty in September! I swear!"

And then he, too, turned tail and disappeared.

The noise level was immediately through the roof, everybody in Arcadia Falls laughing or whispering or saying, "I knew it!" or "He is not my lawn guy anymore!" or "If they get divorced, I'm takin' back that dang toaster!"

Cash's hand trembled in Keelie's. "Did you have anything to do with this?" Cash asked.

"I didn't make Mark a cheating scumbag or Sam a bad friend."

"But the video—"

Keelie squeezed Cash's hand. "Sure sounded like Mark and Sam to me. And photos don't lie."

"Sometimes they do."

"Those did not."

"True. That man loves a French fry."

For a long moment they just stood there, hand in hand.

"Thank you," Cash whispered.

"I don't know what you're talking about, but if I did, you'd be very welcome. Sometimes folks just get what they deserve."

One of Keelie's tables called her over, and trivia commenced, and the world went on spinning. No matter how Cash pressed her, Keelie's lips were sealed. Maybe one day she'd tell Cash about the witch thing, and maybe not. She wanted to talk to Farrah about it, but Farrah was always run ragged on nights this busy.

"That was dirty pool," Eli the trivia guy said as she was cleaning up, once the Arcadia Balls had won again.

"I told you they deserved it," she said before looking up at him, a little guilty. "Can we keep this between us? I don't want my sister to know I was involved."

"I take it your sister is Cassia King, then." He nodded in understanding. "Nope, sounds like the perfect anniversary gift was delivered to just the right people. I don't know where that thumb drive came from." He mimicked zipping his lips and locking away the key. "But maybe you should give me your number, in case I ever need some help with a video?"

Keelie's heart just about exploded, and she gave him her number, and he texted her so she'd have his, and suddenly the world was just a little bit brighter than it had been since Noelle Halloran left town.

When Keelie turned her truck down the drive long after midnight, Gary was there to greet her. But instead of hee-hawing, "My love! My love!" he called, "Welcome home, my dear! Welcome home!"

"Hey, Gary!" she called through the open window, the summer breeze blowing in the sweet smell of grassy pasture, mown hay, and sleeping horse.

In that moment, Keelie decided that she did not mind being a witch at all.

She'd had her revenge, and her leg was going to get donkey-humped a hell of a lot less. That, in her book, was a win.

CONTAINED

Tanya Huff

When he woke and turned on his phone, he had a message from Jack Elson. Sent twenty-three minutes after sunset, the message included an address and a terse Body. Get here ASAP.

Henry considered Jack a friend. In almost five hundred-odd years, there'd never been so many who'd been trusted with the knowledge of what he was. RCMP Inspector Jack Elson had seen a few inexplicable things and—to Henry's amusement—had more trouble accepting that Henry had been the Duke of Richmond and Somerset, the Marshal of the North, and the bastard son of Henry VIII than he did with Henry's being a vampire.

Bottom line, Henry knew Jack wouldn't waste his time. The word *body*, as a sentence on its own, could refer to any number of things, but given the context, its meaning seemed obvious. The body itself—condition, manner of death—had to be beyond the scope of the police.

He wondered what it said about the times that he'd become a de facto police consultant.

At five p.m. on a December Tuesday, the traffic on Marine Drive was appalling. It had grown worse over the years Henry had lived in Vancouver, and he had no idea how anyone without his advantages survived the number of idiots now careening around on the road. He turned left onto Ontario Street, crossed Kent and the railway tracks, and entered a warehouse parking lot a stone's throw from the Fraser River. It had to be the right place given the number of government vehicles.

His headlights picked out two uniformed officers vomiting onto the scrubby grass at the edge of the lot. One had fallen forward onto his knees, back arched as he convulsed and dribbled bile onto the asphalt. One might have been a rookie; the other was far too old. Henry spotted another pair as he pulled into a parking spot, the younger squatting by a squad car bumper with her head between her knees, gulping for air, the elder rummaging in a first aid kit spread out on the hood, tears pouring down his face.

Henry turned off the engine and spent a moment considering the situation. If the police were here in these numbers, if the police were *this* affected, he had to assume multiple bodies rather than the single body implied in Jack's message. Moreover, the bodies had to be in the kind of condition that overwhelmed the coping methods of the VPD. He locked down the potential reaction to what would no doubt be ungodly amounts of blood and got out of the car.

The blood scent was surprisingly faint.

But the strong smell of bleach coming from the warehouse meant nothing good.

Jack stood in the open doorway. The tie he'd been forced to wear since his promotion to inspector had been violently loosened, and he was breathing shallowly through his nose. The rapid slam of his heart against his ribs suggested he'd armored himself in professionalism in order to maintain a semblance of outward calm.

"I have seen some shit, Fitzroy," he said when Henry drew close enough. "On my own. With you." He shook his head and entered the warehouse. "Normally, I'd call Tony for something like this but . . ."

"But he's in San Diego."

"Yeah. That too."

Following Jack between the stacks of crates toward the blaze of what looked like a half dozen circled spotlights hanging from catwalks, Henry breathed shallowly through his mouth so as not to be overwhelmed by the bleach fumes. A pile of crates blocking the end of the passage forced them to turn left down another passage toward an opening marked by a spill of light. A quick glance up at the ceiling suggested the opening would lead to the center of the warehouse. When Henry moved toward it, Jack stopped him.

He ran a hand through his short pale blond hair. "Not yet. You go in there now with *your* eyes, you'll go blind. Give them a minute to . . ."

Before he could finish, all but one of the spotlights up on the catwalks went out.

"Right." He swallowed. "Let's go then."

The remaining spotlight shone into the center of a roughly circular open area three, maybe four meters across. In front of a body propped upright on a low pedestal, a short, heavyset man in a turban placed equipment back into his case with the kind of care that suggested he was barely maintaining control.

Jack cleared his throat. "Doc?"

"I'm done." He closed the case and turned.

"Anything?"

"Alive while it happened. Probably for a while after. Dead

when he was mounted on that post at least, poor bastard." He walked past them, gaze locked on the middle distance, as though acknowledging another person on anything but the most superficial level would shatter his composure. "Now, if you'll excuse me, Inspector, I'm going to wait *outside* for the wagon."

As the doctor's footsteps faded, Henry stepped forward. Once. Twice. Close enough that blood and flesh and terror and pain overwhelmed the bleach. "Saint Bartholomew was one of the twelve apostles," he said. "He was flayed for converting an Armenian king to Christianity. In 1562, Marco d'Agrate sculpted the saint holding a book and wearing his skin like a stole." Confined by the limitations of stone, the sculpted stole was less dramatic than the stole in front of him. D'Agrate had omitted dangling feet and hands, the bristle of chest hair, the face still wearing duct tape over its mouth. Stone genitalia had been covered. Flesh was not. The weight of the skin held open the book.

Saint Bartholomew held a Bible. This non-saint held one of Henry's books.

For the last five years, Henry had been writing graphic novels under the name Henry Richmond.

He took a step closer. Blood obscured all but the panel that held the drawing of D'Agrate's *Saint Bartholomew Flayed* in the Duomo di Milano.

"Figured this is a message for you." Jack's voice sounded muffled, distanced by the fingernail grip Henry had on his control. "Both the book and the . . . extremes the creature went to. So the question is, what's come into my city?"

Henry drew a deep breath in through his nose and exhaled through his mouth, tasting the residue left beneath the bleach. "Nothing."

"Nothing? Are you saying something that could do this has

been here all along and you didn't . . ." The pause stretched. Lengthened. "Fuck me," Jack muttered at last. "A person did this? A basic, non-mythic human?"

"Yes."

"Maybe possessed by, like, a demon or a vengeful ghost or something?"

"No. Just a person. But you're right," he continued, before Jack could respond, "this is a message for me. Both the book and the victim. This body . . ." Once belonged to. Once held. Once was. "It's Kevin Groves."

"The truth guy who writes for the tabloids?"

"The truth guy who writes for the tabloids," Henry agreed. "Kevin Groves. Who knew when he was being lied to. Probably why he got divorced last year. He always said it was a curse. For as long as I've known him, he's been trying to become an investigative reporter and failing. Kept trying though. But more importantly . . ." He could feel his control slipping and turned to face Jack in the hope of containing the Darkness just a little longer. "More importantly . . . He. Was. Mine."

Jack had one hand on his weapon and the other outstretched, as though flesh and bone and willpower could stop what Henry barely held in check. "What now?"

"Now? Now I'm going to find out who sent the message and answer it."

"It'll be a trap."

"I know." He couldn't stop the snarl.

One step back. Almost two, but Jack managed to hold his ground. "What can I do?"

"Clear the way to my car."

"Is it safe for you to drive?"

"It isn't safe to stop me."

⤚⤙

It should have taken Henry an hour and fifteen minutes to get out to the Pitt River Bridge. It took him forty-seven minutes, and he had to force himself to release the steering wheel once he was parked. He didn't know of anyone capable of skinning a man alive, but he knew someone who would. Someone who kept track of the worst humanity could offer. Someone Henry had allowed to hunt around the edges of his territory.

The noise level in the River's Pit slammed at Henry's ears when he opened the door, but the smell was almost welcome. Whiskey and beer and urine and unwashed bodies chased the bleach from his nose. The place was half-full, heat cranked high, blood pulsing under sweat-streaked skin. Two men, their bulk run to fat, shoved each other, back and forth, in one corner. No one paid any attention. A working girl looked up as Henry closed the door behind him, looked hopeful, and hurriedly looked away. Three disgusting pay phones on the wall to Henry's right hung under a handwritten sign that warned potential customers the machines were tapped by the VPD.

The man Henry wanted sat where he had a good view of both exits, his back against the wall, his gaze sweeping the room. He smiled at Henry, a smile that didn't pretend to be anything but a challenging show of teeth. A younger man sat with him, leg jittering, fingers tapping, a scar cutting up the left side of his face almost to his eye. He turned to watch as Henry approached, opened his mouth, and was cut off by a terse "Fitzroy" from his companion.

"Baden." Henry leaned in. "I need the name and location of a man with a skinning knife and the skills to wield it."

"No hello? No 'It's been a long time'? No concern over how I've been?"

"None. Just the name."

"Fuck you. You sure it's a man?"

"Yes. Gender *and* species."

"All right then." Baden leaned back in his chair. "You want to hire this guy or kill them? Don't answer that," he continued before Henry could answer. "You stink of death. You want to rip the world apart right now, but you'll settle for this knife wielder. Too bad. I don't know who he is."

"I do."

Henry turned to the second man, who grinned at him, showing very white teeth, the drugs he was sweating out constricting the pupils of his yellow eyes to pinpricks even in the dim light of the bar. Another shifter. He turned his attention back to Baden, barely holding on to his humanity. "Pack?"

"Reynolds? Not likely. This asshole is another lone. Surprised you haven't run into him, Fitzroy. He's been . . . doing some work downtown." *He's been hunting right under your nose*, Baden's smug subtext added.

"Reynolds." Henry rolled the name past fangs he stopped trying to control. "Tell me what you know. Now."

"Oh, it's not going to be that easy, Lord Cashmere Sweater, virgin wool coat that you don't even fucking need." Reynolds giggled. "You want this guy, Nightwalker, you fight me for what I know."

Baden set his beer bottle on the table and sighed. "Reynolds, shut up, unless you have a death wish."

"Fuck you, Baden. You're not my alpha. I show my neck to no one." Reynolds got to his feet, jittering in place, rolling broad shoulders under his grimy denim jacket. "Well, pretty boy," he jeered, "you got enough balls to fight, or did they shrivel up back in the fifteens with your whore of a mother?"

Henry growled.

The bar fell silent, a nineties country song suddenly foreground and not sounding too happy about being there. These were people who recognized a predator.

Reynolds's yellow eyes glittered. "Fight me, Nightwalker. Let's answer the question, once and for all."

"Outside," Baden snapped, surging up onto his feet. "Now. Whatever happens does not happen in here."

Henry spun on a heel and headed for the door.

"Don't turn your back on me," Reynolds began.

Baden cut him off. "I said, outside!"

Both men were following; that was all Henry cared about right now. Outside. Away from witnesses. Outside. Where he'd release the rage that threatened to split his skin and rip the name he needed out of flesh and blood. He slid out of his coat and laid it on the hood as he passed his car, making his way across the parking lot to a patch of empty ground where dead grass crackled between his soles and the semi-frozen ground.

He turned as he heard Baden and Reynolds leave the gravel.

No one had followed them. Other bars, other places, they'd have had an audience. The people who drank in this bar were damaged enough to know *witness* was another name for *victim*.

Reynolds was already naked to the waist, jacket and shirt discarded in a messy pile. He kicked off one boot, then the other, and stepped out of his jeans. Naked, he drew his lips back off his teeth and changed, man to wolf, as he charged.

Henry released his hold on the Darkness. Kevin Groves had

been skinned alive because of him. Had been skinned alive to send him a message. Henry closed his hand around Reynolds's muzzle, yanked the wolf's head up, and ripped out his throat.

Ignoring death throes that shuddered between skin and fur, he fed.

Replete, he dropped the body and turned to face the other shifter, the world in sharp-edged focus.

Baden sighed, still fully dressed, body loose and relaxed. "Yeah, that lasted about as long as I thought it would. Just don't expect me to bury the fucker. Any dumbass who thinks a few years spent terrorizing humans has a snowflake's chance in hell of winning against five hundred years of experience deserves to feed a few rats. Not to mention that the reaction to headlines proclaiming 'Exsanguinated Wolf' will be funny as shit."

Henry snarled.

"Yeah, fine, whatever. I'll dump him in the river; I owe you for saving me the effort of putting that mangy disaster down. Reynolds was not meant to be lone; he truly sucked at it. Had maybe two functioning brain cells left, and neither of them were within shouting distance of self-preservation." Baden paused, sighed again, and added, "Or species preservation, for that matter."

Anchoring himself to the flow of words, Henry clawed the Darkness back. The night was young, and he had work to do within the human world if he wanted justice before dawn.

"Back with me, Fitzroy?"

He began to answer when he realized what killing Reynolds meant, and the Darkness surged up again.

"Yeah, hard to get the name you wanted from a corpse," Baden agreed placidly. "Not impossible, but necromancers are paranoid bastards. I don't know why you're all Prince of Darkness tonight, but I do know that you need to hunt smarter. Fortunately for you, while I can't name the guy you're looking for, I know who can."

Over the scents of blood and a cooling corpse, Henry could smell wolf and man and beer and leather . . . but not fear. He drew in a deep breath, finding himself close enough to Baden that the shifter's body heat had warmed the air between them. He didn't remember moving. "I could have killed you." His head barely topped the other man's shoulder. Neither of them pretended size mattered.

Baden shrugged. "You got no reason to kill me. Not when you've got a belly full of blood and I'm a joy to be around. Also, I'm not Reynolds. I'm bigger, I'm smarter, and I haven't turned my brain to mush; there's a good chance I'd do some damage before I go down. You can't risk that, not tonight, Nightwalker. Not on the hunt like you are."

He couldn't. Had that stayed his hand? Had he realized he couldn't waste time on Baden, not when he intended to rip the heart out of whoever had tortured Kevin Groves? "I need . . ."

"Don't tell me. My guess, some anonymous asshole challenged you, but I don't fucking care." Baden stepped aside, giving Henry a clear run across the parking lot to his car. "Go talk to some upper-level members of the Pride," he continued, falling in on Henry's left. "Gang's been around for a couple of years, but they're trying to move up. Word has it you stand against them, they send out some crazy fucker with tranks and a knife and that one of the Devil Dogs came to with the sigil peeled off his arm and the skin wrapped around his dick."

"Reynolds was working with a gang?" Henry could feel Reynolds's blood sharpening his focus.

"Fucked if I know. Maybe. Doesn't matter now."

It didn't. "Where do I find the Pride?"

"Generally, downtown. Maybe even in that fancy condo building of yours." Baden's grin showed teeth. "You might want to pay more attention to who's shitting on your doorstep, Nightwalker, and a little less time drawing comics."

⤚⤙

Successful gangs drew wannabe gangbangers like corpses drew flies. With the Pride ready to move up, their circle of hopeful applicants had expanded. The third street tough Henry questioned pointed him to a peripheral member who gave up an address.

The young man stumbled forward, Henry's pale fingers wrapped around both his hand and his weapon. Bone broke against steel. He sobbed out an address. Sobbed out a plea for mercy. Henry left him slumped against a urine-stained building, pupils dilated, every exhalation a terrified sob.

The Pride hadn't set up in Henry's "fancy condo building" but two blocks away. Close enough to be considered "shitting on his doorstep." Fortunately, developers were more interested in profit than safety, and while the bolt on the entrance was solid, the mechanism controlling it was not. A quick twist tore it apart.

He got off the elevator on the fifteenth floor, walked to 1536, and knocked on the door in a parody of unconcern, as if he weren't about to kill anyone who got in the way of the name he needed. Seven heartbeats. Cannabis. Too much cheap aftershave on the man peering out at him.

"The fuck do you want?"

With less than ten hours until dawn, Henry had neither time nor inclination for subtlety. He slammed the door open, grabbed the man who'd answered it by the throat, stepped into the room, and closed the door behind him.

Red-faced and gasping for breath, the man Henry held went for a knife. Trained then. A mercenary acting as first-line defense for people willing to have a man skinned alive. The vicious dilettantes turning to face him hadn't ordered the torture of Kevin Groves, but they'd used the man with the knife on their enemies. Guilt by association.

He tightened his grip, crushing cartilage and stopping air and blood, dropped the body, and counted five guns pointed at him.

No one fired. Gunfire was still rare enough in Canada, even in gang-plagued Vancouver, that neighbors would undoubtedly call the police and the shooters would have to abandon the condo.

Henry could appreciate hanging on to real estate, but they should've fired regardless. If they'd shot him, if enough of them had taken the time to aim, they'd have survived the night.

It was both too easy to kill in this time and too easy to forget how to deal with monsters.

Too easy to forget who the monsters were.

One young man, an open shirt framing the lion tattoo on his chest, raised the hand without a weapon, holding the others in place. "This a revenge thing?" he asked. "One of ours take a shot at you?"

Henry glanced down. His coat hung open, and he'd forgotten about the red-brown stain covering his clothes. It had been years since he'd worn the stain so casually. "One of yours uses a skinning knife," he said.

"Not one of ours, dude. That crazy fucker's contract only. He the one who had a go at you?"

"Not at me."

"Ah, at one of yours."

"Yes."

The speaker nodded, as though he understood. As though he had any idea of what it meant to *have a go* at someone Henry had claimed. "You want him?"

"I do." Two weapons remained pointed at him. The barrels of the other three sagged as the tension in the room began to ease.

"I don't know where he is off the top, you know. But I can find out. If you ask nicely."

Only a heavyset man who'd risen from a leather armchair reacted, his frown flicking from Henry to the speaker and back again. He knew, Henry noted. Both who and, more importantly, where.

The speaker smiled, a smile he probably considered dangerous, and the two sets of heartbeats approaching along the hall arrived at the door. Henry reached back as the door opened, grabbed a heavy jacket in each hand, and slammed the two men together in front of him. Blood sprayed from noses shattered in the impact, and he felt the man in his right hand die, bone shards shredding his brain.

Henry dropped them both, stepped over a twitching leg, and let the Darkness rise.

The only man who might have had a chance to stop him had died first. Four of the five who'd been lounging on expensive leather furniture drinking cheap beer died quickly. He broke the speaker's neck and used the second man as a shield, bullets shattering ribs and shredding organs. In the pause when panicked fingers fumbled to reload, he went up and over the back of the sofa, drove thumb and forefinger through the third man's eye sockets, and, holding him by the skull, used his gun to shoot the fourth. Then he broke the third's neck and wiped the blood and brains off on his jeans.

"Who and where?" he whispered to the fifth man, drinking in his terror.

⤚⤙

James Chin lived in a second-floor flat on Sixteenth Avenue West, an upper-middle-class residential neighborhood. The surrounding houses held children. And pets. And people who'd never suspect that on one of the lower mainland's rare bright and sunny days, he'd skinned someone alive.

In spite of his name, he wasn't Asian. He was a white man in his early thirties with a receding hairline and that ridiculous unshaven look favored by so many.

He wasn't what Henry had expected. He'd expected a skinny man of indeterminate color wearing a stained T-shirt and grimy sweatpants that rose high above bony ankles, squatting ghoul-like in a filthy room in a crap hotel in the worst of the ungentrified parts of the Downtown Eastside. He'd expected a man wrapped in tics and twitches and slack-jawed manifestos. A man balanced precariously on the edge between sanity and madness. An edge Henry would have enjoyed pushing him over.

James Chin slept on his back, alone under a pale blue duvet in a medium blue bedroom in a pleasant apartment that smelled faintly of bleach. Although, Henry acknowledged, it might have been the lingering memory of a smell.

The dichotomy between expectation and reality stopped him at the foot of the queen-size bed.

And then he remembered that this man, this clean, well-fed, comfortably housed man, had taken and tortured Kevin Groves.

Henry reached out and closed his hand around the man's ankle.

And moved so that when James Chin flailed awake, he was there to grab a handful of thick, white, fabric softener–scented

T-shirt and throw him to land half-reclining against the headboard.

"What . . . ? Who . . . ?" His eyes widened and picked Henry out of the shadows thrown by the streetlight. "What are you doing here? Hel . . ."

Henry closed a hand around his throat before the "p" could emerge. "Who hired you," he growled, "to kill Kevin Groves?"

He felt James Chin's Adam's apple bob under his palm. Felt him breathe. Three fast and shallow. One long, released slowly. Felt the fingers clawing at his arm relax, the hands fall away. He saw, to his astonishment, the beginning of a smile.

"You're him, aren't you?" James Chin said gleefully, and Henry felt his rage slide off the other man's total lack of concern. "The one the message was for? He said you'd come in the night, but I didn't think he meant *tonight*. You got here a lot faster than I thought you would. You know, I usually don't get to meet you guys—I get a contract, I fulfill the contract, life goes on. I don't suppose you'd be willing to let me know how you found me? I mean, either way, I'm going to have to reemphasize the point of an NDA, but the details will save me some time." His nose wrinkled. "You smell like blood. I'm going to have to crack a window and air the place out after you go and, in case you've forgotten, it's December out there. Man, my heating bill will be vicious this month."

Henry tightened his grip, feeling the steady beat of James Chin's pulse against his palm.

"Hey! Loosen up, I'm cooperating here. There's an envelope on the mantel under my TV that has all the information you're looking for. You know, information about the guy who actually *sent* the message, because me, I'm just the messenger."

"An easy betrayal . . ."

"What? You think I'm betraying him? Hell no, it was his idea.

'Jimmy,' he said, and I hate being called Jimmy, he said, 'Don't be a hero. When he'—that's you—'shows up, and he will show up, give him this. It's me he's after. Not you.'"

James Chin had turned on the bedside lamp and had rearranged himself into a more comfortable position when Henry returned with the envelope. "You know it's a trap, right? I'll give you that for free."

The envelope held a single piece of paper folded around a name and an address. "What do you assume is going to happen now?" Henry asked, stopping just outside the circle of light.

The answering eye roll was epic. "I assume you're going to go away so I can get the blood stink out of my apartment and get back to sleep."

"Because you're just the messenger?"

"Don't shoot the messenger, right?" He grinned, showing the kind of perfect teeth that in this century meant his parents had had the money for dentistry.

"You killed Kevin Groves . . ."

"Ah, ah, ah." He raised a hand. "Technically, Kevin Groves died while I was doing my job."

Both Reynolds and the man who'd spoken for the Pride had referred to James Chin as a *crazy fucker.* They hadn't been speaking euphemistically; the man was insane.

"Look . . ." He sighed. "He said you won't care about the gun . . ."

"You?"

"Yeah, me. I'm the gun. It's a metaphor." The pale blue duvet rose and fell as he crossed his legs at the ankle. "He said you'll only care about the man who pulled the trigger. Guns don't kill people. People kill people. Right? He said, once you have the information you're after, you'll leave."

"And you believe him."

"I'm a businessman, and there's a certain amount of trust required in order to be able to do business. Particularly our sort of business."

"I'm not in your sort of business."

"Really? Because I somehow doubt that the people who bled all over you were into it." He held up both hands. "Not kink shaming, mind, I just doubt it. Now, since you have what you came for, go away."

Henry had come here to make James Chin suffer. He'd intended to make him pay and keep paying for the pain he'd inflicted. He'd intended to bury him so deeply, wrap him so tightly in Darkness that his screams would echo long after his flesh had decayed. But James Chin would not come face-to-face with his personal demons in the Darkness because he had no personal demons. Nothing lingered behind his eyes.

He'd be found eventually, his heart having stopped while he slept. Depending on timing, if corruption allowed, he'd look mildly annoyed and have a bruise on one ankle and another just under his right ear.

No marks of teeth.

No missing blood.

Henry would rather feed from a rotting corpse.

⤚⤙

With three hours to dawn, Henry walked up and stopped in front of a gated drive. If the size of the lot was any indication, acreage being at a premium in the Lower Mainland, Robert Alistair Kenwick had made a great deal of money in publishing. A quick search had linked his name with multiple newspapers in multiple countries, newspapers that took cash from the credible and had, for the most part, only a passing association with the truth.

The house shouted, *Look at what I am able to do!* as loudly as his father's palace at Greenwich.

⟶⟵

Robert Alistair Kenwick, middle-aged and a little plump, sat in a recliner tucked into a comfortable corner in a second-floor library. He held an open book, no mythic nor modern way to take out a vampire visible. No garlic. No mustard seeds. No holy symbols nor holy water. No stakes. No sunlamps.

There were, however, a great many bits of antiquity sharing the shelves with the books. Not enough to give the British Museum a run for its money, but amulets, rings, carved stone and bone, small idols, and pieces of larger statuary filled every empty place. Asian artifacts, including broken and unbroken jade, covered over half of a huge teak desk. Not unexpected; in that same quick search, Henry had found an article about Kenwick recently returning from "a trip to the Far East with the intention of expanding his empire."

When Henry stepped out of the shadows, Kenwick looked up from his book and sneered. "I see you got my message, Nightwalker. Took you long enough to get here."

Henry curled his lip, exposing fangs.

"You don't frighten me," Kenwick scoffed. "You came when I called."

Henry allowed the Darkness to show in his eyes.

"That Chin boy does lovely work, doesn't he?" Kenwick closed the book and picked up a glass of amber liquid from the small round table beside him. "I wonder how long Groves screamed for you, for rescue, before he died."

And Henry allowed himself to seem only Henry again. The momentary tightening of Kenwick's grip on the glass told him everything he needed to know. "You had no guards in the garden and minimal security. You wanted me in the house. That makes sense—you don't want to attract attention. Once I'm safely out of sight, you'll spring your trap." Henry spread his hands, and dried blood flaked off onto the carpet. "But there isn't a trap, at least not an obvious one. You're alone. Exposed. You know what I am, but you're not afraid.

"James Chin wasn't afraid either, but James Chin was mad. Soulless, although I'm sure modern medicine would make a different, inadequate diagnosis. You know what he did . . ."

"Know," Kenwick scoffed. "I paid him to do what he did. To do something you'd notice."

Henry ignored him. "Having two men without souls involved in attracting my attention is too much of a coincidence." He paused, pulled over a leather club chair, and sat down. "Robert Alistair Kenwick publishes tabloids. Kevin Groves worked at a tabloid. Not much of a leap to assume he said enough about me that you knew what I was. Knew that I was in Vancouver."

"Poor Kevin." Kenwick pursed fleshy lips in a parody of sympathy. "Life is very, very lonely for a man unable to lie."

"Kevin was able to see the truth—not quite the same thing. But we're not talking about Kevin. We're talking about you. About how knowing what I am means knowing my kind are possessive." And how it almost always ended badly. "If all you wanted was my attention, you could have sent Kevin to me with your business card and a threat against him if I didn't respond." A thought occurred and Henry frowned. "I wonder: Did he see the truth about you? Never mind." He waved it off. Kevin was dead. What he'd seen or hadn't seen no longer mattered. All that mattered now was ending the charade. "You didn't just want my attention; you wanted me angry. You wanted me to stop thinking, to allow the Darkness free rein. Why?" The pause lengthened. When Kenwick refused to fill it, Henry continued, not actually needing his help. He had all the pieces now, and he knew what he was building. "With the Darkness released, I'd want blood for blood. A life for a life. You wanted me to attack you. You wanted me to attack you mindlessly. Unfortunate that you got so excited about what you *could* do, you made a mistake."

Kenwick raised both brows and took a drink.

"If you hadn't left the drawing, if you hadn't specifically said the message was for me, the police would have found the tabloid connection. You'd have an alibi, of course, and I doubt they'd have found James Chin—he's a well-camouflaged cuckoo in the nest. After talking to you—rich, alibied—the police would back off. And I'd arrive. You'd admit to having Kevin killed, you'd goad me like you have been, and I'd attack you.

"But when you made Kevin's death specially about me, that ensured I wouldn't wait for the police, and in order to find you, I had to find the man with the knife. In order to find him, well . . ." Henry indicated his bloodstained clothing. "There's a few less gangbangers around." Kenwick didn't need to know about Reynolds. Reynolds was . . . was not his finest hour. And in case this didn't end well, if Kenwick didn't already know about the shifters, well, Henry wasn't going to be the one who told him. "The gangbangers burned off a lot of the unreasoning rage, and James Chin made me start thinking."

"Ah yes, so you said." Kenwick took another drink. "Two men with the absence of a soul would be too great a coincidence."

Henry leaned back and crossed his legs, folding the sides of his coat up over his lap. "I started connecting the dots. Watching you from the shadows, I connected a few more."

"I haven't the faintest idea of what you're talking about."

"Connect the dots." Henry sketched lines in the air. More blood flaked off his hand. "You draw a line from one point to another until a picture forms. You've never done that. You're wearing a man-suit, but you're not a man." He let his hand drop back down onto his lap. "Men don't call me Nightwalker."

Kenwick sighed. "I'm sure they call you any number of things," he muttered.

Henry continued, ignoring him. "You wanted me to attack you mindlessly, so I assume you need blood in order to pass from one body to the next. You want mine because I'm immortal. I expect the late Robert Kenwick picked you up from one of those souvenirs." He nodded toward the artifacts on the desk. "Pricked a finger while buying something old and exotic on the black market, and there you were."

Putting down his glass, the creature wearing Kenwick slow clapped. "Oh, well done."

"Fuck you," Henry said genially. "Why not attack me when it became clear I wasn't following the script?"

"My physicality is limited by the body I inhabit, and this one couldn't lay a finger on you if you didn't want it to." It smiled. "Your immortality is not the only reason I want to wear you."

"Why not transfer to Kevin? You obviously gain the knowledge of the . . ." He paused. Frowned.

"Deceased," it offered.

"Of the deceased. You'd have found me, exposed yourself, and I'd have attacked. You'd have got what you wanted."

"Perhaps." It spread Kenwick's hands. "The whole truth thing made me nervous. Besides, just walking up to you wearing Kevin, where's the artistry in that?"

Look what I can do.

"You remind me of my father."

It inclined Kenwick's head. "Thank you."

"It's not a compliment."

"So where do we go from here?" it asked, curious but unconcerned. "You won't attack me. I can't attack you. You need to be gone before sunrise. At which point I'll acquire a new meat suit and you'll never find me again. Stalemate." It gestured toward the board set up by one of the heavily curtained windows. "Kenwick played bad chess."

Henry smiled. "So do you."

He'd fought in two world wars. He knew how to handle guns, and a target a mere two meters away didn't require precision shooting, not even through the pocket of his coat. He fired eighteen times—the seventeen in the magazine, the eighteenth in the chamber.

Then he waited, leaning forward, forearms braced on his thighs. If he'd been starving, he wouldn't have been tempted by the blood pouring from Kenwick's body.

Where did the thing go when the blood had no contact with anything but a corpse?

Hopefully, back to wherever it had come from.

⤚⤙

"Hopefully?" Jack sputtered, walking shoulder to shoulder with Henry along the Stanley Park seawall.

Henry shrugged. "No way of knowing. I gathered up all the Asian artifacts, and then last night I poured holy water over them . . ."

"Holy water? Seriously?"

"Belt and suspenders, Inspector. Then I encased the artifacts in concrete . . ."

"Do I want to know . . ." Jack raised a hand, cutting himself off. "No, I don't."

"And then 'asked' . . . "

"A vampire making air quotes. Now I've seen everything."

"Asked," Henry repeated, quoting more emphatically, "a young man on a container ship to drop them overboard mid-ocean."

"Yeah, like I haven't seen that plot before."

"Safer than leaving them in Vancouver."

"Fair enough."

They walked a little further through fat snowflakes that melted as they hit the ground.

After a moment, Jack sighed. "So, VPD found a weapon in Kenwick's library, no serial number, no prints, but ballistics traced it to a drive-by shooting we wanted the Pride for. They also found some old blood at the scene that matched one of the victims of a Pride massacre in a condo down the block from yours. The unofficial consensus is gang violence. Same old, same old. A lot of that going around. A lot of the other thing going around too." He paused, then added, "*Your* other thing. Ancient evil emerging from artifacts . . ."

"I understood what you meant." And he wasn't wrong. Like attracts like. Henry could see sinuous shadows moving under the water off the park. It might have been currents moving seaweed, but he doubted it. "I was thinking about moving back to Europe."

"'Was'?"

"After weighing the possibilities, I changed my mind."

"Because you're only *hopeful* that whatever the hell possessed Robert Kenwick is gone?"

“That too.” Henry watched a snowflake land on the back of his hand. After a moment, he shook it off.

Jack watched it float downward. “You know, I said possessed by a demon or a vengeful ghost right at the beginning.”

“In reference to the man who murdered Kevin Groves. And, as I said then, he was just a person.”

“Just?”

“Maybe not *just*.”

“Do we have the sick bastard?”

“No.” James Chin’s body hadn’t been found, but it had only been three days. The cold weather would keep the smell down; it might be weeks. Long enough that there’d be no dots to connect.

“Is the sick bastard going to cut again?”

Not *Did you kill the sick bastard?* Henry noted. “No.”

“Fair enough. This time.”

“You called me.” He thought of adding, *You turned me loose*, but they both knew Jack couldn’t have stopped him.

“Yeah. Well, after what that bastard put Groves through to get your attention, I figured he deserved to reap the benefit of *having* your attention.” The rage in Jack’s voice echoed Henry’s own.

They walked a little further, isolated by the hour and the weather.

“Just so we’re clear though,” Jack said at last, “this was a one-time thing. I don’t want any vampire vigilante shit happening. No matter what that buddy of yours is up to in Toronto.”

“She has no part in this.” She had her own territory. “I was thinking . . .”

“God help us.”

“That I might pay more attention to who’s shitting on my doorstep.”

“And what does that mean when it’s home?”

That people forget who the apex predator is when he stops hunting. When all they have left is rumor, they fill in the silences with what they want to hear. He's not so tough, they think. I can take him. I can take his place.

But all he said aloud was, "Did you know that seven percent of American men think they'd win in a hand-to-hand fight with a grizzly bear? They're wrong too."

DIRT

Jennifer Blackstream

"You had no business trying to do it yourself in the first place. You're not a young witch, you know."

I stared up at the pink pixie peering at me from over the edge of the bookcase. My left elbow and hip throbbed from where I'd hit the floor after falling off the chair. The painting I'd been trying to hang lay a few feet away, its blue sky of fluffy white clouds over a field of wildflowers facing the pixie.

"You're the one who insisted we hang that painting up in the office!" I sat up and hissed as my body made me aware that my left shoulder and knee also hurt, even though they hadn't been part of my collision with the floor.

"I wanted *someone* to hang it up." Peasblossom narrowed her multifaceted pink eyes. "Not you." She stood and climbed over the edge of the bookcase, her glittering wings buzzing behind her as she launched herself into the air to glide down to the painting. "It's February in Ohio," she said, landing on the frame. "One needs a splash of color to remember the dreary gray skies won't last forever." She crossed her arms. "And you almost broke it."

"You're welcome," I muttered.

A knock on my office door forced me to get up faster than my battered body would have liked. I shoved my long dark hair out of my face, trying to smooth it down. With a grunt, I pushed the chair against the wall and grabbed the painting, dislodging the judgy pixie, before hobbling over to my desk.

"Come in," I said, raising my voice.

The door swung open and a petite woman with short blue hair poked her head inside. "I heard you talking to someone, am I interrupting?"

I leaned the painting against my desk and eased into my chair. "No, you're not interrupting. Peasblossom and I were just discussing office decor."

"It's a good thing you're here, Poppy," Peasblossom said, flying over to land on my desk next to the nameplate that read *Shade Renard, PI*. "If she tries to hang that painting again, we might *need* a necromancer."

"Thanks for that." I sighed and turned to my visitor. "It's nice to see you again, Poppy. How's the necromancy business going?"

"It's not." Poppy tugged on her leather jacket with the pink-and-black-striped sleeves, sending a soft rain of powdered sugar and grave dirt onto my office floor. "I'm on temporary hiatus pending my testimony at a trial."

"A trial?" I echoed. "Is everything all right?"

Poppy shrugged and scratched at her jacket collar where another patch of powdered sugar clung to the seams. "Not really. I caught one of my cohorts siphoning life force from people and using it to raise the dead."

I blinked. "I didn't know that was an option."

Poppy stared at her finger and the white sugary dust.

I held up a hand. "Please don't lick your finger."

Poppy wiped her finger on her pants and let out a huff of breath. "Using someone else's life force isn't a *good* option." She crossed the room to the chair in front of my desk, her thick-heeled black boots making a heavy clomping sound with every step. "Using someone else's life force instead of your own puts an extra space between you and the zombie you're raising. You'll have less control over it, and it can be harder to lay it to rest when you're done. Not to mention the potential consequences for the person you took the life force from."

"Then why do it that way?" Peasblossom asked. "Sounds like a good way to get yourself killed by your own zombie."

"There's a theory that if you use someone else's life force instead of your own, you'll live longer. Necromancers use their own life force to raise the dead, and if you're a successful necromancer, you raise the dead faster than your life force can recover. We die young, and not all of us accept that." She grabbed a pen out of the cup on my desk and used it to tap her chin. "The reputation for necromancers turning evil is sadly well-earned. None of us knows what we're truly capable of until we're faced with our own mortality." She dropped the pen on the desk. "Anyway, I'm not supposed to work in an official capacity until after the trial. But that's not why I'm here."

"Why—" I cut myself off as I realized Poppy wasn't alone.

A young man stood in the doorway, unmoving. He was a couple of inches short of six foot, with sallow red skin and short, dark brown hair. Bandages covered his left eye and most of his nose, and his lip was swollen around a deep cut filled with dried blood. Sunglasses perched on his face despite the fact that the sun was already setting, and they sat crooked on his face due to the bandages. He was dressed all in black, including a clingy black fishnet shirt that was completely inappropriate for the cold weather.

Poppy noticed where my attention had gone. "Oh, right, introductions. Shade, this is Alex. Alex Walker. We met the other night. He's the reason I came to see you."

"Why is he wearing sunglasses at night?" Peasblossom demanded.

"The darkness is welcoming to all," Alex responded, his soft voice a deep monotone that was somehow both disturbing and soothing.

Peasblossom smacked her forehead. "Oh, great, he's an emu."

"Emo," I corrected her. "And don't be rude." I folded my hands on my desk. "How can I help?"

Poppy patted the chair beside her, indicating for Alex to sit next to her. "So two days ago, I'm working a cemetery, when Jenkins goes nuts and charges something on the other side of a bunch of trees."

As she spoke, she slid her backpack over her shoulder to land in her lap, and I found myself staring directly at the small skull of Poppy's dead terrier, Jenkins. Jenkins, when animated, was a remarkably spry little terrier, all things considered, and I'd personally witnessed him dragging a zombie back to its grave when things got a little out of hand.

"I chase after him and I see a zombie coming after Alex here." Poppy jerked her thumb over her shoulder at Alex, who, despite her invitation to sit, still haunted my doorway like an imposing Halloween decoration. "I run over to help, and when I'm laying the zombie back in its grave, I notice this."

I frowned as she pulled something out of her pocket. "A lock of hair?"

"A lock of *Alex's* hair," Poppy said seriously. "Whoever raised that zombie sent it after him specifically."

I glanced at Alex and shifted uncomfortably in my seat. "Forgive me, but isn't it also possible that Alex used his own hair to raise the zombie and it got out of control?"

"I don't call the dead," Alex said in the same monotone as before. "The dead call for me."

"I see." I looked at Poppy.

"It wasn't him," she said firmly. "Jenkins caught someone's scent near the grave, but when we tried to follow it, he lost it in the parking lot—probably because whoever it was drove away. Someone raised that zombie and sent it after Alex. I need your help to find out who." She glanced down at my name plaque. "That's what you do now, isn't it?"

"Yes, I suppose it is. All right, then, Alex, do you have any idea why someone might want to hurt you?" I pulled a legal pad from the side of my desk to center it in front of me with one hand and grabbed the pen Poppy had dropped with the other.

"I have a vengeful spirit," Alex responded. "And I help those who need it."

I looked at Poppy.

"Alex has a calling," Poppy said, scooting forward in her seat. "He helps people get revenge."

I frowned. "What kind of revenge?"

Poppy waved her hands, making the chains hanging from her leather jacket jingle. "Nothing serious. It's more—"

"Petty?" Peasblossom suggested, leaning over my arm.

"Well . . . yes." Poppy grinned. "Alex is a college student over in Zanesville. When he hears about someone behaving badly, he helps their victims get a little revenge."

"Behaving badly?" I repeated.

"Yeah. Alex is an engineering and philosophy double major, so he's pretty good at rigging traps and cameras and that sort of thing. For example, there was a woman who was constantly parking in her coworker's assigned space. Alex made a little device that he attached to the nameplate in front of the space and connected to her car's electronics. Whenever she tried to park there, the device would set off her car alarm."

Alex's mouth quirked up in the corner. "Thieves deserve to have their faces bared to the world they victimize."

"I see." I tapped the pen on the legal pad. "All right, then I'd say the first logical place to start is the people you most recently . . . taught a lesson to." I pushed the legal pad across the desk toward Alex and laid the pen on top. "I need a list of, say, the ten most recent people you sought vengeance on."

Alex sank into the chair beside Poppy and reached for the pen. "Sometimes the answer to bringing balance between the light and the darkness is more darkness."

I stared at him, wishing I could see his eyes.

He had to be putting me on.

Alex stared back.

Finally, I smiled. "Words to live by. Now let's just focus on those names, shall we?"

⤚⤙

"Next up are a pair of roommates," I said, reading from Alex's list. "Lauren Reilly and Gabrielle Phillips." I set the list on the passenger seat and slipped the key into the ignition as I looked at Alex in the rearview mirror. "What did they do?"

I couldn't tell if Alex was looking at me because he was still wearing the sunglasses. I guessed it didn't matter though, since the sun had set forty-five minutes ago, and he had to be pretty much blind at this point.

"Gabrielle and Lauren preyed on a doe-faced young intern.

Gabrielle was the doe's immediate superior, and she would force the doe to do all of her work and then claim credit for it. The doe tried to bring it up to management, but Lauren flirted with the manager and convinced him that Gabrielle was the victim and the doe was merely doing the research that was her job and then trying to claim credit for the entire project."

He tilted his head. "I arranged for the doe to be absent the day of an important presentation—with the project she'd done completely on her own safely locked away in her desk at work. Gabrielle broke into her desk to steal it and ended up covered in blue dye with a symphony of greeting card musical inserts blaring. Everyone at the meeting came out to see what was going on."

I frowned as the light turned green, and I eased into the intersection. "Couldn't she just claim that the project was her work and she'd had to get it out of her absent assistant's desk?"

"She tried," Alex agreed. "And Lauren's lover backed her up. But I had told the doe to do this project in her own hand—no electronic copy. Gabrielle didn't know that, and was caught . . . unprepared. And since the manager's bosses were all present, he was unable to save them—or himself. All three were fired."

"Okay, so they could definitely be angry enough to seek revenge." I pulled into a parking spot in front of the apartment building.

Since we had no way of knowing if whoever had sent the zombie after Alex had seen Poppy, both the necromancer and Alex stayed in the car while Peasblossom and I went into the apartment building. As I had on the other visits, I had an official-looking file in my hand that held Alex's "mug shot," a police report I'd printed off the internet, and a blank form for the victims to fill out.

"Ready?" I asked Peasblossom.

The pixie squirmed deeper into the collar of my red trench coat. "Ready."

I knocked on the door.

No answer.

I raised my hand to knock again, but just before my knuckles touched the wood, the doorknob turned. I pasted a polite expression on my face and waited while the door slowly opened.

A girl stood there with one hand braced on the doorframe as if she needed the help staying upright. Her eyelids drooped, and she looked like she hadn't brushed her hair in a couple of days at least. She was dressed in a pink hoodie and matching yoga pants but didn't have any socks on, and there was something about the paleness in her cheeks that made me think she was unwell.

"Hi," I said, carefully. "Are you Lauren Reilly?"

"No, I'm Gabrielle. Hang on a second." She looked over her shoulder, swaying as the movement seemed to set her off balance. "Lauren?"

She sounded as if she'd tried to yell the name but didn't have the breath for it.

She opened the door a little wider. "Come in."

Another girl came out of a room off to the left as I stepped into the shared living space. She had rich brown skin, but even without the paleness, I could tell that whatever was wrong with Gabrielle seemed to be affecting Lauren too. She moved like a woman fifty years older, shuffling forward in fuzzy green slippers. She made it to the couch and grasped the back cushion to steady herself as she looked at me.

"Can I help you?" she asked.

I looked back and forth between the two girls. "I'm here looking for information on a cyberhacker who's been targeting people in the area." I opened my file and pulled out Alex's picture to show them. "Do you know this man?"

Both girls tensed.

"No," Lauren lied. "I'm sorry."

"Who is he?" Gabrielle sidled around the couch and let herself collapse onto the threadbare cushions. "He looks like he got beat up. Is he in trouble?"

"He certainly is," I said, pinching my face in stern disapproval. "This young man has been illegally spying on people on this campus. And we've had reports of him hacking into personal computers and disseminating private information."

"That's terrible," Lauren murmured, sitting on the arm of the couch. "I hope you catch him. Sorry we can't help."

I called my magic, weaving purple energy into my voice before I spoke again. "I think you can help me, Lauren, Gabrielle. I think you can tell me who this is."

Neither girl was in any shape to fight the hypnotic enchantment, simple as it was.

Lauren's eyelids fluttered. "Scales. He calls himself Scales. He . . . I saw him in a coffee shop."

"You were his victims, weren't you?" I pressed, pushing more magic into my voice. "How did you know it was him?"

"Heard him talking at the coffee shop." Gabrielle ran a hand over her face, bringing some color into her cheeks. "Recognized his voice. Such a . . . loser."

"Sexy though," Lauren said, sounding as if she were falling asleep. "Nice abs."

"Don't say that," Gabrielle insisted, propping her chin on her arm where it lay on the side of the couch. "He's . . . trash."

"You heard his voice?" I asked. "When?"

"He called. Said he was . . . *sorry* about us losing our jobs." Lauren closed her hand into a fist. "He was *not* sorry. He laughed."

"You both seem to be a little under the weather," I said. "Are you all right?"

"We're fine."

"She said we'd feel a little tired," Gabrielle added, her eyelids drifting closed. "Nothing to worry about."

"She?" I repeated.

"The . . . witch."

Peasblossom shot out of my collar, and I held my breath until I realized she'd made herself invisible so the girls wouldn't see her. She scrabbled over my shoulder to my neck so she could speak directly into my ear.

"They said *witch*!"

I pressed my lips together, resisting the urge to rub my ear as the reverberations of the pixie's voice made my eardrum buzz.

"What did the witch do for you?" I asked.

Lauren smiled as she closed her eyes. "Revenge. She said she'd make Scales pay for what he did to us."

Gabrielle frowned. "She was supposed . . . supposed to send us a video." She forced her eyes open and looked at Lauren. "She didn't send us a video."

"Maybe it's not ready," Lauren mumbled.

"What did she ask in return?" I pressed.

Lauren sighed. "Just some energy. It's okay, it'll . . . come back. Just need some rest."

"Lots of rest," Gabrielle added. "And time. Just rest and time."

"Energy?" I stepped up to the couch and knelt so I was facing Gabrielle. "What kind of energy?"

"Don't know. She had . . . some kind of dirt. It felt . . . sticky. Like it was mixed with glue."

I rose to my feet, one hand going to my waist pouch.

"What are you doing?" Peasblossom asked.

"I need salt. I need to get a look at these two with my third eye."

"You shouldn't open your third eye here," Peasblossom argued. "You don't know what happened to them. There could be something here, feeding off them."

Neither girl responded to Peasblossom's voice.

I wasn't sure if they were asleep or just that oblivious.

"That's what the circle is for."

I rooted around for the bag of salt, but it remained firmly hidden. I sighed and knelt on the floor again.

Peasblossom watched me remove a pair of socks, an extension cord, and a packet of tissues before letting out a sound of disgust and flying down to land on the zippered edge. "Let *me* find it."

I moved my hands as Peasblossom dug through the enchanted depths of the fanny pack, throwing out a handful of playing cards, a roll of duct tape, and a rain of Q-tips before finally emerging victorious with the bag of salt.

I shoved the detritus back into the pouch and laid out a salt circle, confident neither girl was aware enough to realize I was doing anything strange. I touched the circle and imbued it with a flash of my magic, waiting for the tight hum of energy to tell me it was active before standing.

Opening one's third eye was dangerous business. While it did let you see echoes of the astral plane—very handy if you needed to see spells, or someone's true form—it also required you to rise partially out of your physical body. Which meant two things. One, something on the astral plane with no physical body of its own could take advantage of the opportunity to beat you back into your own flesh and blood, leaving you with no body to return to, and two, anything on the astral plane that happened to be nearby would be in a perfect position to attack your psychic form.

And death on the astral plane was as bad as death on the physical plane.

Safe in the circle, I took a deep breath and opened my third eye, careful to focus only on Gabrielle at first.

I saw the problem immediately.

"Peasblossom, someone took a portion of their life force."

"What?!"

I studied the colors around Gabrielle's body. The shimmering lights of her aura were missing in one large, noticeable chunk. As if something had taken a bite out of the energy field given off by living things.

A quick look at Lauren confirmed she'd suffered the same fate.

I closed my third eye, shifting from one foot to another as my energy settled. "Lauren," I said, raising my voice, "I need the contact information for the witch who helped you."

"I'm not supposed to give it out," Lauren mumbled.

"But I'm going to ask her when you can expect that video," I prompted. "You want to see the video, don't you?"

"I want to see it," Gabrielle said. "I wrote it down. There's . . . the paper is on the fridge."

I broke the salt circle and walked into the kitchen. Sure enough, there was a scrap of paper with a phone number on it.

And a little pentagram drawn next to it in purple ink.

"I'll make sure to have her send the video as soon as possible," I said, taking the scrap of paper and walking toward the door. "Thank you for your help."

Neither girl said anything else as I left.

I paused before leaving the apartment building, giving Peasblossom time to squirm back into my collar so the freezing February wind wouldn't suck the warmth from her tiny body.

As soon as I got into the car, I slammed the door shut and twisted to look at Poppy. Quickly I explained what I'd learned.

"She probably used some of the life force she stole from them to raise the zombie." Poppy groaned and leaned back in her seat. "Fantastic. Another trial. I'm never going to get back to work."

I pulled out my cell phone. "I'm going to call this witch and see if I can arrange a meeting."

"Try to control the meeting place," Poppy warned. "Whoever this is, she left without laying the zombie to rest, so she clearly doesn't care about collateral damage."

Alex nodded slowly. "Those who deal in death hide their faces from the beauty of life."

I shared a look with Poppy, trying to keep my eyebrows down. "Well said, Alex, well said."

⤚⤙

"Alex, you stay in the car. We need to make sure she doesn't see you."

Alex tilted his head. "I often go unseen by those who confuse darkness with despair."

Peasblossom narrowed her eyes at Alex from her position on the dashboard as she slipped on the straps that held the small warming stone I'd given her to her chest. "Do you always talk like this, or are you having us on?"

"I like it," Poppy said, patting Alex on the shoulder. "I think he's poetic."

"All of life's a stage," Alex said seriously.

Peasblossom jumped off the dashboard and glided to my

shoulder, flying lower than usual with the extra weight of the stone. "We need to work on attracting a less weird clientele."

"I'm a witch helping people with Otherworld-related crime," I reminded her, a hint of indignance pushing my voice up a notch. "Weird comes with the job."

"Got that right," Poppy agreed, grabbing her backpack from the floor of the back seat. Jenkins's skull slid side to side, the rustle of the rest of his bones emanating from the backpack. "Let's go take care of this weird so we can move on to more entertaining weird."

She unzipped her backpack and scowled. "Damn."

"What's wrong?" I asked, pausing with my hand on the door handle.

"I'm out of Reese's hearts. All I have left is the regular peanut butter cups my neighbor gave me."

I nodded sympathetically. "The cups aren't as good."

"You know what I really need right now?"

"Reese's eggs," I guessed.

Poppy beamed. "Too right. They're the best."

"Truer words." I rubbed my stomach. Great, now I had a sugar craving.

I opened the car door, turning to make sure Alex was out of sight of anyone passing by before I got out. The gothic young man had obediently slid down in his seat, hiding his head from view.

"Where are we?" Poppy asked as she got out of the car. She looked around the suburban neighborhood, squinting at the combination of neatly kept houses and homes that looked like they were either about to be condemned or were soon to be featured in a Hollywood horror movie. "There's something familiar about this place."

"This neighborhood was a victim of the housing collapse of

2008–2009." I pointed to the house in front of us. "The people who lived here were evicted, but the bank didn't transfer the house title out of their name and never bothered to tell the evicted tenants. It's what people in the industry call a 'zombie house.' Pretty much just an abandoned property."

"So some of these houses have people living in them and some are abandoned?" Poppy frowned. "Weird, but that's not why it looks familiar. I just can't put my finger on it."

We headed up the driveway to the door. There was no car but ours in the driveway or the street in front of the house, so we must have beaten the other witch here.

"My main concern was avoiding collateral damage to other people, and this house has an empty lot next to it." I gestured at the overgrown field next to the house sitting on the end of the block.

"I just hope she shows up." Poppy climbed the stairs to the porch, careful to avoid the broken boards. "Anyone without the sense to stick around to lay down a zombie they've raised is too dangerous to have running around the city."

"If she doesn't show, we'll find another way to track her down," I promised, opening the front door to let Poppy go inside first. I watched the dog skull clinking against the backpack's zipper as she passed me, reflecting that Poppy was one of the most creative necromancers I'd ever known.

Not many people had a zombie-raising service dog.

"Shade, she's here."

"What?" I followed Poppy's voice, picking my way through a litter-strewn living room to the window that looked out over the backyard and the empty lot next door. "I didn't see a car anywhere."

"Maybe she parked close by and walked." Poppy pointed to a

figure standing underneath one of the trees in the backyard. "I'm guessing that's her."

"Oh, great, so we're meeting her outside?" Peasblossom demanded.

"You have the warming stone. You'll be fine."

Peasblossom grumbled but stayed hidden in my collar as Poppy and I made our way to the back door that led outside.

My night vision was much better than a human's, and I was able to see the woman clearly in the light from the almost full moon. She was short, an inch under my own five foot three, with dark skin and long hair twisted into braids. Her blue jeans had a brown leather pouch hanging from the belt, and her hand rested close enough to it that it felt vaguely threatening.

I let my magic rise inside me, humming directly under my skin, just in case.

"Catherine Scott?" I said, when we were close enough to speak without shouting.

The woman smiled. "You must be Shade and Poppy?"

"Yes. Thank you so much for meeting us on such short notice." I gestured behind me to the house. "We could go inside and get out of the wind?"

"I'm fine out here." Catherine looked back at the house. "Any reason you chose an abandoned house instead of a nice warm coffee shop?"

"It will be easier to see if anyone else is around here, and, like I said when we talked earlier, I think I'm being spied on. Someone at work. Which is what I wanted to talk to you about."

"So you said on the phone."

There was something about the smile that never quite left Catherine's mouth that made the hairs on the back of my neck stand up.

"Our friends recommended you," Poppy added. "Gabrielle and Lauren."

"So she said on the phone."

My magic reached through my body to my fingertips.

Something was wrong.

"Lauren said you can raise a zombie," Poppy said, inserting a hint of excited awe into her voice. "Is that true? Could you do it for me?" She scowled. "You wouldn't believe what our boss puts us through. He makes everyone's life hell. He—"

"I could raise a zombie for you," Catherine said slowly, her eyes never leaving Poppy's. "But I'm not sure you'd want me to."

"Why?" Poppy asked.

"Well, what if you didn't approve of the way I did it?" Catherine pouted. "What if you reported me to the authorities? Tattled to the Vanguard?"

"Shade, there's something moving by those trees!" Peasblossom hissed.

"Do I know you?" Poppy spoke slower now, a furrow between her brows as she studied Catherine as if seeing her for the first time.

"It wouldn't surprise me if you did," Catherine said, stepping farther away from the tree. Her voice hardened. "You are so incredibly nosy, after all."

Poppy raised her hand to point at the pouch hanging from Catherine's belt. "Hey, that's not yours. Where did you get that?"

Suddenly a figure lurched from behind the tree Catherine had just been leaning against. It was a woman wearing a cream-colored dress decorated with roses and a strand of pearls around her neck. Her skin looked like thin papier-mâché, and her long white curly hair shifted in the wind.

I knew what she was even before I saw her milky, unseeing eyes.

Catherine had brought a zombie.

The zombie lurched toward us, and Catherine took off at a run through the empty lot, heading for the street on the other side.

"Poppy, look out!" I shouted.

Poppy was already turning to face off with the woman who'd just shambled from her grave. "Now I know why this place looks familiar. There's an old church less than a block away. And it has a graveyard. She must have raised the zombie there and brought it with her." She slung her backpack onto the ground and took the dog skull off the back with one hand while unzipping the bag of bones with the other. "I'll handle the zombie. You go after Catherine!"

I moved a few feet to the side, keeping my eye on the zombie. Her dead eyes locked on Poppy as she shuffled forward, her head held slightly to the side as if her neck weren't quite strong enough to hold it.

"Peasblossom, get eyes on Catherine."

"Right!" Peasblossom wriggled out of my collar and leapt from my shoulder, only the sound of her wings buzzing as she gained altitude telling me what direction she'd gone in.

"Poppy, I don't want to leave you—"

"Jenkins and I are more than a match for one zombie," Poppy said, winking at me as she laid the terrier's bones on the ground. "Even without the sugar rush. Don't let Catherine get away."

"I'm not worried you can't handle the zombie. I'm worried this is too easy and there's something worse."

"All the more reason to catch her."

I cursed and started to run in the direction Catherine had disappeared in, not staying to watch Poppy raise Jenkins. *Poppy is a professional*, I told myself firmly. *She knows what she's doing.*

"Shade, she's over here!"

I followed Peasblossom's voice and spotted Catherine up ahead. She'd parked her car behind the line of trees that edged the street where it met the empty lot, and as I cleared the trees, she reached the driver's side door.

"Not so fast!" Peasblossom bellowed.

I ran faster as Catherine climbed into the driver's seat, trying to get to the car before she could drive away. I was close enough to see through the windshield as Catherine let out a yelp and clapped a hand to her face. She yelped again and jerked from side to side with the familiar motion of someone being attacked by bees.

Or a pixie with a metal cocktail sword.

I stopped ten feet away from Catherine as she half fell out of the car, trying to get away from Peasblossom, and planted my feet on the frozen ground. My magic roared through me as I sucked in a deep breath, filling my lungs with red, glittering energy I could see in my mind's eye. When I couldn't hold any more air, I opened my mouth and let out a scream.

The force of the sound made my throat raw as it surged out of my chest toward Catherine in an eardrum-splitting shriek. Catherine gasped and fell against the car, clutching her head in her hands as she slid to the ground.

"Peasblossom, get the pouch!" I rasped.

Catherine didn't hear me, her ears no doubt still ringing with the effect of the sonic spell. Her eyes didn't even focus as Peasblossom went to work freeing the pouch from her belt using the sharpened edge of her sword.

I kept an eye on the stunned witch as Peasblossom dropped the pouch into my hand and landed on my shoulder.

"Be careful with that," she warned, rubbing her hands together. "There's something about that pouch that makes my wings itch."

I switched my grip on the bag to hold it by the strings. "We'll have Poppy look at it. She seemed to recognize it, so she should know what it is."

Saying the necromancer's name out loud made me look around. "Poppy said the church is less than a block from here. She'll have to take the zombie there to lay it to rest. Fly ahead and make sure she's okay? I'll follow along with our friend here."

Peasblossom tapped her foot on my shoulder. "Do you need help finding the rope?"

I scowled. "I'll find it."

"Mm-hmm."

Judgy pixie tone aside, it did take me a minute to find the rope in my waist pouch.

Fortunately, Catherine still hadn't managed to stand up, though a few metallic thuds warned me each time she tried and ended up falling against the car and sliding back to the ground.

Rope in hand, I put the snack pack of pretzels, Ziploc bag of fireplace ash, and handful of cotton balls back into the pouch, zipped it, and moved to tie up Catherine.

"What's in the pouch?" I asked as I bound her hands behind her back.

"Nothing," Catherine mumbled, shaking her head. "Nothing in the pouch."

I pulled her to her feet and jerked her in the direction we'd come from.

"Careful!" Catherine snapped, stumbling as I pulled her after me. She squeezed her eyes shut. "Oh, my head. What the hell did you do to me?"

"You'll be fine soon, but the headache lingers. It's significantly better than you deserve."

Catherine glared at me. "You don't know me."

"I know you nearly got a young man killed just because he helped karma along a few steps. And you drained the life force out of two young women who were foolish enough to think it was worth it to get revenge."

"Their life force will return," Catherine insisted. "It heals."

"A truth that might as well be a lie." I tugged on her bound hands, making her stumble again. "Did you warn them about the ennui? The depression, the loss of interest in things that used to matter? Did you warn them about the risk of drug use? Of suicide? All the things a person can do when their life force is depleted and they can't feel life the way they used to?"

Catherine sneered. "If they can't handle a few rough weeks, then it's just culling the herd."

I pulled her toward a tree root sticking out of the ground, letting her trip over it. She tumbled forward and hit her knees, hard.

"Let me go," Catherine snarled.

"Attempted murder will be the first charge the Vanguard lays against you," I said coldly. "And if I have anything to say about it, that will be the first charge of many. No one likes an evil necromancer."

"The zombie wouldn't have killed the boy," Catherine muttered, wincing as if the sound of her own voice made her headache worse. "I just wanted to scare him and get it recorded for my clients."

"If that were true, you'd have sent them what you had," I said grimly. "The fact that you didn't send it means either you weren't recording the scared part—because you were waiting for something worse—or you did record the scared part but didn't send it because they were expecting a murder. Not to mention, you left without laying the zombie back. It could have killed any number of people, wandering around free like that."

The corner of Catherine's mouth twitched. "Well, you have to admit, if one gives up part of their life force for revenge, they want something that will last. Something . . . traumatic."

"You—"

I stopped talking, almost tripping over my own feet as the little voice in my head that had been too quiet for me to hear before was suddenly mind-numbingly loud.

"I'm on temporary hiatus pending my testimony at a trial."

"I caught one of my cohorts siphoning life force from people and using it to raise the dead."

"There's a theory that if you use someone else's life force instead of your own, you'll live longer."

"I could raise a zombie for you. But I'm not sure you'd want me to."

"What if you didn't approve of the way I did it?"

"What if you reported me to the authorities? Tattled to the Vanguard?"

"It's a trap for Poppy," I whispered.

Catherine smiled.

Panic sent a surge of adrenaline through my system, and I hurled Catherine onto the ground near a gnarled old tree. She managed to catch herself before she hit her head, but I was already calling my magic, my mouth filling with energy that thickened to a glue-like consistency.

Catherine opened her mouth to say something, but I didn't give her the chance.

I spit on her.

The magic left my mouth and grew thicker and larger as it flew at Catherine, fat strings of gooey dark blue slime that struck her and pinned her to the tree and the ground in a net of tacky, stretchy bonds. Catherine hissed and tried to free herself, but I didn't stay to watch. The spell would hold, and the more she struggled, the more trapped she would become.

"Peasblossom!" I called out.

"Over here!"

I followed the pixie's voice, running as fast as I could. I wasn't a young witch, nor was I a particularly physically fit witch, so when I finally got to the graveyard where Poppy was standing, I was out of breath, my chest hurt, and I had a stitch in my side.

"Trap," I gasped.

Poppy blinked in bewilderment, looking around as if trying to figure out who was chasing me. "What trap?"

"For you." I waved a hand around. "Whole thing is a trap."

"Shade, it's okay," Poppy said, her voice soothing. "Everything is fine. The zombie is in the ground, and there's no one else here." She paused. "Where's Catherine?"

I shook my head. "Tied up. She's not the problem. This whole thing was about getting revenge on you."

"Shade, what are you talking about?"

Suddenly Poppy frowned. She closed her eyes and put a hand on her chest.

"What's wrong?" I asked, my voice rising.

"It's fine, I just . . . I feel a little strange." She tried to smile as she opened her eyes. "Probably just need some sugar. It's been an hour since I had any candy, and that's a long time for me."

"Everything is a joke to you, isn't it?" came a male voice.

I whirled around to see Alex standing by one of the graves. He'd taken off the sunglasses, and there was something about the way he stood there, his feet shoulder width apart, his arms slightly out from his sides, that made him seem on the brink of action.

"Alex?" Poppy asked. "What's going on?"

"His name isn't Alex," I said slowly.

Poppy's gaze flicked from Alex to me and back. "It's not? Then what is it?"

"The necromancer you're testifying against," I said, not taking my eyes off the young man. "What's his name?"

"Reginald Drayton." Poppy's eyes widened. "Reggie? Is that you?"

"Do you feel any shame at all using a familiar name with me after what you did?" Reggie clenched his teeth and took a step closer. "You're going to cost me everything."

"You shaved your beard and mustache. Cut your hair. And the bandages . . . Oh, it *is* you." Poppy took a step toward him, but stopped, wincing as she pressed her hand harder against her chest. "I didn't know you were in college."

"Oh, for pity's sake, I made that name up! And I'm not the real 'Scales,'" Reggie said, his mouth curling with disgust. "I just heard those two half-wits Gabrielle and Lauren complaining in a bar. I got some drunk frat boy to get their numbers, then I called them pretending to be Scales. Just to get them mad enough to do something as stupid as trading some of their life force for revenge. I made up the name Alex Walker for you."

"You're already in trouble," Poppy said sadly. "Why would you make it worse by stealing even more life force?"

"It's worth it if it means making you pay for what you did to me. What you're costing me."

"We have to look out for each other, Reggie. You know that. When we slip, we need to hold each other accountable. There's a reason necromancers have such a horrible reputation, and that's never going to change if we give in." She took a deep breath but still didn't stand straight. "You gave in to temptation. You made someone else pay the price for your magic."

"Life force can be *recovered*," Reggie shouted. "They would have been *fine*. They *are* fine! Why should I die young because I was gifted with power over the grave?"

"Losing life force comes with a price!" Poppy shouted back, anger glittering in her eyes. "One of your victims tried to kill himself. His death would have been on *your* head." She forced herself to stiffen her spine but grunted with the effort it took to do so. "I'm trying to help you, Reggie. It's not too late. You haven't killed anyone yet."

"It *is* too late," he growled. He jerked his jacket sleeves up, baring his wrists.

Tattoos swirled over his skin. Chains edged with runes. I didn't recognize all of them, but I recognized enough to guess what they did.

"They've bound my power," Reggie bit out.

Poppy's face paled. "Reggie . . . I'm sorry. I thought . . . I thought you would have a trial."

"Oh, I'll have a trial. They have to go through the motions, don't they? But the prosecutor has assured me that with your testimony, I'm done. Zero tolerance."

The entire time they'd been talking, I'd been looking around. Trying to find some sign that would tell me what was happening to Poppy.

Though I had a good idea already.

Poppy's voice had been growing less and less vibrant, her eyelids drooping.

Like Lauren. And Gabrielle.

Someone—or something—was draining her life force.

"Poppy," I said suddenly. "Where's Jenkins?"

Poppy looked at the fresh grave a few feet away. "He's fine, he's right—"

She stopped talking, her entire body going completely still.

Then I saw it.

Jenkins sat on the dark, freshly turned earth, his tiny furry face tilted up adoringly at his mistress. But the patches of fur on his undead body were sparser than I remembered. His eyes more sunken.

I didn't look too closely, but I was pretty sure some of his tongue was missing.

Poppy was a much better necromancer than that.

This time when I looked at the grave dirt, I could see it looked a little too thick. Less like dirt and more like tar.

"Everyone is always so impressed with Jenkins," Reggie said softly. "But I can see him for what he really is. A liability. Your own sentiment and foolishness are going to be your downfall." He took a step toward Poppy. "What kind of fool binds themselves to a dead dog?"

Reggie was focused completely on Poppy now, enjoying the horror that came over her face as she realized what he'd done. Jenkins was sitting on a spell. Probably the same ensorcelled grave dirt the witch had used with Lauren and Gabrielle. I would have bet my last set of double-A batteries that the pouch had held that dirt. Reggie had obviously given it to Catherine when he enlisted her help after he'd been bound. That's why Poppy had recognized it, known it wasn't Catherine's.

The full weight of what Reggie had done hit me all at once.

Poppy had used her life force to animate Jenkins.

And now Reggie was draining her life force through the little terrier.

"Don't even think about sending the pixie to free the dog," Reggie said, speaking to me without looking at me. "That spell is quite . . . sticky. It will take Peasblossom just as easily as it took Jenkins."

I glanced at the terrier. Poor Jenkins sat in the trap, completely oblivious to the fact that he was being used against his human mom. The one who literally gave him life.

The one who loved him so much, she hastened her own death to keep him with her.

My throat constricted, making it hard to swallow. Poppy was getting weaker, her body sagging toward the ground.

And still she didn't let go of Jenkins. I didn't know if she *could* break the bond between them.

In any sense of the word.

Hot anger rose inside me, turning my pain into fury. I faced off with the smirking necromancer. I was standing on the other side of Reggie now. He stood between Jenkins and me, stopping me from getting to the terrier or the tar. Probably to stop me from attempting to dispel it.

I smiled.

Perfect.

I pointed my palm at Reggie without moving my arm, trying to move carefully so as not to draw his attention. Red energy flowed down my arm, my magic writhing as it took the form of the spell I pictured in my mind.

Reggie heard me take a breath.

He turned.

"*Ventus!*" I flung an arm out at Reggie, releasing the spell.

A gust of wind shot from my palm with the strength of a battering ram. I held my breath, keeping control of it, softening the power. I didn't want to send him hurtling through the graveyard.

I just wanted him to fall a few feet . . .

Reggie grunted as the wind hit him in the chest, his arms windmilling to keep him from falling. Like a golf ball struck by a putter, he slid back a few feet—and fell.

Right into the grave dirt.

Jenkins exploded into furious yips and barks as Reggie landed beside him, his skin immediately sticking to the spell like flypaper.

Reggie tried to raise his hands to protect himself from the infuriated dog, but his arms wouldn't move.

"You have a choice, Reginald," I said, raising my voice. "You can tell me how to counter your spell, or you can die for your revenge."

Reggie let out a wordless scream of pure rage.

"That's not an answer," I said evenly.

He screamed again, then let out an impressive stream of curse words that made me look for Peasblossom with the urge to cover her ears.

When he was done, I let out a deep sigh and sat down on the ground, ignoring the way the frozen earth immediately sucked the warmth from my body. My heart pounded despite my impressively calm voice. If he didn't tell me how to disenchant that grave dirt, I'd have to figure it out myself. And I was no necromancer, so that would take time. Time Poppy might not have.

I needed Reggie to answer me.

"This is just a guess," I said casually. "But I'm betting the spell will drain you faster than Poppy, what with its connection to you being direct and the connection to Poppy being through a proxy. So you go ahead and have a good long think about how you want to handle this."

Reggie clenched his teeth and pressed his lips together.

"Jenkins," Poppy wheezed, her eyes almost completely closed. "Get him."

Jenkins bared his tiny teeth and lunged for Reggie.

He was too stuck in the tar to move his lower body, but fortunately Reggie was close enough.

Jenkins bit him on the nose.

"Jenkins isn't just a dog," Poppy said, lifting her eyelids enough to give Reggie a rather disturbing look. "He's an extension of my magic. And your spell is draining . . . your life force. A step away from life . . . is a step toward death."

I had no idea what she was saying.

But apparently, Reggie did.

"I'll tell you!" Reggie screamed.

Jenkins released Reggie's nose and sat down, trying to wag his tail. Bits of fur stuck to the tar, but it didn't seem to bother the happy terrier.

Poppy's threat was all the motivation Reggie needed. He couldn't share the method of disenchantment fast enough, and thirty minutes later, the ensorcelled grave dirt was just dirt, and he and Catherine were tied to a tree while we waited for the Vanguard to come and get them.

"Good boy," Poppy cooed, holding a hand out to Jenkins.

The little terrier yipped and barked, his tail wagging so hard I worried it would detach from his little zombie body.

Poppy beamed as Jenkins pressed his head into her hand. "Time to go back to sleep now."

The terrier obediently dropped to the ground, resting his head on his paws. His eyes closed as Poppy withdrew her power from the tiny dog, the magic draining away to leave Jenkins a pile of polished white bones.

"Are you sure you're okay?" I asked Poppy.

"I'll be fine," Poppy said, sounding a little breathless. She scooped up the dog bones and gently placed them back into her backpack. After she fastened the skull to her bag, she pointed at the pouch in my hand, which held the remnants of Reggie's spell. "I'll feel a lot better if the Vanguard can figure out a way to give me back my life force. If I have to heal it myself, that will mean no necromancy for at least six months. Maybe a year."

I sat on the ground beside her. "If that happens, what will you do?"

Poppy's mouth quirked up at the corner. "Actually, I'm learning exorcism now."

"Of course you are." I shook my head. "You are an interesting woman, I'll give you that." I paused. "What were you going to do that scared Reggie so bad?"

Poppy leaned closer and lowered her voice. "It was a bluff. For now. But technically, the closer he got to death, the greater the chance I could flex my magic over him."

I stared at her. "You mean . . ."

"Puppet him like a zombie." Poppy sighed and rubbed her temples. "I'm almost sorry I didn't get a chance to try."

I put a hand on her shoulder. "Poppy, is there anything I can do for you? Anything that will help?"

Poppy's expression turned serious, almost begging. "Yes. Can we stop at the gas station down the road and get me some peanut butter cups? I need a dozen of them."

I grinned and shook my head. “Fine. We’ll get you some peanut butter cups.”

“If they have them, can we get the—”

“The hearts.” I pushed myself off the ground. “This isn’t my first rodeo.”

BLACK BOND

Maurice Broaddus

There will be a day sometime in the near future when this guide will not have to be published.
—VICTOR HUGO GREEN, *THE NEGRO MOTORIST GREEN BOOK*

Rashad Ewing always relished his road trips with his best friend, even after Jerald had died. Slowing through rural town squares—always bookended by speed traps—he was careful to ease off the gas even if he was only doing the limit. Just in case. Despite the quaint cafés and craft shops, the streets were somehow both unwelcoming and uninviting.

"The American flags out here have Confederate vibes," Rashad said.

"Like they wave with a hard 'r.'" Jerald Blufton shifted in the passenger seat, still thin enough for a stiff breeze to send his emaciated hands scrabbling for the nearest handhold to stay upright. Several days' growth of gray and black hair sprawled inconsistently across his face. His glasses kept slipping down his nose. He adjusted the thick, red knit cap that clung to his head.

Rashad couldn't help but wonder why his friend would still need prescription lenses in the afterlife. Perhaps death froze one's appearance for eternity, which left him wondering whether he ought to drop a few pounds in case he had to haunt someone later. This wasn't the rabbit hole of thoughts he wanted to continue down. "Black people got no business 'exploring' southern Indiana."

"Nah, we exploring Lyles Station like we Christopher Columbus: That shit's been discovered and inhabited. Except by us."

"That doesn't make it any better. This trip definitely ain't *Green Book* recommended." Rashad loved history, devouring all such books. *The Negro Motorist Green Book* served as a travel guide for black folks during the Great Migration, outlining the safe places to stay, restaurants, gas stations, and so on. They'd taken a wide berth around Martinsville, the historic epicenter of Klan activity in Indiana, but were cognizant that this area was still full of sundown towns. All white on purpose. Not a place to be after dark; not exactly friendly by day. To be fair, Indianapolis had its share of sundown suburbs. Even sundown neighborhoods.

"Visiting Lyles Station was the good Lord's vision. 'For I, the Lord your God, am a jealous God, punishing the children for the sin of the parents to the third and fourth generation of those who hate me.'" Jerald was always ready with a Bible verse, some word of encouragement. Being dead, he might have had breakfast with Jesus for all Rashad knew. A question he intuitively understood not to ask, since there were probably some answers Jerald wasn't allowed to give. Or Rashad ready to hear. "However, let the record reflect that this nature detour was your idea."

"Let no one ever doubt how much I love you if I'm willing to traipse through the woods with you."

"It was my dying wish. You couldn't deny me," Jerald said.

Fidgeting slightly in his seat, Rashad gripped and re-gripped the steering wheel, unable to shake the disquiet, the unease, in his soul. He'd tired of losing friends. Jerald would make the third one this year. One to violence. One to a random accident. Now one to nature's fickle, yet cruel, hand.

The county road rose over some abandoned railroad tracks before winding through the undulating hills. Shifting into off-road mode, the SUV spat gravel, leaving behind a cloud of dust. Rolling down his window, while not quite slowing, Rashad reached for his camera. His large hand engulfing the camera looked like a catcher's mitt grabbing a child's toy. He aimed in the general direction of a covered bridge and snapped a few pictures. After a dozen in quick succession, he glanced at a sample of the shots. Satisfied, he set the camera back into the nook of his car door.

The overpowering, putrid odor of burning feces filled the vehicle; the last earthly scent that followed Jerald into eternity. Rashad wasn't used to the smell, though he knew better than to comment on it, knowing how it made his friend self-conscious. A mental haze settled on Rashad, accompanied by a vague wooziness. He had barely enough time to pull over to the side of the road before his eyes glazed over and his mind drifted. His spirit viewed his body as if from outside of it. The world went black as his essence rushed down a dark tunnel. On the other end of it, light exploded in a kaleidoscopic flash and . . .

He and Jerald were back in middle school. Eighth period, show choir, the only two boys in the class. At the dress rehearsal for their next performance, the kids practiced taking the risers to arrange themselves on the stand for their concert. He waded through a cloud of too much perfume and Right Guard over underarm funk as they jostled for position. Everyone was supposed to wear a red Polo Ralph Lauren shirt with black pants, but Jerald's family couldn't afford a name-brand shirt. So he wore a knockoff short-sleeve red polyester shirt. One size too large. Bought at a garage sale. None of the students picked on him, but they made a point of avoiding him.

As Jerald swayed in the bass section, his voice often cracked in its attempts to grow into itself. Rashad was a rich baritone, his voice strong and controlled. He scooted over to Jerald, providing a steady pitch for him to tune himself to. Startled at first, Jerald inched away. Rashad held his notes steady, his head bobbing to the flow of the music. In a mix of relief and appreciation, Jerald's tremulous voice found its anchor in Rashad's cadence until the song ended.

To express something approaching gratitude, Jerald offered him a piece of grape Hubba Bubba. "If you're gonna stand that close, at least do something about your breath."

Rashad laughed and popped the gum into his mouth . . .

The strong taste of sour purple-approximating-grape flavor still on his tongue jarred Rashad back to the present reality of the road. He had traveled back to that time. He saw it. He heard it. He touched it. The olfactory memory of the fading scent of Right Guard and armpits clung to his nostrils. The episode reminded him of microdosing mushrooms.

"Could you warn me next time?" Rashad lowered Jerald's window to allow in more fresh air.

"It's not like I can control it. I was thinking about how we first met." His face pallid and drawn, Jerald kept staring out the windshield.

Slipping the SUV back into drive, Rashad continued down the road. He thought about their strange journey together. The good old days. Having fallen in love with it after watching the *Def Poetry* show, Jerald wrote and performed poetry. Leaving to study at Tuskegee University, he thirsted to taste life on his own terms, though he returned to Indianapolis every few years. During one of his open mic blitzes, Rashad volunteered to be part of a film crew to document his shows. From the moment a camera touched his hand, *he* fell in love. Filmed every poem in the competition. Unable to afford a hotel room, they slept in his car for the tour, nothing as nice or roomy as the SUV.

It was easy to romanticize the past.

At the entrance of the park, dogs ran up to the car as it slowed to a stop near a secluded parking lot. Rashad shifted the SUV into park. "We here."

"Snakey Point?" Jerald pointed to a wooden sign.

"I'm sure it's named after a person. There aren't even that many snakes around here."

"*One* is too many. And we in their house. What do I keep trying to tell you?"

"'Nature is designed to kill us,'" Rashad recited with fake annoyance. He opened his door, the dogs sprinting off before his heavy foot hit the ground. His stomach grumbling, sweat trickling down his back and legs, he strode to the rear of his SUV. His body was mostly torso, a barrel of a chest over spindly legs. His ears were too tiny for his head; for that matter, so were his eyes. His full black beard trailed into a bald scalp.

Two stickers marked the door: one in the outline of Indiana filled with prismatic colors; the other, *Star Wars* lightsabers arranged in a rainbow array. He unlocked a case and tucked his holstered IFG Stock Master Defiant 9mm into the back of his pants. "On your six."

"You can't just say 'I'm behind you'?" Jerald asked.

Rashad stalked well-trodden paths along the sun-dappled ridge of a ravine. He wanted to capture the last riot of color from the springtime bloom. A distant train whistled as it passed. Birdsong continued, unbothered by his presence. He stopped at a pond with ambitions of being a lake. Unpacking a protein bar, he had it almost all the way to his mouth when he caught Jerald's disapproving face. He pointed to a sign. NO HUNTING ZONE—U.S. FISH AND WILDLIFE SERVICE.

"Don't act brand-new. 'What we bring in, we take out.'" Rashad crumpled the wrapper and pocketed it. "And 'what's out here stays here.' I know the rules."

"We have signs for a reason."

"It means people done went and fucked something up."

A breeze barely rustled the branches. The leaves crunched softly underfoot. Sunlight filtered through the thick canopy. Three turkey vultures picked at a nearby carcass. As he searched for something to catch his photographer's eye, he noted how Jerald moved as if pressed under a weight, like he needed to get something off his chest. Rashad recognized the burden and gave him space: they were ten years into their friendship before he came out to him.

"Picking up pawpaws, puttin' 'em in a basket." Jerald began singing the folk song when Rashad lifted up a piece of fruit he described as an Indiana banana. "I hope you know how to get us out of here. I'm already lost."

"If there was one thing I picked up in the military besides shooting, it's land navigation." Soon after Jerald left for Tuskegee, Rashad joined the Army, becoming a member of 91 Whiskey Combat Medic, a combat support hospital. While they never deployed, his unit set records for getting stations up and running. But that didn't mean he never saw action: having grown up on the east side of Indianapolis, he'd seen enough real combat. "We did regular exercises. Just a compass, a map, and the terrain."

"I get it. You're a Boy Scout."

Rashad knelt to better take a close-up of a flower from a tulip poplar, its lone huge leaf, bell-shaped and greenish yellow with orange petals. The chittering calls of insects and deep burbles from tree frogs ceased. The gaze of Rashad's camera caught an old forester approaching. His dirt-caked black pants shed dust with each step. His boots were military surplus. Across his T-shirt, the words "When tyranny becomes law rebellion becomes duty" were emblazoned over a Betsy Ross flag: a white Roman numeral three above "1776" surrounded by a circle of thirteen stars against a black background. He had to be a Three Percenter, one of those Far Right anti-government militia types who believe that only 3 percent of American colonists fought against the British during the American Revolution. A new name for the same old hate and their campaign of menace. The name "Monteleone" stitched across his unbuttoned vest, he had gray hair and skin blanched to the color of overripe rhubarb. A perplexed look crossed his rugged and intense face, hardened from playing soldier all day.

"Damn. Even out here, we are never alone," Rashad muttered.

"Because when you're black, white people will always be all up in your business," Jerald said, finishing the adage.

Not overtly hostile, Monteleone stopped well shy of being welcoming. He affected a dull, subtle Southern drawl, his tone attempting to remind them of their place. As if they were somehow trespassing despite this being public land. His suspicious eyes, the shade of frosted wastewater, cast over Rashad. "Are you lost?"

"We . . . I can't be. I was just thinking about how I was good at two things, one of them being land navigation." Rashad thickened his code-switched tone with extra congeniality.

"What's the other?" Monteleone asked.

"Being black." Rashad searched the man's eyes for any signs of ill intent, adjusting the back of his shirt in case he needed to draw his Defiant. Though all about nonviolence, he was also all about self-defense and wasn't going to be made to feel afraid. Or unsafe. Never again.

"What brings you out here?" Creases deepened along Monteleone's forehead. Irritated, he tensed his jaw.

Rashad swatted at whatever buzzed by his ear. Something about Monteleone made Rashad's ass itch. Ready to deploy "What's it to you?" energy while fixing his mouth to cuss the man out, he instead opted for something less confrontational. This was still southern Indiana, he was still all alone, and there were still a lot of trees.

"I'm doing a nature study." He raised his camera for extra emphasis. "Then heading to Lyles Station for a visit."

"Humph." Monteleone felt empowered to intimidate, but he'd picked the wrong one today.

"That a problem?" Rashad went about his business, shooting pictures despite the snide tone.

"Maybe not for you. They're trying to erase us. Forget whose values built this country. Before we descend into complete degeneracy."

"Have we stepped into some weird parallel universe?" Jerald said.

"That's funny." Rashad was about to click the shutter on his camera when he leveled his eyes at the forester. "I was just looking to get out in nature and learn some history."

"We're about protecting our history, real history, and prevent the spread of lies. Including that Lyles Station." Monteleone held up three fingers, an enigma without a hood determined to ruin moments of peace and joy. "Diversity, your multicultural new world order, is your dog whistle for white genocide. You will not replace us."

"Right now, there's no we. Just you. And me." Rashad's free hand twitched near his Defiant, just in case shit jumped off.

A wave of heat emanated from Jerald.

The wind shifted, and Monteleone recoiled. "Jesus, what's that smell?"

"Maybe something died recently." Rashad glanced over at Jerald, who adjusted his cap. And shrugged.

Monteleone relaxed, but only slightly, in the awkward dance of professionalism masquerading as hospitality. Wiping the accrued sweat from his forehead, he pivoted to usher him back toward a more obvious path. "I can show you some of our best trails. Hell, I seeded most of them."

"Nah, I'm good. Thank you though."

"Just don't head that way." Monteleone nodded toward a wood fence with rusted barbwire above it that cordoned off the path. The militia members were careful. Nature shielded them from prying eyes, the dense cluster of trees closer and foreboding. Not even a mat of crushed leaves indicated a path in. The fence blocked off a rickety guard tower of sorts. A sign swung in an unfelt breeze. NOTICE: GOVERNMENT PROPERTY—DO NOT TRESPASS. The words "courage," "identity," and "virtue" had been carved into the wood posts. "It's all power lines and rubble back there."

"No problem. I was about done here anyway."

Monteleone raised his hands in mock surrender. "I'll let you be on your way."

"Deuces." Rashad flashed two sideways fingers at him. Despite his upbeat tone, Rashad hard-eyed Monteleone as he sauntered away. The way one might study a dog skittering past to make sure it was no longer a threat.

Jerald stared down the path toward the Three Percenters' camp. "You'll get yours, you bastards."

Rashad pretended not to hear him.

⁂

Just outside of Princeton, Indiana, scattered houses, barns, and silos dotted the landscape, with less and less open farmland as small towns sold off bits of their soul in the name of development. The quaint town's rural charms didn't fool Rashad.

"Welcome to Lyles Station." Jerald craned about, excitedly taking in as much as he could. "My family goes back five to six generations round these parts. This side of the river used to be the promised land."

"How down bad did someone have to be to want to come to southern Indiana?"

"Folks escaping slavery."

"Damn, man, didn't mean to get all deep," Rashad said.

"It's like we can never escape it. Them." Jerald's voice took on an otherworldly aspect. "Even though Indiana was a Free State, after 1831, black settlers had to register with the county authorities and post a five-hundred-dollar bond as a guarantee of good behavior and to be able to buy land."

"The Black Bond."

"My people came up from Virginia in 1838. Settled at the intersection of the Wabash, White, and Patoka Rivers. Prime farmland. At first they called the place the Switch Settlement but renamed it after a founding family."

"Seems all kinds of deserted now." Rashad studied the empty sidewalks and scattered buildings.

"But in its heyday, Lyles Station was bustling. Had a railroad station, a post office, a lumber mill, two general stores, and two churches. And an elementary school. After the flood of 1912, too much of the town was destroyed. Most folks fled, leaving only a faithful few families still farming. And their descendants."

The haunting stench rose again, and Rashad's world faded into shadows, the way inky storm clouds obscured the sun. His mind fogged, his consciousness flailed, tumbling down a steep, bottomless cavern. He traveled farther down the tunnel this time, a cord tethered to the spirit of his friend in a terrible intimacy of a pain risking being shared. When his vision returned in a haze of baleful violaceous incandescence—the malignant sort of predawn light stabbed through the gray veil—he was on . . .

. . . (Jerald's) great-grandfather's farm, behind its hulking barn and parked hay wagon. A couple of milking cows wandered around, their tails swishing about with mild impatience. The yard a mess of chicken wire and half-built coops, the occasional yardbird squawked at his approach. A story had been passed down—the kind of family lore that became fact after enough retellings—about how Pap joined a group of fellow freed slaves, packing his family's furniture, smoked meat, and all their worldly possessions that could fit in the back of the wagon. Anger fueled him. He'd been a slave on a farm, picking cotton alongside sharecroppers. He dreamt of none of his children—or children's children—ever being tied to a white man's plantation ever again.

"Come on. Just one game," a young boy pleaded with (Rashad).

"I can't play basketball. I have to go home and haul manure." (Rashad) attempted to stretch out his hands, but they didn't respond. His spirit simply hitched a ride in the corner of Jerald's ancestor's mind. The soles sloughed away from his shoes, a casualty of his chores. His toes were too loose in them, so he wore an extra set of socks.

"You'd rather do that?"

"No one would rather do that. But Pap would tan my hide if I didn't come home and do my chores first." (Rashad)'s body reflexively tugged at the sleeve of his shirt, desperate to not draw attention to it despite the overwhelming need to scratch at it.

"Boy, get in here!" (Jerald)'s great-grandfather bellowed. The way he yelled it, (Rashad) nearly believed "Boy" was his given name. He ran into the oak-and-brick cabin his grandfather had built with his own hands. By the time he reached the front room, Pap was already mid-rant, his Sunday lesson voice booming a bit of wisdom to his captive audience, Mamaw. ". . . nothing is free."

"Calm down, you make seventy-five cents a week." Mamaw's voice was comforting as a gospel melody.

"And it's all mine. Earned by my work." Fear was never in Pap; he

wasn't raised with it. Walking with his head high and shoulders back when he spoke, it was with his full chest, nothing kowtowing or deferential. Pap whirled to face (Rashad) with a suddenness meant to catch him off guard. "Show me."

"Show you what?" (Rashad) lifted his cap to wipe away the sweat pooling underneath it.

"Ain't no point in pretending. Mr. Lucas done let me know."

(Rashad) rolled back his shirtsleeve to reveal a red, scaly patch on his arm, a round wound whose center appeared clear compared to its inflamed edges. "What is it?"

Pap turned his arm one way then the next, inspecting the affected area closely with the care of one of his prize hens having taken sick. "Looks like tetters."

"Ringworm? Let me see that. I heard tell there was an outbreak." Mamaw took his arm, her touch gentle yet firm. Her forefinger tapped her chin three times before she prescribed him to "take a penny, dip it in vinegar, and put it on the infection."

(Rashad) couldn't help but breathe a long sigh of relief. He had feared a home remedy involving lye soap or some other strange, foul-smelling concoction since they couldn't afford iodine.

"Mr. Lucas said they're going to have to do something about it down at the school before the epidemic gets out of control," Pap said.

(Rashad) ran his hand through his hair . . .

. . . suppressing a shudder. His friend's presence was a whisper in the dark recesses of his mind. "I'm not sure what's real and what's, I don't know, some weird fever dream from the past."

"My family's past." Jerald shifted in his seat, avoiding his eyes, almost as if ashamed. He wrung his hands, working through a pain. A deep family trauma. "I can't control it. I'm trying to . . . show you my story. I just . . . can you trust me, in me, a little longer?"

Rashad shivered as a distant chill wrapped about his spine. The sun slowly set as he swung his SUV into the gravel parking lot. Lyles Consolidated School—Est. 1917, the painted sign read in bold white script against a green backdrop. "Consolidated" meant students of various ages shared the same classroom. The grounds were manicured like a royal estate. On the opposite side, an American flag flapped in the stiff breeze. At the heart of the sculpted greenery was a stout two-story building with tall windows. The structure itself wasn't imposing, but it had a presence. A solemnity from surviving. Now it was a museum and cultural center committed to remembering its past. Jerald's family name still rang out in these parts as Rashad had been given the code to the lockbox to let himself in.

The foyer was large, the size of two living rooms pressed together as an entryway. The school hallways echoed with each footfall, a soft click-clack of his hard soles against the linoleum. Haints filled its corridors. Framed photographs hung along most of the walls. Images of school leaders facing down the Klan. Rashad recognized the portrait of the school's disciplinarian principal from an identical photograph of him in the Crispus Attucks Museum back in Indianapolis.

Next to a door emblazoned with the words Nurse's Office, an enlarged photo of the nurses' faces shone silvery and spectral as if trapped in moonlight. Rashad skirted it, fearing that any of them might reach out to drag him away. He crossed the classroom's threshold, the air redolent with wood and chalk. Vintage wooden desks filled the room. A chalkboard listed the families: Bells, Cantrells, Nash, Lucas, Freeman, Lyles, Harris, and Blufton.

"I know you're trying to reveal what happened." Rashad studied a picture. Several boys wore caps; some wore beanies, perhaps the latest fashion. Even in the photos of them as adults, they wore either hats or far-too-obvious hairpieces. "Show me."

Jerald led them to an anteroom, little more than a nook near the front of the class that doubled as a kind of stage. Rashad closed his eyes, and Jerald's voice swept his spirit along. There was no tunnel, no light, only the fury of his friend's emotion guiding him to the proper time. "It happened one day in 1927. Ten . . .

. . . students lined up along the wall like they were ready to play red rover. School was a sacred space to (Rashad), even though he and his country self often kicked off his shoes under his desk. Tardiness, punishable by a paddling in front of the class, rarely occurred, not from fear of the sting but of the titters and stares of their friends. In his inattentive rush to be on time, (Rashad) plowed right into their principal, Mr. Joseph Lucas. He was a tall tree in an old-growth forest, majestic and proud, and his sheltering limbs kept his students safe. Mr. Lucas made no attempt to dodge him. (Rashad) shook himself as if he'd run full speed into a brick wall.

"You're cutting it close, Mr. Blufton." Mr. Lucas checked his pocket watch.

"I made it though, Mr. Lucas." (Rashad) attempted a crooked smile, but the principal remained stoic and unimpressed.

"Our ancestors set goals for us, Mr. Blufton. We have the responsibility to do them proud."

Mr. Lucas led the way to class, coming to collect the students to be taken to the Gibson County Hospital, the local sanitarium in Princeton. Marching them to the waiting bus, his face slowly collapsed like he chewed a bite of spoiled lemon meringue pie he was forced to swallow. His eyes glazed with a tincture of uncertainty. And regret.

(Rashad) and his classmates waited outside under the noonday sun for someone to meet them. His arm itched. His knees trembled. Unsure what exactly terrified him beyond the idea of being at a hospi-

tal, he hoped for a salve or a pill, praying that if it came down to a shot, he wouldn't cry. Rubbing his arm—careful not to scratch the ravenous wound—he counted off the minutes in his head.

The metal doors clanged open, and a woman came out. The name "Monteleone" stitched in red thread on her uniform. Tufts of brown hair sprouted from her cap. Her face had a pinched quality to it, made worse by the absurdly bright red smear of her lipstick. A mole dotted the side of her chin; three black hairs budded from it. (Rashad) couldn't stop staring. Her lips twitched with irritation.

Nurse Monteleone led them around to the rear of the hospital, down the stairs into the basement. More nurses clustered in an alcove created by a newly built wall. They stopped their nervous chatter as she paraded the black children toward them.

"You're going to be given a special treatment to stop the spread of ringworm. It hasn't been given to anyone before." Her shadow passed over (Rashad). He shriveled into the tiniest ball he could, the way he'd slouch to avoid his teacher calling on him. "You're special. You get to be first."

She held her hand out, unwavering in front of him until (Rashad) straightened up and took it. Now, he had seen X-ray equipment before, but up close, the machinery seemed like a cold colossus indifferent to their presence. And he was still afraid of it. Sitting him in a chair, Nurse Monteleone began strapping his arms down. Before he could protest, she said, "We need to make sure you stay perfectly still. If you relax, you'll be fine."

Unsure what exactly constituted "perfectly," (Rashad) quit squirming. He even kept his breaths shallow, afraid that deep ones might still be too much movement. Nurse Monteleone placed a cap on him, a kind of beanie with wires attached to it. Once in place, she rushed to join her fellow nurses behind their makeshift lead screen.

"Don't move," she shouted like a soldier from a foxhole.

(Rashad) stiffened. A kind of rattle in his ears became a haunting Klaxon that reverberated in his soul. It grew into a terrible buzz, the sound of electricity charging and leaping about. His scalp felt like someone took a match to it. The sensation spread, a spire of flames shooting down his back. His fingernails dug into the armrests. The air stank of burning hair.

One Mississippi. Two Mississippi. Three Mississippi.

"Oh my God! I gave him too much," Nurse Monteleone cried out.

The machinery powered down to a dull thrum, a predator waiting with infinite patience. When she helped him from his chair, (Rashad) could have sworn that her mole twitched ever so slightly, a satisfied upturn of cruel, too red lips. He staggered up the stairs. Strength fled his muscles, and he steadied himself against the wall. His head blistered, too tender to even touch. He stumbled all the way to the bus before he threw up.

That became their ritual. As each of his friends lumbered to him, they vomited. (Rashad) gathered them, holding hands in a prayer circle. Eyes closed, (Rashad) whispered, "I was . . .

". . . just a little boy, not some sort of test animal." Rashad's head still tingled. He reflexively drew his cap lower onto his head. "How could they?"

"Pap didn't blame Mr. Lucas, you know. Well, no more than he blamed himself. None of them could've prevented it. Just like no one had any idea what their radiation experiment would do to the children." Jerald averted his eyes. "Or their descendants."

"That's how you got your cancer." Rashad's voice hitched. "The sins of the father."

Steadying himself against the wall, Jerald faced his friend. His face downcast, shoulders stooped under the weight of inevitability, he removed the knit cap from his head. Doused in medication, two dressings wrapped the wound. Brown splotches splattered the first layer of bandages, seeping blood having been baked into it. As he peeled off the second layer, the stench of mold and bacteria wafted like a physical force. The wound ate into his skull. Scars, burns that had never healed, mottled his skin, a mix of a bleached scalp and necrotic tissue. Oblong at the top, the wound split along its side like a volcanous mound. Blood trickled from the growths surrounding it. "It's almost time."

"Time?"

"They're almost here. I'm ready to stop fighting. To let my burden go." Jerald's eyes flashed with a fevered mania. "I'm gonna haunt the shit outta the motherfuckers responsible."

Dogs bayed in the distance. The smell of smoke curdled Rashad's stomach. He glanced over at Jerald for any indication of alarm or further explanation, but his friend registered neither. A caravan of torches crossed the lawn, open flames on the march. Monteleone raised a fist, halting his men's advance as Rashad exited the school.

"What are you doing here?" Rashad studied the merciless dance of flames.

"Seeing what you were up to. Making sure our streets remained safe."

"With torches?"

"Sometimes you have to burn out an infection to make sure it doesn't return." Monteleone turned around to appreciate the throaty guffaws of his men. "This is exactly what I've been talking about. They built this school just to terrorize us. Make us feel guilty by association. And it draws . . . undesirables."

"Y'all being awfully bold. Didn't your daddies teach you that without hoods, your sins are more difficult to hide?"

"Don't try to make this a hate thing. This is a justice thing. You'll not besmirch the name and legacy of this great nation."

These men, cloaked in the tarnished veneer of patriotism, were no different than any other homegrown terrorist firebombing a house or church. The intent was the same: to erase Lyles Station's history as a gathering place, its testimony to perseverance in its people's struggles. Rashad refused to give them what they wanted: his fear. His hand inched behind him until he clutched the grip of his Defiant. His posture paused their laughter.

"What you got behind you, boy?" Monteleone's face hardened into a mask of impotent rage.

Rashad heard the word "boy" pronounced with a hard "r." "Why don't you come closer and find out?"

"We don't have to get closer to do what we came here to do."

The men began to spread out. Rashad waited for them to cross the invisible line separating insult from threat. Doing the calculus of violence, Rashad nursed a creeping realization that once he drew down, he could nail Monteleone—and perhaps two others—before the rest descended on him like rabid hyenas. He steeled himself for the inevitable.

"Are you with me?" Pushing his glasses higher up his nose, Jerald appeared next to him.

"Jerald, I . . ." Rashad angled himself closer, his voice softening in a farewell plea to his friend, but was waved off. What needed to be said was already known. He closed his eyes to repeat the last words he spoke when Jerald took his last breaths. "Yeah, I'm with you. Ten toes deep. That's how brothers do."

Rashad counted off the seconds in his head. One Mississippi. Two Mississippi. Three Mississippi.

Jerald removed his cap.

A sudden, deafening roar boomed. The men froze, staring at

the night sky as if a thunderstorm had managed to sneak up on them. The dogs fled. A terrible buzzing, the sizzle of lightning crackling like a living thing, rose from all about them. Confused, Monteleone turned around, perhaps to check for cover. Or run. His men began a slow retreat. A massive ominous plume carried the smell of burning chemicals. Yet it seemed to hover, a thick cloud unmoved by the wind, settling over the Three Percenters like a living shroud.

Panic erupted.

As the men clawed at the air, their screams were choked off by their gagging coughs. The eerily iridescent cloud clung low to the ground, creeping across it like a vengeful lion on a hunt. Some clutched their throats, their eyes bulging, the veins in their necks engorged, desperate to draw breath. They stumbled about, lost in the haze, blinded by the treatment. Monteleone scrabbled toward Rashad but stopped at his feet before collapsing into convulsions. His lips twitched in a cruel spasm.

The plume rose, leaving nothing but agonized bodies writhing on the ground. It hovered briefly above Rashad before it dissipated in the heavens.

⤚⤙

Rashad sifted the black soil of the Blufton farm through his hand, snapping the image of it with his camera. He needed the shot for his exhibit documenting the stories of Lyle's Station. The news reported waves of cancer deaths in Princeton. The Centers for Disease Control and Prevention had dispatched a team to investigate. He couldn't help but be reminded of how when crack swept through his community, the powers that be called it a "crime epidemic," but when opioids ripped through other communities, authorities deemed it a "health crisis." The moral arc of the times changed only in inches.

Dusting his hands off, he swaggered toward a truck being loaded with fruit for a farmers' market. Glancing at a crate, he began to sing to himself.

"Picking up pawpaws, puttin' 'em in a basket."

DOG-EARED

Kim Harrison

Part 1

Al stared in horror at his book, his frock coat's tails swishing as he snatched the demon text from the scratched floorboards where Nicholas Gregory Sparagmos had left it. The need to break the fluid bubble of energy he'd been summoned into so he could strangle the scrawny human became an ache. His book was ruined, the handwritten pages swelled from water and the binding nearly falling off. True, it was over two thousand years old, but it had been intact three days ago.

"What did you do to it?" he croaked, his gloved hands shaking as he found a page bent to mark a favored spell. *Mother pus bucket. How big a cretin do you need to be to dog-ear a curse?*

Thin and heavily scarred, the magic-using human ran a nervous hand over his jeans and resettled himself in the folding chair set to face the well-drawn, blood-enforced circle. The lights were low behind him, probably to hide that his one-room apartment was just above the poverty line—even if it was filled with esoteric books. At least the wizard wasn't summoning him into a closet anymore. "Sorry?"

Al dropped the book in disgust, simultaneously materializing an ornate podium for it to land on. The heavy tome hit with a thump, and Nick jumped.

You should be nervous, little wizard, Al thought, the lace at his cuffs shaking as he cataloged the damage, easing out the earmarks as he found them. "This is not the condition in which I lent it to you," he said, his pretentious, Victorian-age British accent clearly conveying his disgust. The scent of burnt amber rising from the damp pages was making his eyes water. No wonder he had been summoned early. The stench would travel through the thin walls like an ugly argument.

"Oh. Sorry," Nick said again, smiling to show his teeth. "I fell asleep reading it."

"In the tub? You were reading a two-thousand-year-old demon text in the *tub*?"

Nick stood, his motions holding a worried quickness as he went to tweak the ratty curtains shut more certainly. "Are you saying you never have?"

"I have never dropped it!" Al flipped the book closed and held it close, not surprised to feel an ache running through it, stemming from the nearby ley lines. The once-smooth energy flow was erratic. It might even out when the pages dried. It might not. It was as if the book was in pain, and Al forced his jaw to unclench. There was a time to be the all-powerful demon bent on destruction . . . and there was a time to be the helpless slave caught between a salt circle and the ever-after. But really, there was no difference between the two but for attitude.

"I didn't write it," he said, teeth clenched. "Which means I can't repair it. Banish me. We are done, Nicholas Gregory Spargmos. The cost of dealing with you is too high."

Nick's eyes widened as he stood before Al, his fingers twitching. "What's the big deal? You can still read it."

"I assumed it would be returned in the same condition I lent it to you." Al's breath shook as he exhaled, breathing upon the barrier between them until the thin haze of distorted time began to hiss and pop. *Testing* . . .

A smile quirked the annoying human's lips. "You said it. Only an ass assumes. I returned it. It's in your hand. Do you want to know more about Rachel or not? I'm the only one with enough guts to summon you and close enough to her to give you what you need."

Al pulled back from the barrier, his goat-slitted eyes narrowing. It was irritating, but the wizard was right. The man before him was a supreme example of how thin the population of acceptable familiars had become. But all things bow before an all-consuming goal, and Rachel Mariana Morgan was worth a book or two. *As long as I'm the only one who knows* what *she is* . . .

Hiding his ire, Al brushed a fluff of nonexistent fluff from his overdone Victorian finery. It was criminally outdated, but Ceri liked it. Chin high, he snapped his fingers, and both the book and the podium vanished. "That depends," he said with an affected calm. "There will be no more mutilating of my books. And there will be no books at all unless you are willing to give me something truly worthwhile."

Nick's eyes narrowed. "I'm not telling you how she likes her sex, so forget it."

A smile, ugly and mean, cracked Al's expression. He would. Eventually. With the right bait. "Then banish me," he demanded again, knowing it wouldn't happen. Not yet. Nick was too greedy, too selfish. "Or I will claw my way out of this circle and break *your* spine. See how you like me folding your arms backward to mark my favorite parts of your screaming."

Nick paled, and Al's eyes closed as he relished the scent of the wizard's sweat making it through the barrier. "If you could get out, you would have already." Nick settled his feet firmly on the old oak floorboards as if he had control of the situation. He didn't. "What will you give me for how she likes her coffee?"

It was something he was dying to know, needed to know if he wanted to mimic her. And yet . . . "You are slime, Nicholas Gregory Sparagmos," he intoned, the barrier popping when he poked a gloved finger into it. "And I will have you stirring my spells before the year is out. My current familiar is wearing thin and could use the help."

"Stop," Nick demanded, his gaze on the sudden sheen of black racing over the bubble. It was Al's aura, and if the demon took the circle, it would fall. "I said stop!"

Gaze fixed on Nick, Al made a fist, pain arcing through him as he pushed it harder against the shifting band of time separating them. But the circle was drawn in blood, not salt, and he jerked his hand free as dark energy boiled and burned.

"You aren't getting through that alive," Nick said, but his confidence was cracked. It was all Al needed.

"Then we will die together," he vowed, and in a swirl of energy, he dissolved, re-forming as a dog from hell. Snarling, he leapt at the barrier, yelping as it flashed a brilliant green and flung him back.

"Algaliarept, I banish you!" Nick shouted, ashen faced as he retreated. "I demand that you leave this place immediately and go directly to the ever-after. Do not stop on the way. Leave now! Now!"

The strength of the curse shocked through Al, the pain almost sweet as he forced himself to remain despite the pull, slavering like a mad thing as he stared at the loathsome human. It wasn't just that Nick had chained him with a sliver of knowledge. It wasn't that he had ruined another one of his books. The man was slime. Morgan deserved better.

"If you crease my books again, I will rip your throat out," Al said, his canine jaws managing the words as a real dog could never do.

And then he gave in and vanished, letting the ancient elven curse pull him back to the ever-after, the demons' pride and hubris made terrifyingly real.

Or as real as anyone can expect, he thought as he found himself in his library, safely underground and away from the swirling red sands and gritty wind at the surface. It was all that was left of their paradise. Huffing in satisfaction, he wrapped the image of a Victorian dandy about himself once again, shaking out the lace at his cuffs and brushing the green velvet frock coat of the last tingle of magic. There was an intoxicating security here among his books that even his spelling kitchen lacked. The multitude of tomes were arranged in a pattern only he knew, and the scent of power was as tangible as the thin film of dust upon the oldest. Thoughts made real: the original magic, one might say.

"I knew the dog would scare the shit out of you," he said with a laugh—his smile fading when he saw his book, his abused, beautiful book, there on the table beside his chair.

"Ceri!" Al scooped it up, his fingers trying to smooth the creases as he noted what curses Nicholas Gregory Sparagmos had favored with his abuse. "Ceri! Tea!"

"Coming!" came back faintly, the elf's voice holding an unusual amount of bother.

Mood introspective, Al touched the water-damaged cover, silently promising the leather and ink revenge for the violence wrought upon it. The book wasn't alive in any sense of the word. But the pain in him was real.

Perhaps, he thought as he ran a gentle finger across the damaged spine. Perhaps learning how to mimic Rachel in the hopes of tricking her into the ever-after was not worth damaging his library. He could not fix the abuse. *But Newt can . . .*

"Your steps smell of reality."

Ceri's soft, somewhat dry tone turned him around. A fiber mat from the Asia steppe was tucked under one arm, and a clay pot from the Brazilian rainforests was in her grip, two tiny cups stacked atop. She herself was in a flowing silk gown from no era on earth. The elf dressed as if she was still a fey princess, even if she was a slave—favored, but a slave all the same.

"You know I don't approve of mixing eras," he complained.

Ignoring him, she unrolled the mat atop the table and began to pour out the tea. "Why do you let him destroy your books?" she asked, clearly appalled.

Al flipped his coattails and sat in his indulgent chair. "I didn't let him. He claims it's still readable and therefore no foul can be called. Technically he is correct. It is readable." Focus distant, he held the cup under his nose, breathing the fragrant steam. Jasmine. Not his favorite, but it hid the stench of burnt amber better than most.

Taking liberty with her station, Ceri sat on the footstool and sipped at her tea. "I can recopy it. That's it. But it will take me from my other tasks."

His head moved in a slow bob. "The original is not to be destroyed." Al looked at his gloved hands, curling them under into a fist. "I have warned him. He won't do it again."

Ceri eyed him over the rim of her cup. "Don't trust him. You can't convince someone who dog-ears books to not do it again. It's a chronic disease."

Al huffed. "I will keep my own counsel, elf."

A flash of anger lit her, a flicker of her old self, seldom seen anymore. "You say that like it's an insult." Stiff and bitter, she stood, topping off her cup before walking off. "It's not an insult!" she shouted over her shoulder.

He couldn't help his grin at her pique. For all the skills he'd taught her, she was helpless—and his smile widened when he sipped his tea and found it bitter. She'd turned it.

"Little revenge," he whispered, then hesitated, eyebrows high as he looked at his library. "What a good idea."

Nicholas Gregory Sparagmos would summon him again and he would go; the lure to know more about Rachel was irresistible. Besides, he had warned him. If the wizard so much as sneezed on another book, there would be consequences.

But to capitalize on it. That . . . would take some prep.

Coattails furling, he rose, motions fast as he went to his shelves and ran his fingers over the spines to find something he could afford to lose. A wicked smile creased his brow as he drew a badly copied version of a much more valuable tome from the shelf with a dry hiss.

"Ceri?" His gaze fell upon his ruined book, and in a surge of inspiration, he took it in hand as well. "I'm going out!" And then he vanished.

Part 2

Al stiffened as he materialized within a slim circle of silver inlaid upon what looked like imported tile. The circle was barely big enough for his feet, clearly not used for spelling but there to give a person a safe spot with which to jump into and out of. Still, it made him uncomfortable, and he shifted off it as he took in the changes in Newt's underground apartments.

They all coveted spaces that were familiar and comfortable, but only Newt had the skill to turn visions into reality at will, and he wondered how much it would cost to have her spell his quarters so that it looked as if he was at the top of a penthouse gazing out magnificent windows when in reality they were thirty feet underground.

"Newt?" he called as he stepped from the raised entry foyer and into a plush living room with thick carpets and tasteful furniture. He didn't recognize the space, but the era was obviously modern. Weaving among the low tables and couches, he came to a halt before the "window," knowing better than to tap at it lest he destroy the illusion.

Tall ceilings, sparse lines, exquisite furnishings: it spoke of a pleasing wealth, but a frown took him when he realized the view was of the Hollows from downtown Cincinnati.

"Carew Tower?" he whispered, studying the skyline. When had Newt escaped the hell of the ever-after? Or more importantly, how? The sun was up in her vision. She was sneaking out. Minias wasn't doing his job. *Is Minias dead?*

Confused, he studied an unfamiliar building towering in the Hollows down by the river. He would have sworn that building didn't exist.

Yet?

Frowning, he turned back to the upscale apartment, afraid of the answer. Newt was the most . . . inventive of them to the point of recklessness. There had been a time when it had served them all well, freeing them from the elven yoke. A third of his library had been penned by her. But it was that very recklessness that had left her as crazy as a moth on a light. Playing with time left a mark. Destroying Newt's memories to even things out had always had questionable results.

And here I am, he thought as he looked at the two books tucked between his arm and chest. *About to take advantage of it.*

No one, though, had noticed him, and he stood in the center of the room, growing uneasy. "Minias?"

He didn't like the demon. Had argued that he was too ambitious to be playing the part of the subordinate familiar when in truth he was watching the ofttimes erratic Newt, learning her secrets, pretending to be her slave. That she was patterning her apartments after a future Cincinnati did not bode well.

But no one else had wanted the job.

"Newt?" he called, fluffing his lace nervously. Perhaps he should have called, but he was sure Minias monitored her scrying mirror, and he wanted to talk to her alone.

"Newt!" he called again, demanding this time.

A soft and certain thump turned him, coattails furling and eyebrows rising as Newt came tumbling out of the wet bar's cupboard, the ancient demon sporting the slim, pale limbs of a child and her long, curly red hair in a disarming disarray.

"Three, two, one. Not it!" she shouted exuberantly as she swished her dress, changing it from a homespun frock to an elaborate Victorian lace and velvet to match Al's attire.

Not good, he thought as the warning flags snapped.

To treat her as the child she currently was would be a mistake, and he eyed her sourly over his blue-tinted glasses. "Newt, where is Minias?"

The demon's childlike face puckered, her black eyes staring unblinkingly at him in annoyance. She'd gotten them from staring too long into a ley line, or so it was said. He only knew one day she had the red, goat-slitted eyes of a demon, and the next, these monstrosities.

"Looking for me," she said, her voice still high with youth.

"Mmmm." He turned to the window, appreciating the sun—even if it was only a memory. "How long have you been hiding in the cupboard?" He took a steadying breath. "You didn't kill Minias, did you?"

"Not yet," she said wistfully. "We were playing, and . . ." Hesitating at a thought, she narrowed her eyes in anger. "Damn it back to the Turn," she continued, her voice deepening. "He did it again." Angry, she began to shift, her margins blurring as she grew, losing the lankiness of youth when her shoulders broadened and her bare feet became almost ugly. "Minias! You son of a bitch! Get back here!"

Al breathed a sigh of relief. He didn't like dealing with the child. It always got the better of him. "I'd rather you didn't. Three's a crowd."

Newt's anger vanished, her attention diverted as he set the mutilated book down on the table between them with a sliding thump.

Eyeing it, Newt ran a hand over her hair, pulling it out of existence until she was bald. Her proper Victorian frock, too, vanished, leaving her in a gold and black silken spelling robe. Her feet were still bare, and her black eyes just as disturbing, but her hands were now slim with age, her fingers long and narrow as if to fit in tight spaces no one else could manage—as her thoughts often did.

Mood entirely changed, she slumped onto an indulgent couch.

"Reading in the bath again, Gally?" she said as she reached to pull it closer. "This was mine. I don't remember giving it to you."

"You did." She was herself again. Or as close to herself as she generally got, and Al wondered if he should sit. It didn't feel quite safe yet. "The, ah, damage, I'm afraid, is the cost of grooming a potential familiar. Can you . . ."

She pulled her pale fingers from the cover as it began to glow. "Of course." Smiling with her lips closed, she crossed a knee over the other and gestured at the couch across from her.

The table would be between them, and Al took a slow breath and eased himself down. "Will you?" he amended, and the demon they kept balanced between lucidity and insanity laughed.

"For the right price." Her gaze went to the book still in his grip. "Certainly not for a badly copied version of a book already gracing my shelf. Perhaps you could kill Minias for me?" She batted her eyes at him coyly. "He has been dosing me with forget potions again." Her affected smile vanished. "Otherwise I would not be six years old and hiding in cupboards."

"Oh, Newt," Al crooned. "Killing Minias won't change anything. Maintaining your ignorance is the only thing keeping us alive. You will be allowed to recover your entire memory when there's a threat worthy of your talents. No sooner. It was your idea, love."

She bobbed her foot, brow furrowed in annoyance. "Perhaps. But killing him will make me feel better."

"I'm sure it will," he cajoled. "Still, he agreed to the job, and no one else wants it." Al hesitated. "Are you sure you didn't trap him in your oubliette? Should we check?"

"If he was in my oubliette, I wouldn't have been in a cupboard," she muttered, fully aware that she was missing parts of her mind. It was dangerous but necessary, and Al gently touched his ruined book in true regret.

"Can you repair it?"

A heavy sigh shifted Newt's shoulders. "Obviously. But I'm not so out of it as to push a book into the past to fix damage I did not inflict." Her thin eyebrows rose. "Especially if it is not *my* book anymore."

"Ah. I should be more clear." Al touched the ruined cover. "I am here to bargain for a spell to correct the one who dropped my . . . Or is it possibly *your* book in the tub?"

Newt sat up, suddenly interested. "You'll return it? For a spell?" Her gaze fixed on the book as if it might hold a piece of her memory—which, in hindsight, was a possibility. Settling back, she tried to find a nonchalant expression—but he had seen, and a quiver of success shifted through him.

"It would be pleasant to have something under my pillow that Minias doesn't know about," Newt said, eyes still on the book. "He keeps me from my library. Afraid I might . . . remember." She beamed to show her teeth. "What do you propose, Gally?"

She was fully herself, and Al put his elbows on his knees. This version of her was safe. Well, safer—as long as she wasn't pissed at what she still forgot. It was only when she didn't know her mind that she was a danger. Unfortunately, it was getting harder to bring her back. But since she was the only female demon left alive, they pandered to her even as they held her memories hostage, excavating them when needed and burying them when they didn't lest she kill them as she had her sisters.

It hadn't always been such, and Al shoved the guilt down deep. They all did what they needed to do to survive. He wasn't sure why anymore.

"I have a wizard in reality who needs correction," Al said, and Newt nodded, conversant with his skill of luring in and training new familiars for others to use. "My library is taking the brunt of the damage. This last affront would have me abandon him, but he has something I need, and until I have his soul and can force the issue, bargaining for breadcrumbs is the only way to get it. I'm willing to give you this." Al's fingers tingled when he touched the damaged book, satisfied when Newt grimaced, the demon clearly wanting it. "In exchange for your help in spelling this." He set the badly copied book down beside it, wincing at the obvious inferiority of it. Nicholas Gregory Sparagmos, though, wouldn't be able to tell the difference. "I need a whip with which to teach him respect of my books, and you, Newt, are beyond any doubt the most adept at modifying an existing spell to a new outcome."

The flattery fell flat because it was so obviously true. He had once loaned Ceri to her in the hopes that the familiar would return having picked up a few techniques. Instead, Ceri had come home all but comatose, unable to even manage his morning tea. The only good from the experience was that the mere mention of Newt's name brought the uppity woman to a terrified obedience that could last for weeks.

Newt pulled the book closer, her expression puckering as she sent a visible thread of energy through it to feel the unseen damage. "I'd have to fix it before I could use it again," she said softly, her focus blurred as if imagining it. "Ley lines do not run smoothly through water-damaged pages."

She was holding it. A thrill of success traced through him, and he hid his smile. "Damaged goods, but something, as you say, you can fix. At least with you, it will be whole again. With me, it will languish."

"Not enough."

Al's lips parted as Newt dropped the book on the table with a disparaging thump. "Not enough?" he echoed.

The demon arched her eyebrows as if in rebuke for him trying to scam her. "The cost to repair the damage is threefold the damage to me. Oh, I will take the book, but I am tired of Minias's plots. I want a new familiar as well. Ceri will do. You've taught her almost everything you know."

His gaze went to the jump-in-out circle he had arrived in. "Minias . . ."

"Is stealing from me." Newt pulled her knees to her chin, a flash of fear crossing her before she hid it behind a mask of confidence. "You all know it. You all look the other way because to do otherwise might mean you would have to take his place. A memory here, a recollection there. He writes it down, then makes me forget again. You think I was hiding in a cabinet because he was trying to escape me?" Newt scoffed. "I make myself helpless because it's the only way I can keep what I have left. I want him gone before he writes down and erases enough of me such that I am utterly consumed."

"Newt, be reasonable . . ."

"I want Ceri." Newt stared at him with her black eyes, unmoved. "She at least steals with the intent to escape." A smile quirked her lips. "We had such fun the last time."

"Absolutely not." Al pushed deeper into the cushions, frustrated but unable to walk away. "She is my Magna Carta, and you returned her all but comatose. I won't do that to her again."

Newt batted her black eyes coyly at him. "Are you not here to find a whip with which to groom another?" she asked, a gentle hand on the book.

"You had her for a week, Newt. No."

"I need someone with enough skill to stir the spells to regain my memory." Newt pouted. "Minias won't do it. You clearly have no more use for her if you are grooming another."

A sigh slipped from him. Newt thought it was the wizard he wanted, but his real goal was Rachel Mariana Morgan. There was a secret in her he needed to work out, something on the tip of his tongue he couldn't quite taste. But she was wary and smart. The only way to get to her was through the mistakes that Nicholas Gregory Sparagmos made. Al would never gain her without more information. It was his books, or Ceri.

Besides, the wizard needed to be taught a lesson. It was his fault Al had to go to Newt with his hat in his hand. He would have his revenge for his lost book and a new familiar both.

"Loan," he said, immediately regretting it. "When I acquire a new familiar, Ceri returns to me so I may release her as was our original bargain." It had been over a thousand years ago, but it still stood. "And I want the book as well. Repaired. Ceri is worth more than that."

"You intend to release her." Newt grimaced, knowing what that really meant. "Such a waste. Fine. But Ceri is mine from the moment your wizard triggers the spell. You get her back only when you have your new familiar."

"Done." Guilt flashed through him. Ceri would suffer. But her end would be as he promised.

Humming a nonsense tune, Newt drew the book closer, cradling it. "What did you have in mind? To teach your potential familiar respect, I mean."

A smile, wicked and inviting, found him. He had always enjoyed working with Newt, never fully agreeing to the others' plan of keeping her ignorant and helpless. He would take heat for giving her the tools to slip Minias, but this would help both of them. They had been friends, once.

His smile vanished. "I'm so pleased you asked."

Part 3

Six days, Al thought, slumped in his high-backed chair, feet outstretched to his peat fire, brooding with the book Newt spelled for him at his hand. He was beginning to question whether the slavering dog from hell had been too much for the wizard to handle and he had accidently scared him off. Surely he had not underestimated his greed. It had to be cowardice, not guilt, that stayed Nicholas Gregory Sparagmos's hand in summoning him, but it was hard not to feel as if he had made a mistake.

Two mistakes, he mused, seeing as he had brought Newt back to herself in order to teach Nicholas Gregory Sparagmos the error of his ways. Minias was already searching to find out who and demand restitution or assistance in dulling her again. But if Minias had been serious about minding the insane demon, he wouldn't have left her hiding in a cupboard to sneak out for a cup of bad coffee.

Al's gaze flicked to the untouched pot of tea on the side table. "Not that I blame him," he grumbled, eyeing the bitter brew at his elbow. It was all Ceri had given him since he had left that dog-eared, water-stained book with Newt. He *needed* a new familiar. If not Nicholas Gregory Sparagmos, then Rachel Mariana Morgan herself.

Almost as if on cue, a sneeze threatened, grew, and slipped easily from him. Smile widening, he waited for another, his anticipation heady as the pull on the pit of his soul grew. A second sneeze burst forth. It was a summons.

"Ceri?" Guilt flickered, immediately quashed. "Call Newt. Tell her I need her to serve as witness and to come immediately. I'm being summoned, or I'd do it myself."

Ceri appeared in the doorway, silken robes rustling, her face ashen. "You want me to call Newt? Gally, she's insane. Wouldn't Dali—"

"Scrying mirror," he said, pointing at it in the corner of the desk. The summons was becoming painful. "Call her. Tell her. I will be back shortly. This won't take long."

"Gally!" Ceri exclaimed, but the pull across the void had become too much, and he took the spelled curse book in hand and let the summons pull him across time and space.

"Stupid wizard," he muttered, guilt twining about him again as he felt himself dissolve. He would have what he wanted tonight. All of it, and everything. That is, if Nicholas Gregory Sparagmos was as greedy and foolish as Al thought he was.

The soft, almost forgotten sound of rain slipped into his awareness first as he felt himself become solid again, and for a moment, longing hit him, hard and unexpected. Lip curled, he opened his eyes, good mood spoiled at the reminder of what he had lost, what they all had.

"Nicholas Gregory Sparagmos." He practically bit the words off, hating the memories that the smell of rain in the dark had unearthed. Even the sound was wasted on the likes of him. "Does the witch like to be on top or the bottom? Or does she prefer something more adventuresome?"

The wizard stood and stared at him as if wondering if he had made a mistake. Chin high, he ran a hand over his hair to slick it back. He was dressed better than usual, the scent of detergent and pasta making it through the protection circle. *My God. Have they just been on a date?*

"You wish," Nick said softly, but a thrill shivered through Al as he saw the cracks in the wizard's resolve. Six days to search his soul . . . The man was predictable, and with that came success.

"You brought a book," Nick said, eyeing it. "Same deal as before? A day for each piece of information."

Al stifled his smile, then let it flow. "You think she's worth all that?"

The wizard's lip twitched, and he rubbed at his stubble. "I think you wanting to pass as her is worth more than you're giving me. Don't think I don't know what you're doing. But, Algaliarept, there's no way you will ever know how she kisses. You will never be able to be her, no matter how much I tell you."

Six days for a coward to find his greed, he thought. "Perhaps you are right." Motions smooth, he opened the book, angling it so Nick could get a glimpse—and nothing more. "The cost has gone up. Twelve hours for each answered question, provided you answer them to my satisfaction."

Almost had him, and his need to avenge his damaged library swelled.

Nick shifted from foot to foot in indecision. "Okay," he finally said. "What do you want to know? Within reason."

A thrill sparked through him, hidden behind a twitch of his coattails. Nick would want it for two days, bare minimum. *Best to bait the trap with trifles.* "Coffee. Does she have her coffee before or after she gets dressed and her pixy vermin braids her hair?"

Nick licked his lips, his gaze on the door making Al wonder if Rachel had just left. "Before," Nick said softly. "Unless she has to leave, and then it's after." He held out his hand. "That's enough. If I want it longer, I'll call you."

Al shook his head. "Two questions. I can't return until dark to retrieve it. Besides, you're going to want at least two days to copy the text. As before, a picture will show nothing, and there are countless spells here." He hesitated. "Favorite curse word?"

"Crap on toast," Nick blurted. "Unless she's mad at Jenks, and then it's damn it back to the Turn."

"Mmmm." Al brushed his sleeve clean, as if unimpressed. "Pet name for her pixy?"

"For a second full day?" Nick questioned, licking his lips when Al nodded. "Okay. She has no pet name for him. I don't know why, but she has a lot of respect for him."

Al's jaw tightened as he remembered the pixy scoring on his ear. "Perhaps it is because he's not a coward, freely taking his vengeance upon those who threaten what's dear to him." He let the book droop to show Nick a page. "When she's spelling, does she have coffee at hand? Bite the end of her pencil? I need her quirks."

Nick hesitated, clearly reluctant. But his eye twitched when Al snapped the book shut, and the demon patiently waited, smiling when Nick bowed his head. Four days would give Nick time to copy almost everything cover to cover—and they both knew it. The exercise would be good for when he had him—body and soul.

"No coffee when she's spelling," he said softly. "She's paranoid about contamination."

"It's good practice," Al said, impressed despite himself. She would make an excellent replacement for Ceri—in time. *Nearly there . . .* he thought, hiding his anticipation. Revenge was not best served cold. It was best not served at all, but taken. "Last question, Nicholas Gregory Sparagmos."

Nick backed up at his lascivious tone, already shaking his head. "I'm not telling you anything about sex, so forget it."

"Oh, Nicky. You've already given me more than I need," he lied coaxingly. "Indulge my curiosity. Is she a moaner or silent? Aggressive or passive? Does she find a false comfort in the afterglow or fall asleep? I want details. They will make her nights with me *so* much more enjoyable—for me."

The wizard's eyes were bright with defiance. "I'm not giving you that. Four days for four aspects of her. Leave the book as agreed, or I own you."

Al glanced at the book as if reluctant. It had cost him, but if he was right, he'd have what he wanted and his revenge for his damaged library, both. "As you say. But before you banish me, if you tell me what I want to know, you can keep the book. Forever."

A thrill jolted him when Nick visibly hesitated. *Got you, you little pissant.*

"So rare a tome . . ." Al crooned, paging through the book. "So finite. It's one of Newt's. That is how much I want to know about our little itchy witch." Again he snapped the book shut, making Nick jump. "Or do you think you will find yourself one night with my legs wrapped around you?"

Nick's lip twitched. "I'd know the difference."

Al shrugged, waiting.

"You'll give me the book? Forever. Say it."

"It is already yours." Al dropped the book with a loud pop. "But the details must be commensurate with the value of the book, or I leave with it and you get nothing."

Again Nick looked at his door, guilt flashing across him until he visibly shoved it aside, abandoning it like a melted ice cream cone. "She's more adventuresome than aggressive. Playful? Mostly silent unless she can't help it. She enjoys the novel, but always in good taste."

A flicker of masculine pride flashed over Nick, irritating Al. "Does she engage the ley lines?" Al asked, and Nick's man-pride vanished.

"No, but—"

"She would if you weren't afraid," Al guessed, knowing he was right when Nick flushed. "Excellent. Who falls asleep first?" He waited, breathless. He had lost another book, but the information would be useful. Very useful.

"It's always been me," Nick said, head down as if only now realizing what a poor excuse of a lover he was. "I fell asleep last time while she was in the shower," he added as if seeking forgiveness.

Al's lip curled in an ugly smile. Revenge was indeed sweeter for taking its time—the instant of weightlessness at the top of a swing, the catching of your breath when you see a conquest across the room. "Cleanliness is next to godliness," he muttered.

"I've told you enough." Nick stood before him, a somewhat panicked look on his face. "That book is mine. Forever. Say it before I banish you." He hesitated. "I'm never going to summon you again."

Al glanced down at the book at his feet. *Oh, if only that were true, you might survive me.* "This book is yours," he said, a delighted shiver passing through him. "But I warn you. Do not damage it. Understand? It won't take kindly to abuse. That is your only warning." He took a slow breath, knowing Newt was watching this through his scrying mirror. She would be his witness if the wizard should call foul. Demons did, after all, have to play by the rules. "Say it."

"Don't damage the book. Fine." Nick took a breath. "Algaliarept, I banish you to the ever-after, to where you will stay until summoned again. Leave *now*, and go there directly."

"A most secure banishment." Al made a sarcastic, courtly bow before letting the ancient elven curse seize him in a scintillating shower of silver sparks. Anticipation was a ribbon of heat, tempered by the cost of his revenge. Leaving a sacrificial book in reality did not sit well with him, but he was not a cheat. His reputation would not be called into question. Nicholas Gregory Sparagmos had gotten fair compensation for his information. What he did with it after was the beauty of the scheme. Nick was clever enough to know the value of such a priceless artifact and yet idiot enough to trigger the spell Newt had put on it. All he had to do now was sit back and watch. A delighted tremor shook the last of the energy from him as he reappeared in his library.

"Let go! Let go of me!"

Al spun at Ceri's cry, brow furrowed upon seeing Newt holding the terrified familiar by the arm. Ceri's usual finery was gone, and his guilt was a quick flash at the reminder of their agreement. Newt had already dressed Ceri in an insultingly homespun smock. Which raised the question of what Ceri was upset about: Newt's hold on her, or her new outfit.

"It's not finished, Newt!" Al bellowed, and the demon let go, chagrined. But only for a moment.

"You agreed that she was mine," Newt demanded, and Al winced, having wanted to break the news to Ceri gently.

"Gally!" Ceri backed up, her arms wrapped around herself. The look of betrayal on her face went right to his gut and twisted. "You didn't."

"Not until the wizard triggers the spell." A wave of burnt amber rose from him as he fluffed his lace in agitation. Annoyed, Al stomped to where his scrying mirror lay on the table, as Ceri had left it. "He may not." Shoulders hunched, he sat down and pulled the mirror closer. He wouldn't look at her. *Ignore it, and it never happened.*

Bare feet scuffing, Ceri retreated until her back hit the wall. "No. I can't do that again. Gally. Please. Anything. I'll do anything."

Newt laughed, the cheerful sound striking Al as wrong in the tense air. Motions dangerously sensuous, she came to stand over the table and looked down. Nicolas Gregory Sparagmos looked back at them from the mirror, his focus distant as he thumbed through the pages of the book, oblivious to the fact that it had been spelled to serve as a two-way mirror—among other things.

Curious despite her fear, Ceri inched closer, too. "You made the book into a visual portal? Why?"

"Because revenge feels better when you can see it," he muttered.

"Gally . . ."

Her voice was a thin whisper, and guilt finally pulled his eyes up. It might be hours before Nick damaged the book. But he would.

"Gally, you promised you'd release me."

She was kneeling at his feet, her trembling hands on his knees. "I will," he said brusquely. "You are being loaned. Nothing more. You still belong to me."

Anger flickered, returning her to her original magnificence. "You don't want me anymore. Admit it. I bore you."

His eye twitched. In the mirror, Nicholas Gregory Sparagmos bit the end of a pencil and turned a page. "I do want you. But I could not repair the book and buy a curse from Newt without giving her something."

Ceri gasped, jerking her touch from him. "You care more about your books than me!"

He was silent. Across from him, Newt cleared her throat and sat down.

"You are foul." Ceri stood, pale and shaking. "Unclean and heartless. You know what she will do to me, and you'd rather have a book on your shelf!"

Al clenched his jaw, uncomfortable with Newt hearing all of this. "You have a fine enough touch to repair her memory, Ceri. It's my fault that I taught you so well."

"Your fault!" The elf backed up, horrified. "You want me to help repair her memory? She's been made ignorant for a reason. Gally, you don't know."

"I do know!" he thundered, and across from him, Newt settled deeper into the cushions, one finger pulling the mirror closer as if they weren't talking about her. "And if I deem it time for the demons to stop hiding in their caves and take back what's ours, you will do what I tell you to do, and do it well! Newt led us to our freedom once before. It's time for her to remember so she can do it again!"

Newt's attention flicked up from the mirror. "I did?"

She had, and Al stood, suddenly nervous at the memory of what Newt was capable of when she had her back to the wall—and was pissed.

Ceri shook her head, eyes wide in fear. "You aren't captive. I am."

Anger pulsed through him. "Do I look free to you?" he shouted, and her head bowed to try to hide a trace of revenge-ridden satisfaction.

He was not free. None of them were, trapped within this hell created by the waste of a millennia-long war. It had been Ceri's kin who had imprisoned them here, slipping the snare the demons had laid for them to escape to reality.

Perhaps this is a mistake . . . Al mused, drawn to her defiance, intrigued by what might lie under it. Elves were as powerful as demons when all things were equal. But nothing had been equal in several thousand years. "Newt—"

"Look! Look! He did it! He invoked the curse!" Newt crowed.

Hunched, Ceri backed away, terrified.

Al's attention jerked to the mirror, where Nick was leafing through the pages in disbelief. The spell he'd triggered turned them to a blank nothing. "Dog-eared my book again, did you?" Al said, the warm glow of satisfaction finding him. "Use a damned sticky note like a respectable person."

The vision through the mirror shifted wildly as Nick threw the blank book at the wall, the image settling to see Nick, now upside down as he stomped away.

Al chuckled and reached for his tea. "If you don't know the value of a book, Nicky, you shouldn't have any."

Some days were better than others, and this felt like a large step closer to Rachel Mariana Morgan. And Nicholas Gregory Sparagmos? Well, it was doubtful that the little wizard would ever dog-ear another book again. In his experience, revenge was always worth the cost to realize it. Today proved it.

The tea was bitter. Eyes rolling, Al set it down. "Ceri? A new pot of tea for Newt and me to celebrate with!" he called merrily.

But there was no answer, and he looked up into silence, realizing that both she and Newt were gone. His breath of protest caught . . . and then he let it out, his mood crashing. Newt hadn't even given him a moment to say goodbye.

"Just as well," he lied. Flustered, he pushed back into his cushions with his bitter tea. *It was worth it,* he thought.

But as the silence grew and the scent of lilacs faded, he wondered if this time . . . the cost had been too much.

RAZORS AND REVENGE

Faith Hunter

Shiloh stopped in the doorway. The Dark Queen, Jane Yellowrock, sat at a small round table, drinking tea. Eli and Koun were sitting with her, drinking coffee. Eli was the head of security and Jane's adopted brother. Koun was an ancient vampire and the queen's . . . executioner.

Shiloh went still as a statue, hands braced on the doorjamb.

When she woke after the werewolf attack—full of the crazies caused by werewolf prions—Shiloh had nearly killed one of her human blood servants for the blood in her veins.

When a vamp attacked a human, it brought a death sentence.

The three in the small receiving room watched her. Sipped. Silent.

Despite her bloodlust, Shiloh had survived the full moon without going furry, and had found some sanity, some self-control. Was that enough to be allowed to live?

She was still standing, as if glued to the floor. Was there royal protocol for someone about to be executed? Mad laughter tickled the back of her throat.

Panic made her heart beat, forced her to breathe, exhibiting a serious lack of vamp control. Her talons struggled to extend and pierce the wood of the doorframe, which was a dangerous breach of etiquette in the presence of royalty.

The queen raised her eyebrows slightly, her yellowish eyes evaluating.

Shiloh forced the panic down, trying to see everything and everyone at once. There were no weapons of execution in sight. No silver shackles. No stakes. The queen seemed relaxed, her black hair in a single braid down her back, jeans-clad legs crossed, boots. No makeup. Casual.

Jane sipped tea. It wasn't a china cup, used at official functions, but a big lavender mug with a pic of a deeply purple Count von Count on it, the Muppet world's only purple vampire character. No pomp or circumstance. Laid-back.

This wasn't a formal meeting.

Heart rate slowing, she looked at Eli and Koun. Eli's expression was cold. Koun's pale stare was as predatory as the werewolves who had killed Atticus and nearly killed her. Koun had found her. Fed her. Saved her. Later, it was Koun who had pulled her off Rachel before she ripped out her best friend's throat. And Koun might be the only one who knew how nutso, how out of control, she was.

Shiloh fought a shiver. The razors of werewolf prions scored her veins, shredded her nerve endings. The crazies hovered just beneath her skin.

Time was compressing and elongating in her mind. She had stood in the doorway too long. With three steps, Shiloh fell to the queen's Lucchese-booted feet.

No one else moved.

Jane sighed, smelling of mountain lion, tea, and irritation. The Dark Queen of the vampires was a Cherokee skinwalker, not a fanghead. She also tended to operate with a total lack of royal decorum whenever she wanted. No one ever knew what to expect. That pissed off a lot of vampires. All that was why Shiloh liked her.

"Get up, kid," the queen said, her words as unceremonious as her mug. "Sit. Drink tea or coffee. Let's talk."

Shiloh rose, slid into a chair, hope constraining her panic.

She had dressed with special care, her dark red hair up in a French twist, makeup on her vamp-pale cheeks, fancy slacks, silk shirt. Pumps. Even lipstick. *Gah.* If they took her head, it would totally ruin her outfit. The crazy laughter tittered.

Fighting to control her reactions, she clenched her talons into her palms. Pain helped, but her talons drew blood. *Damn it.* Koun shifted in his chair, one hand near his blade as her blood-scent filled the room.

Memories surfaced at the lilac, rock dust, and old ash scent of her own blood. Atticus ripped to pieces by werewolves. Images, smells, sounds. *Blood, fangs, terror. Running. The darkness of a cave. My healing amulets out of power.* Her own inner magic had never been trained or predictable, and her brain had been so messed up with werewolf prions, she hadn't been able to access it.

The stench of Atticus' body had grown each time she woke. With the stench had come pain. *Razors cutting my nerves, ripping through veins. Hunger. Desperate hunger.*

At the queen's tea table, Koun leaned toward her, his vamp scent a mingling of funeral flowers, cold Celtic nights, battle, and safety. Her eyes flew to his. The memories of the attack, of the madness of the nights in the cave subsided, replaced by the memory of Koun entering the rock cavern, the taste of his blood. Soothing words in a language so foreign it was like the burr of a cat's purr and the clash of battle drums.

Koun smiled, the barest twitch of his beautiful lips.

She drew in his scent again. The memory of safety helped, and she shoved down on the crazies. It was easier when she didn't expect to be decapitated.

The laughter threatened again, but she swallowed it down. Perhaps five seconds had passed. She had to do something, so she sat back in her chair.

Her talons withdrew into their sheaths, and Koun relaxed.

Still in the wry tone of her greeting, the queen said, "You earned your bounty."

It took several more seconds before that hit home. The bounty for the werewolf she and Atticus had gone to collect. That bounty paid bills and rent for a year, even in high-priced Asheville. She said, "You found the wolf head?"

Dryly, Jane said, "Three of them. All still in werewolf form."

Blood. Fangs ripping into me. Fighting for my life. Shortsword cutting. Handgun firing. The stink of silver burning were-flesh, the tang of wet dog, nitrocellulose, blood.

The razor sensation cut deep. She wanted to curse, but one did not curse in front of the queen.

Shiloh pulled on the memory of Koun's blood, rich, thick, salty, intense. When he found her, he must have let her nearly drain him dry.

The queen said, "Your rescue party found the wolf heads tied in a tree about thirty feet off the ground."

Three werewolf heads. Dayum. Shiloh poured coffee and gulped it down. The coffee's bitter bite and caffeine hit her like a sledgehammer, easing the pain. That was new. Her mug was decorated with a pic of a fawn, like Bambi, with the words "Fuck guns" underneath. Which was hilarious in the vampire queen's heavily armed, cuss-free household.

"Shiloh!"

Shiloh's eyes flew to the queen. Razors itched along her nerves; insanity danced in her mind. No one knew they were inside her. When she survived the full moon without going werewolf-ish, Koun had unknowingly given her the control she needed, sparring with her in the gym. The zing of adrenaline, the desperation of fight, of trying to stay undead, stopped the razors in her bloodstream, the crazies in her brain. Working with him, she discovered the werewolf attack had left her faster and stronger. Sword strikes—with wooden practice swords—were precise and deadly.

After the first session, she had been able to hide what she had become, but she needed to fight often, the pain scratching just below her skin. In the vampire world, being different brought danger. Exposing secrets could be deadly.

"You killed *three* rogue werewolves," Jane said, "including the one you were originally tracking." She looked proud. And vicious. "*Three.*" Jane's pride disappeared and her voice gentled. "I'm sorry about Atticus. He was a loyal scion. He told the best stories about his pappy and shine."

Shiloh's gaze fell and cemented to the table. Flashes of Atticus fighting, dying, tore through her. The razors sliced, but she had control. For now.

The queen kept talking. "The werewolf saliva was in your system for too long. There was no one to heal you. Koun did his best when he found you, but the werewolves who bit you, who killed Atticus, were psychotic, infected from before the *Change*. No one knows why the *Change* didn't take away the curse from this small pack, but whatever kept the unchanged were-prions active is why you're having trouble adjusting."

Shiloh laughed, a single rough note. *Adjusting. Right.*

The *Change* was the night vamps got back their souls and the were-curse was altered. Prior to then, were-bitches often turned their packs psychotic. *So. This is what it feels like to be psycho.* She ripped her eyes from the table to the queen's.

Jane's gaze rested heavily on her. Shiloh drained her mug and poured more coffee. Caffeine to lull the razors scratching, scratching, scratching for violence.

The queen continued. "Koun smelled a sick, insane bitch-queen but had no time to track her. Getting you to safety was paramount. Tell me what happened."

Razors cut. To ease it, Shiloh gulped the scalding coffee.

Eli's face did something curious, but she didn't know what it meant until he said, "For a fanghead, my espresso is like drinking racing fuel."

"Feels good," Shiloh said. "There was a naked woman in the woods when the wolves attacked. White-blond, scraggly hair, muscles harshly defined. She reeked of"—Shiloh shook her head—"of sickness, putrefying flesh, mangy dog. Violent brown eyes."

Six wolves, all wounded with silver-lead rounds, had surrounded them. She and Atticus had made no kill shots. Even injured, werewolves were fast. The woman whistled and pointed at Shiloh. All six male wolves turned to her, leaving Atticus alone. Shiloh's magazines were empty. She tossed a *hedge* amulet, but it sputtered and died. Undependable as usual, but this time maybe fatal. She took a two-handed grip on the vamp-killer.

A brown wolf leaped on her, shoving her to the ground. Bit into her thigh, piercing her armor.

Atticus charged to help.

Five wolves swiveled on hind paws and savaged him.

From the ground, Shiloh stabbed into the wolf's chest, then to the side, across its heart. Leaped to her feet. It took perhaps three seconds.

Atticus had already been true-dead.

"Shiloh!" the queen said sharply. "What happened?"

Shiloh blinked, her skin clammy, razors scraping, scraping, scraping inside her. They could see she was having control issues. Shiloh said, "The werewolf bitch. I saw her. She made the wolves attack me."

"She spoke?" The queen leaned forward.

Some insane werewolf bitches lost language. "No. Whistled. Pointed. Atticus came to help. Five turned on him at once." She stopped, the queen's stare holding her. "I killed a wolf and got to my feet. Atticus was . . ." She fought vamping out. Fought the burrowing pain. Even Koun's scent didn't calm her now. "True-dead."

"I'm sorry," Jane said again. "I know you two were close."

Sharing jokes. Sharing donors. Sharing everything and moving to being more. Heading to being lovers. "I don't remember anything else."

The wolf-woman's eyes had held nothing but rage and psychosis. The razors and bloodlust in Shiloh were part of that.

Jane said. "You killed two more werewolves. According to the tracks, three badly injured wolves and the werewolf-human bitch left the site together. You secured three wolf heads, carried as much of Atticus as you could find, and crawled into a cave. You were comatose and feverish when the rescue party found you." Jane glanced at Koun. "You did a number on him before he could subdue you. He was impressed."

"I'm sorry," Shiloh said.

Koun gave that almost smile again.

The queen continued. "Werewolf prions shouldn't be able to survive in a vampire, but you're a young vamp, and a witch. A witch-vamp-werewolf is a . . . singularity."

Singularity, hell. She was dangerous. A ravening beast lived inside her. "I should still be chained in a scion room."

Jane chuckled, though amusement never reached her eyes. Her tea sloshed over the Count. She put the mug down and wiped her fingers.

Shiloh wondered if the woman ever smiled like a human. Happy.

Eli wiped the outside of the Count mug and poured the queen more tea.

"Another night in a cell," Jane said, "and your aunts would skin me and pin my pelt on the door. My Beast is too pretty to die."

Shiloh laughed, but it was high-pitched, off-kilter. She finished the coffee and poured another. A servant entered, replaced the empty carafe, and withdrew. Before she realized she was speaking, Shiloh said, "I'm going after the males and the bitch-queen."

Jane's eyebrows rose. She lifted the Count mug. "Would you care to restate that?"

"With your permission, I'm going after the males and the *werewolf* bitch-queen."

"Thanks for the clarification. And no. We forbid it." The royal *we*. A pronouncement.

This had just become an official tea, not that Shiloh cared. "They did this to me," she snarled, her lips curling. Her fangs tried to snap down. She clenched her teeth and, for one hard second, fought the need to vamp out and attack, the razors scraping, the insanity making the room spin. She wanted action, violence. She said, "I want the bitch's head on a pike."

"While we approve of vengeance, *no*." The queen propped her elbows on her chair arms, her tea mug fully hiding her mouth. "Because they bit my scion—you—and killed Atticus, the males you killed each had a fifty K bounty. You earned one hundred fifty thousand dollars. You're injured, so you're done. Three other scions want the bounty on the remaining wolves."

"They'll need me to track and identify the wolves."

"Why?"

"We've been through a full moon since I was attacked. What if the bitch made more? I've smelled the three who attacked us." Shiloh drew on the scent of Koun and repositioned, mirroring the queen's posture. Forcing calm. Negotiating. Hiding the raging wolf slavering inside her. "The werewolf bitch directed the attack. That makes her—what's the word? Responsible, but more?"

The queen said, "Culpable." Without looking away, she asked, "Koun, your evaluation?"

The queen's executioner turned icy eyes to Shiloh. Ancient Celtic tattoos swirled blue above his collar. "She smells, looks, and acts sane, my lady. Shiloh has skills most undead do not. When her aunts evaluated her magic this past week, they found it to be rusty but functional. She can make amulets preloaded with witch workings. Though she knows *wyrd* workings by heart, she has never attempted them. She passed Eli's remedial paramilitary course and is capable of working with a team."

More slowly, his voice sliding like silk across skin, he said, "She killed three werewolves single-handedly. She gave me a black eye. She has untried physical gifts that indicate she is faster and stronger than she allows us to see."

A black eye? Shiloh's eyes darted to his face.

Amused, Koun said, "I approve."

Jane frowned, but lifted her head and spoke into the room. "Alex, record."

From invisible speakers, Alex, head of electronic security, said, "Recording, my lady."

"We proclaim. Shiloh may *go with the hunters*," she enunciated, "to identify the males. But the team will take a trank gun, sedate the bitch, and bring her in, alive, for testing, because she should not be insane after the *Change*." The Dark Queen considered, and added, "We have previously approved a death sentence upon any werewolf who bites a human or one of mine. That proclamation stands."

Shiloh considered the exact words of the pronouncement. She wanted all the werewolves dead. If she had to be bitten again to kill the bitch, that could happen. "Thank you, Your Highness."

The queen made a *pfft* sound and said, "End recording."

"Done, my lady," Alex said.

Shiloh drank her coffee. *It's over.*

"While we're chatting so nicely," Jane said, "tell me how the werewolf prions have altered you."

Shiloh nearly choked on her coffee.

"I've watched vids of you sparring. You're faster, more precise, and holding back to keep us uninformed."

"Beats the hell outta me. I'm a singularity, remember?"

"Language, girl."

"Sorry, my lady."

The queen snorted. "You are *dismissed*."

Shiloh narrowed her eyes at the royal dismissal, stood, and left the room.

Her repaired armor was too tight on her shoulders, too loose in her waist, and short in the inseam. The undead can't grow. Unless starved of human blood, which makes them skinny, their body shape, when changed, is theirs for eternity (or until they're beheaded).

Forever the same. Except her. She'd added two inches since she was attacked.

Armor was expensive, hand-tailored layers of anti-spell Kevlar and Dyneema, to protect against explosive weapons and close-in fighting: bullets, blades, darts, talons, and magic. Because of the damage hers had sustained in the werewolf attack, and her growth spurt, she needed new armor. Instead, she had poorly repaired, blood-stinking armor.

Crappy armor or not, she needed to try out her new abilities, which meant getting in front of the team. She looked overhead at the waning moon and climbed into a tree. "I'm checking ahead." Without waiting for a reply from the others, Shiloh turned on normal fanghead speed and leaped over a storm-downed oak. The trunk was ten feet high. The vamps followed. She cleared a twelve-foot white water creek, landing on the other side. She jumped, gripping a branch fifteen feet up. Feet pushing off the trunk, swinging, she landed in the next tree, five feet higher, like a gymnast on steroids. The vamps made the creek but failed to follow her into the tree limbs. *Interesting.*

Through the winter-dead treetops, she sprinted and swung. Eluding them, she dashed full speed. Seconds into her mad sprint, the nagging razors dissipated. It was so unexpected, she laughed, the sound echoing, brittle and crazy. The air resisted her, a steady crackling and a loud *pop-whoosh* as it shoved aside and filled in behind. She scaled a cliff face like a spider, flipped at the top, and descended, weight on her palms and the tops of her boot toes, reflipped herself, and climbed to stand above her personal rock climbing wall. She was hungry, needed to feed, but adrenaline and speed and a lack of pain created euphoria. She raced on.

She was using vamp vision, her pupils so wide her irises were nearly invisible, the night world bright. Her fangs were secured on their little hinges in the top of her mouth. In control.

This was what she was. Faster, stronger, more predatory and dangerous than the oldest vamps. *Unbalanced? Crazy? Yeah. So?*

Witch, fanghead, with were-prions. If it wasn't for the razors—currently soothed—it would be cool.

A scent trace stopped her cold in a dead tree, fifteen feet up. From a thicket of rhododendrons beneath her rose the sickly sweet stink of rotting blood, faint, after the recent ice storm. *Werewolf. Vamp.* Some of the old blood was hers.

The reek of blood marked the place where she and Atticus had fought the wolves until running out of ammo, too bloodied and exhausted to escape. The memory rose through her again.

The wolves had encircled the thicket, limping, wounded by silver-lead rounds. There was no way they could change back until the silver had been surgically removed from their bodies. But she and Atticus had made no kill shots. Werewolves, even crazy, even bleeding and full of silver, were *fast*.

Her breath came rapid and shallow as the sensations, the remembered fear, engulfed her, a hallucinogenic nightmare. Image upon image, wound after wound.

Atticus, ripped to death by werewolves. He had died, badly.

Shiloh pushed the memories away, reached inside a pocket of her armor, and wrapped her fingers around the *calm of stones* amulet, a cut agate. Its striations were psychedelic, haphazard, but the magic within soothed her crazies. The pain of Atticus' death eased. The lacerating madness faded.

It worked. She hadn't been sure it would.

Shiloh checked her other amulets: *healing* workings; one *hedge of blood*, which could be used as either a shield or, if reversed, a prison; and one *stasis*. Only one *stasis*, the most difficult working in her meager repertoire. If she'd had time, she would have made ten of the paralytic-style workings. Then again, there was no proof any of her own amulets would work. She'd had only hours to make them and no time to test them. As a witch, she was a three out of ten in terms of training, power, and experience.

Maybe a two.

High in the trees, Shiloh circled the rhododendron thicket, spiraling out. The werewolf scent trail moved east. She dropped to the ground.

The guard team caught up with her in little pops of sound. The three vamps—Mi-sook, a mixed-race Korean woman; her wife, Kang, a blond chick who was the closest thing to a friend Shiloh had left since Atticus was killed; and Fred, also white—were winded, breathing heavily, like humans.

Kang sat and rested her back against a tree, gasping, frowning up at Shiloh. "Girlfriend, you run like the wind."

Girlfriend . . . "I'm a little faster, I guess, from the werewolf taint. Prions. Whatever. It'll wear off." Not likely, but no one argued. Shiloh wasn't used to friends, except her human blood-servants, and it felt odd that a vamp wanted to be one. For the last few months, Shiloh had tried to wrap her head around vamps wanting her for herself, and not simply for royal access. Mi-sook and Kang had no interest in getting closer to the queen. Fred just liked fighting.

"I have better tracking skills than you do," Kang said. "And I'm better with sword work. I'll take point when the trail freshens."

Shiloh's sense of smell was better than Kang's. Wolf good. Her sword work was way better than anyone knew. Not that she would share that.

Fred plopped to the ground, propped against a tree, and took a dip of snuff, patting the tobacco inside her cheek. Her weapons were strapped inside and outside her armored overalls, holstered, pocketed. Frederica Crabtree had been married to a successful pig farmer in the late 1800s. When human, she had never flaunted her wealth or been concerned with fitting into society; she was even less interested now. Fred was an excellent tracker and a better shot. She'd been bored, according to the queen, when the team met at dusk.

"Even when you're at point," Kang said, "you should stay in sight."

"Trees are faster," Shiloh said. "And I needed time alone to . . . process."

Kang rolled her eyes and elbowed her wife. "Modern scions need to *process*. When I was human, we did what had to be done. None of this *processing*."

Shiloh had no intention of taking their six. "And you're a well-balanced personality," she said, sarcastic.

"Yes. You stay in sight."

Reminder to self: Kang has no sense of humor.

Moving slower, Shiloh climbed into a tree and jumped to another. "They went this way." In the trees, she left them behind, tracking scents she remembered from the attack. The vamps on the ground followed her own scent in the air above them and the blood-scent below. Once out of sight, she raced ahead.

Half an hour later, the terrain plunged into a crevasse, where the faint moonlight vanished. Hopping to the ground, she vamped out fully; needlelike fangs—indicative of being a young vamp—clicked down. She was under control, the razors distant. On foot, she tracked the werewolves along an animal trail as it snaked down the rock wall of a gorge, deeper into the dark.

The walls narrowed until she could touch the rock face on both sides of the wide fracture.

She reached the bottom, where a springhead bubbled out of the rock, becoming a clear crick. Ahead, the rock cleft widened into a small, hidden forest, brightened by hints of moonlight. Wood smoke hung in tree limbs. A narrow path marked the way.

Shiloh knelt and sniffed. She picked out the original six males and the female. Fresh scents overlapped those: three of the males and three new males. The bitch had indeed replaced her pack members.

Returning to the trees, Shiloh sprinted along the limbs, following the small crick, breathing in short sniffs as the scent trace changed. She caught a whiff of the unexpected.

Fainter, older, was a hint of vampire.

She stopped, arms gripping a tree trunk. Breathing, analyzing.

She knew this scent. It was old, but unmistakable. *Kang.*

Kang had been here before.

Kang had told her to stay in sight. Kang had told Shiloh that she would take point when the trail freshened.

Kang had pretended to be her friend. Playing the long game.

Betrayal stung, clawing through her, sharp as the razors, bitter as wormwood.

If their small group had arrived together, Kang could have obscured her former presence here by simply racing ahead. Shiloh hadn't waited. Kang had to realize Shiloh knew her secret.

Worse, there had been an attack by enemy vamps on the queen's wedding party a few weeks past—and a werewolf had been with them. An ally. Kang was working with the queen's enemies, the last supernats who had vowed to never bow to a Dark Queen. Kang. Maybe Mi-sook. Hell, maybe Fred too.

Kang was a traitor. Kang would die at the queen's order if she was found out, unless the older vamp managed to kill Shiloh first.

She checked her cell. No signal in the narrow valley.

The distant sound of stealthy footfalls indicated the vamps behind her were starting down the chasm. Turning on her new speed, Shiloh kept to the trees to avoid contaminating the evidence trail, following the path. Racing toward the smoke. Breathing in short sniffs to detect other vamps. So far, only Kang.

Step one: Find the outer perimeter guards. Determine entrances, exits, defensive systems, and attack options. Access and/or take out comms.

Eli had trained the queen's scions in paramilitary methods. His remedial lessons in warfare had stuck. *Step two: take out the guards.*

At the highest speed she could achieve without losing the stealth of silence, Shiloh circled a small clearing tree to tree. It was an open-ended, canyon-type, triangular valley, with the narrow end at the source of the water and the other open to forest. The footpath led out. At the open end of the valley, city lights brightened the distant horizon. Shiloh spotted one guard, male, in human form. His two-way radio was clipped to his tank top, the kind of shirt they used to call wifebeaters, and a pair of stretchy shorts, clothes for shifting shape. She knew his scent.

Staying downwind, she completed a full perimeter search, finding a one-room log cabin with fresh chinking, a smoking chimney, no visible electric, no sign of a comms system, and an aromatic outhouse in back. The smell of rotten flesh and viscera came from a pit near the tree line, most likely the remains of their kills. She heard multiple voices inside the cabin, laughter. Too loud to hear heartbeats.

Nowhere had she smelled the scent of other vamps. Just Kang.

Shiloh had started to believe the vamp might become a real friend. Her first real vamp friend. Instead, Kang was a traitor working with the werewolves who had killed Atticus.

Her human need to breathe increased. Her heart beat. Razors scratched, almost gently.

Returning to the lone guard, Shiloh positioned herself in the limbs, downwind of and above the wolf-man, just as he checked in with whoever was on the other end. "All clear," the guard said.

"No shit."

The connection ended.

"Asshole," the werewolf said, clipping the talkie to his shorts.

He carried what looked like a gun in his shorts pocket, and though the pack hadn't used silver-lead rounds last time, they might have learned a lesson during the fight with Atticus and her. His breath blew in white clouds, and a light steam rose from his skin.

Shiloh remembered his smell, his stink, his fangs . . .

Yeah. He was a dead dog. *Vengeance.*

Shiloh heard the faintest of sounds from the bottom of the cliff wall.

The wolf turned toward the sound.

The razors clawed. There was no time to contain them, fight them, control them. For the first time, she reached inside and drew the razor crazies into her. Unexpectedly, the crazies blended with her useless witch magic. It was like fireworks going off inside her brain, a kaleidoscope of light and energy. And power.

She drew her vamp-killer in her off hand. Leaped. Curved her arm across her body, the blade in front of her. At the last second, the wolf-man looked up. Her boots caught him at the hips. Blade at the side of his neck. She cut backhanded, a brutal backswing. Her weight bore him down. Almost in slo-mo. Weird laughter burbled up inside her. They hit the ground. Bounced. His body beneath her, his head a few feet away. The worst of the blood spray missed her, but the wind picked up, carrying the scent back along her original trail, toward her teammates.

Grabbing the head by its scraggly beard, she leaped into the trees and dashed back along her original limb path. Instead of fighting the razors, she embraced them, adding to her strength, speed. Something like ecstasy rode through her veins after the too-short fight. *More*. She wanted more. *Vengeance*.

The three fangheads appeared, Kang in the lead, marking a new scent trail. Covering her old scent trail by jumping from one side of the animal path to the other.

Before she bothered to think, Shiloh threw the severed head underhanded, softball-style. Hit Kang mid-chest. The woman reeled. The head flew. Shiloh swung from the trees at Kang, repeating the same move she'd made only moments past. They crashed down together. Her bloody vamp-killer at Kang's throat. Kang's head arched back, staring up into the sky, held in place by Shiloh's fist in her blond hair.

"Draw your weapons and die," Shiloh said into Kang's ear. Kang spread her arms to her sides, palms open on the ground.

Two weapons made the *schnick* of semiautomatics being readied to fire.

Softly, Mi-sook asked, "Girl? What the hell?"

"Walk up the trail fifty feet and come back," Shiloh said. "Tell me what you smell."

Kang snarled. Began to vamp out, her three-inch fangs clicking down on their hinges. Her pupils went black, sclera flashing red.

Shiloh pressed in. A thin line of red appeared along the blade edge.

"You kill my wife," Mi-sook said, "and I'll bring your head to the queen, you being her favorite or not. Don't care."

What? "Not in my plans, Mi-sook," Shiloh growled, fighting a fanghead response to Kang's fury.

Fred placed the barrel of her gun at Shiloh's head. She said, "Swords are fast. Bullets are faster. Your blade moves a fraction,

Shiloh, and I'll make a couple new holes in your head. One entry, one exit. I'll deal with the consequences of the queen's wrath. Got it?" She spat to the side.

Mi-sook disappeared with a little popping sound.

Favorite? Wrath? Shiloh was tolerated. The queen had favorites among Shiloh's witch family, but none were her.

Moments later, Mi-sook was back, standing behind Kang, facing Shiloh. She had vamped out fully. Tears trickled down her face. Her vamp-killer was drawn, point up. She brought the small sword down. Hard. Fast. The pommel slammed into her wife's forehead. Kang's eyes rolled back. She went lax.

Faster than Shiloh could react, the point of Mi-sook's blade was poking into Shiloh's throat. Shiloh dropped her weapon.

"How did you put my wife's scent here?"

Shiloh slowly raised her hands in the air. "I've been under constant supervision for weeks. If someone planted Kang's scent here, they had to have her sheets, underwear, clothes, and anything they used would also carry your scent. And then there would be the planter person's scent too. Use your brain."

Fred stepped back, lowered her nine-mil to point at the ground. "Well, sheeit." She spat again between her yellowed fangs. The smell of snuff was strong on the air. Werewolves would never know where she was, confused by the snuff spit all over. *Interesting.*

The two vamps stepped back. Still on her knees, Shiloh eased away from Kang.

"How long will she stay down without being staked?" Fred asked, scratching her chin with her off hand.

"No one stakes my wife." Mi-sook sprayed chaw juice over the ground.

Reluctantly, Shiloh said, "I have a *stasis* amulet in my pocket." She had hoped to use it on a werewolf, but if she was right about

Kang, an attack from the rear was possible. She searched the downed vamp while she detailed the particulars of the clearing and the cabin. She took all Kang's ammo, her sidearm, and her blades, strapping them to her own body. Mi-sook didn't quarrel. With her thumbnail, Shiloh activated the *stasis* working, placed the amulet into Kang's lapel pocket, and stepped away. Five seconds later, it initiated, a wave of sparkling witch magic. It worked. She hid her relief.

Retrieving the wolf-man's head, she stuck it on a winter-dead sapling. Bloody. Messy.

"How you want to handle the dogs?" Fred asked.

When Mi-sook turned away, Shiloh realized Fred was asking *Shiloh* to make an assault plan. On the fly. She stared back toward the cabin, her head clearer than it had been in weeks. There were now three vamps against five male weres and their bitch.

"Anyone got a hand grenade?" Shiloh jested.

Fred pulled one out of her overall bib. "Ain't legal. Only got the one. But I also got three flash-bangs. And a pepper bomb." She spat again, her tobacco-stained fangs dripping.

"We drop the pepper bomb down the chimney," Shiloh said, "ram the door open, and toss two flash-bangs."

"Pros to your plan," Fred said, "simple, easy, uncomplicated. Cons: Dogs'll shift. Pepper's too much for their noses. We don't want to fight them in full wolf or hybrid form. We don't breathe, but our eyes will be affected by the pepper, and I got one pair of goggles. I ain't givin' mine up." She spat again, far into the woods. Wiped her fangs on her armor sleeve. "Despite you two being blind from the pepper, we'd have to go in fast and take them down mid-shift. Silver-lead rounds or silver-edged blades."

"Shiloh likes trees," Mi-sook said, her eyes on her wife. "She takes the chimney, tosses the pepper bomb. I'll ram the door.

Fred, with the goggles, goes in first and I'll back her up. Shiloh picks off any runners."

"Done," Fred said. She tossed Shiloh a small can of pepper spray. Neither one mentioned the bitch-queen, or how to handle the three new werewolves who hadn't bitten anyone. Nor had they come up with a *go* sign. *Figure it out on the fly.*

She focused on the pepper spray bottle's instructions. Fred strode into the dark beneath the trees. Mi-sook followed Fred, not looking back.

The pepper spray worked like a grenade, sort of. Pull the tab and it released the pepper in four seconds. Easy, if she could hit the chimney with it. She would get only one try.

Shiloh tucked the pepper grenade into an overfull ammo pocket. She leaped straight up into the trees and ran, swinging from tree to tree, angling toward the metal roof.

When she found a perch that would allow her to hit the chimney—if she was lucky—Mi-sook was already in position. Shiloh pulled the tab and tossed the can. It rattled down the air shaft.

The vamp raced toward the door at vamp speed, air popping behind her.

Shiloh realized she heard no sounds, no laughter, no heartbeats from the cabin. She opened her mouth to shout a warning.

Mi-sook hit the door.

The cabin exploded.

The walls and roof of thc cabin blew out.

⤚⤙

She came to about ten feet lower down, the world whirling, swimming below her in the night, like oil on water. Blinking, she tried to orient herself. Her midsection was sandwiched—part of the metal roof structure above and the tree trunk at her waist below. The tree had sheared off and lay horizontal, precariously balanced on another downed tree.

Pretty sure I'm alive. Undead. Ish.

Deaf. Bleeding. She was a piece of vamp-meat dangling from the trunk.

She vamped out again, the darkness gone, her night vision like day.

A werewolf stood directly below her. He was in fighting form, half man, half wolf, eyes gleaming in the night. He leaped.

She jerked her hands, head, and feet up, banging her head against a roof beam. She saw stars and gagged. *Concussion much?*

He landed on all fours and leaped again.

She pitched her body to the left. Twisting her hands along her sides, she tried to locate a weapon. Nothing was in the right place. She had gotten her hand around a nine-mil and was wrenching it free when the dumbass wolf realized he needed a boost. He dragged up a log. Stepped on it. Contracted his body. And jumped.

Shiloh got her weapon up. Fired. He was dead before he impacted. The shot—and being dead—made him miss his mark. His fangs crashed into the downed trunk.

It shuddered and slid. The metal of the roof cut into her left hammy.

The werewolves had probably detected her during her initial search and had been outside the concussive blast range with their paws over their ears when the cabin blew. Because this was a freaking trap.

She slithered, shoved, and pushed herself out before the gunshot brought reinforcements. She was too slow. Before she freed her feet, she fired at another wolf, this one in full wolf form. No kill shot. The wolf tumbled, floundered, and ran away. *Fast.* Might have been yelping. She was still deaf. But her sense of smell was back. She could smell her own blood and the stench of werewolf.

When she worked herself free, Shiloh fell to the ground in a heap and puked everywhere. She hadn't even known vamps could vomit. Rancid blood. Coffee. She gagged again and the world swirled. She had to get off the ground and pick a shooting position, because she was in no shape to fight close quarters. She beheaded the dead werewolf first, just in case it could regenerate or something, and stuck the head on a shattered limb. Her trademark now.

The world whirling, she limped to the nearest intact tree, a dying fir, and pulled herself up, hand over hand, maybe twenty feet. Saw a muzzle flash—the gun kind, not the wolf kind. Fred stood in the middle of the clearing, twenty yards from her, near the remains of the cabin. The vamp's feet were braced to either side of . . .

She was standing over what was left of Mi-sook. Protecting her. Firing. Firing. Into a ring of three wolves. Two wolves were injured, circling, limping, slavering. The third was closest to Shiloh's tree, in half-wolf form. That one was holding a gun. His finger configuration was wrong to squeeze a trigger, but he worked the tip of his oversized pinky into the trigger guard.

Shiloh had no time to think. She shouted, "*Concretus sanguinis!*"

Misshapen magic shot from her. The working hit a scorched log with a flashing bang. The werewolf's shot went wild. Fred popped in, stabbed the wolf-man in the gut with her silver-plated vamp-killer, wrenched the shortsword up, disemboweling him, and popped back to Mi-sook before the other wolves could react.

The half-form wolf-guy crumpled, trying to shift to human shape, but the silver on the blade stopped the shape-shift. The half-transformed, unhealed wolf writhed on the ground.

Shiloh spoke the *wyrd* again, carefully, aiming the working, and the wolf stiffened, his blood turned to stone. The razors and her magic almost waltzed through her, dancing to the music of vengeance satisfied. She didn't know what the dancing sensation meant, but probably nothing good.

Looking around, she sniffed the air. It stank of pepper spray, explosives, wood smoke, and the stench of regular wolf, silver-burned wolf, entrails, death. Vamp blood, some of it hers. And puke.

Her brain was starting to work. The magic had been instinctive, not prepared. Shiloh vaguely remembered the *wyrd* working from her childhood at her mother's knee. The curse turned an opponent's blood solid. If she had hit Fred with the first misaimed attempt, the vamp would be dead. That's why she never used *wyrd* magic.

Hearing began to return. In the clearing, more shots were fired. Five. A wolf howled.

The world steadied. Her internal clock was missing time since she came to. Not good. For the first time—maybe the second?—she studied the surroundings on the ground beneath her. *Safe enough.* She located and checked her weapons, putting everything where it belonged.

Fred screamed, guttural, coarse. Two wolves had attacked at the same time. One had the vamp's right calf in its jaws. The other had snapped and managed to get its fangs caught in the bib of Fred's overall-armor. That wolf hung from her, jerking her off balance.

On the far side of the clearing, Kang stepped out of the trees, a white wolf bitch at her side.

"Well, that sucks," Shiloh whispered.

The *stasis* amulet had been removed. They were in deep doo-doo if the two joined the attack.

Shiloh dropped to the ground. Landed wrong. Her ankle

snapped. Broke. She righted herself and kicked out, hoping gravity would set it, but she wasn't that lucky. Blood splashed from the forgotten thigh gash. It must have been deep.

Moving fast despite her wounds, Shiloh limped-ran, taking shelter behind a remaining corner of the cabin. She carried a vamp-killer in her off hand, its little strap around her wrist so she could release it, and a silver-lead-loaded nine-mil in her right. Dropping the blade, she steadied her aim and squeezed off a shot at the wolf savaging Fred's leg. He yelped and let go, snapping at his own flank.

Shiloh shifted aim to Kang. The vamp and were-bitch were gone.

Fred gutted the dangling wolf. The vamp seemed to like the gutting move, effective in close-in work with werewolves. Fred took its head. Staggered. Fell to her butt. She shot the wolf Shiloh had injured. It flopped to the ground, keening. Fred began to apply a homemade tourniquet to her leg.

Stepping over entrails, Shiloh took the last two heads. The wolf killed by magic was like hacking through a salt block. Crystalized blood and flesh. *Cool.*

She was breathing heavily, a human reaction to the explosion, battle, and using magic she had forgotten. Magic and battle, together with vengeance, satisfied and soothed the razors.

The smell of vamp blood was as strong on the air as the wolf entrails. Fred was injured. Shiloh was still seeing stars. Mi-sook . . .

"How many?" Fred gasped. She jerked the tourniquet tight around her leg.

"Three wolves dead here, fourth one dead in the woods, that way, the first one dead that way"—Shiloh pointed in different directions—"one injured and MIA, and Kang, working with the bitch." She fell to one knee and checked Mi-sook. The vamp had lost part of both arms and was bleeding slowly from a massive head wound. Shiloh wasn't sure any vamp could fully heal from either, and Shiloh had no idea if she would still be the Mi-sook she had been. But the vamp wasn't true-dead, so there was that.

"I swallowed my snuff," Fred groused.

Shiloh bit off a cackle.

"That shit plays hell on a vamp's digestion," Fred said. She nodded at Mi-sook. "Close her wounds."

Vamp saliva clotted blood and constricted blood vessels. Trying not to gag, she licked Mi-sook's bleeding wounds until they closed, all but her skull. Shiloh wasn't a zombie; brains held no appeal. Remembering the *healing* amulets, she pulled the charms from her pocket and stuck three into the blood pooled in Mi-sook's throat, against her skin, activating them before tucking them into Mi-sook's various wounds. Tossed the fourth to Fred, and stuck the last inside her own thigh wound. Instantly, her blood clotted. That wasn't supposed to happen, but whatever.

Her armor was tattered. But she had weapons and ammo. And magic.

Shiloh scanned her surroundings, still testing her ankle. Broken. "We tracking Kang and the were-bitch?"

"Hell, no. I'm taking Mi-sook to the nearest cell signal for exfil." Fred thumbed at the wide end of the valley and the city lights. "You can come with, or you can track. Don't care. I got indigestion from the snuff and I'm outta here." She tossed Shiloh the trank gun.

Tranks didn't work instantaneously. The only amulet Shiloh had left was a *hedge* working: easy to activate, and she could invert it into a prison cell, a *reverse hedge*. The razor sensation in her veins was an indistinct itch. It wanted to track and fight and use her magic. But chasing a wounded werewolf, a were-bitch, and a vamp alone, with a broken ankle and a concussion, was stupid. She had the spins and couldn't remember the working she had used on the wolf. She hadn't fed. Starvation and blood loss slowed healing, speed, and judgment.

She sat and held her booted foot to Fred. "You know how to set ankle bones?"

"Usually didn't bother when I was a farmer. Just shot and ate the critter."

"I'd probably give you farts. How about you jerk my foot and see if it sets?"

Fred grabbed Shiloh's boot. Yanked. Nearly whipped Shiloh into the smoking cabin ruins.

She skidded into the charred logs and rotated to avoid staking herself on splintered wood. "Son of a witch," she groaned.

Fred snorted with amusement.

Shiloh tried the ankle and it bore her weight. Vamps healed fast. Faster if they got vamp blood. She had taken a taste of Mi-sook's while closing the other vamp's wounds, but the sip hadn't healed her.

Fred was going to need all of her supply when Mi-sook woke, hungry and deranged, batshit crazy, as injured vamps did.

"I'll pile the trophies and help get Mi-sook to safety," Shiloh decided. She piled heads and bodies, and took pics in case something carted them off before they could be retrieved for bounty.

With Shiloh at their six, Fred hefted Mi-sook's blood-soaked body and strode along the footpath. The moon had set. It was dark, even vamped-out. The faint grind of their feet on the dirt was the only sound. It was too quiet.

Halfway to the distant city lights, Shiloh heard a twig snap.

"Run," Shiloh said.

Fred, limping, took off for the horizon and that cell signal, Mi-sook bouncing. Shiloh hoped Mi-sook's brains stayed in place.

A white wolf lunged from the dark. Shiloh shot the bitch.

Fred disappeared.

Kang attacked from the other side. Stabbed Shiloh in the back.

Her knees gave way. As she stumbled, Kang's blade pulled free. Red-hot lightning twisted through every nerve ending, flooding her system. Razors and magic. Power exploded through her.

Shiloh shoved up with her right leg. Pivoted.

Whirled her shortsword in her off hand at Kang.

Kang jumped back. Then rushed her.

False friend. Betrayer. Traitor.

Shiloh shot her. Three rounds. Aiming above her armor.

Kang lurched. Pivoted. Raced into the woods. The bitch was gone too.

Shiloh changed her mag and followed Kang into the night. Razors danced inside her. She still wanted to puke, but she was empty.

She had no idea where the werewolves were, but they were still around. Still insane. Shiloh laughed joyfully, the sound full of the crazies. She was one to talk.

Kang's blood-scent hung on the air, the ground. She'd been hit.

Adrenaline pumped into Shiloh and merged with the magic razor crazies. *Bliss.* Injured, tired, hungry, nauseated, pissed off, and elated all together, she followed Kang's scent.

Shiloh didn't sense the werewolf until her face hit the dirt.

The bitch was on her. Momentum bowled them. Fangs buried in Shiloh's right neck at the shoulder. The werewolf shook her. Ripping.

Faster than thought, Shiloh raised her vamp-killer blade. Reared away. Ripping the fangs from her flesh.

The bitch released, snapped at Shiloh's face. Her bite closed on the blade.

Right arm protesting, Shiloh put the barrel of the nine-mil to the wolf's chest. Fired. Fired.

Yowling, the wolf spun away.

Shiloh caught a flash of movement. Raised her bloody shortsword. Blocked Kang's strike.

She fired at Kang.

Kang ignored the rounds. Stepped over her, legs to either side. Two-handed, the vamp brought down her shortsword.

Shiloh batted at it. Deflected it enough that it wasn't a killing strike. Her armor redirected the blade further until a repaired seam caught it. Sliced into her right side, high under her arm. She fired again. This time into Kang's knee, into the armor joint that allowed bending.

Kang fell to the side. Twisted the shortsword. Tore it from Shiloh. Cutting deeper.

Shiloh made it upright. Crouching. Right hand numb. Right arm paralyzed. Left-handed, she reached for her remaining amulet.

Kang, on one knee, was holding something.

Shiloh felt the faint tingle of her own magic. Her own *stasis* working. *Fuck*.

The vamp pressed the small disc, trying to activate it.

Shiloh ripped her pocket flap. Gripped her last amulet. Activated *reverse hedge*. Tossed it. In the same instant, Kang triggered *stasis*. The two magics met and sizzled, heat and sparks.

Kang was frozen in place for one agonizing second. Slowly, she crumpled to the ground inside the prison.

Shiloh was breathing hard, heart pounding. Agony thrummed through her.

Razors and magic danced, ecstatic.

The wolf bitch was down, panting, eyes full of familiar crazies. Still left-handed, Shiloh aimed at the wolf. "Gotcha, *bitch*."

A thought intruded. She holstered her weapon. One-handed, she lifted the were-bitch and tossed her into the trap with Kang. Magic trap. Magic vengeance. The bitch began feasting on Kang.

"Magic beats blades and bullets." She laughed, fell to her butt, and watched the bitch eat.

Shiloh was bleeding. A lot. It would clot. Eventually. Probably.

From up the path, four gunshots sounded.

"Really?" Shiloh asked the bitch.

A wolf yelped from the same direction.

"*Really?*"

Cursing under her breath, she made it to her feet, gathered her weapons, and trotted down the path. When she found Fred and Mi-sook, near a country road, the last wolf was dead nearby. Fred was on the ground, the injured vamp drinking from Fred's wrist. Fred licked Mi-sook's head wounds.

From a strictly clinical standpoint, it was gross.

"I've called for exfil and blood meals," Fred said as Mi-sook sucked.

Shiloh let herself slide down a nearby tree. The sensation of razors drifted through her, interwoven with personal magic she had forgotten years ago, satisfied with battle and vengeance.

What the actual fuck had she become?

⤚⤙

Four white unmarked mugs, coffee in a big thermos, and a teapot under a pink cozy were on the table. Jane didn't seem like a pink kind of woman, but Jane didn't seem like a queen either.

The door opened. Eli and Koun took places at the table. Neither looked at her.

Shiloh went still, unbreathing, unblinking. *Déjà vu.* Razors scored her nerves, screaming, *Fightfightfight.*

Jane entered. The door closed. The queen took her usual place at the table, poured her own tea, and sat back. "Gentlemen, coffee. Shiloh?"

Eli poured coffee and shoved a mug across the table to Shiloh. "Drink," he ordered.

Shiloh drained the cup and held it out for a refill. She had learned this was Eli's special brew, dark as sin and twice as strong. The razors buzzed happily.

Jane was dressed as a queen, tailored, elegant, her long black hair up in a braided bun. The queen set down her cup. There was no Count von Count on it.

This isn't a casual meeting. Got that. Shiloh should have dressed up.

"You could have killed the bitch *and* Kang," the queen said. "They attacked ones who are ours."

Ours. Royalty speaking.

Pulling up some sketchy court formality from the bottom of her memory, Shiloh said, "Yes, my lady. The bitch bit me."

"Why didn't you? Kill them?"

Shiloh's hand tightened on her mug. "Kang was *your* enemy. What was left of her needed to be bled-and-read for info. The bitch was . . . pitiful. Psychotic. Hungry. Controlled by my queen's enemies."

Shiloh held in a grin. Vengeance had been a magic trap. Letting one conspirator feed on the other had been fun. Not that she would say something crazy like that.

"Capable of rational thought," the queen said. "We approve. How did you feel during the hunt and kills?"

That royal *we* again. Shiloh finished her second cup of coffee, giving herself time to think. Shrugged. "I got vengeance for Atticus."

"Was vengeance worth it?" the queen asked.

"Forgive me, My Queen, but why are you asking?"

"Since you were bitten by multiple werewolves, you're faster, more nimble, more accurate, and less mentally stable, yet you're controlled. Mostly. As *I* once said, like me, you're a singularity. *I* like singularities." The queen's yellow eyes held her gaze.

Shiloh weighed the personal *I* as opposed to the royal *we*.

The queen continued. Or maybe it was Jane talking now. Hard to tell.

"If you don't shift, and if you maintain self-control for two more full moons, it's doubtful you'll shift into a werewolf."

A weight slid from Shiloh.

"If so, we have a proposition for you."

"I'm listening, my lady," Shiloh said cautiously, interpreting the pronoun.

"We are in need of a . . . problem solver," the queen said.

Koun said, "Those who break the queen's law and are within her reach are my duty. Those who break the queen's law but are out of reach still must be dealt with."

Eli said, "She needs someone with a full year of specialized training in security systems, multiple fighting techniques, and magic to carry out the queen's justice."

"Someone like you," the queen said. "Not in our livery. Not in our colors. No written orders."

"An assassin," Shiloh whispered. Magic razors hummed, interested.

"Call it what you will," the queen said.

"Salary?" Shiloh asked Koun.

"All expenses, weapons, armor, a stipend, and bounties," the Celtic warrior said.

Eli slid a folded paper across the table.

Shiloh opened it and read the number inside. The stipend was enough to pay bills, contract with additional human donors, and buy her own home. Add in bounties, and she could fund a long undeath. She tucked the paper into a jacket pocket. "Specialized training?"

Eli said, "Your stipend will begin after two full moons, providing you sign the contract and survive, wolf-less."

Shiloh stood. "I'll take the gig. I'll design my armor. And I'm not going furry." She met the queen's gaze. "Thank you, My Queen."

The queen inclined her head. "You are dismissed."

"You know that phrase annoys the hell outta me, right?"

"Oh yes." The queen smiled, a happy human smile. "When it was used on me, *I* hated it. *You are dismissed*."

Shiloh walked out. The queen's assassin was a pretty cool job title. Yeah. She'd take it.

A CLEAN BREAK

An Alastair Stone Chronicles Story

R. L. King

Alastair Stone expected his motel room to be far below his usual standards.

What he didn't expect was to have roommates.

As soon as he used his key in the rattling lock (no high-tech card-swipe locks for *this* place) and pushed open the door, several small, fast-moving forms scurried beneath the bed like a crowd of six-legged teenagers whose party had just been busted by somebody's parents' untimely arrival. The lingering odors of stale beer, pot smoke, and old urine rounded out the scene's charm.

Stone paused in the doorway, reconsidering his decision.

It's not like you've got a lot of options. This was the last room at any price available in a fifty-mile radius. And it's only for one night.

He edged over the threshold, careful not to touch anything yet. If there were cockroaches, there were probably bedbugs too, and gods knew what else. He summoned a quick spell, sending an invisible wave of magical energy through the space. He couldn't do anything about the rest of the dubious amenities, but at least he could make sure his was the room's only living presence for the night.

He dropped his bag on the sagging bed next to a stain shaped like Texas and was girding himself to investigate the bathroom when his phone buzzed with a text.

Settling in okay?

His apprentice, Verity. This whole thing was her fault, and she wasn't even *here* yet. Define "okay," he texted back.

You know. Fancy penthouse suite, Jacuzzi, hot and cold running spooky groupies?

Not . . . exactly.

Problem?

He glanced at the rusted bars on the window, which looked a lot more substantial than the rickety lock on the door. It wasn't Verity's fault the downtown San Diego luxury hotel where he was *supposed* to be staying had made a mistake on his arrival date and wouldn't have his proper room available until tomorrow. No, everything's fine. Just tired.

I'll let you go then, and see you tomorrow. Thanks again for letting me tag along. I've always wanted to do SD Comic-Con. You have to introduce me to the Blood Offering people.

Verity, twenty-one and goth-adjacent, was far more excited about *Blood Offering*, a soapy new TV series about angsty vampires and other sexy supernatural creatures, than he had been. She'd been the one who'd convinced him to accept the invitation to serve on one of the show's panels at the convention, leveraging his position as a professor of occult studies at Stanford. Ever the realist, he suspected the offer had been due as much to his relative youth, good looks, and British accent as his formidable academic credentials, but Verity had wanted to go, and he couldn't think of a good reason to turn her down.

Until now, anyway. He idly zapped a wayward cockroach that had eluded his last spell, and sighed. I'll see you tomorrow. I'll be

Doc?

He realized he'd stopped typing, leaving her on cycling dots, but that was suddenly the last thing on his mind.

A translucent figure had just drifted through the wall next to the old TV with the SORRY—OUT OF ORDER sign taped to it, crossed the room, and slipped out through the opposite wall.

The phone buzzed again. Doc? You still there?

The figure had disappeared, and didn't seem inclined to return. Stone hadn't even gotten a good enough look at it to determine whether it was a man, a woman, or a stray cloud of smoke creeping in from the potheads next door.

Must go, talk tomorrow, he tapped out, and shoved the phone in his pocket before she could reply.

He stood in the center of the room, shifting his perceptions to allow him to view the magical realm. He'd seen the figure only from the corner of his eye; if it *had* been nothing more than spillover from the potheads, nothing would show up.

Wispy trails of energy, already fading, appeared along the

path the figure had taken. Stone could barely make out the faint, flickering red traces before they dissipated like steam.

Well. At least whatever it is, it doesn't want to share my room.

Normally, a potentially supernatural event like this would have piqued his considerable curiosity. But not tonight. He was tired, the room's AC didn't appear to work, and he was debating whether he wanted to brave the shower—and whatever potential biohazards it might promise—long enough to cool off. Any spectral visitors would have to take a number and get in line.

⤚⤙

His room was at the end of the second floor, about as far from the stairs as it could be while still in the same building. He trudged along the cracked walkway, trying to decide whether to venture out in his rental car or settle for the sketchy mini-mart next door. It was already fully dark, the only illumination coming from a few occupied rooms, the two functional lights in the parking lot, and the flickering neon SUNBEAM MOTEL—NO VACANCY sign out by the street. Even the pool directly below, drained dry with the weathered CLOSED FOR REPAIRS sign on its gate indicating this wasn't a recent condition, was dark.

He still hadn't made up his mind what he wanted to do when a sudden sense of unease took hold of him. Almost a feeling of being watched, even though neither magical nor mundane sight revealed any nearby auras. He hesitated, looking around, then shook his head in disgust and kept walking.

To his right, between two rooms and set well back from the walkway, a heavy chain-link gate spanned a six-foot opening. A substantial lock held it closed. Stone didn't remember noticing it on his way to his room, but he'd been far too busy grumbling about his situation to be in much of a noticing frame of mind at the time. He'd have walked right past it this time too, except as he approached it, the feeling of unease intensified.

He shot a quick glance through the gate. Just his luck tonight, he'd interrupted some clandestine criminal transaction, or a couple of furtive lovers in the throes of a quickie.

But no concealed figures lurked in the shadows. Stone released his held breath in a combination of relief and annoyance.

Parked in an unlit concrete alcove was what looked like a large maid's cart—the kind the housekeeping staff employed to wheel their gear around as they went about their daily chores. It had a sizable central hamper for used towels and linens, several brooms and mops poking up from all four corners, and various bottles, jugs, and rags hanging from hooks along both sides.

Good one, Stone. Spooked by a maid cart. Perhaps getting a drink wasn't the best idea after all if he was letting such things get to him. Maybe he should just go back to his room and try to sleep. Tomorrow, this would be all over.

Still . . . that feeling was coming from somewhere. And the cart *did* look rather sinister, crouching behind the gate like a dangerous beast someone had locked away.

Wait—had it just *moved*?

He stared hard at it for several more seconds, but it remained still and silent.

Of course it didn't move. Seriously, you muppet, stop acting like an idiot and get some sleep. He shifted to magical sight and scanned the alcove, half expecting the cart to burst through the gate and try to tear a chunk out of him.

It didn't do that, of course, because it was a maid cart.

It *did*, however, pulse with the faint traces of the same flickering red energy he'd seen earlier, trailing behind the wispy figure in his room.

"Hey! What're you lookin' at?"

Stone, fully focused on the traces, jerked back like a kid who'd been caught flipping through a dirty magazine and dropped the sight. The red energy vanished. "What?"

The front desk clerk, the same hairy, wifebeater-clad sod who'd so smugly docked his credit card for three times his room's normal rate earlier ("Hey, it's Con, dude, take it or leave it") stood a short distance away, watching him through narrowed eyes.

"What're you lookin' at?" the guy repeated. "You some kinda weirdo?"

Stone considered and discarded several sarcastic replies. Replying would mean he'd have to engage with this man. What did he care what was going on with the creepy maid cart? It wasn't his problem. He'd be long gone by tomorrow morning.

"Sorry," he said. "Just heading back to my room." Yes, the drink could definitely wait until tomorrow night, when he could enjoy it in more appropriate surroundings.

"Yeah. Good idea. I wouldn't suggest wanderin' around. It ain't always so safe around here after dark, y'know?"

⤚⤙

Stone didn't think he'd sleep very well, and he wasn't wrong. Even this close to the ocean, San Diego still got swelteringly hot in late July, and the AC unit did little more than rumble ominously without producing a shred of cool air. All he could manage were brief, uncomfortable dozes, to the point where he'd just about decided to bag the effort in favor of catching up with some reading.

That was when he saw her again.

This time, she—and it was definitely a she—stood at the foot of the bed, watching him. Even to his mundane sight in the darkness, she was clearly visible.

Stone sat up slowly, afraid he might startle her with any sudden movements. She looked more substantial now, and less wispy. “Can I help you with something?”

She didn’t react, but it was obvious she was aware of his presence. She remained where she was, motionless, as if waiting for something.

Stone sat up a little more and took her in. She was a young woman, middle twenties, with plain, weatherworn features and long hair drawn back into a ponytail. A utilitarian maid’s uniform covered her slim form. The two most remarkable things about her were her eyes, burning with a combination of anger and pleading, and her neck, torqued to the left side at a sharp and obvious angle and tilting her head into a position that almost suggested deep contemplation.

This wasn’t anything close to the first time Stone had ever seen a ghost—or an echo, as mages called them, since true ghosts didn’t exist—but it *was* the first time one had surprised him while he was in nothing but his shorts in a manky motel room.

“Can you speak?” He kept his voice even and gentle. Now that she was here, he didn’t want to scare her off. She was the most interesting thing that had happened to him all night.

She made no reply. Her intense, pleading eyes sought his.

“Is there something you want me to do?”

This time, her features twisted in frustration.

Before he could ask her another question, angry male voices rose from a short distance outside the door. Stone couldn’t make out what they were saying, but they were obviously having some kind of argument.

The ghostly maid's face flushed silver with sudden fear, then deeper anger. She shot Stone another frustrated glance and disappeared once again through the wall.

Outside, the voices kept arguing. They didn't seem inclined to stop anytime soon.

Most people would have left it alone and hoped it would go away. Stone wasn't most people. A couple of drunk mundanes held little danger for him, and besides, they'd scared the echo away before he'd had a chance to figure out what she wanted. He pulled on his black Dancing Dragon Inn T-shirt and faded jeans, shoved the door open, and stepped out onto the walkway. "Oi! Want to keep it down out here?"

Two arctic glares settled on him. Stone had encountered the men's type before: the hard gazes, the flashy clothes, the confidence. These were not drunken idiots arguing over whose turn it was to buy the beer.

"You better go back in your room, man," one said, his low, steady voice conveying subtle menace. Colorful tattoos covered a muscular torso in a white tank top. The other one, shorter and thinner, tweaked his denim vest aside to reveal the butt of a gun sticking out of his waistband. Neither blinked.

The display intrigued Stone more than frightened him, but he had no wish to cause trouble that might delay his exit from this hellhole. He assumed an appropriately fearful expression and raised placating hands. "Sorry, sorry. Didn't mean to bother you. I'll just be on my way." Mindful of their eyes still on him, he hurried back to his room. The old-fashioned lock chose that moment to stick—because of course it did. Good thing popping locks with magic was easy. Inside, he immediately peeked through a tiny opening in the curtains.

The two guys had already lost interest in him. They stopped talking and opened the door to the room on the far side of the gated alcove. A moment later it slammed shut.

Well. That was interesting.

Even more interesting: the ghostly maid was back.

This time she was on the far side of the room, and she wasn't looking at Stone.

She was looking at the door.

"Do you know those two?"

She didn't reply.

Stone waited several more moments to make sure the men were going to stay in their room. The echo remained where she was, clearly annoyed she wasn't getting through to him.

"Let's see if I can get some more information, shall we?" he muttered to her. "If you can't tell me, maybe somebody else can."

⤜⤛

He still didn't see the two men as he headed downstairs to the front desk. The clerk looked up in surprise when he appeared.

"Whaddya want now? We ain't got any extra towels, and you missed teatime." He snorted at his joke.

"Just a bit of information."

That thoroughly flummoxed the man, who probably didn't get too many inquisitive Brits around his sterling establishment. "Huh?"

"Has anyone died around here?"

The guy gave him a look. "What the fuck?"

"It's a simple question. Has anyone died here at the motel?"

"Why?"

In Stone's experience, the easiest way to get cooperation in cases like this was by monetary incentive. He pulled out a couple of twenties and laid them on the counter next to a small nameplate that read *Frank—Night Manager.* "I'm doing research."

Frank the Night Manager didn't miss a beat. The twenties disappeared so fast Stone almost couldn't follow the motion. "We had a few, I guess. Couple ODs . . . some guy shot some other guy a couple years back . . . I told you it ain't that safe around here, specially after dark. Surprised some fancy-ass dude like you would even wanna stay here."

"What about the maids?"

"What about 'em?"

"Was one ever killed here?"

Frank glared. "Listen, dude, I don't know what the hell you're talkin' about. Ain't no maids ever got killed here. Why you even askin'?"

Stone had been watching Frank with magical sight as he answered. Auras weren't foolproof lie detectors, but he was good enough he could usually pick up deception. This time, he saw none. Frank wasn't lying. "Just curious. Never mind. You have a good evening."

He was about to turn away and exit the office when Frank called, "Hey."

"What?"

"Gimme another twenty and I'll tell you somethin' about a maid."

Stone turned back around. "I thought you said no maids died here."

"They didn't. But I got another story. You wanna hear it or not? I don't give a shit either way—I got stuff to do."

His "stuff to do" was probably watching porn on his phone, but Stone shrugged and produced another twenty. "Let's have the story."

Frank grinned and squirreled the bill away. "We had one disappear a couple months back."

"Disappear?"

"Yeah. She worked here a couple weeks, maybe. Then showed up one night and by mornin' she was gone. Never saw 'er again after that. She didn't even show up to pick up 'er check the next day."

"Does that happen often?"

"Them not comin' to work? Yeah, sure. Lots of 'em are illegals, so somethin' spooks 'em and they take off, or ICE picks 'em up or whatever. But not pickin' up their check? Maybe this might come as a surprise to a fancy type like you, but round here, nobody skips out on money."

Stone narrowed his eyes. "Did you call the police? Do anything to figure out where she might have gone?"

Frank barked a laugh and looked at him like he was crazy. "For some maid? You're shittin' me. What do I care? Maids are a dime a dozen. Always a bunch of 'em lookin' for work. We had a new one the next day." He glared at Stone. "What diff'rence does it make to you, anyway?"

"I told you—I'm doing research."

The clerk gave him a long, appraising stare, then snorted and waved him off. "You know what? I don't give a shit why you wanna know. I get enough weirdos in here every night, and at least you don't stink. You got what you wanted, now get the hell outta here."

Stone turned to leave, then stopped. "One more question, if I may?"

Frank was already focusing on his phone screen. "*What?*"

"Do you happen to remember her name?"

"Seriously? The maid?" He scratched his ample gut thoughtfully. "Uh . . . it was Luisa somethin', I think. Don't remember 'er last name. Prob'ly fake anyway. Now *out.*"

⤚⤙

She was still in his room when he returned.

She stood in the same place, at the foot of his bed, and turned slightly to look at him as he entered. Her silvery eyes still burned with the same combination of rage and pleading in her bizarrely angled face, though it was hard to tell which—if either—was aimed at him.

He dropped into the room's only chair, which creaked alarmingly even under his tall, slim frame's weight. "Right, then," he said casually. "Frank at the front desk is a bit unpleasant, but he might have given me something useful. Are you called Luisa?"

Her eyes widened.

"Ah. Brilliant. Now we're getting somewhere. Frank says you disappeared one night. But you didn't, did you?" He shot a pointed look at her twisted neck. "Someone murdered you. Here at the motel, I'm guessing, which is why you're stuck here."

Luisa's frustration couldn't have been more obvious. She clenched her fists and drifted back and forth, passing through the out-of-order TV as if she didn't even notice it. The ghostly equivalent of angry pacing.

Her behavior didn't surprise Stone. Most people who believed in ghosts at all got their ideas about how they conducted themselves from too many horror movies or paranormal romance novels. But echoes—the leftover psychic energy of people who'd experienced a violent death or had compelling unfinished business—were frustratingly single-minded things. Communicating with the living wasn't something most of them found easy to do. Sometimes, they needed a little nudge.

"Listen," he said, joining her in pacing. "I want to help you. I truly do. But I'm tired, it's hot as the devil's armpit in here, and I've got an early morning tomorrow. So either give me something to go on, or kindly bugger off and let me get some sleep." To punctuate his words, he sat down on the edge of the bed and reached down to pull off his T-shirt.

Luisa *growled*. There was no sound, but she conveyed the effect just fine in silent pantomime.

And then, before Stone could move or even react, she was there in front of him—and a split second later she'd passed through him. The incandescent rage in her eyes burned flashing, staccato images into his brain, like a stuttering old film reel unspooling almost too quickly to allow conscious comprehension.

Pushing her cart along, whistling a cheerful tune.

Opening a door to what she thought was an unoccupied room.

Two shadowy figures, hunched over a table.

Two faces look up.

Surprised. Angry. Cold eyes.

Killers' eyes.

Drugs and money spread out on the table between them.

Fear. No. Wrong room.

Run! Get away!

She's too slow and they're too fast.

Big hand over her mouth. Rough hand. Can't scream.

Another grips the side of her head.

A sharp, savage twisting motion. A sickening crack.

Sudden pain. She's falling.

Darkness.

And then, just as suddenly, the world wrenches.

Her perspective changes. She's looking down on them from above.

At—her body? How—?

She watches as the men wrap her in a sheet, drag her cart into the room, stuff her in the hamper where the dirty linens go. They move with swift efficiency, expressionless.

She watches as they take her downstairs, put her body in a car trunk, drive off—

Her body leaves, but she doesn't.

She's still at the motel. Watching the red lights recede.

Her abandoned cart stands in the parking lot, and the car is gone.

And she's still here.

Stone's head lit up with pain. Brains—even mages' brains—weren't meant to process that much information in such a short time. He pressed his temples with the heels of his hands, struggling to make sense of the rapid-fire, faster-than-thought imagery.

Someone had killed Luisa—brutally snapped her neck—when she'd accidentally interrupted a drug deal in one of the motel's unused rooms. That much had come through loud and clear. They'd used her own cart to hide her body and transport it away, leaving her echo behind, eternally tethered to the site of her death.

But there had been something else—

He clamped his eyes shut, fighting to recall what was eluding him. Something about the men—

The men.

He'd seen those men. Those same cold-eyed faces.

He lowered his hands and looked at Luisa, who was once more watching him from the other side of the room. "It was those two, wasn't it? They were the ones who killed you and took your body away. This is where they conduct their drug deals, and you walked in on one of them."

She didn't answer, but her silvery eyes never left his face.

"And now they're back. That's why you reached out to me, isn't it?"

The throbbing pain was already beginning to fade. Stone rose and resumed his pacing, rubbing his chin. "I don't know how I can help you, Luisa. The police won't do anything without proof, and I can't exactly go busting into their room and take them down."

She flashed him a challenging look, her meaning clear: *No?*

"Well—all right, maybe I could. *Maybe.* Mages aren't indestructible, you know. But in any case, I'm not going to. I've still got places to be tomorrow, and the police might have something to say about that if anyone catches me messing with those two. Besides, *me* taking care of them isn't going to free you from here. That's not how it works."

Her eyes went wide and fearful.

He shrugged. "I don't make the rules. Me killing them won't bring you closure, and that's what it will take to set you free. It's too bad you can't affect the living. It would be much more satisfying if you sorted out the problem yourself."

She frowned, her brow furrowing. She drifted back and forth a few times, almost as if considering her options. Then she stopped. The fear disappeared, replaced by the rage.

But it was different this time.

Something else had joined it now too, dancing across her silvery face.

Amusement. Relish.

Anticipation.

"Have you got an idea?"

In answer, she merely held his gaze for a couple more seconds, then flitted through the door. When he didn't follow right away, her head poked back through on its twisted neck, as if to say, *Well?*

Stone sighed.

He was probably going to regret this. But then again, he did want to see what she had on what was left of her mind.

Also, it beat trying to sleep while curled up in the arse end of hell.

⤚⤙

Luisa's translucent form hovered just up the walkway, radiating impatience as Stone exited his room. As soon as he emerged, she took off toward the stairs. The way her neck was twisted, she could still keep an eye on him as she moved. If it hadn't been so tragic, it would have been creepy.

No, never mind. It was tragic *and* creepy.

By now, it was after three a.m. The parking lot was quiet; the only light on the second floor came from Stone's room and the one next to the alcove. Either the drug dealers liked sleeping with a night-light, or they were still awake in there.

Stone followed Luisa's echo with more caution, wondering what she was up to. There was nothing to be gained by confronting the two men, since she couldn't physically touch them. Almost without exception, echoes couldn't directly affect the living, only objects directly connected to them—usually, to the circumstances of their deaths. Stone doubted she could frighten a pair of hardened drug dealers by popping through the door and mouthing, *Boo!*

So, then, what was she—

As Stone reached the far edge of the alcove near the door, Luisa's echo turned abruptly and slipped through it. With a sudden brain wave, he caught on to what she was about to do.

He stopped, a lump of anticipatory dread forming deep in the pit of his stomach.

Oh, this was a very bad plan.

She couldn't possibly be—

Luisa popped back out. Stone got a quick impression of a fierce, triumphant grin, and then the door slammed open and the two men emerged, their faces darkened with mixed confusion and menace.

Luisa vanished.

No, Luisa, you didn't—

The drug dealers' searching gazes fell on the only other living thing within sight: Stone.

Their expressions went hard, and then they were moving.

Stone was fast.

They were faster.

The skinny one drew his gun. The buff one with the tattoos and the tank top lunged forward and struck with a cat-quick fist, clocking Stone in the jaw with the effortless aim of a guy who did this sort of thing as part of his daily routine.

Two thoughts flashed through Stone's mind as he flew backward and crashed, stunned, onto the walkway on the other side of the alcove.

The first was that magical shields only worked when you got them up *before* the bad things hit you.

The second was that Tank Top even had tattoos on his *knuckles*.

Apparently, there was no accounting for the things you noticed when about to get your head blown off by two guys you had no personal beef with.

Stone shook his head, trying to clear the static enough to form a spell.

Skinny and Tank Top were already closing in on him. If he didn't get it together *now*, getting out of this dump and back to civilization in the morning was going to be the least of his worries.

Where the hell was Luisa?

And then he spotted her.

She hovered a short distance behind Skinny and Tank Top, floating high enough to give him an unobstructed view of her off-kilter face above them. She caught his eye, and then she did something unexpected.

She cut her silvery gaze sideways.

Very obviously sideways.

Comically sideways, with a level of exaggeration worthy of a *Three Stooges* short.

For good measure she jerked her neck to the same side, which, given her current state, was more unsettling than comical.

Stone's brain got hung up on what the hell she could mean by all of this, but his reflexes did the same thing anyone else's would have under the circumstances.

He looked the same way she had.

This was all happening at lightning speed. The drug dealers hadn't shot him yet, probably because they'd figured out the blast would rouse every sleeping guest at the motel. But that didn't mean Stone wasn't about to be in a world of hurt if he didn't come up with something pretty damn quick.

What was Luisa trying to show him? There was nothing there—certainly nothing he could use as a weapon. All he saw was the chain-link gate across the alcove, the corner of the shadowy maid cart behind it—

And the lock holding it closed.

Popular wisdom states that when you're about to die, you see your life flashing before your eyes in a split second. Stone had no idea if that was true, but something absolutely *did* flash across his mind at that moment. Three thought fragments, in quick succession:

His ridiculous notion, earlier tonight before any of this nonsense had started, that he'd seen the maid cart move behind the gate.

The wispy red energy he'd spotted drifting around it.

And Luisa's vision of her murderers stuffing her body in the cart.

It all came together in a sudden, magnificent bloom of insight, driving the last of the static cobwebs from his brain.

His manic, feral grin must have startled the drug dealers, at least enough to pause before they reached him. Only for a second, but that was all he needed.

He reached out with his magic and popped the lock on the gate, pulling it free and tossing it aside.

Behind Skinny and Tank Top, Luisa's plain face lit up in triumph.

After that, everything happened even faster.

Luisa disappeared again, or maybe she just moved so quickly Stone could no longer follow the motion. Whichever it was, a second later a bright red glow flowered in the alcove. Stone couldn't see much of it from his vantage point on the ground, but that made it somehow worse—as if an unseen portal to hell were opening just beyond his vision.

Skinny and Tank Top got the full impact, though.

They both whirled away from Stone, their eyes bugging out and their jaws hanging open at whatever they were seeing.

The maid cart, suffused with the hellish red glow and seeming somehow bigger than its actual size, erupted from the alcove, smashing the gate into the side wall with a thundering *thoom* that shook the walkway beneath Stone.

Skinny and Tank Top had no time to react. The possessed cart did zero to sixty in a time that would have put a Ferrari to shame. It slammed into the pair of them with far more force than something its size and construction should have been able to manage, driving them forward into the metal safety railing.

The combined weight of the cart and their bodies at that speed proved too much for the cheap structure. It twisted with a wrenching metallic shriek and gave way, sending them flying, arms flailing and legs pumping, over the edge.

A second later, a loud *crash* announced their impact below, bringing an abrupt halt to their screams.

Stone scrambled to his feet, careful to avoid the broken part of the railing, and hurried forward to assess the damage. Around him, lights were coming on in the other rooms.

In the confusion of everything that had happened, he'd forgotten one other relevant bit of the Sunbeam Motel's layout until now. The two drug dealers hadn't fallen into the parking lot, perhaps breaking part of their fall on the hood of some hapless suburban family's late-model SUV. Instead, barely visible in the darkness, their twisted bodies lay in an unmoving heap under the broken maid cart in the empty deep end of the drained swimming pool. A quick glance with magical sight revealed a pair of rapidly fading auras that winked out even as he watched. In a fitting touch, Tank Top—the one who had actually committed Luisa's murder—was at the bottom of the heap, his thick neck bent at an even sharper angle than the echo's had been.

Stone saw no sign of the red energy around the cart.

"*What* the actual *fuck* is going *on* out here?" a voice screamed from down below. A moment later, Frank the Night Manager came trundling out of his office, peering around as if expecting the motel to be under attack.

By this time, more sleepy, confused guests had emerged from their rooms and joined Stone at the railing.

"What happened?" a middle-aged man in an anime T-shirt and plaid boxers asked, holding tightly to a curious boy's hand.

"No idea," Stone said. "I was just looking for the ice machine, and—" He shrugged, as if to say, *I got nothing.* He disengaged from the growing crowd of lookie-loos and returned to his room before anyone else noticed him.

⤚⤙

Luisa was waiting for him inside, floating in her usual place in front of the broken TV. This time, though, the rage was gone. Her smile lit up her face, making her almost pretty if it weren't for her twisted neck.

"You could have got me killed, you know." He shot a sour glare at her but couldn't make it stick. Perhaps it made him a bad person, but he couldn't summon a shred of sympathy for the two dead murderers. He wouldn't have killed them himself, but he couldn't deny they'd gotten what they deserved.

Her smile departed, replaced by something that could only be gratitude. She was already starting to fade, the silvery edges of her hair and her uniform fuzzing out like watercolors in a bathtub.

"Goodbye, Luisa," he murmured. "Good luck on the other side."

As her form lost coherence and drifted away, her silvery eyes were the last to go.

Stone realized he would never even know her last name.

⤚⤙

Of course he didn't get away without being questioned. The Sunbeam Motel quickly became a circus of whirling red and blue lights, overlapping bursts of radio static, and cops and crime scene investigators prowling around trying without much success to make sense of the bizarre situation. Nobody was getting any sleep.

The good news was, no one had seen Stone near the two dead men. None of the guests had been brave enough to emerge when the slamming and shouting had started, and by the time Skinny and Tank Top had made their fatal swan dive, Stone had been nothing more than a fellow curious onlooker.

He could tell the police were frustrated at the lack of living eyewitnesses, but he also got the impression they weren't planning to try all that hard to solve this one. Apparently, he overheard after he'd gathered his gear and joined several other guests in a predawn exodus from the Sunbeam Motel, both men had extensive rap sheets and were wanted on suspicion of at least two other murders.

In other words, nobody was going to miss them.

He was sitting in the back corner of an all-night coffee shop an hour later, sipping a weapons-grade brew and scrolling idly on his phone, when a text popped up from Verity.

> I know you won't get this till tomorrow morning. Just finishing up some packing. Anything you want me to bring?

He smiled, picturing her dashing around her apartment, tossing things haphazardly into bags. No, got everything I need.

Her surprised reply came back fast: Wow, didn't expect you to answer for hours. What are you doing up this early?

You wouldn't believe me if I told you.

Try me? I have time.

The server, surprisingly cheerful for this gods-awful wee hour of the morning, came by and left another cup of coffee. She reminded him of Luisa: young, slim, with long dark hair and a plain, pleasant face. But unlike Luisa, she was still alive. Still in the world.

Still remembered.

Tomorrow, Stone sent back. I want to tell you about someone I met tonight. I think you would have liked her.

GRAVE PAYBACK

A Short Story from the Grave Report

R.R. Virdi

Dying with a lungful of black dust, waterlogged insides, a leg that felt like it'd served as a piñata for an overly enthusiastic minor-league team, while restrained, isn't a good way to go.

But waking up like that is a helluva lot worse.

Trust me on that.

I do this a lot.

Add in the fact that my surroundings were about as bright as the mind of a frat boy on Friday night after rounds of drinking, well, it couldn't get any darker.

Great circumstances for when you return to the living.

I tried to move, only to find something biting hard into my wrists. The wood pressing against my back and my calves let me know I'd been tied to a chair. Another wriggle told me the piece of furniture had seen better days, the way its joints loosely protested the stress. A bit more strength and something might give way.

All of that was a clue in and of itself—the kind to make you worry.

The person whose body I was now inhabiting didn't need to be held long before being sent off to the pearly gates. Either his killer had known they were going to end it quickly, or he'd been left in no state to resist and break free.

Neither were good signs.

The pitch black of the area around me meant the poor stiff was unlikely to be found by anyone who might come looking for them. And I wasn't gagged. That told me whoever had done the victim in didn't care about them crying out for help. I was somewhere that no one would hear me.

Dead. Silent. Emphasis on both parts.

. . . until a rhythmic tapping echoed through the space around me.

That's not ominous.

I shook harder in the chair and cast a wary look around me to no avail. My eyesight hadn't adjusted yet, and I wasn't sure any amount of time would help it do so in these conditions. My lungs burned like they'd been stuffed with rough-powdered glass for a long enough time to leave scars. I coughed, and everything that had already ached inside me doubled in pain.

Something warm dribbled past my lips, leaving the taste of salt, copper, and black earth behind. *Because things weren't peachy before.*

The noise around me intensified, and I realized it wasn't tapping at all but knocking. Small distinction, but those often can make a world of difference in my line of work.

My name is Vincent Graves—paranormal investigator, and soul without a body. The job? Almost as simple as that, and just as complicated as you can imagine. Wake up in the bodies of those killed by the supernatural and find out what ended their lives.

And stop them.

Yet it was never as easy as that. The only small mercy of the gig was that every body I woke up in was nearly restored to a functional enough state just prior to the person's death.

Nearly restored. Like I said, the small details matter.

The knocking loudened.

"Uh, who's there?"

Silence.

"You're supposed to say, 'Knock, knock,' you don't literally do it."

Another stretch of discomforting quiet in the dark.

For all the traits the paranormal might have, a decent sense of humor isn't one of them.

It was a good bet that whatever was making the sound wasn't friendly.

Which meant I needed to get out of my current predicament—fast.

I strained against the chair, new agony lighting up inside me. My mangled leg felt like someone had just introduced it to a fresh current of electricity, as well as placing freshly lit coals along the muscles.

I ground my teeth through the pain until dull pressure radiated through my gums. *Think, Graves.* I had the answer a second later.

The chair rattled under my first attempts to move. As a rule, most modern chairs that people are willing to dispose of aren't that well put together. Shoddy construction, loose joints, and some particulate wood substitute that doesn't hold up to the real thing. If you can exert enough force, or find a hard enough surface to crack it against, you can usually escape.

The floor beneath me definitely met that criteria. I couldn't make it out, but it wasn't a stretch to figure it was stone. Some strong rocking was enough to send me tipping over.

I don't get to choose whose body I end up in, but it's pretty damn helpful if you land in the shoes of someone who, at least by feeling, is built like an ambulatory refrigerator. That much mass matters on impact.

I hit the ground—hard—and for a moment, wasn't sure if the *snap* that filled my ears was my shoulder joint or a part of the chair. Mercifully, it seemed to be the latter. I managed a weak groan, still flooded with whatever this guy had swallowed and some spittle I knew to be tinged with blood.

The knocking now mimicked the percussive beat of an all-drum ensemble. Steady, drubbing me from all sides until it reverberated inside me as much as it did around.

That's totally normal.

I grimaced and wrenched against the chair, managing to break free at the armrest. After that, it was easier to twist and apply the right kinds of pressure to get my other side free. I undid the rope and hobbled to my feet. My pained leg didn't like that much, feeling like it'd been fashioned from hot glass that had taken on too many cracks in the making.

I limped my way forward, figuring moving in any direction was better than sitting still for whatever made that knocking to find me.

Usually, that's a bad idea in a place as dark as this, but there's something that changes that.

No one likes being lost in the dark with a preternatural nasty.

I placed a hand on the nearest wall, realizing it was a rock face. Following it along led me to the first opening I could move into.

Bright whiteness lanced my vision with the sharpness of a freshly honed knife. The world blurred, and a new one took its place.

I'm not sure what the light source was exactly, but it emanated from just above my head. The familiar dirty orange of a hard hat rimmed part of my vision, and the stone tunnel wasn't as illuminated as it should be, but that was because I currently was walking down an offshoot that hadn't been properly expanded into. The way behind me led to a dead end, and I was making my way back toward the main body of the operation.

My head felt like a brass bell that'd just been rung, and the vision faded.

Another part of the job: whatever higher power shoves me into these bodies also grants me access to someone's thoughts and knowledge base, though notably not at my desire. The major downside's been that the years of doing it has left me with a near encyclopedic knowledge of all manner of skills and the memories along with them . . . all at the cost of my original own and my identity along with it.

But the vision had told me something new. The victim I was now inside had known the place well. A routine had been built around it. And now that subconscious information guided me as I walked blindly through the tunnel, wishing very much for that same light that had been in the vision.

I felt my way along until I stepped into a cavernous opening—the main corridor of the stone surroundings that the previous owner of this body had been heading for before. I knew there was a row of high-intensity LED lights above to brighten up the place, only they were now off.

Of course. "At least the knocking's stopped." Just as I'd finished the words, a low, dry rasping echoed through the cave like dying autumn leaves scraping against the ground. And it was close by the sound of it.

There are few options for the intrepid paranormal investigator when confronted by an unknowable and likely supernatural baddie in a pitch-black cave system.

But the best is usually this: run like hell.

I picked up the pace, ignoring every bit of searing pain flashing through my injured leg. It'd be the least of my worries if whatever was making that noise caught up with me. Mercifully, I spotted the promise of light up ahead as it washed through the opening of the cave.

I hobbled outside, taking a second to look over my shoulder and ensure I wasn't followed. The brightness of the outdoors brought sharp pinpricks to my eyes, making it harder to see, but I managed to catch enough.

There *was* something lurking inside what I now realized to be a commercial mine. The knocking returned, just barely audible from where I stood outside—closer to a sound like distant hail on a roof. But there was a darkness lingering inside the already deep black of the cave. Something a shade deeper—enough so that it could pull at all other light filtering into the place.

I couldn't make out any discernible features, but I could feel it when I locked eyes with where I assumed its might be. And the dry sharpness in my lungs doubled, feeling like they'd been freshly wrung clean of breath.

I turned away from the blackness and doubled over, sucking down air. My vision, and the world, soon steadied. Whatever filth had been clogging my borrowed throat and lungs cleared as well. Though, not without a few parting coughs that racked my insides. One last bit of blackened spittle dribbled free from my lips, and I decided that some things are most certainly better spat out than swallowed.

When I chanced another look over my shoulder back toward the mine, I saw nothing. A mild relief, though there was some appeal to the idea of being able to tangle with whatever that was and ending my case immediately.

The dead don't care much how fast you solve their murders. They just need vengeance.

But running in half-cocked against a monster you know little about is a good way to throw your life away.

So I turned to the next logical move I could make: figuring out who the hell I was this time.

The clothes he'd worn before being murdered were what you'd expect of someone who worked in a mine. Heavy safety boots that could break down a door as easily as cave in an ass if needed. Well-worn jeans and an ocher and orange plaid shirt, both of which fit tight on account of the man's build. He had the physique of someone who'd been doing hard labor for decades now and never skipped dessert. Solid, thick muscle with a healthy layer of fat over it.

Not the kind of guy who'd go down without a fight, and certainly not an easy one at that. Which meant whatever had done him in was either terribly strong or clever.

I scanned the surrounding area, most of which was made of hard-packed gravel and loaded with heavy machinery, from bulldozers to excavators. Some caution tape lined parts of the perimeter, indicating the place was now closed. A lone pickup truck sat near a small hovel of a building sporting a faded white cross.

A short look at the vehicle triggered a sharp pang, and a memory followed. Familiar-looking hands gripped an old steering wheel and pushed a cassette into the tape deck. It wasn't a stretch to realize it belonged to the man whose body I now occupied.

Whenever a spot of luck came my way, it was often bad. So the occasional bout of good fortune wasn't something I'd question.

I headed toward the diminutive chapel, stopping just before I reached the pair of double doors. They were the color of dark espresso that had begun to fade to something softer. The place looked as if it had been built nearly a hundred years ago, and on the cheap. Yet it still remained standing. Though I wasn't so sure about the single window near the front, the frame of which sat visibly askew, sagging now due to time and likely the elements.

It wasn't uncommon for mines to have a small chapel like this on-site. It's a tough job, and a dangerous one on top of that. Miners perish every year in some pretty terrible ways.

But those ends usually excluded the intervention of the supernatural.

I pushed through the doors and entered to find the place furnished how you'd expect for an out-of-the-way chapel. Simple carpeting and the usual sturdy pews—all framed by white walls that had been kept cleaner and better maintained than the exterior. A small altar draped in a red cloth stood at the other end from me.

But it was the man with his back turned to me that held my interest.

I moved closer. "Church, that you, pal?"

The figure turned to face me. He had the sort of face that somehow managed to balance softness in features with the right amount of sharp edges and hardness. A look that left you wondering if he was pretty handsome or just handsomely pretty. The guy had the freshly tousled blond locks and icy blue eyes to mirror some of the angelic images in a place like this. If only he didn't dress like an IT guy—from the tucked-in white shirt to the khakis.

The man embodied the idea of geek chic.

"Vincent." He inclined his head in a polite welcome. Church usually had more words for me than just that. While not particularly talkative, he usually made some time for the little niceties in conversation. Then again, I'd once asked the man for his name, and he'd looked around the building we were in and told me to call him the same thing.

No one likes a wiseass . . .

I crossed the distance between us, extending a hand. Church didn't bother with any foreplay. He gripped my wrist instead, brushing up the sleeve of my shirt, then holding tight to the soft skin of my forearm. Mr. IT held me with the strength of hydraulic machinery as the sensation of burning needles pricked along my skin.

I hissed through it.

He released his hand just as I'd adjusted to the fresh pain. My forearm had reddened as if I had actually been burned, but the thing keeping my attention was the fresh number of all black now on my skin.

The number five stared back at me, as much a warning as a motivator. In theory, it represented the amount of time my soul could remain in this particular body. In reality, it was a countdown for how long I had to find the monster responsible for offing this fella, and then put the kibosh on them.

If I failed, I'd be shuffled off to my next case, and someone would go unavenged.

Enough reasons to stop whatever killed this guy.

"Not a lot of time, Church." I nodded to the number on my forearm.

He gave me a tight, thin smile. "It will have to be, Vincent." His voice seemed a bit more strained than the usual light and almost airy whisper. Still as strong and confident, but an undercurrent of rasp just touched it.

I arched a brow. "Everything okay?"

His smile almost widened an imperceptible amount . . .

Almost.

Which said enough.

"I'll take that as a no. What gives?"

In his usual fashion, he didn't give me the answer I wanted. "Your name is Wayland Keeney. Age forty-eight years old. You were a miner born and raised here in Randolph County, West Virginia. There's a bathroom and a mirror, even in this small space." Church gestured to one corner, where an open doorway stood. "You might want to clean up before getting to the case. It won't be as straightforward as some of your others."

I eyed him askance. None of my cases could ever be considered *straightforward*, and Church wasn't exactly *Encyclopaedia Britannica* when I needed him. Though he'd given me a bit more than he usually did. Something I made note of. "Do I want to know why you've already told me the details you have? You're usually more reserved about this stuff."

One corner of his mouth twitched. "This case is problematic in a few ways, and I'm giving you what I can, Vincent. I trust it will be enough." He turned halfway toward the altar at his back, retrieving a pair of leather-bound journals. There was no ceremony as he presented them to me, dumping them into my open hands.

One was a collection of all the monsters and myths I'd come across in my research or on the job. As close to a manual on dealing with the supernatural as I could have. The other served as a recording of all my case files, mostly for my fragmented memory.

I stuffed them into my waistband, taking a step in the direction of the bathroom. Then something he'd said struck me. I rounded on him, opening my mouth as I did. "What's problematic—"

The church stood empty but for me. No sound. Nothing to betray that he had left. Just the sort of quiet in a small building when you're all alone.

I might have grumbled a string of curses about problematic paranormal investigator handlers who vanish on a whim.

The bathroom consisted of a toilet that looked like it came from a gas station, though it had been regularly cleaned, and a sink with a mirror over the top. A quick look at myself revealed a not-so-pretty picture.

Wayland wore every bit of his years and tough labor in his face. Creased like old leather and caked in all the grit a miner would be. Yet the brown of his eyes and natural set of his face spoke of something gentle beneath the hardness. Something that edged on fatherly kindness. The sort of guy who could kick your ass and would probably buy you a drink after.

I washed up and headed outside to the truck.

The world cut out, and I watched a short scene of Wayland's hands wrenching free the cigarette lighter and slipping something into the space. Then he did something with the glove box that happened too smoothly and quickly for me to catch.

At least the vision settled whom the truck belonged to.

I stopped a few feet from it, sighing as I took it in. An old 80s F-250 in what I assumed was supposed to be something resembling the old two-tone style they'd come in. But that works only when you genuinely have a pair of colors. Not ten of the damn things.

The old truck looked like it'd survived a tour in the Middle East and had been cobbled together from the parts of similar survivors, and either a point of honor or likely cost kept Wayland from respraying the other panels to match what I guessed was the original color.

Whatever that was.

Vanilla crime investigators in television shows usually get cool cars, but as a rule, paranormal investigators often don't. Still, you have to be practically a wizard of bad luck to drive around in a beat-up relic with not a single matching body panel, color wise.

I opened the driver's side door, mildly relieved it'd been left unlocked. Then I went about re-creating what I'd seen in Wayland's memory. Removing the cigarette lighter revealed a compartment he'd fashioned to dump his keys in. And something similar in the glove box and under the armrest latch.

That told me Wayland made a habit of this and, given that I'd found his wallet stashed in the glove compartment, that he didn't feel comfortable taking it out of the truck before he met with his death.

It also meant that Wayland had possibly been concerned about needing to hide his identifying materials before he died, which prompted the obvious question: Why?

I didn't have an answer then, but I was certain of one thing: there was a good chance I wouldn't like it when I discovered it. There are seldom good answers in this line of work.

The old truck rumbled to life once I'd started her up and went into gear easy enough. Flipping through Wayland's wallet got me to his license, which gave me his address. Not much good on its own as the man didn't seem to have a cell phone, or a vehicle with GPS. So I ambled onto the only road in sight and took one of the only two turns available to me.

It wasn't long before the small mercy of visions from the guy struck. A familiar bend in the street, and memories of coming down the other way. The images threaded into a montage I recognized from a routine buried deep within Wayland. One I reversed to lead me to a small house just outside of town.

Wayland's place looked like it had been one of many built in the sixties in the pop-up manner to accommodate the population boom the country had experienced as well as returning veterans from the Korean War. A small single-story rambler with pale yellow siding and a single carport.

I parked the truck and thumbed through the few keys in his possession, trying each one until I'd successfully unlocked his front door. "Anyone home?" I kept my voice level as I made the call, figuring one of two things: Anyone who might have been missing Wayland would come to greet him, which would tell me something. Or if there was any sort of trouble lingering, they'd do the same.

Only, there was no answer.

The inside of his home spoke of an old bachelor. Well-used furniture and zero sense of coordination. Everything had been chosen for comfort, and perhaps affordability. Letters lay out in stacks along the small kitchen table, as did a few plastic binders.

I started a slow and thorough search of Wayland's home, making sure I made as little noise as possible in the rare event that something was lurking and had decided to ignore my earlier call.

Mercifully, nothing nasty turned up during my investigation. Though the same could be said for finding anything useful.

My arm tingled, and a look at it showed I'd lost an hour between the drive to his house and my initial search. Just four left . . .

The only bit of information lying about the place was the mounting bills from Wayland falling behind in life, sadly like so many others these days. And the history of what he'd been reading up on: various tragedies the mine had suffered over the near century it'd been up and running.

It wasn't uncommon to hear of in such a dangerous line of work, but the clippings Wayland had gathered pointed to a string of mishaps that possibly could have been avoided. Then there was the stack of notes about a member of the MSHA (or Mine Safety and Health Administration) who'd vanished several decades ago after raising some public outcry about the hazards of the particular site I'd woken up in.

Some of the old newspaper snippets covered local townsfolk murmuring that corners had been cut by the family who ran the mine, and as a result, unnecessary deaths had occurred. Ground falls, subpar respiratory equipment, as well as accusations of other poor pieces of personal protective equipment, or PPE. A few pictures of the mine owner along with a young man near him who could have passed for his son by his looks. Lastly, Wayland had calculated how much a mine might spend on PPE yearly, and what skimping on it might save an owner.

But none of that pointed me in the direction of identifying what kind of monster was behind Mr. Keeney's death.

I ground the palms of my hands against my eyes, more in frustration than anything else. Mining accidents, a missing person from thirty years ago, and something haunting the local mine from the looks of it.

And not a lot of options on how to go about my case. I could march right back to where I'd woken up in Wayland's body and be ready to throw down, but walking in blind to a fight with the paranormal gets a guy killed more often than not.

The best way to win in my line of work is with knowledge.

Which meant I needed to talk to a monster myself.

⤚⤙

I pored as much through one of my journals as I did more of the contents of Wayland's home. My search turned up answers for the empty home, but little to bring me closer to solving my case.

Wayland was a widower. His wife had passed giving birth to

their son, leaving the man a single father with a hard-as-hell day job. Rough circumstances made worse by the fact I'd learned his son had died a few years earlier in a tragic accident . . .

At the same mine where Wayland was employed. Places like this, some folk don't have many options when it comes to work. So it wasn't unheard of for generations of men to toil in the same mine. And it wasn't rare for some to die doing that work over the years.

But losing your son like that? It's a kind of pain no one is prepared to bear. And it had sent Wayland into an obsession with the mine. His home was littered with papers and reports spanning decades back. Any piece of bad press, any concern, any investigation, it was all collected and laid out by Wayland.

Maybe something's not wrong with the mine, but what's in it. The line of thought brought me back to my journal. I stopped turning the pages just as I came across information on a creature from the old world. A mining spirit.

"Perfect." I scanned my writing, taking note of what was required for a gentle summoning. In theory, calling on a supernatural required something (at times many things) associated with their nature or desires. An offering of good faith for their time and knowledge that you might be taking from them.

The old corded phone by the kitchen counter beeped once. Then again. A weak red light pulsed, letting me know a message had been left, and by the looks of it, there were already a few waiting to be checked. Wayland had let his phone go straight to the answering machine and hadn't bothered listening to what anyone had wanted to say.

I figured I'd catch up for him while I went about the space gathering the supplies I needed to talk to a monster. The answering machine beeped again as I thumbed the button to begin playing back the recordings.

The first was from a local librarian who asked if Wayland needed any more help with records on the missing person, a Jeremiah Gibson. He happened to be the MSHA inspector who'd vanished ages ago.

Wayland's fridge had been mercifully stocked before he'd kicked it, leaving me with some apple butter as well as some sort of chocolate spread, some cold beer that came from a microbrewery, by the looks of the labels, and some fruit still in its plastic packaging.

The second message played. "Hey there, Wayland." The speaker had the sort of roughness to their voice that came from years of breathing in sawdust as much as smoking multiple packs of cigarettes a day. It was cracked stone and broken asphalt. "My boy Jimmy said he saw your truck pulling into town. Looks like you came down from the mine way . . ." A pregnant pause, then I heard the man audibly swallow. "I imagine you want to talk. You know how to get ahold of me."

Talk about what? The way the message had been left made it clear it was recent. I had only just driven into the area, and given what had happened to Wayland, it was a fair bet he hadn't been home since last he headed out. In small American towns, everyone is part of a tight-knit community. Even if you don't like someone, you likely know something about their business. When they're gone, where they're going to, and when they come back.

Few secrets in places like this. In normal murders, the victim often knows their killer, but a lot of the usual rules go out the window when monsters get involved.

I just needed to find out which kind I was dealing with. So I grabbed everything I needed and headed out to Wayland Keeney's backyard. Thankfully, most people still believe in the idea of privacy, so a tall wooden fence ran around his quarter-acre property. It'd keep anyone from accidently seeing what I was up to.

As a rule, the supernatural are skittish about letting mundane folk in on their existence. It can lead to all kinds of problems. Monsters generally have an easier time going about their business when people don't know they're going bump in the night . . .

Or day.

A thicket of trees stood at the end of his property, and it seemed like a good enough space to set up. I headed over and laid out the items I'd taken. The apple butter's lid fought me a tad, but I got it open, then popped the top off one of the lagers. I undid the plastic top to the strawberries, the honey followed, and lastly, I sprinkled some salt onto raw earth, taking a clump in my hand before letting it slip from my grip.

"Oh, spirit of the earth—old-world miner of salt, stone, and precious gems, I invoke you. I offer you—"

I hadn't finished the courtesies when I noticed a pair of large eyes staring back at me through the tree line. One moment they were bright as gold. Then they shone like old emeralds. And they drew closer. Soon I found myself staring at something that could have passed for an emaciated man at a distance.

A great distance.

Hook nosed and leathery skinned, the creature had all the similarities to a garden gnome sans the whimsical and bright clothing. It wore overalls that could have belonged to a miner a hundred years ago. Lean limbed and lined in corded muscle, it also conjured the image of a shaved polar bear.

"Is that beer?" asked the mining spirit.

I gave a hapless shrug. "Didn't have mead, figured the honey and this could split the difference?"

The gnomelike being tilted his head, regarding me in silence.

"It's the thought that counts?"

He snorted and grabbed the lager, downing half of it in a single go. "Suppose that's true enough." Then the coblyn smacked his lips after scarfing down two of the strawberries, dipped in honey, whole.

Coblyns are from the Old World, hailing predominantly from Wales. They once lived in mines, deep-earth creatures that, according to the folklore, would look out for human workers underground. They'd lead some to riches. Others to doom. They'd migrated to the New World long ago with the people who believed in them, and then they took root here. If anything had an idea of what was going on in the mine, it'd be a coblyn.

"I was wondering when one of you would grow wise and consult one of us folk." The coblyn tipped back the container of honey, guzzling it as if it were water.

"You know, diabetes is the cause of all blood sugar–related deaths."

The coblyn didn't care much for health advice, finishing off the lager soon after the honey. "So, let me guess," said the mining creature, "you've realized you're in over your head and don't want to end up a dead man." He blinked, then leaned forward, sniffing at the air. "Or . . . you already are. Curious."

Yeah, it was, because as a rule, most things weren't able to sniff me out as easily as that. But I avoided the obvious question behind his realization, turning to one I had in mind instead. "All that means is that you know what's going on?"

The coblyn nodded vigorously before polishing off the strawberries. "Obviously. Wouldn't be much of a mining spirit if I didn't rightly know what went on in 'em, eh?"

I arched a brow, making it clear I was waiting for the answer. The coblyn caught the gesture and replied in kind with a smile.

"I'm tempted to make you bargain for it, human."

I tensed at that. My history with supernatural bargains hasn't been the greatest, and often, it's been a method for them to get their hooks into me long term.

"But answer me this question first: Why do you care? Why do you want to do anything at all?"

I frowned. "It's my job."

The coblyn shook his head as if the answer was unsatisfactory. "It's not your problem, is it? Why make it that?"

"Someone has to get vengeance here," I said.

"And is that what you think you're doing, getting vengeance for the living, if you go after what's in the mine?"

I nodded.

"What about justice?" he asked.

A fair question, but at times, I didn't know just how much of that you could get with the supernatural. But he didn't wait for me to reply.

"You lot have forgotten the old ways. Don't honor the spirits down there anymore. You just dig and blast and tear at the earth, never thinking if you've gone too far, or what you might stir up." The coblyn tossed the strawberry container to the ground.

I couldn't help it; I opened my mouth and recited, "They delved too greedily and too deep."

The coblyn didn't get it, instead jabbing a finger at me in both agreement and accusation. "Exactly. There's a lot of bad things that go on in mining. What men do to profit from the earth. No longer taking care of their own, or those they've wronged. Doing nothing to set things right. That sort of behavior comes back to haunt you, and others. Maybe you're looking at this the wrong way, little spirit."

I blinked, then thought back to the papers I'd seen in Wayland's home. The signs in the mine crashed through my mind next. I knew what I was dealing with, and worse, what had caused it. "Oh . . . son of a . . ."

The coblyn didn't wait for me to say my piece and get confirmation. His eyes widened in glee as he clapped his hands. "There we go! Now go see it sorted, spirit." With that, he vanished into the brush before I could shout for him to stop.

"Fuck." I stormed back inside and pored over all the papers with my journal open beside me. Part of this had stared me in the face the whole time.

And Wayland had done the research. The missing inspector from years ago, and a history of PPE being cut to save what could total tens of millions over all that time. Shoddy equipment leading to accidents that meant death. And if someone had been investigating this before Wayland, it wasn't crazy for a businessman to kill a person to keep that kind of skulduggery quiet. Not with that much money on the line.

And while that might not be supernatural, what happens when you kill someone like that often can be. The knocking and the thing lurking in the mine . . .

There was a spirit of vengeance haunting the place, and I knew just what kind. A tommy-knocker. They were the leave-behinds of those wronged in mining deaths in Cornish folklore. Often, they were good like coblyns. But the more mining became a giant corporation and men died due to recklessness, the more the creatures started popping up as wrathful shades of black.

And somehow Wayland had crossed paths with it at the wrong time. *No*, I realized. He'd been beaten, bound, and left for it . . .

Oh hell, he was bait to get it to come out, and possibly satisfy it. The coblyn was right: I had been looking at this the wrong way. I'd never had a case like this before, but now I knew what to do, and I had one last good card to play.

I picked up Wayland's phone and made a call. The same man from the voicemail I'd played earlier answered. "Wayland, that you?"

"It's me," I said. I'd kept the words flat and neutral, not wanting to betray anything. The man audibly swallowed on the other end of the line.

"You wanna talk about what went down?"

Damn right I do. But I didn't voice that, not wanting to let anything slip. "Funny thing about that, boss, I can't remember a thing. But I found something interesting you're gonna want to see." I told him where to meet me, at the very spot Wayland Keeney had been left as an offering.

"I'll be there. My boy'll tag along too in case we need some extra hands for something."

Doesn't take much to figure out what you're gonna have him there for. I hung up, grabbed the scattered papers that Wayland had gathered, along with the photo of himself and that of the long-gone Jeremiah Gibson.

I checked my timeline tattoo, seeing what was left. Two hours. Shit. I'd lost a lot between my research and talking to the coblyn.

I was sure this time Wayland's boss wouldn't leave things up to chance, or to the discretion of monsters. He'd bring a gun to make sure this ended once and for all.

So naturally I made sure to grab something that'd even the score.

A pack of matches.

⤚⤙

My arm tingled on the drive toward the mine. I rolled up my sleeve and shot it a glance. One hour left. Mercifully, I was almost there. The only problem remaining was how long this would take.

And I have a feeling not long, though that might not be a good thing.

The mine was as abandoned as it had been when I'd started the case, all save for a lifted Dodge pickup that looked decades newer than what Wayland owned. It had the kind of modifications done to it that let you know the owner had several layers of insecurity issues.

I parked the old Ford and scanned the grounds. The place was empty, though. They were probably already in the mine.

The perfect place for them to set a trap. Another part of me wondered, *Is it a trap if you know they've set it?* There's nothing like a healthy dose of paranoia to keep you alive in the paranormal investigator game.

I made my way into the mouth of the mine, deciding that if I was going to be set up, I'd make the first move. So I laid out the photograph of ole Jeremiah as well as what I hoped passed for something connected to him: the corruption and mishaps associated with the mine he'd been investigating. "Here goes nothing." I set to invoking another being then.

"Jeremiah Gibson, if that's really you knocking about in these mines, I'm calling on you. I've got something you want." I swallowed, then added, "Payback." I struck a match and burned some of the materials, then did the same to his photo.

No answer. The mine remained as silent as before.

"Well, shit." I flicked what remained of the match to the ground.

Something crunched ahead and a bright light washed over me, forcing me to blink.

"Shit's right, Wayland." The voice was almost a mimic for the one on the phone, though notably younger, and lacking some of the grit. I managed to squint through the light to catch a silhouette, then another beside it.

Then the voice from earlier spoke. "Not sure how you survived that . . . thing. But damn if that ain't you right there in front of us. We beat you good, left you damn near for dead." The older of the two men sighed. "Shame too. You were a good worker. People respected you. You just had to start digging into my business." The light died, giving me a better look at the pair.

The mine owner was built along the same lines as Wayland, showing signs of once keeping to a good bit of muscle that in his case had been traded in for comforting fat. Watery blue eyes, some hard lines in the face, and thinning blond hair. His son was what the man might have looked like thirty years younger. They even dressed similarly, from their brown and orange flannels to the well-worn jeans.

"And does that business happen to be fucking your hardworking miners out of safety equipment? Killing someone looking into that? The name Jeremiah Gibson mean anything to you?" Each question left me hard, clipped, and with an edge.

The mine's owner cracked a lopsided smile and gestured with a hand, something flashing of polished chrome in his grip. An old revolver. "MSHA inspector long time back. He came sticking his nose in things that didn't concern him."

"Like how you've been skimping on the mine safety and the gear your boys use? Risking deaths, illnesses, and more? How much have you racked up doing that?" I didn't move lest I prompt the man into firing at me. At this close of a range, he wouldn't miss, and I might be able to recover from a lot of things, but bullets can put me down for good just fine.

The man's smile widened as he trained the gun on me, but his son's face tightened into a strained mask.

"Dad, we can't. Not here. It's too close to—"

The older man cuffed his son with his free hand, never taking his eyes off me as he did. "Quiet, boy. Did I give you permission to talk." He hadn't phrased it as an actual question.

But his son answered all the same. "No, sir."

"Kids . . ." the mine owner sighed. "Now, Wayland, normally I'd be mighty curious as to what had you bring us out here, but the amount of trouble you nearly caused me last time has me thinking maybe it's just wiser for me to kill you here and now."

Tap. Tap. Tap. The steady rhythmic noise echoed through the cavern. Then it developed into the more familiar knocking from the stories.

I couldn't help it—I broke out into laughter.

The mine owner scowled. "Stop that, you fucking nut. You know what that is?"

"Yeah, payback, and it's a paranormal bitch." I flashed the pair a toothy grin.

The knocking loudened. It quickened. And soon enough, it evolved into a thunderous drumming.

"Dad?" The boy's eyes widened as he fumbled on his person for something. The flashlight slipped from his hands, hitting the ground hard enough to shatter its lens.

"Jimmy!" his father barked, turning the gun from me toward his best guess as to where the sound was coming from. Too bad the noise echoed from every direction.

I let out a low, maniacal cackle. "It's too late. They're all around us." As a rule, people don't do well when confronted by the paranormal in the dark.

The mine owner whipped back around to face me, his eyes as wide as his son's. "What the hell did you do? You crazy—this thing'll kill us all."

I smiled. "I thought that for a moment, then I realized something: you had to tie Wayland up, leave him beaten and broken almost as an offering, but you were there too. Old Jeremiah has been after you the whole time. When his spirit couldn't have you, he went for what was left, I wager. But now I've got you here."

A wet, gurgling noise filled the immediate area, and Jimmy finally managed to pull free his snub-nosed revolver. It didn't do him much good, as the same dark silhouette from earlier, managing to cast a shadow in the dark, grabbed hold of the boy.

"Dad!" The scream was cut short as Jimmy vanished from sight.

His father spun, loosing shots into the blackness.

All of which gave me a moment to pull one last trick. I laid out the photo of Wayland and his son, muttered the words like I had for Jeremiah, then pulled out a match.

The mine owner fired one last shot before fishing out a speed revolver to reload. Then he turned to me. The revolver shook in his grip, but not so much that he'd miss. "Call it off. Call it off!"

"Can't do that, boss man. You made that tommy-knocker, You and your boy, I'm guessing. Years of ripping off hardworking guys. Putting their lives at risk. Then taking some yourself. It's mad, and there're only two things it wants."

Somewhere in the cave, his son's cries reverberated. "Maybe one more if you don't do something."

"You bastard!" The man thumbed back the hammer just as

another scream rolled through the mine. Then he turned and fired indiscriminately down the darkened way.

It bought me just enough time to finish what I'd planned to do. "Never bring a gun to a match fight." I kindled a flame, touched it to Wayland's photograph, and gently spoke another invocation.

And the mine answered.

A knocking. It then evolved into drumming, and the wrathful spirit of Wayland Keeney arrived. A blackened shade bearing a gaunter version of the man's original face.

"Way . . . land." The old mine owner barely managed the name just as the wronged spirit dragged him away. Gunshots peppered the cavern, drowning out the screams. But eventually, the thundering stopped, and so did the man's cries.

I sighed before pushing myself to my feet, then began the slow, short walk to the nearby chapel to close my case.

⤚⤙

Church waited for me with a patient look of expectation on his face. "Vincent."

I grunted. "You wanna explain what was up with that case?"

He quirked a brow in what could have been confusion, but we both knew he understood what I meant.

"I usually go after the monsters," I said.

He pursed his lips before speaking. "You still did. But I think you're missing the point here."

It was my turn to raise a brow.

"You've often doled out vengeance against the supernatural. Sometimes, justice for the mortals wronged. But what about justice for both at times?"

I blinked, never having considered that.

Church went on. "You brought vengeance against two men who'd killed innocents for greed. You achieved some level of justice for those murdered, but . . . you also helped put their angered shades to rest." He clapped my shoulder twice. "Think on that."

I sat down as a warmth enveloped my arm. When I looked, the tattoo was gone.

And so was Church, without a trace.

So I waited until my soul left my borrowed body, thinking on what he'd told me. Justice and vengeance.

Two very different kinds of payback.

THE BROOM

A Great Lakes Grimoire Story

Kerrie L. Hughes

June 6, 2015
Madison, Wisconsin

A tall, slender young woman with strawberry blond curls, a heart-shaped face, and oddly large aqua eyes waited under a canopy in front of a two-story triangular building. It was located on the corner of State and Broom Streets and had a For Sale sign on the door. The boarded-up windows were plastered with posters directed at the large population of college students.

The unseasonably cold rain whipped a wind off the nearby lake, making her wish she'd worn more than jeans, a light jacket, and canvas shoes. She shivered and fiddled with the charm bracelet on her wrist. Gray days reminded her of her mother; she loved a dreary afternoon and the smell of a cold wind. Eilonwy preferred sunny mornings.

A tall young man with sandy-blond hair and similarly large eyes, but more blue than aqua, joined her. He wore jeans, boots, and a black leather biker jacket and was carrying a blue motorcycle helmet and leather gloves. He looked like their father, but was more like their mother in his enjoyment of stormy weather, and often rode his bike without a care for the elements.

"Taran, there you are. I don't suppose the Realtor called you? She's late," Eilonwy asked her one-year-younger brother.

"She did. I just came from her office, I have the keys," he said while holding out five keys on a ring.

"That's odd, why would she trust us?" Eilonwy asked, even though she suspected it was because her brother was effortlessly charming.

"She told me the building is haunted," he answered with a grin.

"Why are you smiling?"

"She also told me the owner doesn't want to deal with it anymore, he wants to sell it, and it's in our price range."

A whoosh of air came down the pedestrian-only street, and Eilonwy shivered.

"Let's get inside and I'll explain." Taran opened the front door, let her in, and then closed the door and latched it behind them.

Eilonwy found the light switches and flipped them on. The building was as triangular inside as it was outside. A counter split the middle of the room, kitchen on the right, customers on the left. "This isn't as dirty as I expected it to be," she commented.

Taran put his helmet and gloves on the counter and pulled folded papers out of his jacket.

"The history I researched says the place was built in 1888 and has been everything from a shoe store to a pharmacy. It's called flatiron style, whatever that means, and an Italian family bought it in 1964 and turned it into a restaurant. They lived upstairs, but it's since been converted into seating space."

Eilonwy sniffed the air. "I can still smell the spices in the walls, smells delicious."

"The owner retired and gave it to his daughter, who continued the business until she mysteriously disappeared in '94," Taran continued.

"Is that who's haunting the place?"

"The Realtor, her name is Penny, said she thinks so because once the restaurant was sold and converted into a used bookstore, strange things started happening."

"Like what?"

"She wasn't sure, but heard it was mostly noises, moving objects, and a vague sense of unease."

"That doesn't sound bad. Did they do a sage burn and cast out?"

"I didn't ask. She was wearing a Christian cross, so I didn't bring up witch stuff. She just told me this place has a higher-than-normal turnover."

"I remember this being a sandwich shop a few months ago, and a bakery before that."

"It's also been a clothes boutique, a candy store, and an art gallery. Nothing seems to last longer than a yearlong lease."

"And now they want to sell?"

"Yup."

"This is too good to be true."

"Most people don't like ghosts," Taran offered.

"True."

"But we're witches who know ghosts can't hurt you," he boasted.

"They *mostly* can't hurt you," Eilonwy corrected.

"If it were of the Faefolk, we would already know."

Eilonwy frowned. "Don't say the f-word or you'll attract their attention, call them 'fox' or 'foxen.'"

"Right, sorry, this was more your and Mom's thing rather than mine."

Eilonwy was quiet for a moment. "It's been nearly two years since she died. I still miss her."

"I miss her too . . . and Dad."

Eilonwy didn't say anything; she didn't trust herself to keep the secret about their father's whereabouts.

"Do you think he'll be able to come back soon?" Taran finally asked.

"I don't want to think about that right now, we should stay focused. What's upstairs?"

Taran put a smile on his face. "Let's find out."

They walked past a row of window booths, the kitchen, and a handicap-accessible bathroom to the staircase on the back wall. There was a side exit door directly across from the staircase that led out to the sidewalk.

"I like the downstairs layout," Eilonwy said as she climbed behind Taran.

He stopped at the top, where a café table, resting on its side, blocked the landing. "Hang on, I need to move this." He lifted it upright and pushed it aside.

Eilonwy came up behind him and found the light switches by a door with a pebbled glass window and BATHROOMS painted on the glass in gold lettering.

"Wait, don't turn them on all at once. Penny said you can only turn on two at most, or the circuit breaks, then you have to reset the fuse."

"So, we need to have an electrician come in," Eilonwy said as she flipped on the lights numbered *1* and *2*.

"She said they've had several electricians here, but no one can find the problem."

"That seems odd, and expensive."

Eilonwy scanned the room. A door adjacent to the bathroom

door also had a pebbled glass window and PRIVATE in gold letters. The room was redbrick with oak floors and a tangle of tables and chairs piled in the middle. All the windows had deep sills, wide enough to sit on, with heavy, olive-green curtains tied back from them. "The curtains are ugly, but I like the windows, and the view."

"Let's check out the office," Taran said. He unlocked the right-side brass doorknob and pushed the door open.

It was a narrow room about ten feet wide, with two windows and a long bench seat across the back. A surprisingly clean corn-stalk broom lay on the seat. The rest of the room was bare brick, but only five feet deep at the door and three feet deep at the far end because of the triangular outer wall.

"There's nothing in here except a broom," Eilonwy said.

They stepped inside, and Taran looked behind the door. "There's a mirror on the wall."

"Don't look into it," Eilonwy said and pulled him away.

"Why?"

"A mirror behind a door is strange, and it smells like candle wax in here. Can we turn on a light?"

Taran summoned his witch light: "Luminare." A blue orb the size of a child's kickball appeared a few feet above him, glowing as brightly as a flashlight. "There's nothing, only an electrical socket."

"Let's look in the bathrooms," Eilonwy said as she left the office.

Taran unlocked the left-side brass knob and pushed the door open all the way to the wall, where he latched it at the bottom with an attached kick stop.

There were four doors in this hallway, the farthest one on the left labeled MEN, the one adjacent to that labeled WOMEN. They were each a one stall with a sink and a baby-changing station. The doors to the right were solid with no signs.

"Let's check these," Taran said as he unlocked the door across from where they entered. It was filled with bathroom supplies, toilet paper, and paper towels.

"This is a very shallow closet," Eilonwy said, moving some rolls of toilet paper aside. "Look at this, the back wall is wood rather than brick."

"Do you think there's another room behind it?"

"Maybe, let's check the last door."

Taran unlocked that one and swung it open to reveal a small landing and a staircase that went down to another landing, then down to a fire door labeled Exit.

"This is a curious landing," Eilonwy observed. "I saw from the outside that there's a small, recessed balcony above the exit door."

"That would suggest this wall has something behind it."

"Or it's the back of an apartment that belongs to the next building?"

"It might explain the shallow closet," Taran suggested.

"Ghost hunting aside, let's check out the kitchen before we commit to anything. I like the place, but I'm concerned about the electricity."

Just then all the lights went out and the hallway grew cold. Eilonwy and Taran both looked back and saw a mist emerge from the supply closet. It moved past them, through the hallway, across the outer room to the office, and came back out with the broom.

Taran and Eilonwy went into the seating area, illuminated only by the gray day outside. They watched as the broom danced back and forth, sweeping the floor clean. The tables and chairs untangled themselves, one by one, and moved across the floor.

Five small café tables, each with two chairs, assembled into neat settings around the room.

The broom stopped in front of the siblings, the air freezing as they waited. The mist formed into the barest shadow of a human against the darkness. A translucent hand reached out to Eilonwy's face.

Eilonwy put up her palm and stated firmly, "Move away," as she splayed her fingers in an outward gesture.

The ghost moved back a few feet, then tried to advance again.

Eilonwy continued. "My bracelet is made of a silver that will disperse you if you try to enter me."

The hand moved toward Taran, but he raised his arm to show he also wore a silver bracelet.

The mist stopped, threw the broom down, and disappeared. As it did, the tables and chairs all slammed into each other like they were magnetically attracted.

"Well, that was interesting," Eilonwy said.

"What do you want to do?" Taran asked.

"I want to get my ghost kit from home. You get this place's blueprints from the Realtor. Then we're going to camp here until we figure out what this is."

⤚⤙

Two hours later, Eilonwy came back with an overnight suitcase and a large canvas bag with a pillow and blanket inside. She had changed into a long-sleeved T-shirt and switched her jacket for a longer, dark blue canvas coat with a curious amount of outside pockets. She also wore boots and considerably more jewelry. Around her neck was a charm pendant of dawn silver that matched her bracelet. Dawn silver was enchanted with morning light to specifically dispel ghosts—not forever, but until the next sunset. She also wore a shorter, regular silver chain with a protective pentacle that warded her against malicious spell casting. She still had the charm bracelet around her wrist, but it was now joined by a thick silver ring with a shadow sigil on her right pointer finger and a matching ring with a moon sigil on the left index finger, both excellent for spell casting without a wand. She practically buzzed with energy.

As soon as Eilonwy walked through the unlocked front door, she called out, "Taran!"

"Up here! Lock the door behind you."

She closed and locked the door and left the suitcase on the last table before heading upstairs. Hammering accompanied her steps as she climbed the stairs.

She found Taran in the hallway supply closet. He was taking down the shelving to expose the back wall. Three of the four shelves were stacked on the floor, but he seemed to be having trouble with the bottom one.

Rolls of toilet tissue littered the floor, as though children had thrown them around trying to decorate for homecoming. A lamp was attached to the bathroom door handle by a bungee cord.

"I see you've been having a rough time. How long have you been at it?"

"About an hour, but she keeps throwing toilet paper rolls at me. I've been telling her we don't mean her any harm. She calmed down when I told her about where we live, and how you and Mom used to help ghosts."

"How do you know the ghost is a she?"

"When she reached out to you, I could see she had a curvy female form and long hair."

"Interesting. Did you get the blueprints?"

"There aren't any, but Penny says this building only shares the back wall. There shouldn't be any overlap. I walked around outside, and I can't account for a trapezoid shape of about ten feet by seven."

"It seems odd that no one else has figured this out."

"I asked about that, and she agreed with me, sort of."

Eilonwy cocked an eyebrow. "What aren't you telling me?"

"I told her we wanted to spend the night to see if we felt a ghost. She said yes, but she didn't say I could tear into the wall."

"Did you ask if you could tear into the wall?"

Taran grinned. "I did not."

"Are you planning on tearing open a wall with nothing but a mallet and a chisel?"

"No." He laughed and pulled out the last shelf. "I checked for wards, however, and there are old ones right here."

"What kind?"

"A doorway ward. I suspect I just need to unravel it at the corners. I'm moving the shelves first, so I can get in without triggering anything nefarious. I'm not feeling a trap as much as a seal, but sometimes they feel similar, and this one seems to have two layers."

"I'm impressed."

"Thank you."

"Could you wait before you open the door?"

"Why?"

"I want to set up the radio and prepare the spray, just in case."

"You do that. I'm going to eat first."

"You brought food?"

"No, I'm going to run across the street and get the Chinese food I ordered."

"Did you get me egg rolls and fried rice?"

"Of course."

"And green tea?"

"I'll get you green tea," he said over his shoulder as he headed out the door.

Eilonwy busied herself downstairs unpacking a portable AM/FM radio. It was silver with a black handle, and no bigger than a thick book, but weighted at the bottom so it wouldn't tip over. More importantly, it had an antenna, and a dial that could be tuned between stations. Then she took a blue glass spray bottle, one that could hold about two cups of liquid, out of the suitcase and placed it on the table.

Eilonwy could see out to the street through the front and side exit doors. The main windows were boarded, but the doors weren't for fire safety reasons. She could see Taran across the street waiting in line for her tea. Satisfied, she turned on the radio and listened for a specific kind of static, one with a low hum that could barely be heard, and then she spoke.

"I know you can hear me, and that Taran has been talking to you. We want to buy this building and turn it into a coffeehouse. We aren't trying to get rid of you, but we want to be sure you won't scare everyone away. We can't afford to open a place just for it to close in a year."

Taran came back into the restaurant with a white bag and two drinks.

"Here's your tea," he said, handing her a so-called environmentally friendly hot cup with a tea bag tag hanging over the side. "I'll get utensils from the kitchen." He put the bag on the table. Taran hated to use plastic anything, especially single-use items.

"We are going to have dinner," Eilonwy said to the ghost, wherever it was. "You are welcome to join us and chat. The radio is set up so you can have a voice. It's not a trap. The electric charge can help us see you better. I suspect the reason the electricity upstairs is sketchy is because you use it to manifest yourself."

She tapped the spray bottle. "I warn you, though, this is a mixture of vinegar, salt, and dandelion water that will drive you away if you become violent."

"My sister is serious about safety," Taran added and placed wet utensils on a cloth napkin on the table.

"Wait, let me clean the table off," Eilonwy said, and took a box of alcohol wipes out of the suitcase.

"Point stated and confirmed," Taran joked.

They sat at the booth closest to the side door and ate, the radio hissing static nearby.

Between bites, Taran asked, "How are we going to get Uncle Ric to release our money?"

"I have a plan. We will appeal to reason. If that doesn't work, we'll get the Mavens involved. They will intercede on our behalf."

Taran grimaced. "Do we really want to alert the witch council? I know they were friends with our mother, but that might call unwanted attention to us."

"True, which is why he will cooperate. I know he doesn't want us to have visibility now, with Mom and Dad gone, but he may get fetched, and then we'd have to take care of ourselves and Wren. If he doesn't like that, we must have a backup plan," Eilonwy insisted.

She was referring to the Fae practice of the rulers in the homelands banishing some of their fully Fae people to wander the earth and create half-Fae children until they were fetched back. The laws of Fae, however, still applied to them and their children. Parents were required to present exceptional offspring to whichever court they served. In this case their father, Ewan, and uncle, Ric, were brothers from the court of shadows.

Their mother, Joanna, and their mother's sister, Janelle, were full witches and had married the brothers, not knowing they were Fae. Once they found out, they had hoped their children would be safe under their protection. It was a foolish hope.

Ewan had intended to present his talented children to their queen so he could be permitted to stay in the Fae lands, but Joanna objected, and she was more powerful than he was. Ewan then slowly poisoned her so she couldn't hide them. Then he poisoned her sister, Janelle, once she suspected. Ric was furious with Ewan, and it ended badly. Eilonwy knew how badly. Taran only thought that Ewan had been fetched back.

"Wren is taking Aunt Janelle's death hard. I'm worried about her," Taran finally said.

Eilonwy saw a mist form at the top of the stairs but didn't tell Taran. She didn't want to alert the ghost that she saw her. She also didn't want to stop the conversation. Ghosts all seemed to enjoy listening to gossip.

"Aunt Janelle has only been gone for a year, and it was harder on her, knowing how our mother went," Eilonwy said, partly to intrigue the ghost, partly because she was hoping Taran would finally remember what happened.

Taran stopped eating. "I . . . still can't believe Dad poisoned them both."

Eilonwy put down her fork. It was the first time Taran had admitted this out loud. She wasn't sure if she should continue, but she also didn't want to stop him from expressing his grief.

"It's a terrible thing to know," she answered.

"It doesn't make sense," he said quietly.

"You were close with Dad."

He looked at her, his eyes wet. "You were closer to Mom."

"She loved us both the same."

"No, she loved us both, but she liked you more."

"Dad liked you more," she countered in a soft tone.

"He loved you, too," Taran said equally softly.

"I don't think he did," Eilonwy stated.

Taran was about to reply but stopped himself. He looked away, clearly thinking, and not liking the answer he was coming up with.

The ghost drifted closer.

Taran continued. "I've been thinking about this, and I want you to be honest with me. Is . . . is Dad . . . dead?"

Eilonwy had been dreading this question. She wanted to scream "Yes!" but instead she closed her eyes to keep her tears back. Her mother and aunt were dead by the machinations of her father, their father. He was a parent who was deeply selfish—brilliant, but selfish. He could do the most amazing apotropaic magick involving wards, charms, and traps, all to fend off attack. He was also a deeply flawed drunk with an ego and a temper.

"Answer the question," came the static voice of the ghost.

Eilonwy and Taran both snapped their attention to the radio.

"Please," the ghost said.

Taran nodded consent.

"Fine, but first, what is your name?" Eilonwy asked.

"You can call me Haley," the ghost answered.

"Were you a witch?" Taran asked.

"Yes, I was a witch, a real one," she answered.

"How long have you been here?" Eilonwy asked.

"I'll tell you my story if you tell me yours."

Taran waited for Eilonwy to answer the question.

"Dad isn't coming back," she finally said.

"Where is he?"

"You know where he is, you just don't want to remember, yet."

"I do want to remember," Taran said and rubbed his head.

Eilonwy and Haley waited.

Taran rose to his feet; he was calm but clearly experiencing something. "Ric was yelling at Dad in his greenhouse. You, me, and Wren were watching from the first floor. Aunt Janelle was dead in her bedroom, then Dad came back inside. He was screaming at me to pack a bag. I told him no. I told him I knew he had poisoned Mom and Janelle, and I would never forgive him. Then he struck me. You hit him with a spell and slammed him into the wall. Wren was screaming. Ric attacked Dad and was strangling him with a hex. I tried to get them apart. Then I don't remember anything. I just know everyone was crying and yelling and throwing magick."

"And nothing else?" Eilonwy asked.

"No. I thought . . . you put a forget spell on me, to protect me from knowing."

Eilonwy got up and put her hand on Taran's chest. "I would never do that to you. It was Ric. He tried to put one on all of us, but it didn't work on me. Wren is beginning to remember."

"Is that why she's barely eating?" Taran said.

"I don't know, and we have to tell her soon. I was just waiting for you to remember first, I can't . . ." Eilonwy started to say she couldn't deal with everything by herself, especially now that Ric was having a mental breakdown from grief. She stopped herself so she wouldn't cry. They needed to deal with the ghost first.

Taran seemed to sense this and hugged her, then asked the ghost, "Tell us your story, Haley."

"Sit down first, you're making me dizzy."

Eilonwy and Taran both sat.

"I was alive for twenty-one years, and I've been dead for twenty. The short story is that I was a dumb witch girl who fell in love with an idiot goth boy, and when things didn't go his way, he went all spooky and killed me. Then he tried to reanimate me so I'd do his sexy bidding. I'll spare you the details on that."

"Was he a wizard, or a necromancer?" Eilonwy asked.

"No, and he wasn't a witch either. He was a poseur who thought worshipping dark gods would grant him anything he desired."

"Which dark gods?"

"Does it matter?"

"Yes, you're describing a binding, and there are several ways to break those, but it depends on the type of magick and the objects involved."

"He said he was a vampiric druid, he talked a lot about demon knowledge, and he had rare books he was obsessed with."

"A vampiric druid?" Taran repeated. "That seems antithetical."

"I've never heard of one. Did he have any powers that seemed to work?" Eilonwy asked.

Haley sighed. "I didn't think so until he killed me."

"And made you a ghost?"

"He didn't make me a ghost. I refused to cross over. I wanted revenge."

"No offense, but you don't sound vengeful," Taran observed.

"It's hard to keep that kind of energy up," she said.

"I imagine it would be," Eilonwy said, knowing exactly how hard it was.

"Besides, I tried to get revenge, and I failed. Now one of my friends is probably dead."

"Tell us about that," Taran said.

"Her name is Carey. She worked at the sandwich shop that was here last year. She knew me in real life, and I did everything I could to talk to her. I finally used the broom and mirror you saw upstairs."

"How?" Eilonwy asked.

"Items that belonged to a ghost in real life can be anointed with candle wax and used for communication. I worked here in '95, when it was a used bookstore. I would sweep the floor at the end of the night, and that mirror was by the front counter so we could see if the customers were hiding something while at the register. I actually bespelled it to alert me if someone was shoplifting."

"How would that work?" Taran asked.

"It would just sparkle a little. The frame is silver with little red crystals. I used to make them out of thrift store frames and mirrors, then sell them at the craft fairs. I only enchanted a few for friends."

"How long did you work here?"

"About a year."

"You were saying Carey was trying to help you," Eilonwy urged, trying to get the ghost back on track.

"Yes, she was talking to me through the mirror. It took a little work, but she figured out how to make it into a spirit-scrying device—she's a witch, too. Anyway, I told her my story, and she told me he had a store down the street. I was furious! That asshole killed me and tried to bind me to him, but I turned on him. He comes in here whenever a new business opens, and I always try to smack him in the head with my broom!"

"Why would he sell the store? Was he unable to banish you?" Taran asked.

"He didn't own it, he was leasing."

"Do you know who owned it? We heard that she went missing in '94."

"She was his first victim. I didn't know it until I died, but I was the second. Carey thinks he does this every year, because there's a list of women who disappeared on State Street, one each year around Halloween. The same day I died."

"That sounds familiar," Taran said.

Eilonwy felt her temper begin to rise. Madison was the only city she had ever lived in. She and her friends were afraid of the unknown person who was killing local and out-of-town college women. They called whoever it was the Trick-or-Treat Killer and the Samhain Snatcher. They were all fed up with the local police not taking the missing women seriously. They said the women either ran off or that these were unrelated kidnappings, just because bodies were never found.

"Haley, what is his full name?" Eilonwy asked.

"Dante Valentine," she replied.

"Of Valentine's Used and Rare Books," Eilonwy said.

"Yes, have you been inside?"

"I have. The owner is tall, has long dark hair and dark eyes, right?"

"Yes."

"I've been in that shop twice, and he tried to hit on me both times. He's smarmy and smells like incense. I despise incense," Eilonwy said.

"I loved that smell. It's the first thing that attracted me to him. I went into the bookstore that was here, and he had a few witch items like candles, incense, and tarot cards. He was impressed with my knowledge and hired me as a clerk. I resisted him for a few months, but then he . . . Well, it doesn't matter now. Can we get back to Carey?"

"Yes, sorry, please continue," Eilonwy said.

"Okay, so Carey went over to do some reconnaissance, and she never came back. Then Dante showed up here and waited until he knew I was listening. He thanked me for sending her to him. I was so angry I smacked him with the broom and chased him out of the store. I haven't heard from either of them since. I'm worried she's dead."

"Why didn't you tell someone?" Taran asked.

"I did try, but every time I did, the store closed because people are scared of me."

"When did she go over?" Eilonwy asked.

"What day is it now?"

"June 6, 2015."

"I thought it had only been a month, but it's been nearly four. Time is weird when you're a ghost. She must be dead, or worse. Damn it! I'm so stupid, I never should have let her go!"

It was quiet for an awkward minute, only the radio crackling softly with her crying.

"Haley, is there a room upstairs behind the closet?" Taran asked when the crackling stopped.

"Yes. It's where he left my body. It's actually pretty comfy."

"How so?" Eilonwy asked.

"I don't know, it just feels restful and comfortable when I'm in there. It's probably why I can't tell how much time has passed from day to day."

Taran and Eilonwy exchanged a look, one that said they both had ideas.

"What do you want us to do?" Taran asked.

"Could you please find Carey? Without becoming one of his victims."

Eilonwy nodded. "We can do that, but I want to speak to Taran about this outside, privately."

⤚⤙

The siblings stood on the sidewalk near the side exit and looked down the street toward Valentine's bookstore.

"What do you want to do?" he asked.

"I want to help her, without involving authorities if we can, but I'm worried she might be lying."

"Because this has been too easy?"

"Yes. That mirror bothers me, and I want to know what's up with that hidden room. We have to be careful that she's not some kind of lure."

"For a demon?"

"Or something else. I've heard of vampires using ghosts to beckon would-be paranormal investigators into their lairs."

"Do you think she's trying to take one of us so she can get revenge herself?"

"It's a possibility, and I like to cover all the possibilities."

"Could he actually be a vampire?"

"The thought had crossed my mind."

"I say we look in the room and see if we can find out more about him and her."

"That's a good plan. I want to check that mirror, too. We might be able to use it to see inside the bookstore."

⤚⤙

Eilonwy brought the radio upstairs for Haley to use.

Taran examined the back of the closet, running his fingers along the edges. "This is one piece of wood, about an inch thick. Do you know how this opens?"

"No, I've never had to, I just drift through," Haley said through the static.

"What's on the other side?" Taran asked.

"A bed, a bunch of his books, some of my things, mostly stuff he gave me, my body, and jars."

"Jars?" Eilonwy asked.

"Of my blood. He bled me when I was dying."

"Haley, I don't want to be insensitive, but how did he kill you?" Taran asked.

The radio crackled for a long moment.

"I don't like to think about it."

"It could help us?"

"I don't want to talk about this," Haley said, then her mist rose out of the radio and zipped through the wall.

"She seems upset. Maybe we should leave her alone and check the mirror first," Taran said.

"She probably needs a minute. I'll leave the radio here and we can go look at it," Eilonwy agreed.

Taran followed her into the office, turning his blue witch light back on. Eilonwy took a pair of white cotton gloves out of one coat pocket. Then she took out a pair of glasses with pink-tinted round lenses.

"What do those do?"

"They help me see leftover magick while protecting my eyes," she said while putting them on. "I don't want you to look at the mirror while I do this."

"Should I wait outside the room?"

"No, my witch light is too dark, and if something goes wrong, you'll have to pull me away."

"What could go wrong?"

"My pentacle should protect me from most things. Are you wearing yours?"

"Always."

"Do you have salt packets?"

"Yes," he said and pulled them out of his pocket.

"Excellent, now close your eyes."

Taran closed his eyes and listened while Eilonwy examined the mirror. She didn't look directly into it, but looked at the frame, then the glass, without meeting her own eyes. It had a basic, dark shimmer of a scrying mirror.

She pulled a small box of eight spell crayons out of her pocket and selected the dark blue one, putting the rest back in her coat. Then she touched the crayon to the glass in a star pattern while saying, "Scry to me the other side."

As soon as she finished the words, the mirror showed a room with a bed and a book laid on top. It was a cozy-looking space, with floral wallpaper and a reading lamp.

Eilonwy took off her glasses to see better. "Taran," she whispered, then beckoned him to look. She put a finger to her lips, then pointed at his witch light.

He turned off his light and joined her at the mirror.

Dante Valentine strode into the room, stark naked, holding a glass of wine. He was lithe and sinewy, with broad shoulders. His hair was pulled back, and he had a prominent nose, cheekbones, and chin. He put the glass on a side table and got into bed to read. They watched for a minute. He sipped his wine, turned a page, and then sipped again. His eyes seemed to dart toward them for a second, but he just kept reading.

Eilonwy took the crayon and made a cross across the star. The mirror went back to being a strangely dark mirror.

"Why did you close it?"

She brought Taran back out of the tiny office and closed the door behind them. "Because he can use whatever mirror is on the other side to see us as well. Haley may have used it as a focus to talk to Carey, but Dante could also use it as a viewing scry to eavesdrop."

"Do you think there's one in her little room?"

"It's possible."

"We need to see in there."

"Let's be careful. We should treat it as though it's her bedroom. She's upset, and we don't want her to stop talking to us."

They went to the closet, and Taran knocked on the door. "Haley, can we come in?"

The static on the radio answered, "Do you have to?"

"Yes, please, we think there may be things inside that will help us figure out what Dante did to you."

"Do you promise not to dispel me or smudge me out or do whatever it is witches do to get rid of a ghost?"

"As long as you don't attack us," he confirmed.

"Okay, you can come in, but I don't know how to open the door."

"I think I do," Taran said, and stepped up to the door. He tapped the top left corner, then the right, then moved to the bottom right, then the left, and back up to the top left, all while saying, "Wither ward, dissolve your hold, gently I command."

With quiet pops, the wood split down the middle and parted into a swinging door. Taran pushed one side gently, and it moved inward. He pushed it all the way back as Eilonwy held the lamp.

Three feet ahead was a bookcase. It held books from top to bottom, along with a snow globe, a jewelry box, and a few plushies.

"The air isn't terrible. All I can smell are dried herbs and candle wax," Eilonwy said.

"Can just Eilonwy come in?" Haley's voice said faintly through the radio, as though she were far away.

Taran gave her the lamp and stepped back. Eilonwy picked up

the radio with her other hand. She didn't like having her hands full, so she placed the radio on the floor in front of the bookcase.

"I'll make sure you don't get trapped inside," he whispered.

"Thank you," Eilonwy replied, and walked through the door.

The corridor formed by the bookshelf was dark and tight. Just past the shelf's corner was a twin bed with a body on top. She was laid out upon a colorful quilt and under a red satin sheet, her hands folded across her chest, holding a large black feather. Her nails were painted red, a lacy white pillow held her head, and her eyes were covered by a purple sleep mask. Long, honey-blond hair was carefully curled around her face and across her neck. The weirdest thing was her lips; they were still plump. Then Eilonwy realized she had been preserved with some kind of beeswax. It was strangely colorless, or possibly tinted to her flesh tone.

"Welcome to my tomb," Haley said through the radio.

"You are well-preserved," Eilonwy said loudly enough for Taran to hear.

"Thanks. He took a lot of time."

"Is there a light in here?"

Just as Eilonwy said it, a soft light came on over the bed, and another at the end of the room, above a rack of scarves. A curtain was also pulled over a doorway.

"What's in there?" Eilonwy asked.

"A bathroom. It has a window where you can look outside and watch the world go by without you."

Eilonwy took the lamp to the curtain and was about to pull it aside.

"Please don't look in there."

"Why?"

"It's where the blood and guts are. I watched everything he did, and I don't like to think about it."

"It might help me figure out what he is."

"Fine, but I warned you."

A light came on over the medicine cabinet. It was the smallest bathroom she had ever been in. There was the window that overlooked the sink. The lower half had privacy glass, and the top could indeed be seen through. There was a toilet, a pedestal sink, and a tiny tub with a shower stall, only big enough to stand in or take a bath if you bent your knees close. Stacked inside was jar after jar, made of clay and sealed from sunlight. It smelled a little like death, and she guessed Dante had opened the window to air out the odor.

The medicine cabinet was odd. Inside were the usual cosmetics and creams, but behind those, scribbled on the wall in black permanent marker: *You love me. You are the art. We are together forever. This is love. All is well.* Various geometric symbols that seemed familiar, but not quite right, were scribbled on the interior side of the door, and then she realized those were scribbled in blood.

Eilonwy closed the medicine cabinet and went back out to the bed. "I can see why that would upset you."

"It's much more pleasant out here."

Eilonwy looked around the room. There was barely space for anything but the bed, and yet the walls were lined with narrow bookshelves. These were covered in books, knickknacks, and photos. The ceiling, nine feet up, had bunches of dried flowers and herbs hanging from sticks.

"Did you live here when you were alive?"

"Yes. He kept me prisoner after I broke up with him. This was his bedroom when he leased the place. I was locked in here for weeks with nothing to eat but a strange gruel made of marigolds, sunflower seeds, and oats. He gave me cups of green tea that tasted like honey and lavender."

"Did he ever talk to you about reliquary?"

"Yes, he was always going on about the dead and preserving heads, arms, and organs for some kind of honorific worship."

"Do you think that's what he was doing to you?"

"He said I would be his greatest work, but it doesn't make sense. Art is only art when everyone can see it."

It didn't make sense to Eilonwy either, but she knew that people rarely made sense when trying to figure out why they did the selfish things they did. "How so?" she asked so Haley would continue.

"He said he loved me, but he locked me in here, and for some reason I was glad to do what he asked me. I didn't feel like I could escape, and I didn't want to. Why?"

"You were probably mesmerized somehow," Eilonwy offered, not because she was guessing, but because she knew there was no way anyone would submit to this without being mesmerized in some way.

"I've felt shame and embarrassment every day since I died. I feel like I should have seen the signs. He had books about preservation and blood rituals. He wanted me to drink his blood, and I laughed. I thought he was a funny goth guy."

Eilonwy understood. Her family owned countless books of dark arcana. One of the reasons Ric was so grief-stricken was that he knew his brother also had this knowledge. It never occurred to him that Ewan would use it to kill those close to him.

"My mother felt guilty for not seeing the evil around her until it was too late, and she was brilliant. Don't take it hard that you didn't see what was right in front of you, especially when someone is manipulating you with magick," Eilonwy surprised herself by saying out loud.

"I loved him. I loved him, and he did this to me."

"I'm sorry. Sometimes we love people who are terrible," Eilonwy said, her throat hurting from holding back a sob.

Haley was quiet for a long few seconds, and then she started to cry. It was a soft gasp at first, but then she wept. Eilonwy wasn't sure what to do.

Taran poked his head around the door. "Is she okay?"

It was a silly thing to ask. Haley was dead and had been for twenty years. Her brother was as kind as her father had been deceitful.

Eilonwy shook her head.

Then they heard the laughing. It was deep and far away but nearby, from the bathroom.

Eilonwy turned to see Dante's reflection in the medicine cabinet. He looked like an evil bird with large eyes, his head dipped slightly.

Haley stopped crying.

"You are admiring my work? She is quite beautiful, isn't she?" Dante said in a deep voice.

Taran entered the room, holding the mallet and chisel.

Eilonwy's first instinct was to take Taran's chisel from him and break the glass.

Then she realized where she'd seen those symbols before.

He was a raven shifter, one of the dread Fae, but he wasn't supposed to be out of the homelands. If he was here, he was a fugitive, and she could use that to her benefit.

"You are a long way from home, Raven," she said, matching his contempt.

"So are you . . . cousin."

Taran stiffened next to her, realizing this man was a Fae. The shifters were a part of the monstre class of Fae. Many belonged in the court of shadows, but they were not related, not in a way that mattered. If anything, they served as the funeral directors of the court. It all made sense now.

"Were you thrown out in disgrace, or did you escape?" Eilonwy asked.

He laughed like a raven. "Haw ha! As if my kind would be allowed to fly the outland skies!"

"You escaped?" Eilonwy stalled as Taran touched her on the back. He was scared, but ready to fight. He had been trained his whole life to fight and protect. "How did you get here?"

"Wouldn't you like to know?" Dante sneered.

"What I would really like to know is why do this?" Eilonwy said as she gestured at Haley.

"Eternal death is the ultimate form of love," he said.

"It's forbidden to do this to anyone on this side," she replied, even though she was guessing.

"I do as I please. It is my way."

"How many, Dante?"

"Consumed like that delicious morsel Haley sent me, or immortalized?"

"I have time, tell me everything."

"It started—"

"No."

"No, what?"

"Get dressed and meet me downstairs, tell me when you get here," Eilonwy said.

"Why bother when I can do it from here?" Dante asked.

Taran strode to the bathroom mirror and smacked the chisel into the mirror. It shattered into a hundred pieces. The sound felt oddly satisfying to Eilonwy. Then she grabbed the radio and plucked the feather from Haley's hands.

"What's the plan?" Taran asked, following her down the stairs with the lamp and tools.

"Do you know what a raven shifter is?" Eilonwy asked.

"A little. I know they're from the dark court, they eat the dead, and they carry out executions by the order of the queen."

"They also read a lot, and they like to hear the sound of their own voice."

"How did he get here?" Taran asked.

"Probably through one of the portals. Help me move my suitcase. I need to sketch out something on the floor, and I don't want him to know I have ingredients. We also need to turn down the lights."

"He ate Carey, didn't he?" Haley asked.

"Possibly. You need to prepare yourself for when he arrives," Eilonwy said as she sketched out a pentacle on the wooden floor using a dark brown spell crayon made with blood, one that couldn't be seen in the dim light.

"Do you think he's really coming here?" Haley asked.

"Yes, he's too arrogant not to. He'll know it's a trap, but he'll think he can escape."

All the lights on the lower floor went out. The only light left was from the staircase and the streetlights outside.

"I stowed the suitcase behind the counter. Now what?" Taran asked.

"Put the radio far enough away that we can hear Haley, but he can't reach it without exposing himself. Haley, if you can, get your broom!"

The mist of Haley left the radio and floated up the stairs.

"What's the endgame?" Taran asked.

Eilonwy didn't look at her brother, instead scanning the windows to make sure Dante didn't arrive without them knowing. "We need to kill him. If he escapes, he'll keep murdering. If he gets fetched, he'll tell them where we are."

"Is this going to be our life now? Kill to keep killers from killing us?"

"I don't want it to be, but someone has to stop this maniac, and we can't let anyone know what we are."

"Right. What do you want me to do?"

"Stay back a bit, seem unconcerned, don't offer personal information, and know I'm going to lie to him. If I can, I need to get . . ."

The door by the stairs flew open with a bang. A rush of wind and rain announced his arrival.

Eilonwy faced him, hands by her sides, Taran behind her.

He walked in with his arms out, like a rock star showing up to his latest gig, wearing pointed shoes and a grin. He also wore a belted black leather coat, double-breasted, with strangely large sleeves that tightened at the cuffs, and dark, tight pants. He was taller than Taran but skinnier, his features handsome but edging on homely.

"I am Dante Valentine, and *you* are Eilonwy Shaedewell. I am exceedingly pleased to make your acquaintance," he said with a bow and the flourish of his arms in front of him, like a bird touching the tips of its wings together.

She was unsettled that he knew her name; she also noticed that he ignored Taran's presence.

He straightened and placed his hands together, like saying a prayer. "How can I be of service?"

It was all she could do not to roll her eyes. Instead, she placed a polite smile on her face. "Thank you for coming, Dante. I was wondering if you could answer some questions for me."

He returned the smile and put his hands behind his back, cocking one leg out slightly. "I live to serve beauty such as yours. Ask of me anything that would please you."

His smarminess was challenging her patience.

"Have you been hunting in my city?"

Dante was still for a moment, then raised his chin a bit. "How is this *your* city?" The fact that his answer was short told her he was nervous.

Eilonwy answered, "I was born here, I intend to have children here, and I know the elders of the highest coven in the region."

He casually stepped to the left and looked around, toward the front of the store. "You know the Mavens?"

"I do."

"You are a witch?"

"We are," Eilonwy stated, adding Taran to the conversation.

Dante stepped to the right, then back to the stairs, and looked up them. "Was my beautiful Haley a part of this coven?"

"If she had been, we would not have lost her to your kind," Eilonwy carefully taunted.

He looked back to her, leaning against the stairs, his arms crossed. "My kind? We are woven of the same materials," he huffed, a faint caw sound rustling around him.

"Have I offended you?"

"Ha! You offend yourself! You ask if I have been hunting in *your* city. It is my right to take one each Samhain. If you were truly of the court, you would know." The cawing sound grew, as though more birds had landed nearby.

"We are half of the shadows and half of the stars," Eilonwy

stated. Ric had told her witches and wizards were referred to as star children in the Fae lands.

"Fair as you are, you clearly have no powers beyond audacity," he said, trying to anger her so she would prove otherwise.

"You said you would answer my question."

"I answered when I told you it is my right. My people have the highest honor of preparing and guarding the dead. I suspect you know little of your father's people; he undoubtedly only told of the laws and lore." He didn't have to guess her father was Fae. Only the males were allowed to go out and create children; the females had to stay and protect the lineage.

"He told us of the laws that would concern us, and some of the lore, but it still doesn't answer the question of why you think you can murder whomever you please."

"Murder? I *honor* the dead."

"You *murdered* Haley and Carey."

"Haw ha!" he called out into the darkness, his head tipped up and back like a raven. The cawing sounded closer, yet still far away.

Eilonwy hoped he didn't have any siblings nearby.

Dante left his spot by the stairs, stepping slowly closer while he undid the thick belt around his coat. He was shirtless underneath, and his pants rode low. It was erotic in a way that made her want to slap him with a knife for his disrespect.

The cawing grew louder. "Hush, my darlings," he said, and the cawing stopped.

"He isn't alone," Taran whispered, ever so softly, and she realized the cawing was coming from Dante.

He stood ten feet away from her. She needed him to come into the circle she'd made on the floor.

"I will never be alone. I choose the company I keep, and keep them I do. Some I keep better than the others. I made a gorgeous reliquary out of my beloved Haley so she could live forever as a persona," he boasted.

"What is a persona?"

"It is a poor witch who does not know the highest calling of becoming a persona."

"Or you aren't smart enough to explain it to me."

"You are amusing, I might not consume you. I will, however, take your brother."

"I doubt that, but please continue," she countered so he would answer the question.

"Fine, I will explain. A persona is the existence of the soul beyond life, retaining all of their accumulated knowledge so they might pass it along to the next generation. I have the honor of making reliquaries so I can house the greatest minds after death as personas, and they have the honor of teaching what they know."

"Haley is a ghost, and she says you wanted her to do your bidding."

"Haley is a bright little liar who asked me to make her a persona. Her regret is not my problem."

"You miserable *son of a bastard*!" Haley shouted from the radio. A broom sailed down the stairs and slammed into the side of Dante's head.

"Cursed wench!" he called out as he fell to one knee.

"Liar, liar, liar!" Haley screamed, no longer needing to be inside the radio to have a voice through the static.

The cawing rose up. Eilonwy quickly whispered to Taran, "Don't touch him. The sound is coming from his coat."

The broom came down on Dante's head again and again while Haley screamed and cursed and called him names. Her cold mist encircled him until he couldn't see. He stumbled up, opening his coat, his nose bleeding from where she had smacked his face with the broom handle.

Eilonwy took a step back, taking Taran with her.

"HAW HA!" Dante bellowed, and pulled his coat open, his head thrown so far back his spine curved backward as his chest jutted forward. Ravens flew out of his coat and around the room, dispersing the mist, and the broom fell to the floor.

Haley swore at him and retreated.

The large ravens flapped to a rest on every table and counter. There were at least ten, possibly more. One flew up the stairs after Haley.

Dante continued his guttural "haw ha" sounds, and the ravens cawed back in a terrible symphony. He finally threw off his coat, and it landed with a flourish in the drawn pentagram.

"You wanted to meet my murder, well, here they are!"

"These are the women you took over the years?" Eilonwy asked, stunned at the realization. "I count thirteen, if you've been killing every year for twenty-one years, where are the other eight?"

Dante wiped the blood off his nose with his hand, and it smeared across his face. "I have been in this city for twenty-five years. I arrived with my beloved and lost her four years later. A raven without his mate is a painful thing. I tried to date among the humans, but they know nothing of loyalty." He walked to the counter and grabbed a handful of paper napkins from a holder, trying to stanch the flow of the blood. Once again outside the pentagram.

"You started killing women when you couldn't find a girlfriend?" Taran scoffed and stood near the pentagram, but across from him.

Eilonwy stepped back. Taran would take it from here, allowing her to work. She touched the feather in her pocket and searched the floor with her eyes for his blood.

"And what would you have me do? A raven needs either mate or flock."

"Dude, vampires get dates all the time without having to kill them," Taran taunted.

The ravens cawed as though they were laughing.

"Shut up!" Dante yelled, and the ravens stopped.

Eilonwy noticed two things: the flock was scared of him, and he threw the bloody napkins down on the floor.

"Dude?" Dante questioned. "You call me dude? And how many women do you have?" he angrily asked, stepping over to Taran.

Eilonwy couldn't get to the napkins without attracting his attention, and the blood on the floor was impossible to find. Then, one of the ravens hopped off the counter onto the floor and gently plucked up the bloodiest napkin.

Taran saw this but didn't alert Dante.

"I don't need to enslave women to feel like a man," Taran said, his arms crossed over his slightly puffed chest, chin up, two feet from the taller raven shifter, who was hunched enough to meet his eyes.

The second Dante lunged, Taran ducked, punched, spun, and threw the raven shifter down onto his coat in the pentagram.

The raven gave Eilonwy the napkin, and she wrapped it around the feather and uttered her blood magick. "By this blood I bind! On the ground and splayed you'll find!"

Dante's limbs immediately stiffened out, his back to the ground, his legs open. He looked like Leonardo da Vinci's *Vitruvian Man*. "Release me, foul witch! Attack, my beauties!"

The ravens hopped back and forth and cawed in agitation,

and then one flew from its perch on the stairs and landed on his chest.

"I said attack them!"

The raven pecked at his face, biting his lip, tearing it in two. Dante howled and began to lay out a curse. "By my wings . . ." he began.

Eilonwy prepared to silence his spell, but the crow grabbed his tongue, tearing at it so he couldn't speak. The remaining ravens swooped in one by one, each picking, then pecking a spot on him until he was a bloody mess bellowing without a tongue. Blood filled his mouth and nose, making him sound like he was drowning.

Taran ran to the doors and warded them closed, baffling the noise from inside, window by window.

Eilonwy waited.

Haley drifted down the stairs, a crow hopping down with her and perching on the railing post at the bottom. They watched the bloody, writhing raven shifter as he struggled, pinned by her magick. She observed carefully to make sure he couldn't shift to raven.

Taran stood nearby, his brow furrowed. "How far are we taking this?"

"We are letting them have as much justice as they desire."

Dante's flock pecked, tore, gnashed, scratched, tortured, and cawed. It was bloodthirsty work.

Finally, Dante stopped moving.

Haley drifted to the counter. Her voice came out of the radio. "Carey says they will be free when he is dead."

The raven on the stairway cawed for a few seconds.

Haley continued her translation. "She says they don't know what will happen, but they have agreed they would rather be dead than bound to him for life."

"How can she understand them?" Taran asked.

Haley answered, "I understand Carey, but I don't know what the rest are saying."

The ravens continued pecking at the motionless body. His clothes in shreds, his eyeballs gone, they were now feasting on his flesh.

"Do you think we can save the ravens? Will they revert to being women? What about Haley?" Taran asked.

Carey cawed some more.

"They don't know. I don't care either. I'd rather die than live bound to him," Haley answered.

Eilonwy nodded. "So may it be," she said and went behind the counter, coming back with a silver dagger and an empty mayonnaise jar. She unscrewed the lid and put it in her pocket.

"Stand back, ladies," she said in a loud but respectful voice.

The ravens reluctantly, one by one, hopped away and took perches around the room.

Eilonwy centered herself, smudged the pentagram with her foot, and spoke: "From death to dust, and blood to dry." She placed the silver dagger on his body. "I collect your ashes from the sky."

Surprisingly quickly, the body of Dante Valentine dried into a pile of blue, purple, and black sparkly ashes—not even the coat was left—and then gathered up into a swirl. Eilonwy straightened, with nothing left to touch her dagger to, and held the jar out. The tornado of ashes wound tighter and tighter, leaving a trail of silver smoke as it dove into the jar. Eilonwy quickly capped it closed.

The ravens cawed softly and looked at one another, waiting.

"Haley, are you still here?" Taran asked.

"Yes," she answered.

"How are you ladies feeling?" Taran asked the ravens.

They bobbed their heads and hopped around, chattering to one another.

Carey cawed again. Haley translated. "She says they feel good."

"Do you want us to let you out?" Eilonwy asked. "It's nearly summer, and you can see how you will do. We can keep watch if you have trouble. I don't know if you'll change back, but you can come here anytime. My brother and I will be buying this building and opening a coffee shop soon."

The birds all looked at Taran. "I agree—we will watch out for you, and we'll be buying this place. I think we'll call it the Broom."

The ravens cawed in agreement.

Taran removed the wards and opened the side door. He checked the street for people, and then the ravens hopped out, one by one, and flew up into the night sky. They landed in the tree across the street in the green space, waiting for one another. Eilonwy joined him at the window.

"Carey said she would visit," Haley informed them.

"I think you might not be a ghost, Haley. You may be a persona. I'll do some research and see what needs to be done and what your options are," Eilonwy said.

"In the meantime, I'll put the door back on your room, and we'll put your broom back in the office, along with the radio. I think I can fix your mirror, too," Taran added.

"Thank you, but what will you do about his bookstore? There might be bodies in there, too," Haley asked, holding the radio herself.

Eilonwy sighed. "I think we're going to have to tell the Mavens so they can investigate properly. They should know what's been happening in their city."

"Can we not tell Uncle Ric?" Taran asked.

"I doubt it. He needs to know you remember now, and we have to tell Wren."

"Eilonwy, what will you do with the jar?" Taran asked.

"I'm locking it in the cellar with Dad's jar."

Taran put his arm around his sister, and she leaned into him as they watched the birds. "Dad might not have loved you the way he should have, but I love you."

"I know. I love you too, Taran."

ABOUT THE AUTHORS

Holly Black is the #1 *New York Times* bestselling author of fantasy books, including the Novels of Elfhame, *The Coldest Girl in Coldtown*, and her adult debut, *Book of Night*; she is the coauthor of the Spiderwick Chronicles and an Arthurian picture book called *Sir Morien*. She has been a finalist for an Eisner Award and a Lodestar Award, and the recipient of a Mythopoeic Award, a Nebula, and a Newbery Honor. Her books have been translated into thirty-two languages worldwide and adapted for film. She lives in New England with her husband and son in a house with a secret library. She invites you to visit her online at BlackHolly.com or on Instagram @BlackHolly.

Jennifer Blackstream is a *USA Today* bestselling author of urban fantasy and paranormal romance. She is amazed and grateful to have made a writing career out of a master's degree in psychology, hours of couch-detecting watching *Murder, She Wrote*, and endless research into mythology and fairy tales. She firmly believes that whether it's a village witch deciding she wants to be a private investigator or a single mother having a go at being a full-time writer, it's never too late for a new adventure.

Maurice Broaddus is a community Afrofuturist, librarian, and teacher. His award-winning work has appeared in places such as *Lightspeed*, *Black Panther: Tales of Wakanda*, *Out There Screaming*, *The End of the World as We Know It: New Tales of Stephen King's* The Stand, *Asimov's Science Fiction*, *Weird Tales*, *The Magazine of Fantasy & Science Fiction*, and *Uncanny*. His books include the sci-fi novels *Sweep of Stars* and *Breath of Oblivion*; the steampunk works *Buffalo Soldier* and *Pimp My Airship*; and the middle grade detective novels *The Usual Suspects* and *Unfadeable*. He's also an editor at *Apex Magazine*. Learn more at MauriceBroaddus.com.

Jim Butcher is the author of the Dresden Files, the Codex Alera, and steampunk series the Cinder Spires. His résumé includes a laundry list of skills that were useful a couple of centuries ago, and he plays guitar quite badly. An avid gamer, he plays tabletop games in various systems, a variety of video games on PC and console, and LARPs whenever he can make time for them. Jim resides mostly inside his own head, but his head can generally be found in the mountains outside Denver, Colorado.

Delilah S. Dawson is the *New York Times* bestselling author of Star Wars books *Phasma*, *Galaxy's Edge: Black Spire*, and *Inquisitor: Rise of the Red Blade*, plus *House of Idyll*, *The Violence*, *Bloom*, *Guillotine*, *It Will Only Hurt for a Moment*, the Hit series, the Blud series, *Dungeons & Dragons Ravenloft: Heir of Strahd*, the Minecraft: Mob Squad series, *Ride or Die*, *Mine*, *Camp Scare*, and the Shadow series, written as Lila Bowen and starting with *Wake of Vultures*. The story in this anthology is from the world of Arcadia

Falls, a new series penned under the pseudonym Isla Jewell and beginning with *Books & Bewitchment*. Delilah's comics backlist includes *Ladycastle*, *Sparrowhawk*, *Star Pig*, and works in the worlds of Marvel Action: *Spider-Man*, *Firefly*, *Adventure Time*, *The X-Files™: Case Files*, *Rick and Morty*, *Labyrinth*, and *Batman: The Brave and the Bold*. With Kevin Hearne, she writes the Tales of Pell. Delilah lives in Atlanta with her family and enjoys Olympic lifting, mountain biking, gluten-free baking, and long walks in the forest. Find her online at WhimsyDark.com.

Kim Harrison is best known as the author of the #1 *New York Times* bestselling Hollows series, but she has written more than urban fantasy and has authored more than two dozen books, running the gamut from young adult to accelerated-science thriller to several anthologies, and has scripted two original graphic novels set in the Hollows universe. She has also written traditional fantasy under the name Dawn Cook. Kim is currently working on a new Hollows book between other, unrelated urban fantasy projects.

Kevin Hearne is the *New York Times* bestselling author of the Iron Druid Chronicles, the Ink & Sigil series, and the Seven Kennings trilogy, and is the coauthor of the Tales of Pell. He's into heavy metal, nature photography, and beard maintenance. He likes to plan road trips and sometimes even takes them.

Tanya Huff lives in rural Ontario, Canada, with her wife, Fiona Patton, two dogs, and, as of last count, nine cats. Her more than thirty novels and seventy-five short stories include horror, heroic fantasy, urban fantasy, comedy, and space opera. She's written four essays for BenBella's pop culture collections and the occasional book review for *The Globe and Mail*. Her Blood series was turned into the twenty-two-episode *Blood Ties*, and writing episode nine allowed her to finally use her degree in radio and television arts. Her latest novel is the cozy horror *Direct Descendant*, and she is the author of the Peacekeeper series. She can be found on Bluesky @TanyaHuff.bsky.social and on Facebook. Four collections of her short stories as well as six of her older novels are available pretty much wherever e-books are sold.

Kerrie L. Hughes is a paranormal girl in a way too normal world. She's primarily known as an anthologist and short story writer but has recently ventured into novels. Cauldron: A Great Lakes Grimoire is her first series, featuring witches, wizards, shifters, dragons, spirits, and, of course, the Fae. In her spare time she researches art, history, and psychology. She has been known to cast spells, read fortunes, and meet ghosts. She may even know a vampire or two.

Faith Hunter is a *New York Times* and *USA Today* bestselling author and a 2018 winner of an Audie. She writes dark urban fantasy, paranormal urban thrillers, paranormal police procedurals, and science fiction. Her long-running, bestselling Skinwalker series features Jane Yellowrock, a hunter of rogue vampires. The Soulwood series features Nell Nicholson Ingram in paranormal crime–solving novels. Her Rogue Mage series—dark, postapocalyptic fantasy novels—features Thorn St. Croix, a stone mage in an alternate reality. She also writes a sci-fi novella series, Junkyard Cats. Under the pen name Gwen Hunter she has written action adventure, mysteries, thrillers, women's fiction, a medical thriller series, and even historical religious fiction. As Gwen, she was part of the WH Smith Literary promotion for fresh talent in the UK, and she won a Romantic Times Reviewers Choice Award in 2008. Under her various pen names she has more than forty books in print in thirty countries. For more, including a list of her books, see FaithHunter.net and GwenHunter.com. To keep up with her, like her fan page at facebook.com/Official.Faith.Hunter.

R. L. King has been writing since childhood, mostly for two reasons: because other people weren't writing the things she wanted to read and because she likes getting inside the heads of all sorts of different characters. She is the author of the Alastair Stone Chronicles urban fantasy series (an increasingly misnamed trilogy that's rapidly approaching forty books), including two spinoff series set in the same universe, as well as two novels and numerous bits of in-game material in the Shadowrun RPG universe. When she's not writing, she likes hanging out with her understanding and very supportive spouse and her three impossibly cute cats. You can find her online at RLKingWriting.com.

R.R. Virdi is a two-time Dragon Award finalist, Nebula Award finalist, and *USA Today* bestselling author. He is the author of the urban fantasy series the Grave Report and the Books of Winter as well as the epic fantasy novels *The First Binding* and *The Doors of Midnight*. His love of classic cars drove him to work in the automotive industry for many years before he realized he'd do a better job of maintaining his passion if he stayed away from customers.